"Do not believe all that the bards sing, young man! I have heard those songs myself; they summon ghosts to Troy, heroes dead for centuries raised up to fight in battles they never knew. Bards! Do they mourn for Troy, the great city laid waste? They sing of heroism and glory and forget the pain, the shame, the suffering."

"You were there?"

She sighed with the wind. "I was there."

"You knew him also? Achilles?"

"Oh yes. I knew Achilles."

Her voice came again as a whisper, hardly audible over the wail of the wind and the babble of rain. "They sailed to Troy. They ravaged many lesser cities first, gathering chariots and horses, before closing in on Troy itself. None sacked more fair towns than Achilles and his Myrmidons."

She sighed deeply. "You ask if I bedded with a warrior? I tell you I bedded the greatest of them all. Listen, and I will tell you how it was at Troy."

DAUGHTER OF TROY

SARAH B. FRANKLIN

HarperTorch
An Imprint of HarperCollins*Publishers*

This is a work of fiction. Names, characters, places, and incidents are products of the author's imagination or are used fictitiously and are not to be construed as real. Any resemblance to actual events, locales, organizations, or persons, living or dead, is entirely coincidental.

HARPERTORCH
An Imprint of HarperCollins*Publishers*
10 East 53rd Street
New York, New York 10022-5299

Copyright © 1998 by D.J. Duncan
ISBN: 0-380-81830-2

First HarperTorch mass market printing: March 2002
First Avon Books trade paperback printing: May 1998

HarperCollins ®, HarperTorch™, and ● ™ are trademarks of HarperCollins Publishers Inc.

Printed in the United States of America

Visit HarperTorch on the World Wide Web at www.harpercollins.com

10 9 8 7 6 5 4 3

THIS BOOK IS FOR
JESSICA WYNNE DUNCAN
MAY SHE LAUNCH
ALL THE SHIPS SHE WANTS,
NEITHER MORE NOR LESS.

CONTENTS

CONTENTS

DAUGHTER OF TROY

The Troad c 1250 BC

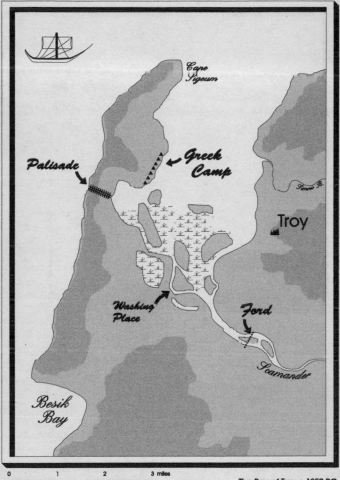

The Bay of Troy c 1250 BC

PRINCIPAL CHARACTERS

Briseis, the narrator.
King Briseus and *Queen Nemertes,* her parents
Sphelos, Enops, Bienor, her brothers.

Aeneas, leader of the Dardanian host, a cousin of Briseis.

Paris, Hector, Polydorus, sons of *Priam,* King of Troy.

Achilles, prince of Thessaly, greatest of the Greek heroes.
Patroclus, his friend and deputy.
Agamemnon, Great King of the Greeks.
His brother, *Menelaus,* king of Sparta and his wife, *Helen.*
Odysseus, king of Ithaca.

Mynes and *Epistrophos,* sons of *Euneus,* king of Hire.

A **complete** list of People and Places will be found at the
end of the book.

PROLOGUE

Nothing remained of the day except a red wound between earth and sky. Dark and Storm were rushing down together from the peaks as I stumbled through the ruins of Mycenae—thorns and thistles, fallen walls and gaping cellars whose charred timbers still bore the rank stench of a funeral when the pyre is quenched.

My destination was the skeleton ruin of the citadel that crouched on the hilltop above me like a sphinx guarding the pass. My chances of reaching it before the storm struck seemed slim. Between cursing my bruised shins and wrenched ankles, I called out prayers to Hermes, reminding him of the lamb I had sacrificed to him that morning. The Pathfinder must have heard me, for as I passed a tangle of thorns a voice spoke almost at my ear.

"Traveler?"

I jumped wildly and grabbed for the hilt of my sword. With my eyes full of tears, I had completely failed to see the speaker, and all the terrible tales of perils both human and inhuman that beset travelers flashed through my mind. I decided with relief that she was merely a very ancient woman, bent under a bundle of faggots, leaning on a staff. The wind roiled her dark gown and wisps of snowy hair.

"Grandmother, you scared me!"

She cackled shrilly. "Then you are timid indeed. I had appraised you as a most valiant hero, seeing as you seem bound for the palace."

"I seek shelter for the night."

"You will find a resting place for all eternity if you venture into that den of brigands."

"I heard it had fallen on hard times," I admitted. "Fabled Mycenae, rich in gold? My grandfather went there once, entering through the Lion Gate. He passed by many fine houses and the graves of fabled heroes on his way up to the palace. He marveled all his life at the splendors he saw there."

"Gone now! Sacked, rebuilt, and sacked again." She repeated her sinister cackle, sounding well pleased. "Aye, its walls will stand there until the ending of the world, but its kingly halls are destroyed. Those who dwell upon that hill now will cut that slender throat of yours for the cloak off your back, let alone the sword you bear."

I wondered if her eyes and wits could possibly be sharp enough to recognize just how valuable my sword was, for it was of the new sort—iron, not bronze—traded from valleys of the far north. Unfortunately, my skill with it did not match its quality.

"I am no Heracles to clean them out," I admitted. "You suggest I look elsewhere for hospitality?"

"I recommend it strongly." She waited for my offer.

"The gods enjoin charity to strangers."

"The gods know naught of hunger!"

The rain was starting, so I decided to trust her, although for all I knew she was housekeeper to a dozen brigands worse than any dwelling on the hilltop. I was very young in those days. "If you have a roof to share, Grandmother, I have a bag of beans and a lump of cheese. Lead me to your palace, that we may converse in comfort."

"Palace? I have dwelt in palaces in my time, lad, but the latest is not the greatest of them. Come then." She lunged forward with an awkward, scuttling gait, moving her three legs in a pattern complicated enough to puzzle the Sphinx itself. In moments she vanished, faggots and all, into a hole like the mouth of a beast's lair.

I followed, slithering down the remains of what had once been a staircase and crawling under an ox hide drape to find her on hands and knees, blowing up a tiny fire. The sickly gleam was enough to illuminate her entire residence, part of a large room whose ceiling had fallen bodily except in this one corner, where it now curved overhead like the roof of a tent. Even a heavy rain might bring the rest of the load crashing down. The place reeked of rot and smoke.

"Welcome to my megaron, stranger!" she croaked cheerfully. "Admire the frieze of griffins and lions behind you. The floor mosaic depicts an octopus motif in the Cretan style, although I admit it isn't visible, so you must take my word for it. But relax your limbs on a soft couch and I shall call the bard to sing for you."

There was barely room for two of us in her smelly kennel, together with a few smoked pots, a heap of rags to serve as bedding, and the sticks she had just brought in. I made myself as comfortable as possible on a fragment of masonry, my back to the wall.

My hostess raised herself painfully. "Beans, you said?"

I tossed the bag over the fire to her. "Beans and cheese. No wine, no flesh. Praise the Immortals."

She uttered her peculiar chuckle again and fumbled with the cord. Already my eyes watered so hard in the smoke that I was barely less blind than she.

"So who rules now in the halls of Atreus?" I demanded. "Who sits on the throne of Perseus?"

For a moment she made no reply, one claw scrabbling to locate a crock. At length she mumbled, "The Kind Ones."

I shuddered, thinking of Orestes. "*Hush,* woman! Do not speak of them lest they hear you!"

"Bats, then. Hawks mew in the halls of Agamemnon."

The storm hammered on the ruins, its lightning flashes through the chinks showing that she was indeed ancient—her face a wasteland of cruel wrinkles, her hands twisted like knotted cords, white cobwebs of hair about her shoulders. Yet, she was still tall. I wondered how she had seemed in her youth, before time flattened her dugs. In the flicker of the fire I tried to replace the lost flesh, smooth out the wrinkles, straighten the joints. Her eyes were dark, so I imagined her hair black. Long and shining. She did not bear herself like a slave nor speak like one. Once, certainly, she had been young.

"Have you lived long in golden Mycenae, Grandmother?"

"Too long."

"Knew you Tisamenus, the king?"

"Well, seeing from afar is not knowing. But, yes, I was here when Orestes' son ruled, and also Orestes himself, of unlucky memory."

She was even older than I had thought, then, for Tisamenus reigned in my grandfather's day. "Tell me of those men! Or tell me of yourself. Had you a husband? Did you bear no sons to ease your old age?" It was a thoughtless query, for gory Ares had sent many goodly men to the halls of Hades in her lifetime.

"No sons." She bared her gums in a Gorgonian leer. "Many men have entered me, but none ever emerged. Lovers aplenty . . . Nay, one love and many men. But enough man-juice to water all the Argolid never quickened my womb. Seeing me now in my decrepitude, stranger, are you surprised that my body once inflamed men's desires? Does the thought disgust you?"

"No, no!" I said hastily. "The maiden who cannot inflame men must be a fearful hag, and I do not believe you were that. You have a nobility of speech that tells me you were not the child of a swineherd."

"Ah, you seek to turn my head with flattery." She went back to stirring the crock in the fire.

It must have been a lifetime since she had smelled flattery, and no perfume is cheaper. "Grandmother, you have not always dwelt in such humble surroundings. Deny that once you ate off gold in palaces and adorned the bed of a noble warrior."

She cackled. "That is more true than you would believe, stranger. Hordes of great warriors have struggled to subdue my frail flesh, thrusting their spears into it until they were exhausted, and yet I always survived to vanquish the next. King Theseus of olden times never laid low so many heroes as I. Were I to tell you the truth of it, you would suppose my wits to be as wasted as my womb."

"As Father Zeus is my witness, I swear I shall not doubt a word you tell me. Come, then," I coaxed, "was it Orestes himself?"

"The mother-slayer? Aye, he was one, although so drunk he thought I was a man and treated me as such. I doubt he remembered by morning."

"It is true, that tale? He killed his own mother?"

"He did, and just for killing his father! She cut down her

husband when he returned from the Trojan War. I would not blame her for that. Agamemnon was a boor."

I laughed. "Oh, come, my lady! You do not expect me to believe that you knew Agamemnon, king of men?"

Her stick rattled angrily in the pot. Thunder roared directly overhead, shaking a shower of plaster from the looming ceiling. I flinched, as well I might.

"Alas! Here I vowed to the Lord of Storms that I would believe everything you said and then at once foreswear myself. Tell me, and I shall not doubt. You knew the son of Atreus?"

"I knew him," she mumbled. She twisted around painfully to grope for another pot. "Two sons of Atreus—Agamemnon, king of men, and red-haired Menelaus, lord of Sparta. I knew them both. They shared a royal gift for getting into trouble over women." Wrapping a hand in her rags, she lifted the crock from the fire and pushed it a small way across the floor in my direction. She laid an empty bowl beside it.

My scalp prickled. "But if you knew Menelaus, just how old are you, lady?"

"Too old to waste time talking about times that are forever dead."

"Nay!" I cried. "Those times shall live forever! The bards sing wondrous tales of the great heroes who went to Troy. Their deeds will never be forgotten while the wind blows, the great days before the palaces burned. Menelaus and Agamemnon, Diomedes and Ajax, the ingenious Odysseus—glorious heroes all! You knew these giants?"

When she did not answer, I reached for my supper. I first took out a mouthful on the stick and tossed it into the embers for the gods. Then I tipped out a fair share into the bowl for the old woman—not a half, certainly, but a good third. Suddenly her voice rang out louder than I had yet heard it, lit by a scorn I could not have expected.

"Giants? Heroes? They were but men who ate and pissed and slept as you do, who fornicated as you would like to. Do not believe all that the bards sing, young man! I have heard those songs myself; they summon ghosts to Troy, heroes dead for centuries raised up to fight in battles they never knew. Bards! Do they mourn for Troy, the great city laid waste? Do they count the slain or the wretched captives? They sing of heroism and glory and forget the pain, the shame, the suffering."

"You were there?"

She sighed with the wind. "I was there."

"A thousand ships!" I cried. "Ten years they fought below the walls—"

"Faugh! You have been listening to the bards, boy. There were never a thousand ships. That would mean fifty thousand men, and who would feed them? Nor did the struggle last ten years, although it may have seemed that long to some of the wretches who had to fight in it."

"Oh," I muttered, chastened. "And you say that Agamemnon and the rest were not giants, not great heroes?"

"I say that the bards sing only of triumph. They do not tell you that Agamemnon almost lost the war." She mumbled angrily and reached for her supper, snatching the hot food from the pot with her gnarled fingers and mashing it with her gums.

"There was another we have not mentioned," I said. "The greatest of them all—Achilles, sacker of cities and more than human, for his mother was a goddess . . . or is that an exaggeration also?"

She looked up then, her eyes shining like a cat's in the last glow of the dying embers, so almost it seemed that the brightness in those eyes was a glow of power and her size was that of an Immortal. I cringed back with my former mockery bitter in my throat.

"No, little man. The son of Peleus was more than all of the rest of them put together. There has never been a hero like Achilles, nor will be again. To see Achilles was to look upon a god."

"You knew him also?" I whispered. "Achilles?"

"Oh yes! I knew Achilles."

"You speak marvels in my ear! The storm still rages, and we have a long night ahead of us, lady. Take pity on a young man born in times so much less than yours, for there are no such heroes now. I shall never see men worthy to tread on their shadows, so tell me what manner of people they were. I know that Paris, son of King Priam, stole Helen, the wife of Menelaus of Sparta, and carried her home to Troy. I know that Menelaus's brother, Agamemnon, king of men, rallied the Greeks to go and bring her back, and thus the war began—that much surely is true?"

"It is not the whole truth. Even the sons of Atreus could not raise all that much trouble over a woman. But that tale will serve."

"Oh? So the Greeks sailed after her to Troy . . . ?"

She sighed and settled herself upon her leprous bedding. Her voice came again as a whisper, hardly audible over the wail of the wind and the babble of rain. "They sailed to Troy. They ravaged many lesser cities first, gathering chariots and horses, before closing in on Troy itself. None sacked more fair towns than Achilles and his Myrmidons."

"And you knew the son of Peleus?"

"I knew Achilles, little man. Truly a great spearman!" She sighed deeply. "Even mother-naked, he was a great spearman! You ask if I bedded with a warrior? I tell you I bedded the greatest of them all. Listen, and I will tell you how it was at Troy."

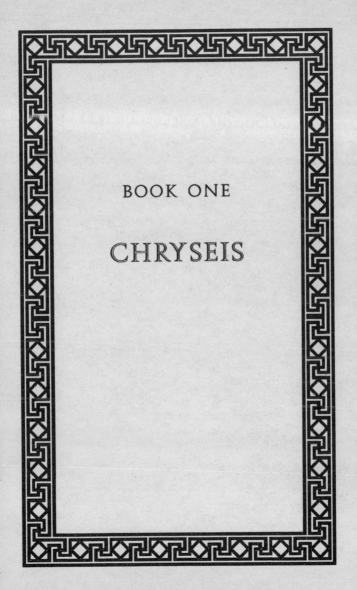

BOOK ONE

CHRYSEIS

1

"And who might you be, child?" demanded the Great King.

"Most noble son of Atreus, my name is Briseis," I said proudly.

"But whose woman are you?"

"I have the honor to be consort to Prince Achilles, my lord."

"Consort, indeed?" Agamemnon raised his shaggy brows. His followers laughed. "How fortunate you are! And how fortunate he is to have won so glorious a prize."

A chance meeting? Just a casual word spoken after a funeral? Nay, it was the gods themselves who brought about that slight encounter, for it was to bring much sorrow and the deaths of many splendid young men. I knew Agamemnon by sight, of course, as I knew all the leaders of the Greeks; he did not know me. He had seen me once, but he did not recall that first encounter, because it had been so arranged. He was not to forget this one.

Pestilence had struck the army camped before Troy. For days the deadly arrows of Smintheus, whom the Greeks call Apollo, had been striking down both pack beasts and men, noble and commoner alike, causing balefires to blaze day and night. Unlike Trojans, the Greeks would rather bury their dead than burn them, but they refused to lay their comrades in foreign soil, nor could their spades have kept pace with the awful toll. It was as he was returning from lighting a funeral pyre that Agamemnon first knowingly set eyes on me. Surely great Zeus himself decreed that inauspicious meeting.

I had left the camp and was on my way to sacrifice to the Mistress of Winds, whose altar stood on the hill south of the bay. I had suggested this to Achilles that morning, explaining that the Lady frequently granted relief from sickness. Although she was not a goddess known in Thessaly, he had agreed that I should go to her, because all gods must be honored and it might be that she was angry at being neglected. He had ransacked his storeroom and found a vial of rare perfumed oil for me to take.

I was not alone, of course. I had an armed escort and a following of fifty or sixty women, all bearing loads of laundry on their heads and many accompanied by children. We wound our way south from the camp, glad of any excuse to leave its confines for a while. I supervised the Myrmidons' women in their work, and washing clothes in the river was a large part of that work. Truth be told, I had very little to do by day during those months I spent at Troy. At night I was certainly kept busy enough—most enjoyably so—but by day I sometimes found the shadows turning slowly. I had no loom or spindle to busy my fingers in the spinning and weaving that had filled my hours at home in Lyrnessos; but I had run the palace there and running Achilles' camp was no harder.

Being the lady of a great sacker of cities had much to commend it, especially in the choice of wardrobe. Chests of booty were stacked to the roof in the porch of Achilles' house, and he had told me often that it could find no better use than to adorn my beauty. In ten years, I could not have exhausted the riches there. When I had thoroughly explored one box, I would ask Patroclus or even Achilles himself to lift down another. They laughed at me for treating them like porters, but they would always oblige, just to demonstrate their strength and win a kiss of thanks.

To honor the goddess I had dressed in the finest garment I could find—a gown of wool fine as gossamer, woven in red and gold and sea purple, with a wide flounced skirt, short sleeves, and a tight bodice that left my breasts uncovered in courtly style. Old Maera anointed me with oil and scents and arranged my raven hair in trailing ringlets. She helped me into the gown and set gilded shoes of soft calf leather on my feet. Scorning gold and silver as too showy for such an occasion, I looped four strings of rock-crystal beads around my neck and laid a fine veil over my head. Hanging a fleecy cloak upon my shoulders as protection from the inevitable wind, I strode forth with Maera shuffling at my heels.

The women were waiting for me, bantering with grinning spearmen, who at once lost all interest in them and turned to gape at me with flattering amazement. Since coming to the camp, I had never sported such finery outside the privacy of Achilles' lodge. If their reactions were typical, it would be an interesting outing.

Although Patroclus admitted the Trojans were well locked up within their walls, he always insisted on providing an escort, and that day the leader leaning on his spear aloof from the rest was his own charioteer, Alcimus son of Polyctor. Alcimus was the palest person I ever met, with milk-white hair and baby skin, and in consequence he looked like a child. He never smiled, although he sometimes pulled back his lips to display his teeth, and then he looked like a corpse. He was good at killing Trojans; but I never liked him, and the men feared him.

With no more greeting than a cold stare, he led the way southward along the beach where the ships lay, the older children running ahead of us and the youngsters clinging to their mothers. Horses grazed among the tents and huts of the army to our right, while eastward lay the silver-shining bay with the plain beyond and Troy itself, the towered citadel on its hill. The day seemed perfect, yielding no hint of the evil it was to bring.

We took a path that wound between marsh on the right and the bay's mud flats on the left. In places it had been built up with heaps of brushwood, and in others it was still swamp—impassable for chariots and not exactly a convenient road for walking in gilded shoes but a practical shortcut. The alternative was to go around the marsh by the chariot trail, but that was longer. In the distance, smoke drifted from the morning's pyres.

Halfway along this trail, we saw a band of men approaching, led by the Great King himself. I had no especial fear of Agamemnon and no great wish to meet him either. He was attended by four of the most senior Greek leaders— on his right his brother, red-haired Menelaus; on his left

Odysseus, king of Ithaca; with Achilles and the Greater Ajax following behind them, those two towering over everyone else. At their backs came fifty or so lesser men, although most would have seemed outstanding in any other company. They were variously clad in kilts or tunics or breeches, but every man wore bronze greaves on his shins. Sunlight gleamed on their oiled limbs and clean-shaven faces; the breeze played with their long, trailing hair.

Achilles was declaiming so vehemently about something that he did not notice us, but Agamemnon did. Where his brother was ruddy and Achilles gold, the king was swarthy. He lacked Achilles' giant stature or the breadth of Odysseus, but he was an imposing man, one who stood out even in that company. Take away the gold-studded scepter he bore, the rich purple tunic with its gold beadwork, the jewelry adorning his neck and arms, and a stranger would still have known him at once for the Great King. His shadowed eyes fixed on me at a distance.

Alcimus selected a tussocky patch of land, a tiny island, and ordered us to stand clear of the path so the Great King could pass. I sank to my knees and the other women copied me. The men raised spears in salute.

I saw that Agamemnon had noticed me, and more than my attire had caught his eye. I was then in the fullness of high-breasted youth and as tall as any of the spearmen. My lips were wide and so red that I rarely painted them; as were my nipples and aureoles. My hair was as black and shiny as jet. Any true man would notice me.

The Great King halted. They all halted. Achilles stopped talking. I expected him to smile at me as he usually did, but he merely looked me over and nodded as if approving my choice of jewels. Agamemnon gestured for me to rise, so I rose and let them all admire me from a new angle. No one would speak before the Overlord did, but there was much nudging and pursing of lips going on. Achilles would be pleased. Like any successful warrior, he welcomed a chance to display the fine bedmate and other treasures he had won with his spear.

The question was asked: "And who might you be, child?"

Any other woman in the Greek camp might have hoped to attract the Great King's fancy and win a promotion, but

Achilles was the greatest warrior in the army. I had absolutely no desire to change my station and no fear that
Agamemnon would dare even suggest such a thing. I proclaimed my name and that of my lord proudly.

The dark eyes glittered. "Indeed? How fortunate you are!
And how fortunate he is to have won so glorious a prize." He
glanced inquiringly at Achilles.

Achilles said, "Lyrnessos."

The heavy lids hardly moved, and yet a mask came over
Agamemnon's dark eyes. He was a hairy man, with matted
arms and a black hedge at the neck of his tunic; for a moment he seemed like a stuffed bear as he stood there, pondering. Achilles was hairy, too, but the sunlight turned the
red-gold haze on his great chest and arms to flame, making
him glow like an Immortal.

"Strange!" murmured the Great King. "I do not recall seeing this goddess at Lyrnessos."

"She was there with the rest, son of Atreus."

"Indeed? And is she as good as she looks?"

Achilles' blue stare became suddenly deadly. "Every bit
as good."

Agamemnon chuckled majestically and strode off without
another word, the rest hastening after. I saw Patroclus go by,
frowning at me in a way I could not remember him ever
doing before.

That was all that happened, and yet, like the little mouse
god Smintheus who can lay low an army, that brief exchange
was to lead to the death of many splendid warriors.

2

The washing place was busy that sunny morning, with hundreds of women trampling clothes, churning mud, spreading
garments out to dry, and squabbling, screaming, laughing,

and flirting with the amused soldiers who guarded them. Not a few had already disappeared into the reeds and rushes, but I made sure that the Myrmidons' women behaved themselves—they got quite enough excitement after dark for the good of their health. Children swarmed underfoot.

Most of the women were lowborn, of course, or even slaves by birth, but some were of noble blood, like me; and I had resolved to invite a few of the better ladies to accompany me on my visit to the goddess. Observing Hecamede and Melantho in conversation under a solitary willow that had somehow escaped the army's scouring of the plain, I picked my way over the marshy ground to join them.

Hecamede was from Tenedos and could claim a distant cousinship to Antenor, one of the great Trojan leaders, but the relationship was too distant to have produced a ransom for her. Despite her mature years, her wit and breeding had moved old King Nestor to choose her as his camp consort, his interest in women being more intellectual than the younger men's. Melantho was widow of the king of Larisa and still agile enough to have won Menestheus of Athens as her patron. Although both much older than I, these ladies were charming company and had helped me greatly in my first days in the camp, while I was adjusting to my new life.

They were still complimenting me on my attire when Chryseis slunk over and invited herself into the discussion. Her husband, Pollis son of Eëtion, had been a prince of Thebe—another city sacked by Achilles—but she was an uncouth brat, a mere priest's daughter. With her stringy red hair and a figure astonishingly voluptuous for her years, she was the Great King's current favorite and thus a very good demonstration of the unreliability of men's judgment. I smiled at her politely enough and continued.

"Ladies, I am on my way to sacrifice to the Mistress of the Winds. I hope that she may be persuaded to cleanse us of the pestilence or may send us a sign so that we can understand how we have offended. Perhaps you would care to accompany me and add your prayers to my own?"

Melantho nodded approvingly. "I shall do so gladly, although I lack your god-given gift of reading omens."

"And I also," said Hecamede. "I only wish I were more suitably clad."

Reluctantly I looked to Chryseis to include her in the invitation.

She smirked back at me. "Is that dress meant to be like that, darling, or have you burst out of it?"

Such a remark could be ignored, for Hecamede and Melantho knew well enough what ladies wore in high fashion. "The day is unseasonably warm," I said.

"Will not your lovely ivory tits turn brown as walnuts?"

Melantho murmured reprovingly, but I decided that a lesson was needed. "Pay no attention to her, ladies. Her spite arises from boredom. I hear that the Overlord has not called her to his bed in a month."

Chryseis's shriek must have alarmed the watchers on the walls of Troy, miles away. "That is not true! He always calls for me when he retires. He may send for other girls later, for he is strong and lusty, but he always takes me first!" She was admitting that she lacked either variety or stamina, for I was mortally certain that Agamemnon could not catch Achilles' dust in matters virile, and Achilles had not laid hand on another woman since he first embraced me. I would not have cheapened myself by saying so, even had she given me time to draw breath.

"He swears," she screamed, "that after the war is over he will take me back to Mycenae to live out my years in his palace and please him in bed."

"I am sure Queen Clytemnestra will be delighted to meet you and give you pointers on technique," I replied with dignity. "The son of Peleus will take me home to Thessaly. It is admittedly a lesser land than Mycenae, but he does intend to marry me."

Flushed like a robin's breast, Chryseis aimed her nails in my direction. "Oh, so that is why you favor that butcher Achilles, is it? The monster who has slain so many of your countrymen, sacked a dozen cities, shed torrents—"

"Twenty-three cities," I said, with commendable dedication to detail. "Twelve by sea and eleven by land."

"You pray to the gods to aid the Greeks against your own people?"

Her logic escaped me. I smiled at the ladies to show how I disdained this petty bickering. "Warfare is men's business. The outcome of the war is the gods'. My interest is that the Immortals have given me to a man who is universally recognized as the finest warrior and most godlike hero of all. Furthermore, he loves me as much as I love him, knowing I will satisfy him gladly, no matter how strenuous his demands. I thank Aphrodite for her kindness to me. What happens on the battlefield is none of my concern."

Before the brat could utter another shriek, I added, "Why? Do you favor the Trojan cause, Chryseis? If that is where your loyalty lies, then surely your duty is to slide a knife between Agamemnon's ribs when next he covers you."

Hecamede and Melantho both gasped in horror. Even the priest's whelp was momentarily at a loss for words.

But not for long, alas. "The gods need no help from me!" she screeched. "Do you not see that the Greeks' cause is doomed because they abducted me? They spurned my father's pleas and refused his ransom, so he took my cause to Smintheus, who sent this pestilence. I tell you, the Greeks are paying for my suffering!"

"You utter blasphemy, child!" Hecamede cried.

"Oh, let her continue," I said. "Speak a little louder, darling, so the whole army can hear you."

The listening soldiers were already glaring. Realizing that she had said too much, Chryseis glanced around nervously. "You will see!" she spat, and off she went, splashing through the marsh.

"There really is no accounting for some men's tastes." I sighed. "Even kings'."

Accompanied by Hecamede, Melantho, and a few other noble ladies, I set off across the plain to the altar. Spring was a dazzle of color, from the new foliage on the distant oaks and willows to the fresh green of the flower-spangled grass underfoot. The spearmen Alcimus sent with us followed at a respectful distance, not crowding around to indulge in vulgar flirting as they did with the lowborn women. Old Maera slowed us, but Melantho drew me a little ahead of the others for a private word.

She seemed worried. "Do you suppose Chryseis is truly the cause of the god's anger?"

"Why not? It seems likely that the goddess has already spoken to us out of her mouth. Yet she has been here many months, and it is not many days since the pestilence struck."

"That was just after her father sought to ransom her. The Great King refused and sent him away."

I had not heard that. "It could not have been much of a ransom."

"It is said to have been prodigious."

Truly, the sons of Atreus had a knack for getting into trouble over women. However mysterious the ways of the gods, it made sense that Smintheus had sent the pestilence because his priest had been insulted. Chryseis was the problem, so Chryseis must go. That was the gods' will, and I should be happy to arrange it for them.

The altar was a simple pair of stone horns, set on a bare hillside that was surely the windiest spot around, although the Plain of Troy is notorious for wind. I offered wine and barley and tipped out Achilles' perfumed oil from a silver rhyton, explaining who had sent it. My companions aided me in singing a hymn or two, and we danced for the goddess. The wind began to bluster, roiling our gowns and hair and making us stagger and laugh—normally that wind would be a sure sign that the Mistress had heard our prayer, but the wind always rises in the middle of the day at Troy. No, it was the solitary bird that sat in the lone oak tree behind the shrine and chirped its infuriating song the whole time that told me our prayers had been answered. None of my companions seemed to notice it; but the ability to read omens is granted to few, and I was one of those few.

3

As I headed homeward with my charges and guards, I mulled over the Chryseis problem. If Agamemnon had in fact angered a god by refusing a ransom offer for the red-haired slut, I would not be the one to tell him so. Like me, she was a prize of honor, although why carroty hair and pointed tits turned men's wits so was beyond me. No, the suggestion would have to come from Calchas, the Great King's own soothsayer. He would be believed. I decided I must arrange that.

The long cape was a natural stronghold. Its hills had been pared clear of trees, and even the scrub was disappearing now, for great herds of animals roamed there: pigs, goats, cattle, but above all horses—the famous horses of Troy, rounded up by the Greeks. The Myrmidon camp was at the extreme north end, so I had to walk the whole length of the Greek army, with tents and shacks on my left, beached ships on my right: Cretans, Spartans, Mycenaeans, Arkadians, Boeotians, and innumerable lesser contingents. Even the dogs that barked at me had their own accents.

When I first arrived, a year earlier, I noted that Achilles' camp was in the safest possible location, as far as possible from any Trojan attack. I dared to question Patroclus about this curious fact, because I could not believe the son of Peleus would ever shun danger.

"Danger?" Patroclus said with a laugh. "When he's around, danger hides under the bed. But do not feel bad if you fail to understand." Chuckling, he told me the story.

"In the first days after the landing, when we realized that we could not take Troy by storm and must settle in for a long stay, Ajax son of Telamon claimed the south end of the line, closest to the foe. As soon as he defined the place of honor, all the other leaders were honor bound to dispute his right to it. While no one denies that Ajax himself is the greatest fighter after Achilles, his Salamisians are a small contingent. Leaders like Diomedes and Idomeneus who had brought the most ships felt entitled to the honor, and every one of the others tried to find compelling reasons why he should have it—some of their arguments being extremely ingenious.

"Finding he had a major squabble on his hands, Agamemnon called a council of war to settle the matter. At first it solved nothing, for no leader would support anyone's right except his own, although they were in agreement that the Great King's natural place was in the center, all being mindful of his notoriously delicate temper. Achilles just sat and said nothing, but no one noticed his silence except Odysseus son of Laertes, who is a man of subtle mind. At last he rose and took the speaker's staff.

" 'My lords,' he said, 'we could argue here all day, while the Trojans lick their wounds and sharpen spears. The dispute must be settled quickly and harmoniously. We might, for example, agree to choose positions by lot, so the gods decide for us. To save time, though, may I respectfully point out that the son of Telamon was the first to ask for the most southern position and we should honor his request. Furthermore, the son of Peleus, who is universally acknowledged to be an even greater fighter, does not seem to contest his right to that location. May we inquire what his own choice is?'

"So he passed the staff to Achilles, and Achilles rose and took it.

" 'Son of Atreus,' he said, 'and all your lordships, let the son of Telamon have the south end by all means. As no one seems to want the north end, I shall be happy to camp there.'

"At that he sat down, leaving the entire council speechless, for they could not believe that the bellicose son of Peleus would seek the *safest* place to put his Myrmidons. Nevertheless, the Great King quickly accepted this arrangement, and so the matter was settled!"

"An amusing tale, my lord," I said, "but a mere woman such as myself cannot possibly understand what moral it bears."

"Quite simple," Patroclus answered. "The Trojans have

ships, do they not? They fish, trade, go raiding just as Greeks do?"

"Indeed they do."

"But their fleet was nowhere to be seen! We still have not found it. Now the Dardanelles to the north of us is a strange branch of Ocean, a saltwater river that flows always to the west. Even a crude raft can always sail *down* the Dardanelles, but on very few days each year do freak winds allow even a strong crew to traverse it eastward, against the current. Achilles therefore surmised that Hector must have moved the Trojan vessels to safety in those eastern lands of which we Greeks know little—home of the Phrygians, Amazons, Paphlagonians, and Halizones. And whether the Trojan ships are lurking there or not, many Trojan allies certainly are, all of them capable of building rafts or paddling boats. Thus the Trojans can launch an attack down the Dardanelles and into the Bay of Troy at any time. The north end of the camp is at least as dangerous as the south."

"I see. But from my experience of Hector, he will never think of such a strategy."

Patroclus's eyes twinkled. "He has many wily brothers to advise him, I understand?"

"Oh, yes!" I agreed, with a sigh of nostalgia. "Some of his brothers are as wily as foxes."

At the Myrmidons' encampment I encountered real signs of life, for Achilles would never allow his men to mope. He knew every one of them by name and drilled them constantly, so that they were the best and most versatile fighters in the army. If he had nothing better to do—meaning no one to fight—he would be out there with them himself, but today Peisander and Menesthius were shouting the orders, supervising a mass team-wrestling contest in the water. Hundreds of men were churning the sea to foam, choking, cursing, but mostly laughing. I recalled that Achilles had suggested that exercise to Patroclus the previous evening. Alcimus and his squad speedily stripped and raced into the water to join the melee. I ordered the women to stop gaping and start preparing the midday meal.

Bidding Maera to move faster, I left the beach and passed through the tents and parked chariots to the paddock. Beside it stood the fine wooden lodge the men had built for Achilles, and there I paused to catch my breath while the dogs came sniffing and wagging to greet me. Often Achilles would stand right here, staring across the bay to distant Troy, planning how he would throw down its proud walls and fire its towers. Sometimes, though, he would venture on westward and climb the higher ground along the coast. From there he could gaze at the booming sea itself—not to admire the view of Imbros or the blue peak of Samothrace beyond it, but because westward lay Thessaly. Homesickness was a universal pestilence among the Greeks, and even the greatest warrior was not immune.

Another month, they had said when I first came to the camp—Troy would starve by the next full moon. But the moon waxed and waned, winter came and went, and now there was talk of allies slipping in through the hills with supplies and reinforcements: Thracians, Paeones, Lycians, and others. They would be more mouths for the defenders to feed, but also more spears to defend the city or assault the Greek camp, which is what Achilles was expecting Hector to try soon. Thanks to that little carrot-haired bitch, the Greeks were laid low by pestilence!

I went in without waiting for Maera to catch up. There were two big rooms. The first was termed the porch, although it also served as kitchen and storeroom, and boxes of loot were stacked high along both sides. There was even more stored in the ships; and yet all of it, Achilles grumbled, was only a fraction of the wealth he had collected. Agamemnon kept most of the booty for himself.

The megaron beyond was large and high-roofed, but dim, for it had no windows and the clerestory roof let little light in and less smoke out. This big chamber was cool in summer and reasonably warm in winter, and had it been furnished tastefully with a handful of battle trophies and a few stools grouped around the central hearth, it could have been an imposing warrior's hall. Alas, it was overwhelmed by its contents. Glittering cataracts of bronze weapons sheathed the walls. There was scarcely room to move between tables, chairs, footstools, and ornate chests, all inlaid with ivory or silver, every piece worth a fortune. When I had first arrived, a year earlier, I tried to simplify this pirate's lair, only to discover that Achilles liked it the way it was. He exulted in his ostentatious litter of riches. He kept adding to it.

Old Maera came hobbling in, tiny and bent, a black beetle of a woman.

"Hurry, now!" I told her as I shed my gown. "We must go out again."

"You're meddling, my lady!"

"I have a right to meddle."

She crunched up wrinkles in a smile. "Just because you saw an omen, yes?"

I should have known it would not have escaped her notice. Maera was as blind as a mole and small enough to vanish in tall grass, but she could see important things better than most people.

Swathed in a drab brown robe, with my head covered by a shawl, I set out to find Calchas. No law said I must not wander around the camp. Patroclus might fret about my safety, but Achilles certainly saw no point in winning a prize of honor and then shutting her up where other men never saw her. He wanted them to lust after me and it would never occur to him that anyone might dare harm anything of his. He would not approve of what I was about to do, though. Caution was required.

Young men accosted me several times. When they were polite, then so was I. If they were obnoxious, I was curt. Mostly I felt sorry for them, those young farmers, herders, or woodcutters dragged away from their homes and families to fight a war that did not concern them. Why should they die to help the king of Sparta reclaim a wife he had not been man enough to keep in the first place? So I would smile sadly and say that their interest flattered me, but I could not oblige them, because I was the consort of the son of Peleus. Then they would jump like grasshoppers and back away.

I certainly could not just march along the shore to the

Mycenaean contingent and inquire where the famous augur was. No, I decided while passing the Lokrians, I must not interrogate any man at all. The women were unlikely to gossip to their masters about Achilles' lady going around asking questions. They all knew who I was and who I had been.

Unfortunately, it turned out that very few of them had ever heard of Calchas son of Thestor. I could trudge up and down the cape all day, but Maera could not. Other methods were required, so I spread out my arms and said a prayer to the goddess who was guiding me. Then I watched the birds.

They led me to the western cliffs, where the land dropped steeply to the noisy foam. They did not take me to the exact spot, though, and I had to wander along the edge for some time until I found a narrow path angling down to disappear under an overhang. Handing my shawl and cloak to Maera, I began my descent. The trail narrowed until there was barely room for my shoes. I had to work my way along sideways, holding on to the grass and weeds with both hands, while the wind tore at my dress and the waves raged on the rocks below. Around the corner, I came to a hollow in the cliff face—barely a cave, for the floor sloped so precariously that no one would have dared sleep in it. There, brooding by himself with his elbows on his knees, sat Calchas.

He was long and gaunt, wrapped in a ragged cloak that flapped loosely around his cadaverous limbs. His shriveled cheeks and sparse white locks bespoke great age, and his bony jaw worked all the time, as if he were trying to chew his tongue. He rolled his eyes at me angrily.

"Daughter of Briseus, you will bring great sorrow upon the Greeks!" His voice had a hollow, ghostly timbre, echoes from a vaulted tomb.

"Such is not my intention, honored son of Thestor."

"But such will be your consequence."

I sat down as comfortably as possible on the rubbly slope beside him, although I felt as though I were about to tip out and fall to the surf. "Then aid me to avert that consequence."

"You are reputed to be a seer. Think you that you can turn aside the gods' will?"

"Of course not." I discovered that he had effectively

ended the conversation, which is a problem when arguing with someone who thinks he knows the gods' will better than you do. "How did you know who I was?"

"From dreams. From the flight of birds. How did you find me?"

"From the flight of birds. Have they also told you why the Archer sent the pestilence?"

He rolled his god-crazed eyes at me. "You know the cause."

"That Chryseis slut."

"Why do you call her that?" His jaw worked, and he slavered. "Because her round arms are whiter than yours?"

Tempted to point out that his face was the color of raw liver, I remained calm and more respectful than I felt. "Because she admits it. A god spoke the words through her mouth. And I made an offering to Our Lady of the Winds, who sent me a sign."

He glared. "What sign?"

"A cuckoo, sitting on a tree by the altar, twittering away; 'Cuckoo, cuckoo.' "

He rocked, waved both arms in the air, clasped them around his head, and generally behaved as if he were about to have a fit. "Cuckoo! What sort of omen is that? There are thousands of cuckoos around just now, woman—it is spring! And they all say 'cuckoo'! If it had recited hexameters to you, now, or hooted like an owl, that might have been a sign."

"I have *heard* the thousands of cuckoos, son of Thestor. The difference was that I *saw* this one. Cuckoos haunt the deep woods. They do not sit on exposed branches and watch women dancing. What the goddess was telling us was that we have a cuckoo's chick in our nest—who else but Chryseis?"

He snarled and stared furiously at the sea.

"Am I right?" I asked.

He nodded angrily.

"Then why," I persisted, "do you not advise the son of Atreus to mend his ways?"

Calchas chomped his gums and rolled his eyes. "Because

the woman was a prize of honor. Because I fear his rage. Even if he does not smite me as I speak, he will store up hatred for me in his heart. The lowborn cannot contest with kings."

"If you speak with the good of the army in mind, Achilles will certainly defend you."

"You commit the son of Peleus, do you? He jumps to your bidding?"

Infuriating old trickster! "Of course not, but I know he is a man of honor and high principle."

"He can also be a hotheaded young fool, lacking respect for his elders."

No fool like an old fool! "Such words are hardly the way to win his support. I can tell him . . ." I thought for a moment. "I shall explain the problem to Patroclus son of Menoitios, Achilles' companion. He will explain it to Achilles."

"And advise his dearest friend to spit at the king in public?"

"Er . . . Achilles will do whatever is best."

"What is best for all the Greeks will be for Achilles to put away the woman Briseis."

My answer verged upon a screech. "How *dare* you! The son of Peleus loves me. He has sworn he will take me back to Thessaly and marry me!"

Calchas turned his time-ravaged face in my direction, chewing even faster than before. "No, he will give you up."

"You are talking nonsense! If he promises to protect you from the king's anger, will you speak?"

"I will speak, but you will rue what you are doing, woman."

I rose, balancing precariously on the slope. "I trust Achilles!" I snapped, and departed.

4

Achilles' favorite recreation was feasting with the kings and captains in Agamemnon's hall, and his next best was entertaining his own followers in the lodge. I preferred the nights he spent with just Patroclus, Iphis, and me. I enjoyed the singing, for both men had fine voices and played the kithara with skill, but even more I liked the lovemaking, which would begin early and go on a long time. Tonight he had invited the Myrmidon leaders. I did not intend to bring up the Chryseis affair with him, not directly. He looked to me for relaxation from the stress of war, and I would not soothe his cares by chattering politics at him.

Long before sunset, I sent the other women away to tend their masters, for Achilles did not hoard his captives as some leaders did. He had not merely assigned women to his senior followers but had distributed the rest among the war bands. Now every tent had at least one, making the Myrmidons the envy of other contingents. Maera tottered off to deliver a baby somewhere, so only Iphis and I remained. Iphis was little older than I, with lovely thick hair and lustrous dark eyes like huge pools of starry sky. She was always eager to please, and if Patroclus was satisfied with a dimwit as a bed partner, it was none of my business. He was patient with her—never mocking, as most men would.

We set everything ready for the meal and laid out clean garments that had been aired in the sun all day, smelling of new grass. We put cauldrons of water to warm on the hearth. Finally we prepared ourselves, donning simple linen chitons clasped by a single pin at the shoulder; we combed and arranged each other's tresses. Now all we needed were men to tend. That evening I ordered Iphis to remain inside the megaron, while I kept watch in the porch.

To my delight, Patroclus appeared first, walking alone

through the ships. He was a tall man—although he did not seem so when he was close to Achilles—supple and well-shaped, moving always with the grace of a trout in a pool. His hair was the brown of acorns and so curly that it would not trail down his back as most of the Greeks' did, but bunched up around his head and neck in a mane. He had an easy smile and a soft voice. No man could be so dazzlingly handsome without being aware of it, but I never saw Patroclus make use of his beauty the way attractive people often do. He did not flaunt it by adorning himself with excessive amounts of gold and jewels, nor did he collect boys, although he could have had half the army for a smile. He was closer to Achilles than his shadow, yet I never saw them exchange intimacies other than the hugs of greeting any men share. If there had been physical passion between them in their youth, they had grown out of it and diverted their lusts completely to women, as Iphis and I could cheerfully testify.

That night he seemed preoccupied. His tunic was dusty and bedraggled, his face sweat-streaked and even dustier, but when he saw me, it lit up with one of those smiles that make a whole day seem worthwhile. As he stepped through into the shadows of the porch, that smile dimmed like a flower-decked meadow shadowed by a cloud.

"That was an unfortunate meeting this morning, Briseis."

"Yes, my lord. Er . . . has Achilles said anything?"

"No. I don't think he will."

We were discussing Agamemnon, of course, and not saying everything we might have said.

"What else have you been up to, lioness?"

"Up to, son of Menoitios? Me? Attending to my duties, of course."

He shook his head in wry disbelief. "You want to ask me something before Achilles returns. Speak quickly, then."

I had not expected him to bare my soul quite so speedily. Patroclus was a wonderful person, the second best man in the world, but I must not let him think that I was conspiring against his prince.

"I learned something that he ought to know," I explained. "Probably just idle camp gossip, but—"

"But it is none of your business and you want me to do your dirty work. What is this scandal?"

"I heard a rumor that the pestilence was sent by the son of Leto because his priest has a daughter who—"

"No, it is not your business! Everybody knows that."

"They do? Well, I didn't. Not till today."

He shrugged. "Suspect it, then. No one speaks of it."

"Does Achilles know?"

"Perhaps, perhaps not. You are not to tell him, do you hear?"

I bowed my head in assent, but I whispered, "Shouldn't someone do something about it?"

"Such as tell Agamemnon to send her home? Will you volunteer?"

"No, my lord. But Calchas son of—"

Patroclus took my shoulders in his fine, strong hands. His eyes shone like well-polished olive wood. "Briseis, you have been meddling!"

"No, no! Not at all—"

"If you shame Achilles, then he will have to put you away. His honor will be in question, and he will have no choice. The least he can do then is send you to the slave market on Lemnos."

"I just happened to run into Calchas!" I protested.

"No one has seen Calchas for days. The king has turned the camp outside in looking for him, but you just happen to run into him?"

I blurted it out. "The Lady led me to him. He will not speak unless Lord Achilles shields him from Agamemnon's anger!"

Patroclus frowned. "That would be open defiance."

"I merely repeat what I was told, my lord."

"Oh, Briseis, Briseis! Achilles is the only man who might dare challenge Agamemnon like that, but it would have to be done in a council, and Achilles is not the most patient man in council. The son of Atreus is distrustful and treats any complaint as insurrection. Stay out of men's business! Besides, it is not safe for you to go tramping around the camp like that. Have you any notion how one glimpse of you can drive men mad with desire?"

I knew how it could inspire Achilles, and the compliment made me smile. "You seem quite sane to me at the moment, my lord."

An arm the size of a ship's mast went around me and its mate around Patroclus. "What foul conspiracy do I find in my house?" Achilles demanded cheerfully. "Who is seducing whom?" He kissed my forehead, then beamed down at us with eyes bluer than the sky.

"Your fair lady is setting her cap at the king," Patroclus retorted. "Didn't you see her try to trap him this morning?"

"Never!" I cried. "I wouldn't serve the son of Atreus if he whipped me from here to Crete."

Frowning, Achilles released us. "He is the Great King, appointed by Zeus. Do not speak of him so."

I pressed my hands against his back and laid my head on his chest. "Forgive your errant slave, my lord. I am spoiled for all other men."

At my back, Patroclus groaned loudly. "I feel in need of consolation. Where is that filly from Skyros? Iphis, come here and love me!"

I heard her squeal of joy as she came running, but I wasn't really listening. Achilles was kissing me again, this time with more attention to detail, but I sensed that my remark about Agamemnon had offended him. My heroic lover was lordly and gracious, and I adored him. Most of the time he went through life with the simple joy of a small boy masquerading as a Titan; but sometimes I would catch glimpses of the other Achilles, the ruthless sacker of cities, and that one was absolutely terrifying.

Now followed the ritual I enjoyed every evening, when I had him all to myself. He removed his sword and helmet, dropped his kilt, and sat on the stool I had set beside the hearth. After I had removed his greaves and boots, I took a sponge and washed him from head to toe, and rinsed and combed his hair. Usually he made conversation while I was doing that, inquiring after my day, my troubles, my wants. Once I had expressed a desire for a gold bracelet, and he straightway strode out to the porch, naked and soaking, and came back with four. He never discussed his day, because that was men's business; but that evening he was unusually silent, either still upset by my criticism of Agamemnon or troubled by other matters. Iphis and Patroclus were going through the same procedure on the far side of the hearth, with quiet chuckles and lustful whispers that I pretended not to hear.

When I had dried Achilles, I rubbed him with perfumed oil, and that evening I had selected a vial scented with cypress, one of his favorites. There was a lot of him to anoint, and it was a procedure I always found enjoyable and even exciting. If he had been exercising, he would lie down so I could massage away the stiffness, but that day he just sat on the stool, so lost in thought that I began to feel quite worried. I attended to his wide back, his great chest, the hard muscles of his arms. I was kneeling beside him, working on his thighs, when he seemed to realize how taciturn he was being.

"My love, you made a great impression on the kings, today. Half of them thought some goddess had come to visit us. I was wonderfully proud of you."

"I am happy to know that." And relieved also. "Do you wish me to dress like that every day?"

He chuckled and shook his head, although he was probably tempted by the idea. "No! You'd tantalize them to death. But wear it for our guests tonight. Did your sacrifice go well? Is there anything you need?"

"Just this." I fondled his member, deliberately provoking it. It jerked at my touch, coming alive. Taking his silence for consent, I bent my head to kiss it and it reacted even more. Excited now, I continued to tease, making it grow larger and warmer. When I reached down to stroke his scrotum, he parted his thighs for me. Very soon I had raised the great spear of his manhood fully erect. Rising, I put my lips first to his nipples, raising them also, and then to his mouth, feeling the familiar throb of anticipation in my own loins. He unclipped the pin of my chiton so the cloth fell away. He stroked a great, killer's hand up my thigh, sending waves of delight surging through me.

Very few men, in my wide experience, will ever allow a

woman to take the lead in love. Most of them insist on being master, on being on top and in charge. Achilles was sometimes an exception. Soon I put one leg over and stood astride him so he could kiss my breasts. Clutching his head to them, I began to impale myself, inch by inch, easing over that magnificent phallus; sword slid into scabbard, man into woman. I moaned when I came to rest on his lap, holding all of it within me—no other man was ever as filling or fulfilling as Achilles. Even then, he just sat there with his eyes closed, his hands caressing my breasts and thighs but letting me find my own pleasure. I rose and sank back again. As my movements became more urgent, he began to breathe faster, his fair-skinned face grew flushed and bedewed, but still he allowed me to set the pace. I have known no other man who would do that.

Some men enjoy hurting their bedmates, but Achilles never did, at least not deliberately. He was as considerate as lover could be, and yet his size and enormous strength, even his bloody reputation, brought a fearful zest to his lovemaking, a sense of bedding down with a full-grown tawny lion, eager to romp but capable of rending a playmate to shreds by mistake. Often I would find myself bruised and aching afterward, although I never disliked what was happening at the time or regretted it later—I was no shirker in such encounters and inflicted many scratches and bite marks on him in turn. But to be given that wonderful body to play with, as I was that evening by the fire, was the greatest joy for me. I rode him without mercy, I galloped him like a Dardanian warhorse, and when at last my whole being exploded in ecstasy, he clutched me to him with a shuddering gasp of simultaneous joy, and I felt his storm break within me.

He held me tight while we recovered, our sweat mingling, our hearts thumping in unison. I could hear that our example had provoked Patroclus and Iphis to similar exertions, but I did not look to see what procedure they were following. At that moment, I cared only that I was clasped in the arms of the man I loved and had pleasured him.

He had guessed the secret I shared with Patroclus and had forgiven me.

5

Patroclus carried out the cauldrons and tossed away the water. Iphis and I tidied up towels and discarded clothes, and also cleaned ourselves—Achilles was always generous with his gifts, and I was wet to the knees. When I tried to help him dress, he told me to attend to myself, so I knew he was eager to open his treasure box and start decorating me. He loved doing that, weighing me down with gold and precious stones. That night he used mostly jaspers and chalcedonies, about a score of them, all exquisitely carved and set, plus chains and bangles of gold and a filigree diadem that had belonged to a king. I cried out that I would collapse under the load, and he laughed and added more, his blue eyes flashing with delight.

When he was satisfied that I was sufficiently adorned for the prize of a great warrior, he chose a gold-studded belt and a heavy gold pectoral for himself and let me fasten gold bands on his arms. Then he settled on the only chair that really fitted him, a carved olive-wood throne studded with ivory carvings of heroes and monsters. It had belonged to King Lethos of Larisa, who had no use for it now. I brought cool Thracian wine in a silver cup ornamented with flying doves so realistic that they seemed ready to coo. Laughing, he pulled me onto his lap again—less intimately than before, of course—and shared the wine with me, sip by sip. I snuggled my head against his shoulder, enjoying the mingled scent of cypress and man.

"How fared your visit to the goddess?"

"It went well, son of Peleus. I am sure she heard our prayers."

"Let us hope she will intercede with the Archer to withdraw his plague, then." He held the cup to my lips. "And now you must advise me. What gifts shall I present to my

guests tonight when they depart?" He grinned happily, for
he loved showering wealth on his followers. "Horses, armor,
gold? Women? But we're out of women now, aren't we?"

"You have given them all away. Most of them are bearing
already."

He caught the anger in my tone and kissed me. "Your time
will come! No one so favored by Aphrodite can possibly be
barren."

"You really think so?" I peered closely at the clear blue
eyes, looking for signs of deception. I suspected Achilles
would be a very poor liar; but I had never known him to try,
so I couldn't be sure. At the moment he seemed supremely
confident and honest.

"Of course I think so!" he said. "And I am very happy to
wait until I am home in Thessaly before I have to watch you
swell up like a wine jug." A tiny smile crinkled the corners
of his eyes. "Life back at Phthia will seem very boring after
Troy. I'll have time to make love to you more often."

"It isn't possible!"

"No?" he said with a confident smirk. "So what shall we
give Phoenix and the rest?"

"Furniture."

Two flaxen eyebrows shot skyward. "Furniture? For warriors?"

I laughed. "You're a warrior, and I've never known anyone collect stools and tables as you do."

He shrugged, intrigued by the thought. "Well, why not?
They don't have much of that, I admit. All right, choose
some. For Phoenix?"

"The boxwood table with the bulls' heads in ivory and
rock crystal." I particularly disliked that piece, because it
had come from Lyrnessos. If Achilles remembered that, he
did not comment.

"And for Alkimedon?"

Cradled in his arm, I thought as always that the gods had
never blessed a woman with a stronger or more beautiful
lover. Iphis, similarly entwined with Patroclus, was the second most blessed.

*   *   *

Soon after that, alas, barking dogs announced that the Myrmidon knights had begun arriving. The first, anxious not to be late and with every freckle sparkling, was Automedon son of Diores, a tall and gracious youth, auburn haired and snub-nosed. He had dimples that made him seem no more than a boy when he smiled, but he was a tough and proven warrior, who often went into battle as Achilles' charioteer, although he was a sworn knight himself with his own war band. Achilles strode out to the porch to greet him and lead him in by the hand. Iphis fetched another wine bottle.

Close behind Automedon came Alkimedon, who was a little older and slightly shorter but twice as thick and broad, a young bullock with rippling black tresses and the sort of brooding good looks that could turn female heads like potters' wheels. The reverse was not the case, though. He had never once smiled at me or addressed me, and he was far more interested in his charioteer than he was in the woman Achilles had given him. Fortunately for her, the charioteer had wider interests.

Next came Peisander son of Maemalus, an austere, humorless man in his thirties, who had the reputation of being the best spearman after Patroclus and Achilles himself. I could never bring myself to like him because I had seen him slay one of my brothers, although it had been a completely fair fight. With him was Menesthius son of Borus. His mother was Achilles' half sister. He flashed the same bright blue eyes and golden hair as his uncle's, but in size he was not much beyond enormous. He had the shoulders of an ox and much less intelligence.

Patroclus had failed me in the Chryseis affair, so my next appeal must be to Phoenix son of Amyntor. Under the pretense of seeing to the food, I stepped out to the porch, hoping that the gods would favor my cause and give me the chance to speak a quick word with him when he arrived. I was annoyed to see him coming around the corner of the paddock with Eudoros, the grandson of Phylas.

Eudoros's lack of a patronymic meant that he had been born out of wedlock, of course, and he was reputed to be a son of Hermes. Such explanations are fairly common when daughters of noble families produce otherwise unaccountable offspring, and only the rash or impious would question them. It is well known that Hermes frequently assumes the form of a beautiful young traveler. Eudoros was godlike enough in appearance and an honored fighter, yet somehow not well trusted—whether his reputation was attributed to his paternity or vice versa, I never learned.

As the two men drew close, I took up the largest log from the woodpile and staggered toward the door. I caught Eudoros's eye and smiled ruefully.

"You will ruin that gown!" he proclaimed, taking the load from me in spite of all my protests. He strode inside with it balanced on one hand, and I heard shouts of laughter from the others—jokes about bringing gifts and not letting porters mingle with the nobility. In truth, it was an Olympian miracle to see a Greek knight behaving so, and the Myrmidons would do such things for me only because they thereby honored Achilles.

I surprised Phoenix by catching his arm as he reached for another log.

"The gods be with you, my lady," he said uncertainly.

"And with you, my lord." I eased him aside, away from the door. "I have a problem on which I need your advice."

Phoenix was twice the age of the others. His features had lost the chiseled angularity theirs had, his hair was scanty, and his tunic bulged above his belt, although he was still a feared warrior. He had been Achilles' tutor in the arts of war. Achilles regarded him as another father, second in his respect and affection only to Peleus himself. If anyone had his complete confidence, it was Phoenix.

I explained quickly, while Phoenix frowned at the grass. "Calchas dreads the Great King's anger," I concluded, "and will speak out only if he is granted protection. I fear that Achilles may hear of this and do something rash."

"That is grave news indeed, my lady. But obviously someone will have to raise the matter, and who better than Achilles? No one else could protect the seer. It may be his duty—nay, it is his duty."

"But the danger!"

"There are procedures. Achilles will have to call a council."

I recalled that Patroclus had said the same. "I thought only the Great King himself could—"

"Not a council of war." Phoenix had a tendency to lecture. "It is a Greek custom. When a man takes issue with another of equal rank—some matter that may require an oath or payment of reparation or even resolution by combat—then he calls a council of their peers to witness their discussion and whatever means of settlement they agree on. Agamemnon knows that his army is nothing without Achilles, so he will not dare antagonize him. You have not told him?"

"No, my lord. I did not think it right for me to meddle in such affairs."

He nodded. "Very wise. Let me think about it. I am grateful to you for mentioning this."

He went into the hall. I followed as soon as I had shed my smile.

At first the talk was purely social. These Greeks were endlessly curious about the Dardanians' habit of riding on horseback and often questioned me about it. How fast could they go and for how long? How could they hold their legs up to avoid banging their feet on rocks or catching them in bushes? How could they stand the painful jolting in their crotch? I explained again that the riders strapped fleeces on their mounts to cushion the shock.

"But how do they control the brutes?" Menesthius demanded, scowling.

I could recall telling him that at least twice, but his resemblance to his quick-witted uncle was entirely external. "They train them to respond to commands from the riders' knees and feet."

The lout snorted in disbelief and drained his goblet. Achilles caught my eye and grinned faintly. We both knew that no horse ever bred would be able to carry him for long.

"You could not wield a spear on a horse!" Phoenix protested. "You'd fall off! Nor aim a bow, even."

"The Hittites are said to do so," Achilles remarked thoughtfully.

"A man could ride a horse to the battlefield," Automedon suggested.

Patroclus shook his head. "Then who holds it while you fight? It would take two men and two horses to deliver one fighter, so why not just stick with chariots?"

As the talk drifted to matters of war, Iphis and I withdrew to the porch. We could hear what was being said, though. Most of it concerned the Trojan allies who had been driven off before winter. Now that spring was returning, so were they. They had been seen in the hills.

"Agamemnon expects to march out and storm the citadel," Achilles said, "but I think we'll have to fight our way to it again."

"Hector must know of this sickness," Menesthius growled. "Why does he not attack us while we are weak?"

"Because he hopes it will do his work for him?" Eudoros suggested. "Or else he has plague of his own in Troy."

I waited for Phoenix to bring up the Chryseis problem, but he held his peace.

"The Trojans are backed to the brink of disaster," Menesthius said. "They will fight desperately."

Achilles' voice boomed out. "They have always fought desperately, but the greater shall be our honor for defeating them. By the beard of Zeus, you're a glum lot tonight! You sound like a pack of village elders sitting around a market-place complaining about their bladders. Is that your ambition? You want to go home and rot in the fields, break your backs cutting grain? Here at Troy we have a chance to win enormous riches and everlasting fame. How many men are ever so fortunate?" He laughed but not unkindly. "Would you rather live long in poverty and be forgotten?"

Menesthius protested that he had not meant that at all, and Automedon gallantly commented that the son of Borus had won no little reputation already.

"Beans!" Achilles said. "Crusts! What we have achieved so far is nothing compared to what lies ahead when Troy it-self falls. Wealth and women and glory! This will be a far greater sack than Thebes, and think how those heroes are remembered." He grew louder. "What is life for, if not for this? To eat, toil, die, and be forgotten? You are warriors, aren't you? You swore your knight's oath, didn't you? This is the greatest war since the Titans stormed Olympus. There may never be a greater war than this, a greater chance for glory."

And so on. By evening's end, he would have put fire in all their veins, but I knew what was troubling him—the Myrmidon knights were not the baying, bloodthirsty pack they had been when I met them a year ago. A long winter of inactivity and then the pestilence had blunted their edge, and this was true of all the army. The war was taking too long.

Eventually Patroclus came out for the meat—a pair of tender lambs already butchered—and carried it inside to roast on the great many-pronged forks. Iphis and I took in the wine jars that had been chilling in damp cloths where the wind could blow on them. We also had some fish that a soldier had caught that afternoon and been glad to offer for his prince's table, plus fine white wheaten bread from the Pylosian camp. Their men seemed to be better bakers than the Myrmidons, but we had better Thracian wine, and Hecamede was glad to accept that in exchange. We had goats' milk cheese, beans, lentil mash, nuts of many sorts, and dried figs and plums. Achilles served his guests, passing out laden golden bowls and laughing as Eudoros and Menesthius flirted with me and I bantered right back at them. Jealousy and distrust were foreign to him, for why would any woman who could have him ever prefer another?

There was no talk of the present war while we ate, although many older battle yarns were spun. When everyone had eaten and drunk to contentment, Iphis and I again withdrew to the porch while the men reminisced about their lives back in Thessaly—which basically meant about childhood, for only Phoenix had much more than that to look back on. Cool moonlight lit the pallid walls of Troy and scattered silver across the bay. From the twinkling fires amid the tents came a rumble of male voices like distant surf on a rocky shore, and doubtless they also spoke of home. Here and there a singer, a woman laughing shrilly, a throb of drums for dancing.

I heard Calchas's name mentioned. Phoenix was speaking. Then Achilles, angry. "Ransom? I never heard of that!"

Chryseis was as good as gone, but Phoenix talked for some time, and his voice was less audible than the others', so I did not hear what he was advising.

Then sounds of anger surged up from the camp. Metal clashed. I jumped to my feet, but there was no need to alert Achilles. He came hurtling out with his six companions at his heels. Roaring, they all disappeared in the direction of the quarrel.

They had gone unarmed. Iphis clung to me in panic.

"The Trojans?" she cried, her eyes like bottomless wells.

"No, not Trojans. There would be gongs and trumpets. Just the Myrmidons themselves."

"Fighting one another?"

I heard Achilles' thunderous bellow.

"It is war weariness," I explained. "Too many sieges, ambushes, battles, too long away from familiar things. Men act strangely if they are pushed too far. Even the strongest man can break."

"Not Patroclus!"

I laughed. "No, nor Achilles. Let us go and tidy up."

A few minutes later Patroclus returned, looking winded and annoyed. Iphis bleated the unnecessary question: "My lord, what happened?"

"Just a brawl. A family matter." He took her in his arms and kissed her tenderly. "You'd think they got enough fighting without quarreling among themselves! The others have gone to their tents. You can lay out the bedding now."

Needing no further encouragement, we cleared spaces near the hearth and spread fleeces and blankets.

"Idiots!" Achilles said, slamming the door. "Squabbling children!" The incident could not have been so trivial if it had caused him to forget the gift-giving he had planned. His feet were dusty and scratched, and I cursed myself for not having foreseen that.

"My lord, I shall prepare hot water."

"No. Come here." He clasped me in his arms, my head on his shoulder. I could feel his great heart thumping. Other men might break, but Achilles was indestructible. "You raped me this evening, you Trojan vixen! Now I shall take my revenge."

I snuggled closer. "Do your worst, you beast."

Chuckling, he began to strip the treasure off me, dropping it on a table. "Your struggles will be useless!"

"As long as you promise to win," I said, untying my laces.

He dropped my gown around my feet, lifted me like swan feathers, and laid me on the bedding. His hands explored me in the firelight. "Gorgeous creature!" he said, "sent by Aphrodite to drive men out of their wits. How I long to return to my father's hall to display the finest prize I won at Troy!"

He bent to run his tongue over a nipple. My body arched in joy. No one had thought to scatter the fire. As from a great distance, I could hear Patroclus and Iphis whispering urgent words of love to each other, but I had learned not to pay heed to what happened on that side of the hearth. There was more than enough going on at my side to keep me occupied.

6

Far from diminishing Achilles' exertions in bed, my exploits on the bathing stool inspired him, and that night he displayed the superhuman ardor I expected on his return from battle. It was almost dawn before he was satisfied. Not surprisingly, I overslept.

When I opened my lazy eyes at last, full daylight was streaming down from the clerestory and someone was shouting in the distance. I sat up to listen and concluded that I was hearing the cries of heralds in the camp, proclaiming a council. Iphis continued to sleep on the far side of the hearth— hardly surprising, for Patroclus had been inspired to follow his leader's example and had not been badly outdone in exerting his manhood. Both men were gone, perhaps long gone. They would have been amused to leave us two lying there like corpses on a battlefield.

Phoenix had not mentioned women attending councils, but I felt a proprietary interest in the fate of the insufferable Chryseis. I dressed quickly, wrapped myself in a drab brown cloak, and ran out to meet a glorious morning. The Myrmidons were streaming away southward, along the line of basking ships. A quick inspection of the swallows who nested so auspiciously under the caves of Achilles' house revealed nothing amiss, so I hurried after the warriors, keeping my eyes open for omens and seeing nothing untoward.

The army had gathered in a shallow hollow a short way back from the Great King's hall, and the discussion was already in progress. Encouraged to see that all eyes were aimed at the proceedings and that women who had crept in around the edges were being ignored, I huddled close to some bare backs, being all innocent and inconspicuous. I was taller than the longhaired men in front of me and had a good view of the assembly—men sitting on the slopes, men standing around the rim, thousands of clean-shaven faces. Few wore armor, many were bare chested, but every one had greaves on his legs, and most were armed with swords or long daggers. My father would not have approved, for any crowd is dangerous and one like this could be deadly. But such was the Greek way.

The lowborn were only spectators. The real assembly was the double circle of knights seated on benches in the center, all wearing tasseled mantles and ceremonial helmets made of plates cut from boar's tusk. I located the senior leaders among them—Achilles, Menelaus, Diomedes of Argos, Odysseus of Ithaca, Idomeneus of Crete, the Greater Ajax son of Telamon, and the Lesser Ajax son of Oileus. They all glittered with gold and precious stones, showing their prowess as sackers of cities. Behind Achilles sat his followers—Phoenix, Eudoros, and the rest—and directly opposite him, Agamemnon presided on an impressive laburnum-wood throne that Achilles had looted from Pedasos.

Robed in red and purple, the Great King sparkled with more gold than any: a spiked diadem on his head, rings and bracelets, many-stranded necklaces, and in his hands the studded scepter of Mycenae, topped with two lions. His heavy-featured face brooded in a dangerous scowl, and even at that distance, I could tell that the road so far had been rocky.

The speaker in the center was the emaciated, bedraggled Calchas. As I strained to make out his words, Agamemnon cut him off with a roar. "Liar! Charlatan!" The king leaped up and ran forward, brandishing his scepter. "Foulmouthed, croaking harpy!"

The seer spun around and fled toward Achilles with an agility remarkable for his age. Achilles began to rise, but the old man squirmed past him and vanished into the crowd like a mouse in a mouse hole.

"Purveyor of ill omens!" Agamemnon yelled after him. He laughed, and the knights joined in, but their mirth was a bleating of sheep. The king waited for silence, then let his great voice boom out.

"Give up the prize of honor you awarded me? My lords, is this fair? The girl is a treasure. She surpasses my wife, Clytemnestra, in mind and body, in wit and skill—and she's a lot younger too. I plan to take her home to Mycenae with me, to give me joy for years." He peered around carefully, then sighed at the lack of response. "Well, if we have displeased the god, I suppose I must make the sacrifice."

It seems absurd to say that I could see a ripple of relief run through the assembly—but I did. Achilles rose to his feet and walked forward, smiling. Agamemnon tossed him the scepter but remained where he was, in the center.

Achilles caught the staff nimbly, as if it weighed nothing. "I called the council, so it is my joyful task to thank the son of Atreus on behalf of all of us. My lord, your acceptance is gracious, as befits a great warrior."

While the other knights cheered these words, he walked over to Agamemnon, gave him the staff, and started back to his place.

"Of course," said the Great King, "it is only right that I be allowed to choose a suitable replacement."

The onlookers exchanged shocked glances. Achilles spun around and stared in bewilderment.

"Replacement? From where? Have we some secret store of undistributed booty? You will have to select from your own hoard." His fair face reddened. "Every scrap of loot has already been apportioned—most of it to you, as we all know."

Agamemnon aimed the staff at him, perhaps as a sign that he should not be speaking without it. "I was awarded first choice, and now she has been taken from me. I shall choose another to take her place."

"Scrounger!" Achilles bellowed incredulously. "You would force someone to give you charity? Take instead an extra share when we sack Troy. You will anyway."

Patroclus had warned me that the son of Peleus was not noted for his patience. *Achilles!* I thought, *be careful!*

Kings' tempers are often quick and Agamemnon's was notorious, harder to hold than an oiled piglet. He lost it with an even louder bellow. "You dare give me orders, boy? You think you can cheat me so easily? Either I am voted a replacement, or I shall take one—from you or Ajax or Odysseus . . ." He stopped abruptly, as if feeling the ground move under his feet. He caught the piglet again with a laugh. "But never mind that now! Come, let us haul out a ship and send the wench home with a rich offering to Apollo."

I thought, *Triumph!*

I had forgotten that Achilles had a notable temper also. He reached Agamemnon in three long strides and snatched the golden staff from his hands. "Oh, no! You expect us to trust you after that remark?" He was half a head taller, and he could glare down at the Great King as at an errant child. "To fight for you on those terms? I have no quarrel with the Trojans; they never did harm to Thessaly." He paused to draw breath, or perhaps he was astonished to realize the scale of his own indignation. "You despicable cur! You threaten to steal our honors from us? We came here to aid you and Menelaus. We risk our lives fighting for you, and yet whenever we take a city, you claim first pick of the women and the biggest share of treasure. Brothers?" He looked around the assembly of knights, and it seemed as if not one of them would meet his eye.

This lack of support encouraged Agamemnon. "It is my right. I am Overlord—which you too often forget. You are insolent, son of Peleus! I shall take your prize to teach you respect."

He reached for the staff, and Achilles swung it away. "Overlord? How often do we see you putting on armor and venturing into battle? Not very often! That's dangerous, isn't it? No, you show up when it's time to share out the loot. Why should I fight to make you rich and win no honor for it? I'd sooner go back to Thessaly!"

The Great King hunched his head down like a bull preparing to charge. He prodded Achilles' great chest with an insolent finger.

"Go then! Run away if you want. You're the worst troublemaker in the army, my boy, good for nothing but brawling. Go and take your Myrmidons with you. We don't need you. But since the god is taking my pretty girl, I shall come and take that Lyrnessos hussy you flaunt around—just so you will remember where Zeus bestowed the power!"

Achilles threw down the scepter and reached for his sword. Sunlight flamed on the bronze. Blinded, I covered my eyes. When I looked again, not a leaf of grass had moved, not a finger, not a muscle. The two men stood frozen in the middle of a valley of statues—Achilles with his blade half-drawn and Agamemnon staring at sudden death. If either man died, the bloodbath that must follow would take half the army to the underworld. In such moments we sense the presence of gods.

I wanted to scream, *Don't do it, Achilles! Don't do it!*

In the end, it was Agamemnon who moved first. He turned his back on death and returned to his throne, moving with dignity, ignoring the needle point that could have run him through at any instant. It was a stunning display of courage before his assembled host, and nothing could have better dismissed Achilles' words as empty bluster.

Achilles thrust the sword back in its scabbard, and five thousand men drew breath together. He stooped to take up the scepter and raised it to point at the sky. His voice was a peal of fury.

"Then I fight for you no more, you dog! The day will come when the Greeks will fall like hay before the wrath of Hector and cry out for the strong arm of Achilles. And I swear by Our Lady Athena and the throne of Zeus that it will not be there!" He glared contemptuously around the shocked circle of knights. "Go fight the Trojans without me, all of you. Send in my stead this craven, scavenging drunk, who lies abed counting the loot that others have gathered at the cost of their blood, or else goes slithering through the camp stealing heroes' honors. You deserve him, you *insects*!" He hurled the staff to the ground and stalked back to his stool.

After a moment of shocked silence, a nervous herald hobbled out to pick up the scepter. Before he could return it to Agamemnon, up rose old King Nestor, who had ruled in Pylos for so long that no one living could remember a time when he had not. His hair was white as sea foam now, his face all bone and sunburned leather, but his back was still straight and his voice resonant. He held out a gnarled hand for the staff and then brandished it overhead as if threatening the gods.

"Shame, shame! Oh, how Hector and the Trojans would rejoice to hear this unseemly squabble! I am greatly burdened with years now, but in my time I knew mighty heroes, greater men than any here: Caeneus, Perithous, Exadius, Dryas, Polyphemous, and many others. Godlike men and supreme warriors, all! No one today is fit to put sandals on their feet, those heroes of yore. And yet they listened to me when I spoke and prized my words. So should you, my lords. So should you listen to me. Here, then, is my advice. Noble son of Atreus, keep your hands off the girl who is Achilles' symbol of honor, for he earned her well. And you, young man, must apologize for your rash words to the Great King, whom Zeus set to lead us."

He sat down. The army waited tensely. Red-faced, Achilles just glowered across at the Overlord. Agamemnon glowered right back, looking as if he could hardly contain himself; but when at last he spoke, he had his voice under control.

"The gods made the son of Peleus a mighty warrior. That does not entitle him to set himself up as Overlord and rule us all."

Of course Achilles could deny any such intention. It was not a rope he was being thrown, but it was a thread, and a careful tug might have found a rope on the other end of it. Alas, Achilles was neither patient Patroclus nor crafty Odysseus, and his fury was still on him. He sprang to his feet, bellowing like a tortured bull.

"I will not stay here to endure your insults! What do I care if you take the woman? You think it is the woman that concerns me? You think I am so besotted with her? Take her! I have won a hundred girls and they are all the same. It is not female flesh that concerns me, it is honor! Take the girl if you will."

I cried out in shock and disbelief as I heard the prophecy of Calchas fulfilled. *Achilles was giving me away to Agamemnon!*

"But nothing more," he added, "not a goblet, not a cushion! Nothing else! And if you do this thing, son of Atreus, I will fight no more for you, nor for any of the rest of you sheep either."

Alerted by my cry, the nearest men were looking at me curiously. If I were recognized, I would be dragged down there and handed over to my new owner without delay. I turned and fled.

7

Take the girl if you will! How could he have said those words? They spun in my head like moths as I raced home along the cape. Herds of stocky brown ponies whinnied and fled from my path. He had told me he loved me and would take me home to Thessaly when the war ended. Flocks of white gulls battered up into the wind at my approach. He was the greatest warrior in the army, a sacker of more cities than even Odysseus, yet he had given me away without a fight.

Gasping for breath, I stumbled into the house. It was deserted—meaning that the women were neglecting their duties and had either gone to watch the assembly as I had or were tussling in the scrub with soldiers. That did not matter anymore. The household of Achilles was no longer my concern. *Take the girl if you will!*

Nauseated by my exertions, I reeled through the forest of tables and stools and threw myself down on the soft bedding I had not bothered to put away earlier. Never again would I cry out with rapture there in Achilles' embrace, dying of joy. How could he have been so cruel? How could the gods be so cruel—giving me to such a man and then tearing me away again? I had nowhere to go, nowhere to hide. I was a prisoner, after all, a chattel. I could not hope to escape from the camp unseen. Even if I did, I would be caught on the open plain by the Greek patrols, and then my fate might be very terrible without Achilles' name to protect me. *Take the girl if you will!* How could his lips have said it, so soon after kissing mine?

I had not wept for Mynes or my brothers, but now I wept convulsively, choking and retching in my misery.

When I ran out of tears, I turned to anger instead. Achilles would never trust the king's men in his house unless he were present, so he would come for me himself. I must make myself presentable, wash away the redness of weeping, arrange my hair, don the most sumptuous gown I could find—let him see what a prize he had surrendered so callously!

As I completed my toilet, though, I had second thoughts about the dress. All those fine garments belonged to him. I owned nothing at all—even my body was his to give away. Yet I did still have the ragged shabby servant's smock I had worn on the day he claimed me as his prize. I had hidden it when I first came to his house, and although I had not looked at it since, it would still be where I had put it, a secret memento of my lost home in Lyrnessos, the only thing I had been able to salvage from the ruin. He would recognize it.

I retrieved it from where I had concealed it in the porch the year before, then scampered back into the hall and put it on. The fine hair I had just arranged, I tangled up and rubbed with ashes. I smeared ashes on my face and arms, too, until I looked like a swineherd's slave. That was how I had been when he chose me—let him remember!

The sun was higher. Why had nobody come yet? What was happening? I went out to the porch again to see. There were no men in the Myrmidon camp or among their ships. Out in the bay, a solitary ship went by, heading for the sea with its banks of oars sweeping like wings. Farewell, Chryseis! How the little dog-faced vixen would be laughing, knowing that I must take her place in the king's bed! Southward, the wind was trailing streamlets of smoke from fires burning on the beach, and I could see distant crowds there. That meant the army was making sacrifice, offering bullocks to Apollo and feasting on the carcasses. I no longer cared. Let Troy stand or fall; it was nothing to me now.

I ran into the hall and shut the door.

It was a long time before I heard male voices rumbling in the porch, and the door squealed open on its pivots. Brightness, then something blocking the brightness . . . The door closed. I was sitting with my back to it in Achilles' great ivory-plated chair.

"Did you go to the assembly?" Patroclus said.

I nodded, not looking around. "Yes."

He came into view and settled on a stool. He ran a hand through his curls and then for a while just sat and stared at the helmet he was holding, as if he had never noticed how the plates of boar's tusk were sewn on the leather backing. At last he sighed. "I was sure Agamemnon was dead when Achilles drew on him. Some god must have stayed his hand. I have never seen Achilles angrier. It shows how much he values you."

"Values me? Values me! Yes, he values me as a sign that he's a better killer than other men. I thought he loved me, fool that I am. He gave me away!"

Patroclus's forearms swelled; his eyes were suddenly deadly. "Of course he loves you! He was going to take you home with him and marry you. Would he have planned that if he did not love you?"

I sniffed and hated myself for doing so. "He never said so!"

"Oh, yes he did! I've heard him, many times."

"He said he would take me to Thessaly and ask his father's permission to marry—"

"*Briseis!* Do you think for a moment that old Peleus would refuse anything in the world to his glorious son? Or are you hinting that Achilles was deliberately misleading you—because I've never heard him utter an untruth in his whole life, and I've known him since he was eight years old. Your tongue spins evil words, woman!"

Another despicable sniff escaped. "I'm sorry. I'm not myself. I didn't mean to upset you or insult the son of Peleus . . ."

He smiled, but his knuckles stayed white. "Perhaps I'm not quite myself either. Can't you find anything better to wear than that rag? Do you really want the army to think that Achilles threw you out looking like that?"

"I—I didn't think of it that way."

"Hurry up and change then. The Great King's heralds are waiting—and don't be hard on them, because they hate this business just as much as you do. Their names are Talthybius and Eurybates. They're nice old codgers."

I went over to the water jug, ripped off my horrid rag, and began to clean myself. I was well aware that Patroclus was watching, but we had lived together in Achilles' home too long for such things to matter between us. He was like a brother to me.

"You told Phoenix about Calchas," he said softly.

I scrubbed my face vigorously.

"I warned you Achilles was not patient in council, Briseis."

"I didn't tell him."

"Mmph!" *How dare he disbelieve me!* "Achilles tried, you

know. When he told Agamemnon to come and take you—he was trying to make up."

I turned to stare at him. "Make up what? 'Take the girl?' That sounded very straightforward to me, son of Menoitios."

He sighed and looked away, completely unaware that he was displaying the second most beautiful profile in the Greek army. "And to Agamemnon too. What he meant was that you were only a symbol. The other captains would not be sympathetic if they thought he was making a fuss about a girl. Any man can become infatuated by a woman, but only weaklings like Paris let it lead them into dishonor. Achilles wanted to make it clear that the matter was one of principle, of honor. How could he have known that Agamemnon would be so petty as to take him at his word? He didn't see that the son of Atreus had no choice by then. It had become a matter of principle for him too. After all that had been said, the Overlord would have had to come for you with the army at his back. We Myrmidons are the best fighters the Greeks have, but would it be right to kill us all just to save you? Achilles had to give you up."

I threw down my washcloth and went in search of a dress. I was disappointed in Patroclus.

"But he was trying to make up," he repeated. "He told Agamemnon he could come and take you—which was perfectly obvious. He thought Agamemnon would back down, once he'd won that concession."

" 'But nothing more, not a goblet, not a cushion!' It warms a woman's heart to be worth less than a cushion."

Patroclus shrugged. "If Agamemnon had tried his tricks on Odysseus, he'd have talked him out of it and then talked him into giving him four or five women of his own. Achilles doesn't have the slyness it needs. A quick temper is a virtue in a warrior but a handicap in council."

"And now you are all going home to Thessaly?"

"I don't know. He hasn't ordered the ships made ready— not yet." He rose and came over to help me with the laces on my dress. It was finely woven, but not in the courtly style I had flaunted the previous day. I would not go to Agamemnon in anything like that.

"Where is he?" I asked. It would be better if I did not see

Achilles. Then it would be as if he had fallen in battle, as I had so often feared he would. Many sleepless nights I had known in this hall, worrying about him when he was away raiding. Better not to see him.

"He went up on the ridge."

Without even saying good-bye? Heartless! "Gone to commune with his mother the goddess, I presume?" I said angrily.

"Very likely." Patroclus had found a comb from somewhere; he set to work on my tangles.

"You don't believe that . . . *Ouch!*"

"Don't I? Whatever did you do to yourself? This is a stork's nest, woman! I have never met a man like Achilles," he continued quietly. "He is greatly favored by the gods, because he honors them with many rich sacrifices. Now Agamemnon has shamed him intolerably. If he prays to the Immortals for recompense, will not they listen to their favorite?"

"I suppose they will." The Immortals were fickle.

"Then you must not give up hope. There, that will have to do. We must not keep the heralds waiting any longer, or they will wonder what we have been up to, you and I. Now, dear Briseis, demonstrate again that noble breeding of yours, the courage that amazed us all at Lyrnessos."

I turned and hugged him, my cheek against his. "I detest Agamemnon. He has dogs' eyes."

"Then snore in his ear! The gods have always smiled on Achilles in the past. Why should they stop now?"

A sudden shrill chattering made us jump apart and look up. A swallow wheeled and swooped among the rafters, chattering furiously. Then it flashed up and vanished out the smoke hole.

"A sign!" I cried. "It is Potnia!"

Patroclus paled. "Athena? Are you sure?"

"Yes, yes! Swallows are one of her symbols. She was telling us that the gods will listen to Achilles!"

He tapped the back of his fist to his forehead in salute to the daughter of Zeus. "I believe you. And perhaps you will be their agent."

"Me?"

He smiled wryly. "You disposed of Chryseis very neatly. See what you can do to humble Agamemnon."

I avoided his eye. "I am only a slave. He is the Great King!"

"You are a king's daughter, and you, too, are greatly favored by the gods. Come along."

What could I possibly achieve against the Overlord? Patroclus was only trying to cheer me up. He escorted me out to the heralds. For the second time in my life—for the second time in a year—I was led away into slavery.

BOOK TWO

PARIS

1

If you think of the war as a great storm that wrecked and sank everything within its reach, then I was warned about it when it was no more than a speck of white cloud on the far edge of the sunlit sea. I knew it was coming while all its other victims still went happily about their business, living their lives in peace and trusting their gods. Men expect protection from their gods in return for the offerings they give. Alas, other men may make richer sacrifices and win greater favor. The Immortals never explain their decisions, but once in a while they warn of them, and they warned me of the coming of the Greeks.

I was thirteen, youngest of four children, survivors of eight births. My father, Briseus son of Mydon, was king of Lyrnessos, where the sea washes the toes of Mount Ida. Other girls of my age were all hard at work or even married, so I was a solitary, lonely child. My scalp was still shaven in child fashion, leaving only a short lock in front and a slender ponytail behind. I was gangly and ugly, all legs, a human heron. I had no grace, no skill in adorning myself or wearing fine clothes as they should be worn, and I lacked the patience for spinning and weaving and other womanly pursuits.

Do not think I went around talking with gods as an everyday occurrence. When younger I had seen dryads dance in the speckled sunlight under the olive trees and heard the whispering of nymphs in the chuckle of the streams. When breakers thundered on the rocks, I had watched nereids dancing in the white spume. All children do, but at thirteen one no longer admits to such perceptions, although even adults usually notice when a god is present. A sudden hush stilling a noisy room, silent echoes when idle words suddenly take on special significance, the certainty that something has happened before, although it cannot possibly have happened before—only fools ignore such signs. What happened that day was very different.

The olive harvest had begun, so the beach had been left to the gulls and terns, and our little fleet of fishing boats rested high on the strand beyond the greedy reach of breakers. Zephyrus brought us a storm from the west.

Confined indoors all morning, I was even more restless than usual, prowling around the palace, seeking warmth in the busy pottery where the kilns glowed hot and clay came alive in the potters' hands while boys spun the wheels for them. I went to the metal shop, where glowing bronze was run into molds like liquid fire, but the smiths chased me away, threatening to complain to Father or Sphelos, my oldest brother. I inspected the women's weaving. I supervised fullers, flax workers, furniture makers, and silversmiths— commenting, criticizing, and asking endless questions. I suppose they all considered me a dangerous nuisance, a meddling, pampered brat who might overhear and repeat gossip and must be treated with undeserved respect.

Joyful smells led me at last to the kitchens. In that turmoil of hurry and boiling cauldrons, a royal pest was never welcome, especially one accompanied by a large and boisterous dog. I had barely time to burn my fingers on a hot roll when a deep voice said, "My lady?"

I looked around and said, "Yes, Daos?" most graciously, although Daos was only a porter. He seemed very manly and muscular to me, but he could not have been much older than my brother Enops, for they had been childhood playmates. Two or three years make a huge difference at that age.

"Um," he said. "We have an offering to go to the Mistress of Trees, and I, um, wondered if you would take it. I mean, I'll carry it, but it needs a lady to, um, you know, do the giving. The rain's stopped . . . ?" He glanced across at the pastrycook to see if he had got it right.

I knew that this was a ploy to dispose of me, because it had been used before. The prospect of some fresh air appealed, though, and so did the chance to visit with old Priestess Maera.

So I told Daos, "Of course I will. I'll meet you at the tannery."

I ran upstairs to find my warm cloak and my shoes, then went down again and out by the porch, where Daos was waiting for me, holding a large basket. Off we went together, Gorgon bounding ahead through the mud. The rain had merely paused for breath, not stopped. The air was full of thick, leafy smells, wet on my face, and I pulled my cloak tight about me. Daos shivered, having just come from the kitchen and wearing nothing except a cloth. I laughed at all the dark hairs standing up on his arms and legs and told him he looked like a bear.

We did not have far to go. Lyrnessos was a tiny place. The palace stood atop a small hill, and several hundred women and children dwelt in its slave barns. The freeborn lived down in the town on the shore, but most of them trudged up the hill every morning to work in the palace, except when they had to tend their own little fields. Mostly we thrived on trade and our craftsmen's skills, but what land we had was bounteously fertile—fields and vineyards and olive groves cramped between the beach and the higher pasture and forest. Mount Ida sheltered us from Boreas and so gave us a climate far kinder than the bleak plains of Troy. They say that Zeus often visits the summit of Ida, and a god wanting an earthly home could find nowhere finer.

In those days there were many altars and shrines around Lyrnessos, sacred to many gods and goddesses—some only minor spirits, like the little stream gods, others worshiped throughout the whole world, although often by different names. She whom we called Mistress of the Trees, for example, may have been the lady known to the Greeks as Artemis, although they claim that the olive is sacred to Athena. Maera said it did not matter what names we used, as long as we were respectful and gave offerings. Alas, no one tends those altars now!

The six olive trees of the sacred grove were ancient and massive. Within their calm gloom stood a xoanon of the goddess, a gnarled shape of cypress wood stained black by centuries of oil and wine. It was so old and weathered that the Mistress's shape was more hinted at than stated, but in the hot silence of summer or the restless winds of winter, I could always sense her presence in that holy place. I rarely went into the grove itself, unless I was with Mother. Usually I just called at the priestess's hut nearby and handed over my offering.

Sometimes old Maera would be crabby and send me away with a curt word of thanks. If she was in a mood for company, she would invite me in and feed me honey cakes or other treats that looked and tasted astonishingly like the ones I had just brought for the goddess. The rest of the food she ate herself or distributed to the old and infirm within the town. Not that she needed my help; she was quite capable of walking into the palace to help herself to whatever she felt Our Lady needed, and frequently did so.

If she was in an exceptionally agreeable mood, she would entertain me with tales of places far off and times long since, of beautiful princesses who had been loved by gods or rescued from monsters by great heroes. In her own youth, centuries ago, she had been a priestess at some shrine near Miletus, far to the south. She knew more about the ways of the Immortals than anyone. Mother, who was resolutely opposed to nonessential exertion, delegated many of her sacred duties to Maera. I approved of the old crone in a way I did of few adults. She never pestered or lectured, and even Father never gave her orders. Most people were rather frightened of her, which was funny, because she barely came up to my shoulder and was older than Egypt.

That day she was not at home. I took the basket from my escort and looked over to the sanctuary itself. Even at that distance, I sensed the holiness. The grove seemed alive. Rainwater dripped, the wind sighed in the wet leaves, and birds were angrily mobbing something perched in the branches—an owl or a hawk, probably, that had taken shelter from the storm.

"Just look at that rain coming! We'd better hurry home, boy."

"Yes, my lady." If Daos guessed my fear, he knew better than to comment.

Happily depositing my load inside Maera's door for her to deal with, I hurried off toward the palace. A gray cloak of rain was sweeping in along the coast. Then it happened. Gorgon uttered a huge howl, unlike any noise I had ever heard her make before, and took off into the woods like an arrow.

I yelled, "Gorgon!" and "come back here, you crazy mutt!" and other useless things. I gave chase. In a few minutes the rain came roaring in, causing me to swear all the bad words I knew. Nose to the ground, my dog tore down the slope, where the trail wound through fruit trees. The flats beyond were shaded by more great olives, and I would certainly have lost her had she kept to a straight course, but every few minutes she would lose the scent and start twisting and looping like a congregation of snakes. As I drew near she would find what she wanted and take off again. Normally during harvest time the groves were crowded with women, but that day I saw no one I could call on to head her off. She had *never* behaved like this before! Some god must be playing tricks on me.

Daos jogged along at my side. "My lady? Where are you going?"

"To catch my dog, of course!"

"She's just scented a squirrel or something. She'll come back on her own. You'll get wet, my lady."

I was wet already and he could not have been wetter if he'd been diving for octopus. "You go back." I panted. "That's an order, boy! Go home."

He responded no better than Gorgon. Would no one obey me? He just frowned and chewed his lip and kept up his easy barefoot lope. If he left me alone in the woods, he would suffer for it. If he laid a hand on me, he would suffer much worse. He would probably suffer now whatever he did, or I did.

"Can't leave you, my lady," he concluded.

"Then go and catch Gorgon!"

"She won't let me."

He was right, and I had no more wind to argue. Every time I thought I had lost her, I would catch another tantalizing glimpse. The country climbed steeply now. Soon the trail would emerge from the olives into the fields and pastures above, clumped with oak and pine trees. I slithered and stumbled in the mud, for the downpour had turned the trail into a minor river. I prayed silently to Our Lady of Trees, to Hermes, and especially to Potnia.

Daos, infuriating man, still had breath left to talk. He prattled about wolves and wild boars and the lion tracks that had been seen last winter. He tried demons. He tried, "There's bad men up here! Woodcutters and herders. Dardanians."

That stopped me. I had never come so far on foot before, and never without adults to defend me. Father had driven me up into the hills once or twice when he was inspecting his herds and I had been taken on visits to the Dardanians a few times, that was all. Lyrnessos lay between the Kilikes to the east, the Leleges to the west, and the Dardanians to the north. In my childhood the land was at peace, but just because my father the king had no trouble did not mean that I would not.

"You'll defend me," I said between puffs, rubbing the stitch in my side.

"Why?" My brawny companion folded his big arms and waited for me to come to my senses.

"What! Of course . . . you'd . . . defend me!"

He shrugged. "Don't have a weapon, and if I hurt a freeman even a tiny bit, I'm like to die of his wound. You, now—a princess would fetch a big ransom, a really big ransom. Twelve oxen, maybe. Or more! I'm worth two oxen or twelve sheep, if I'm biddable, being young and stronger than most. Why should I fight for you? I'd salute and say, 'Yes, masters!' "

"If you won't defend me, then you're no use. Go back to work!" I took off up the trail again on aching legs.

Daos followed. Eventually the rain slackened, became a miserable drizzle, and then stopped altogether. With astonishing suddenness, the sun came out, painting every thistle and rock with pearl. A few hundred paces ahead of me, and only a long bowshot from the edge of the real forest, Gorgon lay on the grass beside a boulder, licking her paws. She looked up, tongue lolling, tail wagging.

"Stupid brute!" My wet cloak hung on me like an ox hide. Passing near a tree, I stooped to pick up a stick.

"Don't beat her!" Daos said sharply. "She won't understand."

"Are you giving me orders?"

"No, my lady. But if you beat a dog when you catch it, it won't ever let you catch it again. Tell her she's good and pat her, so she'll come to you next time."

I considered this advice for a moment, and reluctantly dropped the stick. "That makes sense, I suppose."

"Slaves know all about beatings, my lady. Me, of course, you can tell what it's for."

I flopped down on the boulder, and gave Gorgon's ears a perfunctory rub. I was still too mad at her to do more. As soon as I caught my breath, I would head home for a hot bath.

Daos was still standing. "Used to tend sheep up here."

"You like being a shepherd?"

His face went blank.

"Don't play stupid with me, boy."

"Liked it better than some of the things I have to do in the palace," he admitted.

Remembering whispered gossip I had overheard in the kitchens, I guessed that he was referring to certain tasks he performed for Sphelos. I had only a vague idea what these duties entailed, and I should probably have demanded details had my attention not been diverted. I saw a sail.

Above us, the great wall of Ida hid within draperies of rain. Southward the town was invisible, blended into the shore, and even the flat-roofed palace on its hill seemed no larger than a slab of cheese, with a few crumbs of outbuildings. To east and west the coast was a crumpled tapestry of stubbled fields, vineyards, and olive groves, hemmed with white foam, rising to the folded hills. Lesbos was completely hidden, and only a few patches of gray sea showed between the blurs of squalls.

I jumped up. "Look!" I cried.

Daos shrugged. "Nothing we can do."

The little spit that sheltered our beach in most weathers

was a hazard in a westerly, but even if the captain could turn the point, he would pile up at the eastern end of the gulf very shortly, because there was no good harbor anywhere on that coast. Perforce, therefore, he was heading in. The chances were that his vessel would capsize—I had seen that happen twice, and my memories did not go back very far. If men and horses were standing by to help, they might be able to pull her up on the shingle out of the breakers, but not even Father's tax collectors would be looking out for visitors in this weather. If I sent Daos, he would never arrive in time.

"We must pray!"

"You pray, my lady. Slaves have nothing to offer."

Feeling very self-conscious, I raised my arms. "Father Poseidon, Sea Lord, Earthshaker, if you will save those mariners, I will ask my father to sacrifice a horse to you, a fine young mare. You lifted the rain so that the ship did not go right by Lyrnessos without seeing it, and it would be very unkind to give men hope like that and then wreck them on the shore to drown. I do promise, and I think my father will do as I ask."

Daos saluted the god. I had no sense that the Lord of Horses was present or had heard my prayer.

The ship was not wrecked, of course—I wish it had been! Then all the strife and suffering would have been avoided. The gods may show their purposes by portents, but sometimes what they fail to do is even more revealing.

"Come along, boy!" I was freezing. "There's no use staying around here to be eaten by . . ." I turned to lecture Gorgon, and Gorgon had gone.

She was three hundred paces away, racing across country again, nose down and this time heading eastward. I forgot all about the ship. I shrieked at her and was ignored. Howling in fury, I took off after her again, leaping and stumbling over the tussocky hillside, through thorns and thistles and long wet grass, wondering how far she was capable of going. In theory, we should eventually come to Thebe, the Kilikes' town. King Eëtion was on friendly terms with Father but would make him pay a stiff ransom for me, just on principle. He would certainly keep Daos.

Another rain cloud came after us, spattering drops on my scalp. We were no longer following a trail, and clumps of oaks and pine trees were crowding in. I resolved that I would keep up the chase only as long as I had Gorgon in sight. As if to prove me a liar, she immediately disappeared over a rise. I forced myself to one last effort, wincing at the pain in my side. When I reached the top, there she was, at the bottom of a gully, drinking from the stream. I slithered and skidded down the wet grass until I could grab her.

Daos slid down the bank after me. He broke off a willow stick and stripped it to make a long hook, which he slipped through Gorgon's collar. He was trying hard not to grin. "You want me to hold her?"

"You keep her. I want to wring her neck. Let's go."

"Um. My lady? Shouldn't you, um . . . Shouldn't you thank the god?"

I turned and saw what I had missed. Beside a small spring that dribbled from the bank stood an altar, a large flat rock supported on several smaller rocks, half buried in reeds. The surface of the stone was crumbly in places and coated with moss in others, suggesting great age.

"Oh! Do you know whose shrine that is, Daos?" My question came out in a whisper, because suddenly the mist-sodden air seemed to throb with the same sort of holiness I so often sensed in the grove.

"I was told it belongs to Our Lady Dictynna." He was whispering too, embarrassed at having to instruct me. "I used to make sacrifice from my rations, and the goddess looked after me."

"I wish I had something to give her." I knew nothing about the holy Dictynna, but I might have sacrificed a dog to her if I'd had a knife handy.

Then came the omen.

A gray bird came fluttering down from the sky to settle on the altar, and a moment later another joined it. There was nothing earth-shattering about seeing pigeons around Lyrnessos, although if they ventured too close to the town they would find themselves in a pie very quickly—and yet my scalp prickled. No doubt these two were planning to take shelter under the table of the altar, but the way they had chosen to visit that particular holy spot just when Daos and I were gazing at it was decidedly odd.

My thoughts were already turning over the idea of *portent* when a shadow flashed overhead. The pigeons hurtled into the air in a thrum of wings, but too late to escape the dark death falling from the clouds. One of the doves died instantly, without as much as a scream. A huge eagle landed on the altar and crouched there, the glare of its golden eyes challenging us to dispute its right to the victim clutched in its talons. My teeth jangled. I had never seen a living eagle at close range, and it seemed much larger than a dead one. It spread wings so wide that I thought of a servant stretching out her arms to fold a blanket.

It launched itself right at us. I yelped and fell to my knees. *Thump . . . thump . . .* the great wings beat the air, passing close over our heads. I craned my neck as the huge bird rose—up, up . . . And then yet another struck it. *Two* eagles screamed and clawed and tumbled in the air above us. The body of the pigeon went spinning down into the scrub. The eagles followed it, locked in combat, falling into the gully around the next bend. A moment later, one of them rose up and flew away.

I buried my face on my knees, shivering uncontrollably in the mud and swampy grass. Rain beat on my head and drummed in the stream. Obviously I had been shown an omen, a very potent omen—but what did it mean? What was I required to do?

"Mistress," I whispered, "I do not understand."

In the hush, my heart thudded and raindrops splashed, then Gorgon shoved a wet muzzle in my ear.

"You all right, my lady?" Daos was pale, and his teeth were chattering, but that was probably only from cold.

I scrambled to my feet. "We have been shown an omen!"

"You have, my lady. Slaves don't get omens. The dog led you here, didn't she?"

That was a throat-tightening thought. A god had led Gorgon to this place so that I would see an omen! "I suppose so. Let's find that eagle."

I looked briefly for the pigeon, but it was lost in the weeds. Daos soon found the eagle, ripped and bloodied, but he absolutely refused to touch it. Surprised how light it was for its size, I dragged it back to the altar and laid it there as an offering. I said a hasty prayer of thanks to the goddess of the shrine, another to Potnia, and even one to Smintheus, just to be safe.

Then Daos and I set off home with Gorgon trotting ahead of us, perfectly behaved now the god had done with her.

2

Two rainstorms later, I shivered my way in through the gates, across the outer courtyard, where the palace dog pack greeted me raucously, and into the shelter of the porch. The day was already dying under the mantle of gray-black clouds, although the hour could not have been much past noon.

"You'd better go," I said. "If you have any trouble, tell them you were obeying my orders."

Daos said, "Thank you, my lady," doubtfully and ran for the kitchens. I took off my shoes and trudged across the inner courtyard to the portico.

The vestibule beyond was where all paths crossed, but there were far more people than usual hustling around there. Cups and wine flasks and dishes were being carried into the megaron, as if a feast were being prepared, but there was no feast due.

The only person present who wasn't in a hurry was my least-favorite brother, Bienor, shaven-scalp collection of strings, sticks, and brown skin, with scabs on his knees and elbows. Although he was my twin he was shorter, and I could rub his face in the dirt when he needed it, which was often. I stalked by him while Gorgon and Griffin greeted each other with wags.

"You missed all the excitement," he said offhandedly.

I turned. "What excitement?" He wore only skimpy white shorts, as usual, but surprisingly unfilthy and untattered.

"Oh, nothing much."

I advanced with intent to cause harm.

"A ship came in."

I had quite forgotten the ship. It made things much worse, for now I owed the god a horse. My promise had seemed a very safe offer at the time. "I'm glad it made it in safely."

"Father saw it first! He sent Sphelos and Enops down in chariots to round up the townsmen to pull it in. There are *very important* visitors on board!"

"Who?"

Bienor's eyes gleamed like Orion's dog. "Strangers are never questioned until they've been fed—don't you even know that much?"

"Then you're just guessing."

He wasn't, though, because Griffin was as wet as Gorgon. If there had been an exciting rescue down at the beach earlier, a plague of wild boars would not have kept Bienor away, and he would have certainly gossiped with the sailors or eavesdropped on other people doing so. He wouldn't be able to keep quiet about it. I turned to go.

"Am not guessing! A prince!"

I turned in my tracks. "What prince?"

Bienor was well aware of my interest in princes. Mother had often told me, "One day, when you are grown-up and a beautiful princess, handsome princes will flock to Lyrnessos, driving their chariots, and they will ask for your hand in marriage. And your father will choose the bravest and fairest to be your husband." At thirteen, I was not old enough to marry, but I was certainly old enough to be betrothed—or baited.

"I don't believe you!"

"It's true! Come to the shrine and I will swear before Potnia."

Even my despicable twin would not lie before Our Lady, so I must take his news seriously.

"Prince of where, then? What's his emblem?"

Bienor glanced around and whispered, "A single horse!"
Troy! A solitary horse was the emblem of Troy.

King Priam of Troy had fifty sons.

"I'll believe it when I see it myself."

"Father ordered an ox slaughtered!"

I regarded my brother and he regarded me. The glint in his
dark eyes told me that he was thinking what I was thinking.

"I must go and change," I said.

The glint brightened. "We haven't been invited."

"We haven't been forbidden, have . . . No, don't tell me.
Nobody has told *me* I can't attend." We were growing up—
I was, anyway; Bienor wasn't, not yet. For the last year or so
we had been allowed to watch formal court affairs from the
balcony. "I must get ready."

That was the best exit line I could think of. I went off to
find hot water and dry clothes, conscious of a very large
emptiness in my insides, and not just from hunger. Most
likely the ship had just been blown off course, but there were
other reasons why a prince might come to Lyrnessos.

At the top of the stairs I ran into a scent of roses that
would have choked a billy goat. In the center of the miasma
came Mother, displaying finery she flaunted only at the
greatest festivals—voluminous skirt with seven layers of
many-colored flounces; crimson, short-sleeved bodice open
in front; even her crown, a flat felt cap embroidered with
thousands of gold sequins in a spiral pattern. Carefully
oiled tresses dangled behind her head, with another in front
of each ear reached down to her copious breasts, which
were powdered with chalk, her nipples stained red. She
sported silver bracelets, her precious carnelian brooch at
her shoulder, loops of many-colored beads around her
plump neck, carved sealstone rings on her fingers. She
filled the corridor.

At her back came Alcmene and Anticleia, two of her
cronies—Anticleia tall and stooped and cadaverous, with an
irritating sniff; Alcmene short and even tubbier than Mother,
blond hair and skin fading evenly to gray. Both ladies were
dressed as if invited to Olympus, and I was totally beneath
their notice.

Mother stopped and blinked at me abstractedly. "There you are! We have been looking everywhere for you."

"I saw an omen—"

"You must hurry and get ready. They will be here any moment."

"There's an old altar—"

"The dress with the red and yellow beads, I think, dear."

"Yes, but—"

"Get your scalp shaved; you're a half-plucked goose. You look absolutely frozen. You really ought to be more sensible at your age. Hurry now. Watch carefully, so you will know how things are done, but I don't want you and Bienor disgracing yourselves up there."

"Two eagles and—"

With a fading, "Yes-dear-tell-me-tomorrow," Queen Nemertes of Lyrnessos clutched up her skirts and waddled down the stairs. Anticleia and Alcmene followed.

She had not specifically said I was to watch from the balcony, only that I was not to disgrace myself there—and that could best be avoided by not going to the balcony at all, naturally.

The chances of finding a bath attendant were clearly remote. I ran to my room, stripped off my soaked clothes, rubbed myself dry. The coincidence of visitors' arriving just after I had seen the portent was disturbing in the extreme, but the interpretation of omens was not something a thirteen-year-old girl should even attempt. As soon as I felt respectable, I hurried back down to the vestibule, and there my wrist was grabbed by Bienor.

"Come *on*! We're late. They'll be here any minute." Dragging me after him, he pushed his way into the megaron.

3

That night the weather had gone from bad to horrible, but most days, year-round, the palace was airy and bright, filled with sunlight like a haze of rainbow. True, it was only a rambling flat-roofed house of timber and plaster, but whenever I try to imagine the Immortals at home on Olympus, I can visualize nothing finer than a slightly larger version of the palace at Lyrnessos. Bienor and I once tried to count the rooms in it. We started to fight before we completed the ground floor and so never settled the matter, but twenty downstairs and about fifteen on the upper level would not have been far wrong. A great many of them were only storerooms or giant larders, but there were dozens of outbuildings too.

What turned this warren into a palace was that every surface was coated with fresco in white and carmine, cobalt and gold, vermilion and sea blue. Beams and ceilings, even floors, were patterned in a myriad shape of intricate repetition: birds and leaves, shells and spirals, waves and checkers, chevrons and rosettes. The walls bore pictures, mostly depicting scenes of animals or people. A dozen dolphins might sport on one side of a corridor while charioteers pursued stags on the other. To walk through my father's house was to wander in a wonderland of warriors and hunters, eagles and octopuses, bulls and dogs, lions and griffins.

The megaron, by way of contrast, was normally cool and deep shadowed, full of the mystery befitting a sacred place. On even the brightest of days, little light filtered down from the clerestory roof past the wide balcony that flanked all four walls. On feast nights, as now, a great fire would blaze on the open hearth between the four thick columns in the center and illuminate the finest murals of all. My favorite scene was the hunt with dogs and men fighting lions; but Bienor preferred the battle, a besieged city on one side and the attackers' camp on the other. A procession of male and female worshipers bore offerings to Potnia, recognizable by her sword and her great size; and there was a sea scene, with a dozen dolphins romping with octopuses, although no mortal ever saw dolphins in those colors. The megaron murals were repainted every few years, as they became dimmed by the smoke.

The hall was crowded and loud, with dozens of people standing around drinking wine from painted beakers. Bienor towed me behind him, staying in the shadows where we might hope to escape detection but obviously intent on getting close to the throne.

"Let's stay here!" I protested.

"No, come *on*! I want to *see*!" He pulled harder.

Already many spectators were leaning on the balcony rail, lesser folk who had come to watch the festivities and hope for a taste of the leftovers. To have been relegated to their company as usual would have been bad enough, but to be evicted in front of all these witnesses must be fatal.

Blazing pine logs sputtered on the circular hearth. No one was very close to them except some kitchen slaves roasting chunks of meat on long, six-pronged forks and being almost as well cooked themselves. Standing well back from the heat, the important people of Lyrnessos chattered like swallows: Mistress of Textiles Lede, Master of Bees Amphimedes, Kreion the creaky old captain of the guard, Master of Bronze Poias, the Keeper of Records, the Masters of Dyes, Grapes, Wool, Perfumes, and many more senior officials and artisans of the palace. The richer farmers and herd owners were there, and ship captains, but also all the priests and priestesses, for they were the same people. Being appointed to holy office was a mark of rank and royal favor, much sought after because every shrine had its own dedicated lands, herds, and groves.

The really important place to be was before the throne, and there stood our parents, of course, and Mother's ancient aunts, Melite and Klymene, plus a few special friends. Bienor and I paused at the edge of the human forest and peered out warily at this assembly.

Father was swathed from elbows to ankles in a fine wool robe of red and white and sea purple. Around his shoulders hung his blue mantle, displaying the dolphins of Lyrnessos and trimmed with knights' tassels. As he wore that only for formal state occasions, it made a mockery of the pretense that no company was expected, and it implied that he thought his guests would be knights also. Just in case the visitors might still be uncertain who he was, he was holding the scepter, a polished oak staff studded with a few dozen gold nails. He wore his agate sealstone bound to his left wrist, a necklace of amethysts, and jeweled anklets. His beard was inlaid with silver. I had not seen him in all his regalia for some time and thought he looked very impressive—fully as majestic as Zeus himself. Of course Zeus probably did not keep biting his lip like that, but if the Father of Gods and Men had to keep watch on the whole world the way Father was trying to keep watch on everyone in the megaron, then his eyes might well flicker around all the time too.

Bienor said, "Ha!" as if a god had sent him directions. He dragged me over to the aunts.

"I'll never forget the time he brought Queen Hecuba to visit," Klymene screeched.

"Yes, dear," Melite bellowed. "I never said so. It was spring."

"I distinctly remember wearing my amber beads."

"She couldn't have been. Enops wasn't born yet."

The aunts could keep that up all day. It was a long time since I had seen them in formal court gowns, and I found the sight unnerving. Some things are better left covered.

Being excessively winsome, Bienor caught Klymene's eye. "I put a dead pig in your bed, Aunt."

She simpered toothlessly. "Thank you," she shouted. "You look very smart yourself."

Mother spun around in a swish of skirts. "Oh, no! Who said you . . . ?"

Bienor smiled, and I saw what he had realized—now we were in, she would not make a scene by sending us out. Her painted eyes narrowed angrily, but she was stuck with us.

"Briseis, I told you to get your head shaved. Oh, dear, what will the princess think of us?"

"Princess? What princess?" The prince was already married? I shot an angry glance at my brother, who stuck out his tongue at me.

Mother sidestepped the question adroitly. "And why didn't you put on your silver bracelet? Here." She quickly slipped off one of hers and handed it to me; brazenly removed an amethyst necklace from a startled Aunt Klymene and dropped it over my head; lifted a string of clay beads from Melite, who did not seem to notice the loss, and put that around Bienor's neck; then gave him one of her own rings—all in one fast flurry of movement like a goose collecting her goslings. She took hold of our elbows as if we were ewers and removed us to a safe distance.

"Stand here and for Ares' sake behave yourselves." She hurried back to Father's side.

I turned to smirk triumph at my fellow conspirator and met a ferocious glare. Bienor hated ever having to stand near me. It did no good to explain to him that girls were often taller than boys at our age and he would grow out of it. He thought I enjoyed being a human stork.

Mother's cryptic slip about the princess proved that my infuriating brother had been telling the truth—some of the truth—and of course kings did not lay on banquets for penniless vagrants, whatever the traditions said.

"Who are these royal visitors?" I demanded, "and why are they here?"

He smirked. "Told you—nobody knows."

"You do! You went down and talked to the sailors, and I'll bet that Sphelos knows too!"

"It's possible, I suppose," he said thoughtfully.

A sudden hush warned us that the guests were arriving. Fussing with her skirts, Mother settled herself on the throne, a monstrosity of shiny olive wood inlaid with silver and purple faience, while Father took the ivory-trimmed chair beside it; for in Lyrnessos we clung to the old ways. Our home was sacred to Potnia, Goddess of the Palace, and the queen would grant hospitality—or in theory refuse it, although I never heard of that happening.

My two oldest brothers led the procession in through the great double doors. I thought they looked very fine in their bright-patterned kilts, their gold and jewels. True, Enops's whiskers still left a lot to be desired—especially by Enops—but in the last month or two he had outgrown Sphelos. Sphelos was a maiden's dream. His beard shone, his chest bore swirly patterns of black hair. Put a sword in his hand and he could have passed for one of the idealized knights in the frescoes.

Hand in hand, prince and princess trailed them into the smoky, fire-lit megaron with its rich, mouthwatering odors. At their backs came three followers, knights in boar's tusk helmets and tasseled mantles. On any other occasion, even one of those legendary warriors would have created a sensation in peaceable Lyrnessos, but that evening no one had eyes for anyone but the royal couple. Forgetting that they were officially blind to the presence of strangers, the spectators whispered and muttered at the idea of a woman traveling by sea at that time of year.

The newcomers advanced into the central square between the four thick pillars, then turned to the right to face the throne and the royal family. If they were surprised to see the queen occupying the throne, they did not show it. The prince appraised the situation at a glance and chose to stop beside the blaze of the hearth. He unpinned his mantle and tossed it to one of his followers. For a moment he stood there in the hot firelight, smiling very white teeth at his audience and letting us admire him. He wore only a simple tunic of pure white, its short skirt dangling red tassels at his knees, but he had a gold diadem on his brow, a gold sealstone ring tied on his wrist, gold at his throat and wrists and ankles. He did not seem outstandingly tall or broad or muscular, although a careful look showed that he was all of those. His hair was dark and wavy and shiny, but not unusually so, and his beard was trimmed close. No single characteristic was exceptional in itself, but the total effect was breathtaking: male beauty incarnate. He would have drawn all eyes had he been clad in nothing but a slave's rags. If god became man, he could look no better.

Then he lifted away his lady's head cloth and cloak to let us see her also. A sea sound of appreciation rumbled through the hall. If the man was a god, then here was a goddess. She was very tall, of course, and her seven-tiered skirt was a rainbow of miracle weave below a bodice of plain sky blue, open at the front, displaying perfect arms and breasts whose striking pallor was complemented by the burning auburn of her hair. Like her escort, she did not need the treasure she wore to overawe. Her simple beauty made everyone else in the megaron seem inadequate, either dowdy or garish, mallards around a swan.

She floated across the floor and knelt to my mother, laying one hand on her knees and reaching up to clasp her chin with the other in the traditional manner. "My lady," she declared, "we offer our blessings on this house, upon you and your lord and your children, in the name of the mistress of this place, mother of its hearth and roof. We travelers come in friendship, seeking shelter from the storm until we may once more be on our way."

"Two doves at an altar!" I muttered.

Bienor said, "What?"

I had seen two doves land on the altar and now two strangers sought shelter in my parent's house. Their knightly followers might be powerful landgraves, but they did not count in this. The gods would not stoop to act as heralds, announcing the arrival of visitors—not unless the visit was in some way vitally important. So who were the eagles? And which dove would die?

Mother stared down at this goddess for a moment in silence, thrown off balance in a way I had rarely seen before, then rallied her wits with an effort that reminded me of Gorgon shaking herself dry after a swim. "Welcome, strangers, in the name of Potnia, our mother!"

My father strode over to take the man's hand and lead him forward. Servants produced ornately inlaid chairs and footstools, laying fleeces on them. More servants flocked in with stools and three-legged tables for all the other guests. Yet others brought the great silver mixing bowl that was perhaps Father's dearest possession and began to blend wine and spices and honey. Servants poured water over the strangers' hands and ladled a few drops of wine into their goblets. Again the woman took the lead, tipping out the first libation to Potnia. Her escort offered one to Father Zeus for hospitality and another to Poseidon for fair sailing. They knew their manners, these beautiful visitors. The servants filled the cups.

My parents knew their manners also; and though I watched them making small talk with their guests, I could tell nothing from their faces. The newcomers were more transparent, constantly exchanging glances and smiles. Young as I was, I knew moon-sick lovers when I saw them. Melite and Klymene were arguing about people long dead, shouting down each other and everyone else like gulls squabbling over a fish bucket. I was the only person in the hall who even suspected that there was anything wrong, and I was a child. My head throbbed.

Or perhaps I was not alone. The beautiful woman listening so attentively to my mother bore a strangely forlorn expression for one so gifted with beauty and wealth. She responded brightly enough, smiling when she spoke, and the prince could smother her in bashful blushes with a single glance; but yet I sensed that her happiness was no thicker than the delicate skin on her cheeks. In the background, Enops was staring at her with his mouth open. Sphelos, I was annoyed to notice, was gaping idiotically at the prince.

The stewards were running out of furniture—Bienor and I were provided with chairs but no footstools and only one little table between us.

"Tell me who these two are," I said.

Torn between the joy of keeping a secret and the pleasure of telling it, my brother hesitated, then dropped his voice to a villainous whisper. "Paris, son of Priam. He's on his way home from Greece."

Which one of the fifty was he? No matter; he was a son of Priam. A vein throbbed in my throat. Doves were sacred to Aphrodite, and if ever two people had been blessed by the goddess of love, it was our royal visitors. One of the doves had died. What would happen to Lyrnessos if a son of Priam came to grief in our house? Lyrnessos was a swallow's nest compared to Troy. Holy Troy ranked with Mycenae or Knossos or Egyptian Thebes—at least in our minds it did. Troy was only two days away for a strong runner and could send an army of chariots against us. Lyrnessos had no army at all.

"Who's she?" I asked.

"Mustn't gossip."

"I need to know. I saw an omen."

Suspiciously, Bienor said, "What sort of omen?"

"You first."

The conversation degenerated swiftly, until he pinched me and I stamped on his toes. Some god whispered a warning to Mother, who turned her head to glare at us. The wine stewards were coming around again, so soon it would be time for Father to offer meat to the gods and then his guests. I was frantic to solve the augury before it was too late, although what it would be too late for, I had no idea. Something was awry and unnatural.

Lubricated by the wine, Bienor could not withstand the internal pressure of his big secret any longer. "Queen Helen of Sparta!"

Queen? I looked at the cooing turtledoves and then turned back to him in shock and disbelief. "No! Truly?"

"Truly!"

"What is a prince doing with a reigning queen?"

Bienor snickered lewdly. "I expect he takes her clothes off and . . . well, you know!"

"No. Do tell." I was certain he knew no more of the details than I did. "Old ways or new ways?" The wine was making my head whirl like a spindle. For a prince to go off and find a wife in foreign lands and bring her home with him was correct behavior under the new ways—although she ought not to be another man's wife. I knew that Troy itself followed the new ways, because Priam ruled there as his father, Laomedon, had ruled before him and one of his many sons would rule after him. Paris had followed the old ways in sending Helen to appeal to Mother, but that meant nothing. A prince would know such things and respect local custom. I asked again. "Does Sparta follow the new ways or the old ways?"

My brother's glee became conspiratorial. "It has to be the old ways, because her mother was queen before her and she has two brothers."

So she was queen by right. Under the old ways, the prince did not take his bride home; he stayed to succeed her father as king. Bards could sing you a dozen instances at the twang of a kithara, and our own father was one; but a queen's consort should remain at her side, honoring her bed and ruling her realm until the end of his days. Paris had stolen another man's wife and his right to reign as well. If my sprat of a brother knew all this about the visitors, then my parents certainly did. Could they not see the danger?

"But then her husband's lost his claim to be king of Sparta. He'll demand her back! The Trojans won't keep her, surely!"

Bienor chuckled, showing man's teeth too large for his boy's face. "That's up to old Priam, isn't it? It could mean a war!" he added cheerfully.

I thought about the eagles. *It could mean a war.* I looked again at my twin, who had turned his attention back to the visitors. He seemed quite unaware of the terrible words he had just spoken, but they rolled through my head like an echo of thunder, and for the second time that day I recognized a message from the gods. The meaning of the augury suddenly became sickeningly obvious.

I leapt to my feet. At that moment, a sudden hush fell over the entire megaron. My goblet shattered on the floor. Everyone turned to peer through the smoke in my direction, and only the sizzle of the fire marred the silence. The gods had stilled the room for me, and I did not know what to say.

I gazed in dismay at my mother, who had extended hospitality to these troublemakers, with all that that implied. She could not compare to the glorious Helen beside her—haggard mouth, droopy neck, puffball arms. Only the cunning artifice of the bodice held up her meal-sack breasts, and paint colored her nipples. The sight raised no pity in me, only anger, as if I had been betrayed.

Similarly, my father on the tall chair beside her—I had always thought of him as big and masterful, venerable king and sage. Horrors! Seen beside the divine Paris, he was old, potbellied, spindle-shanked, absurd in his knight's mantle. The gods had sent me omens of war, but whatever the king of Lyrnessos had been in his youth, he was no warrior now. The wine had addled my senses, for I felt as if sunlight had broken through a mist and I was seeing my parents clearly for the first time.

At their side, my two older brothers—Enops still a fuzz-faced boy, Sphelos . . . even Sphelos could not bear comparison with Paris. In that godlike glow he seemed disgustingly ordinary, too bony, too hairy. Too small.

"He was very high-spirited," one of the aunts shouted, "but he had the sweetest nature. One white ear and one brown."

"Oh, it takes years, you know," said the other, "and a lot of them never root properly."

Everyone else was staring at me. Paris could guess who the only children in the hall must be. "Your two fine sons we have already met, my lord. Do present the rest of your family."

Obviously Father had not noticed us until then, and the glare he flashed at Mother showed that he assumed it had been her idea to include us. Reluctantly, he beckoned us forward into the light. Wishing I could vanish from the megaron like the sparks of the fire, I began to move. Bienor was there already.

"My youngest son, Bienor, my lord."

"A promising lad!" the prince remarked with obvious lack of interest. Then his gaze fell on me and he raised his shapely brows. "And this budding beauty?"

Young as I was, I knew mockery when I heard it. "My name is Briseis," I snapped. "You and your companion are not welcome here." My effrontery was so unexpected that my parents were struck speechless. "Today the gods sent me an omen concerning you. I saw two doves—"

"*Briseis!*" Mother's voice thundered through the hall as

Potnia's did when the goddess was manifest to us. "We are not interested. Return to your seat."

"Wait!" With that royal command, Paris brought silence. Only the aunts talked on, oblivious. He fixed me with eyes that could have stopped a stooping falcon. "Let the child speak."

I could not have stayed silent had I wanted to. Shivering and stuttering, I gabbled out the story the altar, the doves, the eagles, the message from the gods. I did not know in those days that such things must be discussed with caution, if at all. I must have sounded like a maniac. My parents glared, Sphelos glared, and Enops had his mouth open. The whole megaron heard me, even the servants frozen in place.

"Don't you see, Mother? It means that you must send these strangers away or anger the gods! And war—"

"We do not see anything of the kind!" my father roared. "You bring shame on our house by insulting—"

"Wait!" Again Paris obtained silence with that one word.

"So she took it all off," Klymene proclaimed, "and we saw she was a Thracian."

Paris blinked at her and then looked back at me. "Omens are serious matters. My sister Cassandra would like to hear of this. She's a noted augur. You know who I am, girl?"

"Paris son of Priam."

He leaned back and gazed languidly at Father. "What the girl says seems very reasonable. Only the Thunderer displays his intentions with eagles. If Father Zeus did send her such a sign, then her interpretation is credible. It may well be that my wife and I trail war behind us, Briseus son of Mydon." He shrugged and laughed. "But there are always wars! If you wish to send the strangers back to their ship, then I shall naturally understand your caution. One mustn't ignore warnings from the Immortals, must one? On the other hand, your daughter may just have an excessively vivid imagination. You will know that better than I."

"She is babbling, my lord." Father gave me a ferocious glare of dismissal and waved at the servants to continue their work. Sphelos stepped forward, but I did not wait for him. I turned and fled from the hall.

4

A river of servants flowed in one side of the doorway and another flowed out. I was swept into the vestibule, where my elbow was caught by a set of bony, horny fingers. I looked down into the dusky prune face of old Maera, tiny and twisted, swathed all over in dull black. Her smiles were always gruesome affairs of writhing wrinkles and wet, pink gums; but this one seemed well meant.

"I did not hear all of that, my dear. Tell me the whole story."

I was on the lip of tears. "I don't want to talk about it!"

Technically Maera had absolutely no authority outside the sacred grove and no business inside the palace, but she was Mother's confidante, and no one ever questioned her. She pulled me over to a stone bench against the wall and sat me down. Perched beside me with her feet dangling, she spooned the whole story out of me, even to Bienor's fateful prophecy, nodding her head up and down like a barnyard pigeon.

"You believe me?" I whispered.

"Oh yes."

"Mother didn't! Father didn't!"

"They didn't admit they did."

"But if they believe what the god told me—"

"Goddess, child. That shrine belongs to holy Dictynna, whom some call Artemis."

"Paris said that only Zeus sends eagles."

"What matters is that you saw an omen."

"But did I interpret it correctly? Does it mean war?"

"Eagles fighting? I think so."

"I wish you would convince Father, then. He should do something!"

"What can he do, Briseis, mm? Insult a son of Troy by throwing him out of his hall?"

"You mean there must be war whether Father believes me or not?"

Maera sighed. "If the gods prophesy war and you can avert that war, then the prophecy would become false, wouldn't it? You expect to make liars of the gods, girl? The Moirai spin our destiny when we are born. If it is war, then war it shall be."

It is hard for children to accept fate; they expect justice. "And we can do nothing about it?"

"That is why the gods so very rarely tell us the future. So why did they reveal it this time? And why to you?" She squirmed down from the bench. "Come to the kitchen and I will find you something to eat, since you are no longer welcome at the feast."

I stayed where I was, shocked by this new problem. "Why? Why did the gods speak to *me*? I'm the youngest. I'm not important."

I didn't believe that. My mother's second child had been a daughter, whom she had joyfully hailed as the next queen of Lyrnessos, but the babe had died two days later, so now my parents never discussed the succession. The future lay with the gods, they said, and mortals who tried to foretell it were being presumptuous, risking their anger. Bienor could jeer that it was time for Lyrnessos to start following the new ways and let Sphelos succeed Father as king, but I assumed that the old ways would prevail and I would be the heir.

Maera's age-slimed eyes looked sadly up at me. "The gods favor whom they favor. They warn whom they warn."

"That's no answer! If they sent me a message, then they must have had a reason. Explain why I was shown that omen. Why me?"

She laid a crooked hand on my arm. She was standing, I was sitting, and yet she had to crane her neck to look me in the eye. "Think about it. The war you cannot avert, but if you have been advised, then the advice must concern something you can do or will do or will not do. Is that not reasonable? A choice you must make? You are very young, and female, so what can you do, what choice must you make? Stay here and think about that until I come back."

She scuttled off before I could argue. I sat on the cold bench and watched the servants hurrying by, bearing dishes and wine jars. I could hear the roar of the feast growing louder, although the roar in my belly made fair to drown it out at times.

Maera returned, thrusting a heaped bowl at me—cheese and bread and fruit. She pulled herself back up on the bench again.

"It is terrible to be young," she said sadly.

"Worse to be old," I mumbled, mouth crammed.

"No. It is good to be old. Nothing bad can happen to me now. A strong wind would blow me away, so I take every moment and care nothing for the next. But you . . . you have so much life ahead of you, so much to fear, so much you may suffer. Did I ever tell you of my mother?"

I shook my head.

"Ah. She did not eat as you eat, because her father was a swineherd and she had six sisters. But she prayed and gave what tiny offerings she could, and her prayers were answered. One day, when she was hoeing in the fields, a knight drove by in his chariot. He was not a king like your father but a goodly landgrave, a follower of the king of Miletus. He was young and strong. He saw my mother and stopped to talk with her."

"Just talk?" I asked with my mouth full.

"I don't know. I wasn't there yet!" Maera cackled at her own wit. "Talking or tumbling . . . one way or another, she pleased this handsome knight so much that he went to her father that very day and offered cattle for her. He took her to live in his palace. She ate much better after that, and so did her sisters, I expect."

"He married her?"

"Oh, no! She was lowborn. But he treated her with honor, sired children on her, cherished her. The gods were kind to her, yes?"

"I suppose so."

She chuckled and patted my knee with a spidery hand. "Ah, but knights go to war and sometimes do not come back. The king gave his lands to another, who preferred to choose his own women. My mother was too old and I was too young. She went back to the fields and I went to the goddess. I don't know what happened to my brothers."

"You're a slave?" I was shocked. I had not realized that a priestess might have been bought and sold.

"I am a servant of Our Lady of the Grove," Maera said placidly. "One day I'll tell you about my travels. But now do you see?"

"No. Not at all." I paused in my eating. "You mean I need a husband? But I do not bleed yet; I'm only a child!"

She shrugged. "You won't be one for long, and royal matches are not arranged overnight."

The notion did have appeal. A dashing husband waiting outside the bedroom door might add zest to life. "When the time comes, my parents will choose a husband for me."

"No doubt, no doubt. But perhaps they should start looking out for one."

"A knight to fight for Lyrnessos in the war?"

She shook her head with surprising vigor. "If that was what the gods meant, they would have sent the warning to your father."

I ate two figs while I puzzled it out. Bienor liked to sneer that a tiny place like Lyrnessos was too unimportant to waste a real prince on. A royal bastard, just maybe, he said, but I shouldn't count on even that. Bienor was often right, but not always.

I swallowed the last fig. "Troy? The gods were warning me against Troy?"

"At least that. Or more. If Greeks come against Troy, they may do other damage too, child. War is like fire—it spreads. You know only palace life, but the world outside is harsh. Do what my mother did. Find a strong warrior who can defend his woman and her children. And go with him to his own country."

I cried out in shock. "Give up the throne?"

"That is how I would read your omen," Maera said. "Leave Lyrnessos while there is still time." She slid down off the bench and crept away without another word.

5

The following morning I awoke before Dawn did. For a moment, all things were as they should be. Gorgon's warm weight lay over my right foot; the rain had stopped. Then memories came drenching in to wash away my contentment—the augury, the dread message it contained, my folly in the megaron. I writhed in shame as I recalled how I had embarrassed my parents in front of the royal guests and loyal subjects. Could I ever again look them in the eye or face my brothers? Could I even live in the palace anymore?

Deciding I was hungry, for I was always hungry in those days, I rose and dressed and crept off downstairs without awakening a single squeak. By sepulchral corridors I came to the kitchens, still warm from the previous day, littered with sleeping slaves and dogs. I gathered some fruit and scraps of stale bread, but I did not linger to eat them there, for soon the drudges would waken to their chores. I went back out to the vestibule and from there into the megaron, which was silent and black, smelling of wine and ashes and burned grease. Edging between the tables and stools that had not yet been returned to storage, I headed for the great hearth, navigating by the glow of a few last embers and the radiant warmth on my face. I sat down on the curb to eat and rue my folly some more.

Gorgon's tail thumped against my foot. I heard a movement, rather than saw anything, then realized I had company on the far side of the big round hearth. I wanted desperately to be alone. I was about to rise . . .

"They call you Briseis," she said quietly. "Have you no name of your own?" Helen herself sat on the curb opposite me.

I did, of course, but I had always hated it and thrown such tantrums that even Bienor never dared use it. "I am not ashamed to be my father's daughter, my lady."

"A good answer. You are young for what happened. Have the gods ever spoken to you like that before?"

"Oh, my lady, I am so ashamed! I did not mean to say all those terrible things."

"Why not? You were merely passing on the Immortals' message as you should. Every word you spoke was true." Helen's voice was sadder than the mew of a hawk, and I remembered the wistful expression I had glimpsed on her lovely face the previous evening. "The gods spoke through you. It is true, all true. I was queen of Sparta, daughter of Queen Leda. I succeeded her in the old ways as keeper of the royal shrine."

She sighed. "Then the son of King Priam came on embassy. He is beautiful, isn't he?"

"Yes, my lady."

"Aphrodite stole my heart and gave it to him. I left my realm. I left my husband. I even left my daughter, Hermione, and that was hardest of all, but she belongs to the land. I hoped that Menelaus would be satisfied to rear her and rule through her. Now I fear not. You told me otherwise."

"I?"

"The gods." Helen fell silent for so long that my hand quietly lifted the crust up to my mouth. Then she sighed again. "Aphrodite drove me into the arms of Paris. She forced me to abandon my people and so defy Athena the Protector. She forced me to defy Hera, for it was in her name I honored my husband as king of Sparta. Ah, how demanding and insatiable is Love—the fire, the ache, the longing! At her command I have offended two great goddesses. I fear their jealous anger. You know those goddesses?"

"I know of them, my lady. We call them by other names, that is all."

This was a tricky point around the palace. My father often referred to Potnia as Athena. I changed the subject.

"I thought the Greeks followed the new ways, my lady."

"The old ways hang on yet in some places."

"They are better!" I insisted. "Strong kings may not breed strong sons to follow them. If a daughter inherits the realm, then her father can choose a valorous knight to be her husband. It is a better way."

"Is it? In olden times the king would be put to death when his strength failed and the queen would take a younger lover. Do you approve of that custom too? You say that Paris should have slain Menelaus and claimed the throne of Sparta?"

Bewildered, I merely stuttered.

"I was joking," Helen said, "but I should not joke. I have been very foolish and I still am, but it was the goddess who sent that folly. Ah, Briseis, you have not yet tasted the sweet wine of love! I could renounce my folly, stay here in Lyrnessos, and send my beautiful man on to Troy without me, couldn't I? Then I could go home in the spring to clasp my husband's knees and beg his forgiveness."

I gulped, remembering that Troy had many chariots and many knights. Paris and his followers could probably take over the palace and town by themselves, anyway.

"But my fate is determined," she said firmly. "I have chosen and will not falter now, no matter what men may say of me. I shall not impose upon your parents. I only hope that Menelaus does not do anything rash."

I could think of no safe comment. I sucked a corner of my crust in silence. When she spoke again, I had a feeling that she was speaking more to herself than to me.

"But from what you told me last night, he obviously will. Agamemnon dotes upon him. Menelaus cannot bump an elbow without Big Brother rushing over to dry his eyes. There is no knowing what folly those two may not devise between them. Will the Trojans send me back as sensible men should, do you think? They are reputed to be a proud race. Will the Greeks be headstrong? Sparta and Mycenae between them could launch many ships. . . . We shall see. Why did the gods speak to you, though? Why you?"

"I don't know, my lady." I waited for a moment, but Helen waited too. "It may be . . . I talked with a wise old priestess last night, and she says I should ask my father to find me a husband as soon as possible."

The princess sighed. "She thinks that Lyrnessos is dangerous for you? A fast marriage and a move to a faraway city, yes. Go and live in Greece. But, oh, Briseis, do not forget love. My parents chose a noble husband for me, a valiant warrior to guard and rule my realm. Many, many were my suitors, but they chose well. I could not have asked for a better man than Menelaus. He is strong and virile and upright . . . and oh, so dull! See what trouble that has brought on us all? New ways or old ways, make sure your father picks out a man who has joy in his heart. You are going to be a great beauty too."

That last remark made even less sense than what had gone before it. I decided that she must be joking again, for it was the sort of thoughtless thing her prince would have said. I laughed as politely as I could.

"I mean it, Briseis. Soon there will be suitors around you like gulls around a fishing boat. I pity you, in a way. Beauty should bring happiness, but it doesn't always. Don't be foolish like me and start a war, will you?"

"I shall try not to, my lady." Reviewing my answer, I decided it was every bit as idiotic as her question. As for my ever being a beauty . . . absurd! I took a noisy bite from the crust. The openings in the clerestory showed as scraps of gray now. I could make out her shape, the thin veil draped over her cascading hair.

"Watch for the gods' signs, Briseis. To those who have been granted the ability to see them, they are everywhere. You will learn when to speak of them and when to remain silent. But never deny the gods." Helen rose and came around the hearth toward me, as vague and silent as a reflection moving on dark water. "May you serve the Immortals well and long, child. What is your real name?"

I stood up. "Panope, my lady." I had told her before I realized that what had always just seemed ugly and pretentious now had abhorrent implications—*the All-seeing*.

Helen made a surprised noise and then laughed. "What did I just tell you? Oh, Panope Briseis, see well for your people's sake. We must both bear our burdens, you and I. With your royal birth and your beauty, you will certainly be a queen—if not for Lyrnessos, then for somewhere else. Whatever realm you rule, may you be a better queen than I have been for Sparta. Now I must go. My lord will need me when he awakens. May Aphrodite bless you."

She embraced me briefly and then floated away into the dark.

6

The wind had shifted in the night, so the guests' ship could leave. My father pressed them to stay much longer. Paris declined with appropriate semblance of regret, and who could blame his eagerness to deliver his bride to the home he had not seen in so long? More food was served in the megaron, nibbled as hurriedly as decorum permitted. The hall filled up as everyone came to watch the gift giving.

My father promised to send a jar of wine and a white ewe to the beach so that the travelers could sacrifice to Poseidon before embarking. He added a bronze cauldron, two footstools inlaid with ivory carvings, and a gold mixing bowl embossed with an octopus design, while each of the prince's three followers received a carved sealstone ring. Mother presented Helen with a handsome chest, inlaid with silver and niello, containing a rhyton of serpentine carved in the shape of a bull's head, an ostrich egg with a silver stand, and an agate sealstone engraved with a lion attacking a doe, set in a ring of iron, more precious than gold.

The spectators cried out in appreciation as these riches were displayed. I was very impressed and very disturbed. I had never seen Father be so lavish. The standard gift for a departing guest was a cloak made of the incomparable wool that comes only from the sheep of Mount Ida, which Mother usually said she had woven herself—a total fabrication—but Trojan weaving was famous, so Father would not offer cloaks to Trojans. If he had been forced to empty his treasure room to appease the guests' anger at me, then he would never forgive me.

I watched from the balcony, but I left before the visitors did. The first slaves and flunkies who had stirred in the palace had fled from me like gulls on a beach being chased by a barking dog. Pausing only to put on my shoes, I fled also—out through the town and off along the shore with seabirds wheeling overhead and Gorgon loping joyfully ahead. She, at least, did not care that the gods now spoke to me. I wandered the shore until I saw the ship sailing away to the west. Only then did I turn my reluctant feet homeward.

I plodded through the town along muddy alleys. Lyrnessos was not great Troy of the wide streets, just a random huddle of mud-brick hovels and wooden shacks. Child-draped women chatted in their doorways, with spindles whirling; men went by me in twos or threes, bearing burdens. I felt as if they were all pointing at me and whispering behind their hands. I climbed the hill and entered the palace through gates that were never closed or guarded. Crossing the big courtyard, I thought every servant I passed turned to stare at my back.

As I reached the stairs, Bienor came trotting down. He stumbled when he saw me and backed up a step, his eyes wide. Years of injustice suddenly cried out for retribution. I remembered knots that had appeared mysteriously in my weaving, dead fish in my clothes chest, nettles in my bed. Who would not be revenged? I raised my hands in talons.

"Woe!" I proclaimed. The sound echoed off the painted plaster of the walls. "Woe!"

His mouth fell open. He paled! "W-what?"

"Woe to Bienor son of Briseus, for the Moirai have spun his thread. In darkness the Kind Ones shall come to him crying out for vengeance!"

My intolerable twin uttered a shrill shriek of terror and went hurtling back up the stairs. There were definite possibilities in this, I decided. I was about to follow him and rattle his teeth a little harder, when a male voice boomed out below me, "Briseis!"

There, fists on hips, stood Sphelos, my manly, chiseled, so-handsome brother. I stopped where I was, one step up, so my eyes were still higher than his. I felt like a cat treed by a fierce dog. Sphelos would not be intimidated like Bienor. Sphelos' tidy mind did not store sisters on the same shelf as gods.

"You call me, son of Briseus?"

"You're not the gods' herald now, girl. To speak of the Mist Walkers in jest is dangerous folly! Suppose they hear you?"

I shivered and tried to look penitent. "Yes, Sphelos."

He scowled at me. "You have caused quite enough trouble already. Father's talking of sacrificing two heifers to Zeus, just in case there may be something in what you said."

Two heifers! He would never forgive me. Even if he did, Sphelos wouldn't.

"I am sorry," I said automatically. Then I had second thoughts. "Don't blame me for the heifers—I did nothing to anger the Thunderer! I agree I was tactless to speak to the prince as I did—I suppose that's why Father had to give him all those valuable guest gifts?"

"What? Of course not!" My brother's tone implied that my ignorance was willful stupidity. "A guest must be given gifts worthy of his own wealth. Now that Father has a guest friendship with him, one day he will visit Troy, and of course Paris will have to give him gifts even more lavish than those Father gave him today."

"Oh." Would the visit to Troy involve negotiating a betrothal?

My brother's expression chilled. "But what's done is done." He leaned against a red dolphin and folded his arms. "What you said last night was true? You really saw eagles fighting?"

I nodded.

"And you think it means war?"

To be believed was astonishing enough. To be consulted on what the omen meant as if I were a learned augur was even more so. I saw that his anger sprang from worry, and that worried me even more.

"Maera does."

He sighed, staring at the floor. "You were wrong to say what you did when you did, Briseis, but there was truth in your words. I did warn Father that Paris must have violated

Menelaus's hospitality, but I did not realize Sparta followed the old ways and Helen was an apostate." He looked up at me defiantly. "But what could we do? Turn away a son of Priam?"

"I don't know," I whispered, close to tears. I was being blamed for something that was not my fault.

He shrugged. "Well, Mother wants to see you."

"Good! I want to see her."

He cocked a shapely eyebrow. "Why?"

I had said too much already, but Sphelos's reaction would warn me how our parents would respond to my strange request. "I want a husband." I waited for the hurtful laughter.

But my brother did not laugh; he scowled. "She'll tell you you're far too young. Father will make the final decision."

"Of course." To be taken seriously was frightening.

"And he'll have to consult Alcathous."

"The son of Aisyetes?" What did the king of the Dardanians have to do with it? "I don't want to marry some dung-scented herdsman. I want to go and live far away from here—that's what the gods are telling me. It is time for Lyrnessos to change to the new ways and—"

"*No!*"

I gaped at the unexpected anger. "You don't want to be king?"

"Found you!" said Enops, appearing at his back.

"Mm. Well, good luck." That was not what Sphelos had been about to say. He was still glowering.

Enops flashed quizzical looks at each of us. "Did you tell them to stack the smoked fish in the oil store, Brother?"

Sphelos swore luridly. "No! Make sure our family seer goes straight to Mother, will you?" He went dashing off.

Enops grinned and held out his arms for me to fall into. His beginner's beard tickled my cheek as he hugged me. Then he kissed me. Enops had recently developed a passionate interest in the younger palace women and knew what he was about in kissing. I struggled free and said, "Stop that!"

He grinned again, unrepentant. No rain ever fell near Enops. Sphelos was lean and saturnine, but Enops was

chubby and cuddly. Where Sphelos was industrious and un-
tiringly persnickety in helping Father keep track of the vast
palace stores—a prowling leopard stalking the slightest
shortfall in the barley crop—Enops was as indolent as a cat
on a hot afternoon. He seemed to have no ambition in life
beyond a wineskin and good company, which until a few
months ago had meant hunting with the boys, then
overnight became chasing the girls. A prince rarely had to
chase very far.

But when he asked, "How are you, gosling?" he genuinely wanted to know.

I sniffed. "Well enough."

"My baby sister had a frightening experience."

"I shamed everyone!" The tickle in my nose was fast becoming a prickle under my eyelids.

"Not at all. Having a genuine oracle speak in the megaron
for everyone to hear was a great honor, but I'm sure it wasn't
pleasant for you. What's rocking Sphelos's boat?"

"I don't know. Did they really put the fish in the oil
store?"

"I don't suppose so. Is there going to be a war?"

To be everyone's soothsayer was terrifying. I shivered and
nodded, wishing he would hug me again.

"Praise the gods!" He beamed, showing every tooth in his
head. "This is a wondrous augury, my sister!"

"Wondrous? War is terrible!"

"Not to kings' younger sons, it isn't! How long will it last?
How soon will it start? Will I be old enough to fight in it?"

"I don't know! I don't want to know."

"I do." He laughed, putting an arm around me. "They
wouldn't even let me go boar hunting last year, but they
can't keep me out of a war—what else are sons for? Mother
has half the kingdom hunting for you. Come along. How
long until it starts, this war of yours?"

He led me away, babbling all the time about the great adventure I had foretold for him.

7

The first person I saw as I went in was Maera, like a tiny, shriveled raisin. What had the old priestess been saying about me?

The queen's hall was smaller and simpler than the megaron. Its frescoes were more vivid, its windows framed a vista of the town and the sea on one side, orchards and honey-stubbled fields on the other, with a backdrop of brooding Mount Ida. Usually the floor was cluttered with baskets of dyed wool, joyful as flowers; and there were always three or four tall looms standing around, their hundreds of weights tinkling softly in every breeze. The output of finished cloth was small, though. Mother spent her days pretending to weave complicated tapestries displaying scenes of valorous mythology, but mostly she just gossiped with her women and nibbled honey cakes. It was from Queen Nemertes of Lyrnessos that Enops had inherited his royal sloth.

In the sunniest corner, Klymene and Melite were in full croak as usual.

". . . dolphins and starfish on the sides, but the handles were blue."

". . . told her I wouldn't be pushed around, no matter how hot it was."

Omens were easier to understand than those two.

Mother was on her favorite chair, half hidden by a loom. I was relieved to see that last night's illusion of age had passed. The droopy arms and neck were still evident, but if I had not noticed those sooner, it was because she had taken to wearing clothes that hid them. So why had she not yet shed the jewelry and formal gown she had worn to say farewell to the visitors?

Father, who rarely came there, was on a stool facing her,

stiffly erect and as out of place as a bull in a herb garden. He, too, was still in his finery, his mantle and boar's tusk helmet lying by his feet. His hair was tangled.

"Here she is at last!" he said, frowning. He held a ball of blue thread in his hands, turning it over and over.

Mother beamed as if my arrival was a relief to her. She stretched out a plump arm to offer me a half hug as I kissed her cheek. "Where in the world have you been, my dear? We were becoming quite worried about you. You've been keeping us all waiting."

"Keeping the gods waiting, too!" Father growled. His disapproval seemed oddly unconvincing, a thin coat of anger painted over worry.

I apologized, inspecting him surreptitiously. Yes, he was the imposing royal father I knew, the silver in his beard depicting wisdom and maturity, not decay; and yet I could detect traces of the lesser man I had glimpsed at the feast—pouches under eyes, paunch under robe. Coming to see one's parents as human beings must be a part of growing up, but most people do it more gradually than I did.

Maera said nothing, her beady black eyes peering warily out from her wrinkles like a squirrel from its hole.

"Well, now she's here, we may as well begin," Mother said firmly. I wondered what my arrival had ended, what they had been arguing about.

Father said, "Yes." He twisted the ball of wool.

"Sit down, dear. Tell us the whole story."

I began at the beginning again. They frowned when I spoke of Daos, then listened to the rest with a concentration I found flattering. I came to a difficult part when I told how I had seen the ship.

"I prayed to Lord Poseidon, Father. I promised him if he would save the sailors I would ask you to give him a horse, a fine mare."

He grunted and glowered at me under his shaggy eyebrows. "Oh, did you?"

I nodded timorously.

"Well, go ahead."

"What?"

"You promised you'd ask me, right? So ask me."

"Oh. Please, my lord, will you offer a horse to the Earth-shaker?"

"No." He smiled grimly. "There! You've fulfilled your oath."

"That was all you promised, wasn't it?" Mother said, patting my knee. "To ask? You don't really think that you deflected the gods from their purposes, do you? Whatever they planned for the prince and the—er—princess would have happened no matter what you said. Now stop worrying about it and carry on with your story."

That seemed a very slick way out of my obligation, but if my parents said it was all right, then of course I believed them, and I was certainly relieved to be rid of it. I talked on and they asked no questions until I told how the god had spoken to me through Bienor.

Father snorted skeptically. "Bienor brays like a lost goat. Why do you think that was a god?"

"I don't know how I knew, my lord. I didn't when he said it, but then it seemed to echo, somehow. Just those last words."

"You were tired, you were drinking. How long since you'd eaten?"

"Oh, don't be so disbelieving!" Mother snapped. "Even if you don't believe that a god spoke to her through Bienor, how else would you interpret the omen she saw?"

Father twisted the fraying ball of wool harder. "You went up into the woods with Daos?"

"Yes, my lord . . ."

"And whose idea was that?"

I doubt if I even knew what was being suspected, but any child can recognize disapproval, and I did not want Daos to be punished. "Mine of course. You think I do what a slave tells me? I had to go after my dog and didn't want to go alone."

Looks were exchanged.

"That was very foolish of you!" Father said. "People will talk. You're not a child any longer. You mustn't go running into the woods with slaves."

Mother contradicted him, "She is still a child." Then she backed him up, "But people don't know that. You must not cause a scandal."

"I went to catch my dog!" I protested.

"You should have sent the slave to fetch the dog," Mother said sternly. "Princesses do not consort with slaves."

"He didn't touch me. I didn't touch him."

"We believe you, dear, but other people may draw the wrong conclusions."

"What's wrong with Daos? He's very—" About to say, "handsome" I changed it to, "civil. And Enops *consorts* with slave girls all the time." So did Father, for that matter. Sphelos did something similar with the boys.

More looks were exchanged, darker looks.

"And you want to bear a few slave babies, I suppose?" Father said. "Weavers and bath attendants? Don't you understand the difference between men and women?"

"My lord!" Mother protested. "Briseis and I will discuss this privately."

"Do so!" Father growled. "What do I tell the priests? A black bull to Poseidon, of course—and a silver bowl? Our Lady of the Spring . . . a bronze cauldron and a ram? A heifer ought to do for Apollo, and—"

"You can be more generous than that, surely? Why don't you let them advise you?"

Father groaned and threw the badly tangled ball of wool over his shoulder in obvious exasperation. "They'll suck me dry!" He had no liking for priests and priestesses, although he chose them all. He called them beggars and extortionists in public. He grumbled and growled whenever they came to collect their gods' portions, especially the rich offering that went to Smintheus on the seventh day of every month.

Mother exploded at him in a way I had never heard before. "Briseus! Can't you recognize an emergency? Go and drill the army instead, if you'd rather. Briseis and Maera and I will deal with the palace and Dictynna."

He glowered at her. "And Chthonia?"

Mother flinched but set both her chins stubbornly. "There is still time to think about that. Off with you now!"

I blinked, never having heard the king dismissed like that before.

I doubt that he had, either. He snatched up his mantle and helmet and rose to his feet in a black sulk of complaint. "You would also like me to summon your chariot, I suppose?"

"You may pass the word if you wish. Don't bully the priests!" This assertiveness was a disconcerting note I had rarely heard before from my mother, who normally preferred riding at anchor to breasting waves. If Helen had not turned the world over yet, she had certainly given it a tilt.

"You simply can't imagine what she said then," Melite bellowed.

No, Klymene couldn't, because she was snoring peacefully.

King Briseus snorted and stalked away. Maera had been as still as a cat during the exchange, but now her toothless mouth twisted in amusement. I wondered why the dread Chthonia should be involved.

"Don't mind your father, dear," Mother said complacently. "He's worried about trade."

I suppose I looked as blank as a freshly rolled clay tablet.

"Shipping, dear!" she explained. "If Troy has a falling out with the Greeks, that will be bad for business. Piracy and so on."

I thought my father was worried about a lot more than that, and so was she. He could not go and drill the army, as she had so waspishly suggested, for he himself was the only knight in Lyrnessos, and the nearest he had to a war band was the palace guard, a rabble of aging spearmen led by Captain Kreion, who was not even of noble blood.

"Now," Mother said, "we must go and give thanks to Our Lady for sending you the augury."

I did not feel especially grateful. "Yes, Mother."

"The palace shrine first, and then we'll drive up to the altar where you saw the eagles."

"Mother, do you think there will be a war?" If Father was willing to throw heifers and rams and gold bowls around, then he obviously thought the matter gravely serious. "And was our house profaned by giving Helen hospitality?"

"Tush! We could not know, dear! We shall ask Potnia how we should purify the palace and the city again. She will not be hard on those who offend in ignorance."

"Won't she?" Maera cried shrilly, bursting into our conversation so abruptly that we both jumped. "What about Actaeon? He didn't know he had wandered into Artemis's sacred grove, and look what happened to him, just for watching her bathe! What else would a man do? I can think of many people who affronted the gods without meaning to and still had to pay the penalty. How about Oedipus? He married Jocasta because she was queen of Thebes and he wanted to be king, not because she was his mother. He didn't know he was doing anything wrong! He didn't know the king he'd killed was his own father."

My mother's robust confidence swayed a little and then steadied again. "Those are very old stories."

"It's the act that counts!" Maera said fiercely.

"Well, Our Lady sent us a warning through Briseis, so she means us well, and we shall ask what is needed."

Maera smirked toothlessly. If she was not going to mention her interpretation of the omen, I would have to mention it myself.

"Mother, the gods were telling me I need a husband."

Mother recoiled as if I had butted her. "A *what*?" she bleated.

"A husband. The gods were warning me to find a protector, a knight who will marry me and take me away to—"

Her plump cheeks had paled under their paint. "Oh, nonsense! No! No! No!" I had never seen her so shaken. "You're far too young to be thinking of marriage. Why, even Sphelos isn't married yet! Don't be absurd. That can't possibly be what the gods meant." She glared at Maera and made an effort to compose herself. "Now, is my hair all right? What offering can you take? A weaving?"

"I have the one with the dolphin on it."

"Not very appropriate! Let's see, you did help Alcmene with the lily and hyacinth one, so that's sort of your work." Queen Nemertes heaved herself up from the chair to go and look for it.

"Well?" I asked Maera, meaning, *Your interpretation isn't very popular in these quarters, is it?*

The old woman ignored my question. "She is eternal maiden," she chanted in her creaky old voice. "She is eternal lover. She is eternal mother." She rocked on her stool, beaming her toothless gums at me.

She was referring to Chthonia

8

The royal shrine was a dim and poky cellar with one wall of bare rock and several pottery gods and goddesses standing patiently on plinths. It had no need to be large, because Potnia's great festivals were affairs of state, held in the megaron itself. At those, the goddess would appear to us in the flesh. This was a much lesser ceremony. Prompted by Mother, I made an offering of wine and barley and honey, and then of the cloth I had woven. The rancid fumes of the lamps made my eyes prickle. I fought against a surging dread that the goddess herself was present, listening. By the time I emerged into daylight again, I had a headache.

Fresh air soon disposed of that when we set off to visit the altar of Our Lady Dictynna. Mother's chariot was waiting for her, all very splendid, made of elm and pearwood with ivory inlays on the box and silver fittings on the harnesses; the wheels were rimmed with bronze. Both the main pole extending from the floor and the upper pole from the rail were painted purple, while the yoke and the horses' neck straps were crimson. She threw a queenly tantrum over dust on the ivory inlays. Three stable hands hastily wiped the whole vehicle with handfuls of straw, while Maera got in their way, fussily loading supplies on board.

The other chariot was a workaday car of plain wicker, very drab by comparison. I reached it before old Anticleia, who picked her way fastidiously over the muddy ground, huddling a warm cloak around her emaciated carcass— Anticleia could be relied on to disapprove of stable yards, just as she disapproved of everything else. By the time a slave had handed her up, I had a firm grip on the reins. She looked at me distrustfully.

"I'll bring you home safely," I promised cheerfully, "but if you want to promise an ox to Hermes, I'm sure it won't hurt."

She took hold of the rail with both hands and muttered something that might have been, "A hundred oxen!"

Mother declared herself satisfied and climbed aboard. Maera was already there. The sun shone, the shaggy little horses seemed eager to please, and soon we were heading uphill through the olive trees, following the trail.

Chariot driving is never restful, but it can be more pleasant than walking. Lyrnessos was not the Argolid, with its fine paved roads on which chariots can hurtle along at a trot. Going across country, or up a rutted track as we were, a gentle walk by the horses was enough to bounce us around like flails on a threshing floor. Any pace faster than that would hurl us out bodily and usually upset the chariot itself; or the horses' throat straps would start to choke them, they would panic, and total disaster befall. If Mother's long tresses blew out behind her that day, it was entirely due to the wind, not any headlong velocity.

We climbed into the hills until the forest came in sight again, and then turned to the east. I worried that I might not be able to find the shrine, but of course we came to the stream and that led us to the right place easily enough.

I knew at once that the goddess was not there. The holiness I had sensed the previous day had disappeared, and so had the eagle's body. I explained confidently that some predator would have carried it off, and when we gathered around the ancient stones, I pointed to fresh scrapes on the moss and a few specks of what I insisted was blood. There were gray pigeon feathers among the reeds, too.

"We don't doubt you, dear," Mother said politely.

Perhaps not, but the previous day's events now seemed

like a bad dream, so those feathers were welcome. Much had changed—I was no longer the unimportant child I had been. The gods had spoken to me. Unless Maera was very wrong, they had warned me to find a strong husband, to renounce my claim to be future queen, to go and live somewhere else. Yesterday I had longed to grow up, but now I shied back from the implications.

The ceremony did not take long. I offered barley and honey, wine and oil, and Mother prompted me through a prayer of thanks. The wind carried my words away. I had no sense that the goddess was present or that any immortal heard. Anticleia, who fancied herself a herbalist, began wandering around, peering disapprovingly at the vegetation. In a few minutes we boarded the chariots again and so began our journey home.

BOOK THREE

AENEAS

1

We had no augur to explain the portent to us, but it was obvious that Paris, by stealing Menelaus's wife while he was Menelaus's guest, had broken the laws of hospitality all civilized peoples observe. If we, by taking him in as our guest, had brought the wrath of the Immortals upon ourselves, the god most likely to have taken offense was the Thunderer himself. In his aspect of Zeus Xeinios, he is god of hospitality. Next morning Father sacrificed to him in an effort to avert his rage. Even in little Lyrnessos the Cloud Gatherer received offerings almost every day, but this was to be something special that would calm all the people alarmed by my outburst.

Mother had a favorite chair carried to the outer courtyard and sat under the shade of an olive, holding the scepter. I stood among the young women, hearing girls of my own age whispering about their love affairs and sniggering over those of absent friends.

The two heifers were handsome animals, sleek and fat after a good summer's grazing, groomed and adorned with wreaths of wool, their horns gilded. First, Father cut a lock of hair from their heads, and cast it into the fire. Then he raised his arms to address the clear blue sky, calling out his dedication of these fine beasts. He sprinkled water and barley on the pyre and on the ground. He took up the knife. I held my breath and I suppose others did, also.

The first one went well. Four men clung to the ropes that held the heifer's legs, two men lifted its head, and Father made a clean slash across its throat. The beast staggered and went down. You know how the blood spurts out with every beat of the dying heart, but Sphelos caught it neatly in a silver bowl. We all cried out, as was expected of us.

While other men attended to the messy butchering, the

second heifer was brought close. Alarmed by the fire or the smell of blood, it began to resist. Father bungled his first stroke. The victim bellowed, understandably upset at this wanton violence. He cut again, quickly. The heifer tried to go elsewhere and dragged its handlers several paces before they could steady it for a third blow. That one did bring it down, but it kicked over the bowl in its death throes. By that time everyone was soaked with gore. It was an inauspicious performance.

Worse was to come. When the thigh bones had been wrapped in fat and laid on the fire, the smoke of the sacrifice seemed strangely reluctant to rise. Then a flight of cranes came from the north, from Mount Ida. An omen! Nearer they came, very high, flying steadily. If they went straight over it would be good—even very good, according to the lore of augurs—and of course they should have done so, were they only cranes doing what cranes do. Just before they reached the palace, they abruptly veered. A great moan surged through the courtyard as the birds turned to the west and vanished into the distance, following the shore toward the direction of a setting sun. Bad, very bad! No one needed the family seer to announce that the offering had been refused.

After that portent, the feast was sodden and unfestive. Oh, we all partook of the juicy meat gladly enough, but what should have been a divine delicacy was clay in our mouths. Father ordered more and more wine brought out, but even that could not raise the crowd's spirits. The dancing and singing seemed dreary and joyless.

Despairing, I left the revelries and returned to my mother for comfort. I was surprised when she beckoned me close, for I was not one of her usual confidantes. When I leaned over her chair, she clasped my wrist with pudgy fingers.

"You were correct," she whispered. "We have angered the Immortals."

For a child, a parent's first apology is a memorable triumph, but I found no joy in it. "I'm sorry," I said, as if it were all my fault. "What can we do? Should we seek out a soothsayer? Surely there must be learned augurs in Troy who can advise us." I think I had some faint hopes of being allowed to accompany an embassy to Holy Troy.

She gave me the sort of look that darkens a child's world, but fortunately I knew that this time it was not provoked by any misdeeds of mine. "I need no mumbling white-bearded Trojan to tell me when my house has been profaned." She glanced around as if to make sure we were not being overheard. "There are those who know the gods' will more surely. Go and tell your father that tomorrow I will seek guidance from Chthonia's realm."

"No!" Chthonia is mistress of the dead in the Troad. Father identified her with the Greek Demeter, but she is more fearsome than the Earth Mother. "I do not know this ritual."

"I have only seen it done once, when I was about your age. The dead know all."

I half expected my hair to stand on end, but it didn't. "You can make them speak?"

She shrugged uncertainly, and I was shocked to realize that the prospect frightened her as much as it did me. "They cannot be called back after they have crossed the river. And those who cannot cross . . . if they have resided too long with the Mistress, their memories of daylight will have faded." Mother pulled a face. "They must be most recently dead."

Before I could confirm that this meant what I was afraid it meant, she heaved herself to her feet, nodded to Alcmene and Anticleia to follow her, and stumped away—bent and care-laden and smaller than usual.

2

I felt dismal with apprehension and early-morning chill as I climbed into the chariot, and the dawn chatter of the birds sounded ominously discordant, like a knife on pottery. Sphelos jangled the reins, I grabbed at the polished ash-wood rail, and we rolled forward toward the gate. Enops was still fussing with his car, which meant he was giving us a head start and setting up a race.

Trails on the dewy grass showed where the wagon and other chariots had gone ahead of us. Sphelos held the reins in both hands, balancing expertly on the leather webbing as it rolled underfoot like a sea swell. His cheekbone was puffed and purple, but when I asked what had happened, he refused to explain.

"You don't need me," I grumbled. "Why do I have to come?" I had no desire to speak with the dead.

My grown-up brother rarely acknowledged my existence, but this time he gave me a civil answer. "Because you're the heir, of course."

"Why? Why am I the heir? Why doesn't Lyrnessos change to the new ways? Maera says that's why the gods sent the omen to me—they were warning me to marry a man who will take me away to live in a safer place."

"Nowhere is safe from war. War is everywhere." He snorted. "I hope you're not suggesting I should be king after Father?"

"Why not? Father says you know more about how the kingdom is run than anybody."

He shot me an irritated glance but seemed to conclude I was offending out of ignorance. "That may be true, but it isn't important. Well, it is important. Without the procurator and his staff, the kingdom would collapse. I can never be king, Briseis, because noble blood is not enough. A king must be a knight, and I'm not big enough. Can you see me running around in plate armor? I couldn't ram a spear through an ox-hide shield, let alone a cuirass behind it. That takes weight and muscle and sheer size."

I could not tell if this confession hurt him. I had no comfort to offer—the Moirai spin our fates. His mantle had been woven for him by Mother herself. It was one of her better creations, but it bore no tassels.

"Alcathous would never accept me," he added.

He had mentioned the king of the Dardanians before. "What's Alcathous got to do with it?"

Enops and Bienor went by us at a trot, bouncing wildly and shouting derision. Racing was beneath Sphelos's dignity. He smiled contemptuously after them, not looking at me. I wondered what he had done to his cheek. I wished I were home in bed.

"Things are not always what they seem, Little Sister. Every year King Eëtion sends Father a tribute of fifty oxen. King Altes gives him a hundred wethers. Do you know why?"

"No."

"So that Thebe and Pedasos may trade with each other along the coast road. Anyone else has to pay tribute to pass by Lyrnessos. But why do they bother? We have no army, just a few lowborn spearmen. The Kilikes and the Leleges are big tribes, with many warriors. Either of them could overrun us in a morning."

I was in no mood for puzzles or lectures. "Don't know."

"Because," he said with the exaggerated patience adults use on ignorant children, "the Dardanians want free access to the sea. They can trade through Pedasos or Troy, but Altes and Priam might squeeze them if they didn't also have us as another outlet."

"You mean the Dardanians defend us?"

"The Dardanians own us, although no one is rude enough to say so openly. Father claims to be an independent king, but in truth he holds Lyrnessos on Alcathous's sufferance."

The morning had darkened even more. I knew the Dardanian royal family and liked most of them, but I had believed them to be our equals, not our masters. Queen Hippodemia was Mother's cousin, a few times removed.

"So Alcathous will decide who succeeds Father—long may that day be delayed, of course. In these troubled times he will want a strong warrior. The family connection is wearing a little thin, so he'll probably choose some nephew or cousin."

"No!" My hopes were set on a handsome, cultivated prince along the lines of Paris, not a loudmouthed tribal drunkard. Besides, Dardania was even closer to Troy than Lyrnessos was. This was not what the omen had meant.

Sphelos laughed. "You will lie in whatever bed Father chooses, my girl, and he will choose as Alcathous tells him to."

We were almost at our destination already. The path tipped steeply downward into the shadowing trees. Sphelos pulled back on the reins to slow the horses.

"If not you, then Enops?" I said.

"Enops? Enops may have dreams of grandeur, but he's as lazy as Mother, and he's too young. Bienor is even younger. You're the heir, Briseis."

"I'm even younger than Bienor!"

"Only by the length of time it takes a pot to boil. Besides, women are different. You could be betrothed today, married very soon. A man doesn't reach his full size until he's at least twenty, and even then he may have trouble making older men follow him. Your prophecy about war coming only makes things worse. Let's hope Mother learns otherwise today."

The horses were fretting as the chariot tried to run away with them on the hill. The clearing was in sight through the trees ahead. I could see the wagon and half a dozen chariots, plus twenty or so people. I shivered and forgot my marriage problems for the time being.

Sphelos jerked the chariot to a halt alongside the wagon, where soldiers were unloading firewood. I stepped down and went forward to hold the horses.

In all Lyrnessos, this was one place where children never played and no birds sang. Only rank grass and a few reeds grew near the cave mouth, the portal to the realms of death. The droopy willows had lost their leaves, but the great limbs of the oaks stretching overhead still held theirs. The canyon was cold and dark, dank with scents of rotting vegetation. Even the palace guards, who were normally as raucous and vulgar as magpies, were going about their work in awed silence. It could have been worse, though, because Mother had wanted to perform the ritual after dark. Father had told her the men would refuse to come and he might not even turn up himself.

In all her priestly finery she sat on a folding stool with her women fussing around her. Old Anticleia knelt at her feet, preparing a potion of wine and other arcane stuff in a silver bowl, mumbling incantations. Father stood in menacing silence, supervising the soldiers building the pyre. Enops was at the wagon, helping the men unload all the things Mother had ordered: billets of wood, a silver bowl for catching blood, the bronze knife, amphorae of wine, a bundle of oiled torches. The black ram had been unbound and tethered to a wheel; it was grazing contentedly. She had specified that it must be totally black, for only the perfect could be offered to the gods, but even at a distance I could see matted patches in its fleece that I suspected might be paint. A pure black animal is rare, and there had been little time to find one.

And who else? Reluctantly I looked where I had been carefully not looking—at the young man sitting on the tailgate of the wagon, legs a-dangling, conspicuously idle amid so much activity, just leaning back on thick arms, gazing happily up at the cliff. His scalp had been shaved to leave only a forelock dangling down to his eyes, his bronzed limbs were clean and oiled, he wore a white loincloth and garlands of white wool around his neck. *No!* Before I knew it, I was running.

"Daos? Oh, Daos!"

He tilted his head down and gave me a bemused smile as if I were some beautiful vision he could not quite understand. Before he could say anything, a man grabbed me from behind and put a hand over my mouth. I kicked, squirmed, and bit. Hard. He yelled, and I realized that it was Sphelos. I stamped on his foot. I might have broken loose and made a scene if Enops had not joined in. I was helpless against the two of them, and they dragged me away.

"Stop it!" Enops said, in a much harsher voice than he normally used. "There's nothing you can do. There's nothing you should do. Do not anger the gods any more than . . . than they are angry already."

They marched me over to Bienor, who was sitting on a rock in the cool shadow of the cliff. There they released me but stood close on either side, ready to grab if I tried anything. Everyone else was ignoring the four royal children.

Sphelos examined his bleeding finger. "Vixen!"

"Does it hurt worse than your black eye?" Enops sneered.

I was sobbing. "He didn't do anything! He came with me to protect me! It was pouring, he was frozen, but he came because he thought it was his duty. I told him not to, but he thought he should."

"Ha!" Sphelos put a mean twist on the sound. "That wasn't what you told Father."

"He was trying to help me. He did help me. He did nothing wrong. This isn't fair!" My protests would do Daos no good—but they could certainly do him no harm in his present situation. I clenched my teeth and tried to control my heaving sobs.

"It had nothing to do with your trip up the mountain. Father told me to pick out the finest, so I chose Daos. I didn't even know then that he was the one who went with you that day. It would have been Daos anyway."

"But why?" I shouted. "He's a good worker, isn't he? Everyone likes him."

"Some like him very much," Enops said.

Sphelos scowled and made an effort to assert his authority. "Because he's growing too big, that's why. Males can be dangerous, and he's shown a temper once or twice. It's this or the slave market, and we wouldn't get much for him, because everyone would guess that he was getting out of hand. He's also started pestering the women."

Of course he would pester women—that was what young men were for, at least in the women's view of things. I thought of Enops and his daily rampage. But Enops was a prince.

"He flirts, you mean?" he said. "What real man doesn't, Brother?"

Sphelos flushed bright scarlet. "The reason Daos was the obvious choice is that he's beautiful! Only the best are good enough for the gods, and he's the finest we have to offer."

"Quite!" Enops snorted. "If he'd really wanted to hurt you, he'd have broken you in pieces."

Memory can play odd tricks. It was only then that I recalled how big Daos's fists were and how I had seen a swelling on his knuckles when they rested on the cart. I stared accusingly at Sphelos's matching cheek. He glared back at me and then at Enops.

"That had nothing to do with it. That happened only after I suggested him to Father!"

"Kissing him good-bye, were you?" Bienor sneered, breaking his unnatural silence.

Not many months ago, Sphelos would have beaten him purple for such insolence. Now he just spun around and stalked away. He held his head high, but if he'd had a tail, it would have been between his legs.

"Fungus!" Enops growled, scowling after him.

"Father takes boys sometimes," I murmured, not understanding.

"So do I. Fun is fun, and no harm in it, but a prince should not try to make a slave into a *lover*! He has no shame at all. If Daos were noble, even just freeborn . . . Oh, never mind about Sphelos. Behave, please, Briseis! You can only cause a scandal or anger the gods. You're the king's daughter—set an example."

This calm, authoritative adult was so unlike the chirpy Enops I knew that I just stared. He turned and followed Sphelos. I wiped my eyes. My throat ached.

Bienor stood up. "I feel like you do." He took my hand and squeezed it—had all my brothers changed into strangers overnight?

"Do you think he knows why he's here?" I muttered, gazing at the wagon. Daos had not moved.

"He must know what the wool means, but Enops said he's been given enough poppy to stun a bull. So he knows but doesn't care, I suppose."

"I wish they'd chosen some farmhand I'd never met."

"Me too," Bienor said. "They're ready. Come on."

The spearmen stood back, doubtless all rejoicing that they were not required to participate more closely in the ceremony. The rest of us gathered before the mouth of the cave, with Mother in the center. Seeming even more gaunt and cadaverous than usual, Anticleia handed her a goblet. She drained it. Anticleia refilled it and brought it around to each of us in turn.

"Just a sip," she whispered as she held it to Bienor's lips, repeating the same words for me. I caught the sickly scent of poppy, but the taste was astringent and vile.

Daos, though, was given a full goblet all to himself. He quaffed it obediently, bemused but blissful. He might never have tasted wine before or know that it was drugged, but even if he was aware why he had been included in this noble company, he followed orders as he had done all his life. He was already unsteady on his feet, just conscious enough to be embarrassed by that, being supported by Father on one side and Sphelos on the other. Neither looked as if he was enjoying himself.

We took our flaming torches and paraded into the cavern, chanting the invocation we had been taught for this occasion— Mother first, Alcmene leading the ram, Daos and his two royal attendants next, Maera, various priests and priestesses . . . and the rest of us, with Bienor and myself at the rear. We had been told we did not have to go all the way down, only far enough to watch the ritual, but neither of us would give in first, so we went with the group as it descended into the dark, into the halls of the undergods. *I shall come here again,* I thought, *when I die.* I did not know then that there are other portals in other places, so that not all souls pass that particular way. Not that it matters, I suppose. We all go there in the end.

The arch dwindled behind us and soon I could see nothing but my companions and the leaping flames of their torches. I hoped the faint twitterings overhead were only bats. The floor was so thickly padded with their droppings that our feet made no sound, but the brands hissed. My heart pounded in the overwhelming holiness.

Whatever was in the goblet was potent. Daos was barely able to walk now, leaning heavily on Father and Sphelos. Like a universe of bad eggs, the stench made my head throb and my eyes reel until the torch flames danced in pairs before me. We halted where the ground dropped away steeply into a pit. Mother chanted at blackness ahead, pouring out the offerings of honey and wine and water. Soon, surely, the ghosts would start to come, the empty shadows who roam the underworld in endless sorrow.

I moved closer to Bienor. He put an arm around me. Grateful, I gave him one. Someone was coughing painfully.

The ram died with its head over the bowl that Mother held. She rose, calling on the goddess to receive the offering and hear our prayers. Two priests dragged the carcass away to be burned.

Together Father and Sphelos took hold of Daos's arms and kicked at the back of his legs. He slumped to his knees with a bemused protesting mumble. "Sirs!" Father pushed his shoulders down, pulled his head up by the forelock, and brought the knife around to cut his throat. I tried to close my eyes; they refused my commands. Blood sprayed out in black torrents, never ending. There was a terrible amount of blood in him. I repeated to myself, over and over, Sphelos's assurance that he had not been chosen because of anything I had done. Had it not been Daos, then it would have been some other husky boy.

Mother straightened triumphantly with the brimming bowl, dark shining blood slathered over her breasts, her eyes huge and filled with the flames of the torches, a nightmare of how Chthonia herself might look if any artist ever dared depict her. I buried my face in Bienor's neck, he put his arms around me, and I felt him shaking. The twitterings were all around us, a whirling smoke of bats alarmed by the torches, but among them I could hear the squeaks of lost souls coming to the scent. The homeless dead crave blood, and a taste of it can give them just enough form to speak.

"Daos!" The voice was guttural and strange. "Daos!"

I forced myself to look and saw her advancing deeper into the cave, offering the bowl before her in both hands, stumbling down the felted slope, and almost invisible. The shades danced around her, through her, incorporating glimpses of darkness that the torches could not banish. They twittered and gibbered, a rustling lamentation like dry leaves.

"Daos, come to me. Come and I will pour this blood for you. You must answer my questions before I will let you go. Answer me, Daos, and we shall give you proper rites, so that you may enter the Fortunate Land. Be silent and your corpse will lie here for the rats to spoil, so that your soul wanders forever in the dark."

Someone was crying, "Release!" but I could not tell if it was Mother promising or Daos demanding. Flames leapt, and the shadows flitted around me, through me, thinly wailing in my ears. The cave swayed.

The next thing I remember with any clarity is the hurtful glare of daylight in my face as Sphelos carried me out through the arch. I mumbled, wanting to retch.

"Easy, now!" He trudged across the clearing to the trees, away from the underworld reek. He was panting with effort, his face wet and flushed, yet he set me down gently enough on a bank of cool ferns. I lay there gagging until the world might steady. Others were emerging from the cave—Father and Anticleia supporting Mother between them, Bienor leaning on Enops. And the rest.

"Did it work?" I whispered. "Did he tell her?"

"She got an answer," Sphelos muttered into his arms. He sat doubled over.

I choked and discovered that I was weeping. My brother looked at me blearily and patted my shoulder as if it might bite him. "You've scratched your cheek. Are you a mourner?" He seemed to find that funny.

"Murderer!"

He flinched and turned away. After a moment he spoke toward the nearest tree. "Don't pity him, not now. He was a slave, a chattel. His mother could not even tell him what his father looked like, let alone name him. He was ours to give to the goddess like a silver cup or a ewe lamb."

Because you can did not mean *so you must,* but I stayed silent, and Sphelos went on muttering incoherently to the empty air: "Daos, Daos! What did the world have in store for him? Nothing, nothing at all. And nothing after it, either. Who cares for a slave's soul? Now he will have noble rites, with a king presiding, go to the Fortunate Land. Given provisions for his journey, possessions to take with him, things he never owned in this life. Died for a goddess—will she not welcome in her halls, honor forever? What more

could he have wanted? What better could life have brought
him?"

I answered that. "Length of days."

"As a slave? No, Briseis. I pitied him when he was alive,
but I don't pity him his death."

"I liked him!"

Sphelos groaned. "I loved him. I doted on him. He was
the most beautiful creature I have ever seen, and he could
not love me. Only submit. I loved him. I promised him
wealth, even a woman of his own, but he could not love me.
I gave him this because I loved him."

I wiped my eyes so that they could confirm what my ears
were telling me, that Sphelos was weeping, too. I could not
see his face, but his shoulders were shaking and his voice
kept breaking. He rambled on, making less and less sense. I
did not understand and I doubt any woman could have understood the sort of love he was trying so clumsily to describe. It sounded like childish spite—if you can't have it,
break it—and I was frightened to discover that grown-ups
could think that way. I'm sure that wasn't what he meant; I
still don't know what he did mean.

When he mumbled into silence, I asked, "What answer
did he give Mother?"

My brother groaned again, looking over to where the
body was being laid on the pyre, with the ram at its feet. "He
told her to arm her young men, to set her women weaving
shrouds, and to beware the son of a goddess."

3

The men remained behind to preside over the funeral pyre.
Mother was taken back to the palace in the wagon.

I was thirteen years old and recovered quickly. I had never
known her to be sick, not ever, but when she was brought to

her room that day, she was very sick indeed, retching, coughing, and brightly flushed. The women made light of my terror. This was a normal reaction to the potion, they said—she would sleep now and be better when she awakened. Mulishly refusing to be chased away, I sat by the bed and held her hand.

The chamber was one of the largest in the palace, with wide windows facing the sea and net-draped doors leading out to a balcony on the landward side. The bed was large, too, and the thought occurred to me as I sat there that I must have been conceived on it. Father's quarters lay across the passage, and his bed was smaller. Sunlight crept slowly around the walls, highlighting faded frescoes of fishermen holding up their catch on one wall, warriors offering to Potnia on another, a traditional Cretan scene of boys leaping over bulls on yet another. I wondered how old those images were and who had specified their subjects—why so many scantily clad young men in a queen's bedroom?

Father looked in briefly after the funeral. Maera and Alcmene fussed in and out. Mother barely knew us. Her eyes seemed inhumanly bright, she drooled incessantly, and still her face was the color of ripe pomegranates. The words she babbled made no sense, although I suspected that Maera was listening carefully as she dabbed at my mother's brow.

Suddenly my hand was squeezed so tightly that I yelped. Mother's head rose from the pillow, her eyes staring right at me, brilliant as enormous gems. "Euneus!" she said very clearly, very urgently. "I need Euneus now!"

"Yes, Mother. Who's Euneus?"

Her eyes rolled and she fell back, asleep again. I caught glances pass between Maera and Alcmene.

"Maera, who's Euneus?"

Maera mumbled toothlessly, "Don't know. Just maundering. Doesn't mean anything." She went scurrying across the room like a bent little beetle and busied herself with folding Mother's gown and packing it into the chest. I was quite certain that she did know, though.

After a while, I decided that Mother was sleeping soundly

and I had a job to do. She had told me she needed Euneus, so I must find him. I released her hand gently.

Demodokos was the one to ask. At that sleepy time of day, he could often be found on a stone bench in a shady corner of the outer courtyard. Sometimes he would play his kithara and sing, and then people would gather around to listen until Father or Sphelos appeared and ordered them all back to work. Usually he just gossiped with a collection of cronies as old as himself. That was what I found him doing that day, seven white heads bent in a circle, bobbing like ducks on a pond. There was much to discuss in Lyrnessos then.

Divining my destination, Gorgon bounded ahead of me like a shaggy black herald. One of the ancients yelped in alarm as a cold nose snuffled his arm. Then all the faces turned in my direction, and I could tell from the way they looked that I was at least one of the topics under discussion. I stopped under the next tree but one and called, "Bard!"

Demodokos rose stiffly to his feet and hobbled over to answer my summons. I did not think he would have so honored me three days ago. The change was both pleasing and worrying.

He said, "My lady?" and he had most certainly not called me that before. He was no taller than I was, a stooped little owl with a hooked nose netted in fine red veins.

"Do you know a man called Euneus?"

"Euneus, my lady?" His watery eyes blinked a few times. "Er . . . that is not an uncommon name. Can you be more specific? I could probably call to mind some I have met myself, and even more mentioned in songs." He exuded evasion like a stench of garlic.

"Cite instances. Parade them in glittering congregation before my wondering gaze, designating their rank, paternity, status, and accomplishments."

His smile faltered. "The king of Lemnos has a brother, Euneus son of Jason. There is a ship captain from Rhodes who calls here most years. . . ."

"Continue."

"I can't think of any more offhand, my lady. May I inquire why you are asking?"

He could inquire, but I wasn't going to tell him, any more than he was going to answer me. First Maera, now Demodokos!

"Let me know if you remember the one I want," I instructed him, and walked away. I glanced back as I entered the porch, and he was still standing where I had left him, staring after me.

Sphelos's authority would soon bring Demodokos to heel, even if Maera might defy him, but Sphelos was off supervising the olive harvest. That left Father, and I had other matters to discuss with Father anyway. It was time I asked him to find me a husband.

At this season, Father and Sphelos spent much time in the treasury that made up so much of the palace. Everything that came by sea or land to Lyrnessos found its way to the treasury to be tabulated before being used or stored away. Some rooms were stacked to the roof with bales of flax, rope, leather, finished cloth, or raw wool, while others were crammed with chests or shelves bearing painted pots, plates, perfumes, spices, tools, or fruits. Huge jars sunk in the ground and floored over with tiles stocked oil, wine, wheat, barley, lentils, beans, or smoked tunny. I found all this excessively dull, although Father had explained its importance to me often enough.

"Suppose a potter wants to eat fish, but the fisherman does not need another pot. Must he exchange his wares for flax and then exchange that for something else that the fisherman will accept? No one could ever achieve anything, because everyone would be haggling all the time. This way, people turn in their produce to the palace and the palace sees that every family has enough food, clothes, and time to cultivate its plot. Without the procurator, the kingdom would collapse." Many realms have discovered the truth of that in the years since then!

Just inside the main door of this beehive was the tablet room, where the various officials kept their accounts by making marks on strips of wet clay. After the tablets had been dried in the sun, they were stored away in baskets until the year drew to a close, as now. Then the totals were added up and written out on rolls of leather and stored in mouse-proof jars. This was a huge and temper-testing task, but only thus could Father be sure that no one was stealing from him or from the gods, who had to receive their share of every-thing. Sphelos boasted that every lamb and olive tree in the realm was accounted for, every slave, every loom, every ingot of bronze. I confess I sometimes wondered if the Olympians had a similar system to keep track of us mortals, but I was never rash enough to put such blasphemy into words.

I found the tablet room deserted except for Amphimedes, the master of bees, who was sitting astride a bench writing notes on clay with a thorn, and so engrossed that he did not notice me. Not even the girl who prepared the tablets was there. As I hesitated, wondering where to try next, I saw Gorgon staring along the corridor, wagging her tail. Excellent! Her brothers hunted deer and wild boars, so why should she not find a king for me?

"Track!" I said. "Find Father!"

Usually she would interpret any unfamiliar command as an order to leap up and lick my face, but in this case she set off at a lope into the gloom. I followed and was led right to my royal sire, at work in a chamber I had never visited be-fore with a couple of brawny male porters and a keeper of records holding an oil lamp. All four were crammed into a very small space by the door. The rest of the room was packed with wooden chests, tables, stools, huge pots, poles, nondescript wicker hampers, and a waist-high stack of hide-shaped bronze ingots. Some of the furniture was damaged, some of the pots were chipped, but it was not a junk store, because the bronze alone must be worth a knight's estate. Dust danced in pearly shafts of light from the tiny, thief-proof window.

One of the boxes had fallen apart and lay as a pile of bro-ken boards and dull metal objects at their feet. Another stood open beside it. Crouching there, my father was inspecting a curved plate of very dusty bronze. He was low enough to be vulnerable to a friendly slobber from Gorgon.

He cursed. "Gorgon? Briseis! Your mother?"

"Sleeping. I think she's all right."

He sighed with relief. Then he looked at me oddly, rather the way Enops did if I met him on his way to the women's quarters late at night. I realized that the metal things on the floor were arrowheads, hundreds of them, and the other box contained plate armor.

"So what do you want?" His tone was unpleasantly sharp.

"Mother says she needs someone called Euneus, but I don't know who he is."

"Euneus?"

"Yes. Euneus."

"What else did she say about him?"

"Nothing. I'm not sure she knew what she was saying."

He grunted. He obviously knew who Euneus was and just as obviously did not want to discuss him. His minions were staring at nothing the way slaves do when pretending to be totally deaf.

"Ponteus, Chariseus, go back to your other work. Leave that mess on the floor for now. Phylo, I want this door sealed."

All three hurried away. Father himself closed the door and tied the ropes over it. Phylo returned with damp clay, with which she covered the knots, and he stamped it with his seal-stone.

"Now bring that damned dog out of here," he told me, "before she eats our winter fish."

4

He led me upstairs to his private balcony, which was not overlooked from anywhere and yet had a fine view of the town, the harbor, and the coast road. This was his favorite spot for private chats and his sleeping place in warm weather. He sank into a chair, waved me to another, but then just scowled gloomily at the sea, saying nothing. Truly the name of Euneus provoked most curious reactions!

The outside of the palace was white plastered with the woodwork accented in bright colors. The sky was blue and white. Brown grooms were putting brown horses through their paces on green pasture. The fishing fleet lay on the beach far below like basking seals, by a sea of startling cobalt, speckled with white surf on the rocks. Only three days ago, Paris and Helen had narrowly escaped death on those. If they had died, then Daos would have lived and my father would not have gone in search of his armor.

The wine came, rousing him from his reverie. After he had rinsed his hands, he sent the women away and poured it himself into stemmed goblets made in our own pottery, glazed with curves and spirals. It was good Rhodian wine, too, not our bitter Lyrnessos stuff.

He sighed and glanced briefly at me under his heavy brows before directing his frown back on the scenery, which had done much less to deserve it. "I owe you an apology, littlest one. I did not believe you when you told us of the omen."

"I owe you one, my lord, for I should not have blurted out the news in public." I thought that sounded like a very adult sort of concession.

He snorted, which was probably an adult sort of agreement. "It seems there will be war, as you prophesied. Lyrnessos is such a little place! We have no great walls, no armed knights. Ask Demodokos for an epic tale of the founding and he will blink at you like a drunken owl, in that way he has. But mention Troy, or any Greek city, and he will make the strings of his kithara smoke. The original rulers, whoever they were, were certainly not ancestors of yours. They were mostly traders."

"And slavers?" Slaving involved fighting and danger, and was much more honorable than mere trading.

Father nodded and sipped wine. "In your great-grandmother's day, the Lyrnessians used to raid all their neighbors indiscriminately, exporting the women and children. The Dardanians took offense and seized the town. They put in a king of their own."

Aha! This was getting close to what Sphelos had told me. "Why?" I asked. "I mean, why did they not just kill everyone and come to live here themselves?"

He shrugged. "They don't care for cities. They would rather wander the wild uplands of Ida with their herds. In winter they huddle in their little villages, or in Troy. But don't underestimate them! The Dardanians are legendary fighters.

"They need us. They bring us wool and hides, which we send south to Miletus, Rhodes, or Tiryns. Our ships bring back many things that we cannot produce ourselves, such as ivory and bronze. These the Dardanians obtain from us. We process some of the wool into cloth and some of the bronze into tools and weapons. Lyrnessos is the bridge between the Dardanians and the Greeks. We are such a little place! I hope that we would not be worth even noticing in a war, but I fear that is not how wars work. If Troy refuses to give up Helen, then I suppose there will be war. But which side will the Dardanians support?"

Astonished, I said, "Troy, surely?"

He smiled fondly at my naivete. "Not necessarily! Neighbors are not always friends. And if the Kilikes or the Leleges choose opposing sides, we shall be a bone between hounds."

He probably wasn't asking my opinion, but I gave it to him anyway.

"Then you must be guided by King Alcathous!"

He poured more wine for himself and watered it. "Ah, if it can only be that simple! If he supports the Greeks, then what of the guest friendship I forged with Paris? If he supports the Trojans, then how will he protect us from the Greeks? They could sail a fleet here and the first the Dardanians would know of it would be the smell of smoke in the wind."

I was learning that adulthood involved more than sharing the best wine. "Is there no one else who will give us protection?"

"Who? We have little contact with Crete, and King

Idomeneus is a Greek anyway. Egypt does not know we even exist. Nor do the Hittites, I am sure. Thebe will certainly support the Trojans, because Eëtion's daughter is married to Hector." He turned to face me and smiled. "I should not be worrying you with all this! War is men's work."

I took a deep breath and said quickly, "But this one may be my business, my lord, for why else did the gods send the omen to me and was it not a warning to me that I ought to marry soon and go and live in a far country?"

His face darkened. "Desert Lyrnessos?"

"I don't think I shall ever make a warrior, my lord."

"Indeed not! You are young to be thinking of marriage."

"Some girls are betrothed in the cradle."

He forced a humor-the-child smile. "True. And I was not very much older than you when I set out to seek my fortune. I never really expected to become a king, but it happened. Ah, youth!" He leaned back to stare at the sky. "I dreamed of winning great fame as a warrior and settled for a throne instead. My brother trained me, but he had no place for me at his hearth. I became a wanderer, a free lance without lord or land and, in my case, no followers and no arms except shield and spear. That is a stony road to walk, Briseis, for no one trusts a wanderer. His honor will not let him earn his bread by toil, so folk fear that he will take what he needs by force. Other knights see him as a danger to themselves or their people. Like many others, I set forth in search of a convenient war, where I might earn a reputation and find glory."

That was about as much as he had ever told us of his origins. He rarely spoke of his ancestors, even, except to say that he was a grandson of the king of Enispe, in Arcadia. Bienor and I had concluded that he was either a royal bastard or else his father, Mydon, had been. There must be thousands of such men strutting around Greece all the time—landless, masterless knights looking for trouble to profit from.

"I was on my way to Thrace," he said pensively. "The Moirai brought me to Lyrnessos, where I discovered a beautiful princess in need of a royal husband—and she truly was beautiful, you know, very beautiful."

"She still is," I said, trying not to think of her scrawny neck and flabby arms.

"Yes, she is, at least to me. There was one problem, though." He raised his bushy eyebrows, smiling through his cobwebby beard.

Now the sun broke through. "Euneus!"

"Euneus son of Selepus." My father reached for his goblet and drained it again. I suppose the wine was bringing out the story, although I may not have realized that then. "He was here before me, pressing his suit. He was a mighty fighter who could trace his lineage back to Ares. I did not think I had a chance, and if he had thought otherwise, he would have skewered me on his spear like a tunny."

I clapped my hands. "And Mother fell in love with you?"

"Mm. Well, not quite right away." He examined the design on his goblet as if he had never seen paint before. "Of course, your grandfather would not have forced her into a match she truly disliked. He bound both Euneus and me to abide by his decision. He specifically bound us not to fight each other, which would have been the natural solution and certainly the way Euneus would have preferred to settle the matter. In return, though, he promised that he would choose one or another of us, excluding any others who might appear. After a month or so, when he had observed us both and your mother had indicated that she could accept either of us, he called us in and said he had a problem. I guessed right away that this was a test, but I don't think Euneus did.

" 'Thebe has seized one of our fishing boats,' he told us, looking very worried. 'The king has sent word, demanding twenty oxen as ransom. He says that the boat was poaching in his waters. What should I do?'

"Euneus saw a chance to prove his valor and win the princess, and grabbed it like a hungry babe grabs its mother's teat. 'Let me gather the young men, my lord!' he cried. 'I will lead them against those pirates and so smite them they will never trouble you again.' "

My mother had said: *I need Euneus!*

"And what did you say?"

"Well . . . This is not a heroic story, Briseis, my dear. Euneus had given the obvious answer. It was a very good answer, not stupid at all—don't think that. Knights who do not stand up for their people soon have no people left. But if I gave the same answer, then there would just have to be another test, wouldn't there? So I gambled that there must be another, better answer.

" 'Does the king of Thebe have any right on his side, my lord?' I asked. 'Have there been oaths sworn?' "

"Euneus showed his teeth in disgust, but your grandfather stroked his beard as if to hide his lips, and said, 'There may have been oaths, a long time ago. It is certainly custom that our boats shall not fish beyond Killa, nor Thebe's boats this side of it.'

" 'Then,' I said, 'I think that it would be safer to assume that there was an oath, for the gods will certainly remember, even if mortals do not. The fishermen must be aware of the custom and of the trouble they will cause if they do not observe it. Were I in your place, my lord, I should send the king's herald back with the message that he may seize the boat's cargo as tribute—which he will have done anyway before the fish spoiled—and sell the captain into slavery as a warning to the rest of our fleet, but that you would take it as a sign of friendship if he were to be content with that and let the boat and the rest of its crew return, chastened or even chastised, but otherwise unharmed.'

"Well! I thought Euneus was going to choke on his scorn. He laughed so hard he turned purple. But your grandfather sent us both away, and the next day your mother and I were betrothed. Poor Euneus! He never did understand."

This was certainly not the sort of tale Demodokos sang in the great hall, but I could see the humor in it, sort of. Nor had it mentioned the Dardanians. Anchises had been their king in those days—had he been consulted? Father and he were close as paint and plaster, but perhaps their friendship had developed later.

"Was there a fishing boat?" I asked, a little wistfully.

He seemed disappointed by my reaction. "I don't think so. The fishermen go where they please. Your grandfather knew that Lyrnessos did not need a warrior king, my dear. It needed someone to nurture trade and keep peace with neighbors. He chose me, and under me the town has prospered."

Mother had said, *I need Euneus!*

"If the old man returned from the halls of Hades," Father said, "he would not recognize his palace. It is larger and grander by far than it was in his time. Lyrnessos has waxed rich in my reign." He sighed and stole a glance at me. "One of Paris's followers asked to meet my host leader. I had to admit that I am still my own host leader, because your grandfather gave me the title when I married your mother, and I never appointed anyone else when I came to the throne. Even kings who lead their own armies usually have a host leader to blame if things go—to look after training. Kings too old to fight in person must be very careful where they put command of their armies."

He was too old to fight. He had no army. The young men of Lyrnessos rowed boats or chopped trees or guarded herds.

"We are a small realm." Father sighed. "There is so little to share! After the gods have received their portion, we have hardly enough left to support the palace. Even one knight would require his own war band; a house and servants and lands to support them."

"That's all right, Father!" I took a deep breath and gabbled, "Maera says the gods were telling me I should marry in the *new* ways—go to live in my husband's country."

My father glared mightily, like Zeus gathering thunderbolts. "He would still expect me to give him an enormous dowry! Do you think the treasury is packed with silver bars, child? Briseis, your mother and I will find a suitable match for you when the time is ripe. Until then, it would be more seemly if you did not discuss the matter."

"Yes, my lord."

He relented a little. "However, I will send a messenger to Troy and ask for an interpretation of your omen. They have several fine augurs." He rose to his feet, ending the audience. "Ahem . . . How many people heard your mother mention Euneus?"

"Just Maera and Alcmene." No need to mention Demodokos.

"Arr! That Alcmene has a tongue like a snake." He turned on his heel.

"What happened to Euneus?"

He paused without looking around. "Don't know. Went back to Greece, I suppose. He's probably been dead for years. Sooner or later those rough types always pick a quarrel too big for them."

5

Mother recovered in a few days. She and Father began disappearing together for long private conversations on his balcony. Raised voices were overheard, although I could not make out the words even when I happened to be harvesting olives in a tree very close. Something was afoot.

One morning I was in the queen's hall, all alone. I had decided to catch up on my weaving in the hope that this unusual dedication to duty would help restore my popularity. Besides, skill with the loom was an essential attribute for a prospective bride.

I was already bored when in came Xanthus, one of the junior heralds. He had the same lean good looks as Sphelos and some of Enops's cuddly charm, too. He was widely believed to be one of my half brothers.

"My lady, the lord king commands your presence in the megaron."

"You're very formal today, Hermes."

He gave me Bienor's smirk. "You'd rather I dragged you there by the ear? I can't find Enops."

"Amphitrite around?"

"She went down to the spring with the washing women."

"Chloris?"

"In the kitchens."

"Mm!" I thought again. "Try the hayloft above the mule shed."

"A boy?"

"Two of them."

Rolling his eyes at the luck of princes, Xanthus departed.

In the megaron, I found Father on the throne, bare feet and hairy ankles resting on a stool and a preoccupied scowl on his face. He was wearing an everyday robe and no regalia except the sealstone on his wrist. Five chairs stood in a semicircle before him, and Mother was already sitting straight-backed and high-chinned on one. When she held her hands like *that* and her mouth like *that*, there were storms ahead. Glancing from one parent to the other, I decided that whatever argument they had been having, its hide now hung on Father's wall. The silence remained unbroken.

If this was to be a private family meeting, why the assorted bric-a-brac on the table at Father's hand: lamp, empty goblet, wine flask, two rolls of kidskin, and a flat gold dish containing red wax?

Bienor came hurrying in, and Mother's finger directed him to a seat a safe distance away from me. Enops came next, flushed as if he had been running, seeds and hay on his tunic. Sphelos was last to arrive, annoyed at being called away from his current task of overhauling the fishing fleet.

Behind him came Xanthus and the even younger Perimedes, Father's cupbearer—tall and slender, slinky bronzed muscle and very white teeth. I found him amusing, Mother disliked him, and Sphelos absolutely detested him, perhaps because he was unavailable.

Father now sat up straight and adjusted the hang of his robe. He poured a few drops of wine into the goblet and offered them to Athena, without explaining why he had chosen her. "You wait outside," he told Xanthus. Then he handed one of the vellum rolls to Perimedes. "Read."

Perimedes read surprisingly well, rarely stumbling, although he had apparently not seen the text before: "Run, Perimedes, to Altes son of Molion, king of Pedasos, and say to him . . ."

Twice Father corrected him, and each time the error turned out to be the fault of the scribe. The text outlined the events of the past few days—the omen I had seen, the arrival of Paris and Helen, the warning of the dead.

"Very good," Father said. "Extremely good! Deliver it. I expect you back by sundown tomorrow."

That would test Perimedes' beautiful legs. He bowed and ran from the megaron. Xanthus replaced him and was given the other letter, which instructed him to deliver the same message to King Eëtion of Thebe. He made more mistakes and had to repeat the whole thing three times before Father was satisfied and sent him off. Then the family was alone.

"Who wrote for you?" Sphelos asked.

"Iphimedeia."

"She has a good hand."

"She did very well." Father leaned back on the throne. "It seemed neighborly to pass on those warnings to Thebe and Pedasos—and I don't want them jumping to dangerous conclusions if we start arming. We are in no immediate danger, but a wise ruler must always look to the future. It his duty to his people." He glanced at Sphelos, who nodded curtly, as if he had better things to do than listen to this lecture.

"The Dardanians are another matter, for they are our kin and allies. I will not trust my business with them to a mere herald, and I have no idea where to find Alcathous at this time of year. He may be a day's walk away or in Troy itself. The matter is serious enough to send you, Sphelos."

My eldest brother stiffened and his face reddened. He said, "But . . ."

"But?"

"Nothing, my lord."

Father frowned and let it go. "Very well. This is the message. You will, of course, explain all that has transpired in your own way, but these are my words to him. 'Briseus son of Mydon, king of Lyrnessos, to Alcathous son of Aisyetes, king of the Dardanians: Greetings to you and the holy Hippodemia. I remind you that our two houses have long been joined by ties of blood and friendship, and beg you to accept these gifts as tokens that Lyrnessos wishes always to be the ally of Dardania. Know that we have received guidance from the gods that we must prepare to defend our hearth against the wrath of Ares. Having no knights of my own, and being encumbered with years, I humbly ask that you will send me a man of valor and honor who will lead my host in battle. He will be well rewarded.' "

Bienor caught my eye and stuck out his tongue. My heart galloped. The hand of the princess and half the kingdom, with the other half to follow in due course? This was what Father had explicitly told me he was not prepared to offer. What had changed his mind so suddenly?

And what sort of mountain bumpkin would answer the summons?

Sphelos moved his lips in silence as he thought.

"I shall repeat the message," Father said, and did so. "Now, can you?"

Poor Sphelos—one minute happily counting ballast rocks and the next a mere herald! He shot angry looks at the rest of us, especially Bienor, who was grinning wildly.

" 'Briseus son of Mydon, king of Lyrnessos, to Alcathous son of Aisyetes, king of the Dardanians . . .' " That was the easy part. " 'Greetings to you and . . . er, Queen Hippodemia—' "

Father corrected him.

Father corrected him several times.

He grew steadily more heated, like a cauldron on a fire. "My lord!" he burst out at last. "Heralds practice this! By all means, if you feel that this message is more important than the oil crop or the seaworthiness of the fleet, then send me off to climb Mount Ida. Gladly will I take your gifts to the king, but surely you can spare a herald to accompany me?"

The atmosphere was suddenly icy.

"Alcathous will wonder why I bothered to send you."

My brother bared his teeth. "Then let me write it down."

"You would stand in front of the king and *read*? Like a clerk? Have you no pride at all? Repeat the message."

It was then I noticed that Mother's lips were clenched white, and I knew I was missing something. Bienor was enjoying the performance. Enops was strangely intent.

Sphelos tried again, and this time he only stumbled twice.

I could see his forehead gleam with sweat. " '. . . well rewarded,' " he concluded.

Father nodded. "Good."

There was a pause. What were we waiting for?

Enops. "I could say it better."

Father turned to him. "How would you say it?"

"I'd say, 'My lord, make me a knight.' "

Sphelos gasped. Bienor almost dropped his eyeballs out of their sockets. Enops waited tensely to hear what reaction his presumption would provoke. I thought of the fishing boat story.

Father stroked his beard. "How soon can you leave?"

My middle brother released a long breath and grinned wildly. "Now. There will be sunlight on the grass for hours yet."

"Hold!" Sphelos barked. "You didn't tell me to change the message, you just told me to repeat it!"

"I didn't tell him to do either." Father frowned. "When you were his age, I asked you if you wished to seek the tassels, and you declined."

"You wouldn't even let me drive your chariot! It was your decision, not mine!"

"It was the correct one. You don't have the temperament. Besides, you have made yourself invaluable as procurator. We cannot spare you. Your brother performs no useful function around here, but he has just shown that he is quick to seize an unexpected opportunity, and there is no talent more valuable to a warrior than— Wait!"

But his firstborn was halfway to the door, running. He had not asked permission to leave, and he did not heed Father's command. Exit Sphelos.

We all turned back to stare at Enops as if he had suddenly grown fangs.

"He is too young!" Mother shouted furiously.

"I have told you already, Nemertes, he is almost too old! Son, are you quite sure? You are embarking on a stormy sea."

Enops had gone from pale to flushed as he recovered from

the first shock of what he had said. "Quite sure, my lord!" Where was my indolent, playboy brother now?

"It may break your heart. Many fail, you know. A man who tries and is found wanting loses everything. He is spurned evermore by high and low alike."

"I won't fail."

Father stared at him for a long moment. "Do you understand what success will bring? Rank and honor and respect, yes. Often wealth. But if you do prove worthy to wear the boar's tusk helmet, you will find that it cuts you off from all other men. Those who live by death are a brotherhood apart. Most men fear war and flee it, but the warrior must always seek it—to justify the privileges society grants him and to prove his worth to himself, to his peers, to the gods. Very few live to enjoy old age, as I have done. You never asked for this before."

Enops licked his lips and said, "I am asking now, my lord."

The king sighed and then smiled. "Very well. I find I am proud of you already and expect to be more proud in future. How will you travel?"

"Oh, on foot! I don't know the country well enough to risk taking a chariot and it might tempt . . . and, well . . . I can't defend it yet, can I?" His grin was boyish, nervous, and heartrending, all at the same time.

That was the right answer again. Father nodded approvingly. He took the pan and held it over the lamp for a moment to soften the mixture of wax and dye. When it was warm, he dipped his sealstone in it and Enops held out an arm to be marked with the dolphin of Lyrnessos. He would speak in the king's name.

"Done!" Father said. "Let us go and make an offering to Athena, then I'll drive you to the edge of the forest."

Cocky as a rooster now, Enops inspected his herald's blazon, let Bienor admire it, then graciously allowed Mother and me to hug him before he headed off to gather what he needed for his journey: shoes, cloak, dagger, and probably nothing more. Bienor was dispatched to order Father's chariot prepared, leaving me alone with my parents, who were

staring at each other like strangers. Father announced he
would seek out something inconspicuous for Enops to take
to Alcathous. Mother muttered that she had a headache and
must lie down for a while.

They were gone before I could summon enough courage
to ask them about my own future, but it would have done no
good. The gods had blinded them. Having just been cheated
of one babe, Mother would certainly not part with another.
Father could not condone the expense of providing a dowry
or the risk of designating a successor. He had contrived another plan, one that seemed totally unrealistic to me. The
war would not wait for Enops to grow up—and what could
one boy do against the Greeks?

6

Thus my brother Enops departed in search of glory, as a
prince should.

Father did not ignore the warnings of the gods completely. In theory, every freeman in the kingdom kept a
spear and an ox-hide shield beside his hearth and taught his
sons how to use them, but long years of peace had left Lyrnessos easy prey for any flock of crows. Now he put Sphelos in charge of the host. Reluctantly foregoing his endless
counting in the records room, my brother rounded up all
available young men for training. Soon squads of herders,
woodsmen, farmhands, and even apprentice artists ran up
and down the hills carrying poles. Arms that could swing
an oar or a bronze ax all day were already capable of ram-
ming a spear through an oak, so all that sweat made little
difference, but I suppose it made them think of themselves
as warriors. Father organized games, supplying generous
prizes.

We always had half a dozen chariots in use. Ransacking

long-neglected stores, he unearthed about twenty wheels and almost a dozen cars. Most were in a state of advanced decay, but he set the carpenters and wheelwrights to repairing and replacing. Leather workers toiled to turn out shields, smiths fashioned arrowheads and spear points, furniture makers were set to shaping shafts, and unguents makers assembled harnesses. The stockmen were run half to death training horses.

My own life changed, too. Mother stopped her perpetual nagging at me to get my head shaved. I would have been happy to be left in peace just to grow hair, but she also took my religious training in hand with an unusual outburst of energy, showering offerings on the gods so that I could learn the proper rituals. I was drilled in herb lore, taught the care of the holy serpents, even dragged out to assist at births, which made me ill for days after. Suddenly my childhood seemed like a golden age.

Bienor, who already showed skill as a driver, was set to work in the chariot force. I was willing to concede there were matters in the stables that he was uniquely talented to handle, but we had slaves to do that. He exercised the teams, and sometimes I managed to accompany him. Slinking past the paddocks one afternoon, a fugitive from Mother's determination to rehearse me in the proper invocation for Potnia Theron in time of famine, I saw him driving out—and in Father's own silver-decorated chariot, no less. I took wing. Before you could say "Phoebus Apollo!" I was up beside him.

"Drive on!" I cried. "Run down those fleeing Greeks so I may smite them with my man-killing spear."

He snapped the reins expertly on the horses' backs, and I grabbed the rail to save myself from an ignominious return to the turf. Gorgon and Griffin followed in loud pursuit.

"Charioteers don't use spears," Bienor said, navigating through the orchard. "And today I'm a Greek. We're chasing Trojans."

"Whomever," I said, ducking branches of fig, pear, and apple trees. "They are despicable cowards, barbarians, worshipers of wrong gods. I shall shoot them with—" I bounced knee-high and my feet came down on the leather webbing hard enough to buckle my knees and make me grunt. "How do I manage a bow and hold on, too?"

Apparently we were not just heading down to the beach, which was the only place flat enough to risk anything more than a sedate walk. From personal devilment, or to impress me, my madcap brother was heading inland. Olive trees hurtled by us, wheels yammered on loose gravel.

He spoke through clenched teeth. "You don't. The only thing any archer could hit from a moving chariot would be ten thousand men in close array. What army is stupid enough to give you the chance?"

My all-knowing brother was not as well-informed there as he usually was. A long time later I was told by a real warrior that Egyptians and Babylonians do shoot arrows from chariots. They live in very flat lands.

"What use is a chariot, then?"

We went up in the air and came down so hard I thought the wheels would fly off. The poor horses gasped and choked in their neck straps, and Bienor belatedly kicked out the heels to slow us. At the bottom he yanked the cord to bring them in again and we went rushing up the next hill. Chariot driving was exhilarating. Soon we were out of the trees, Mount Ida straight ahead. A herd of sheep took flight, shepherd boy and dogs in angry pursuit. I hung on and laughed aloud to tempt Bienor to more daredevilry, aware that if Father heard of this, he would hang my brother's skin on the wall.

He knew horses, though, and soon slowed the pace to spare the team. By then we were almost as high as I had climbed that unforgettable morning I saw the eagles. We could scan the whole coast, laid out like a staked hide, and Lyrnessos was small below us. The sea was an unfriendly gray-green, white tongues licking at the rocky cliffs. Kites or eagles floated high over the drab hills in the winter-pale blue of the sky, riding the wind that chilled my heated face.

"Where are we going?"

"Up to that shrine of yours." He had just thought of that and shot me an impish glance to see if I approved.

I was in no mood to be outdared. "We should take an offering."

"I brought wine." He gestured at a long leather tube strapped to the inside of the cab.

I peered inside and confirmed that it did, indeed, contain a stoppered flask. I wondered what he had been planning to do with it before he thought of the shrine, or whether one of the stable hands had hidden it there. "What is this thing?"

"The quiver, of course. To hold spare javelins. If you see a Greek, you can throw a javelin at him. Then we'll load his armor in the chariot and drive home."

"I thought we were the Greeks."

"Trojans, then. Dardanians will do."

"Why not spear them?"

Bienor hesitated, which meant he knew he was right but had to work out why. "You'd need a lance as long as a ship to hit anything in front of the horses."

I conceded that much. "It would wave around like a reed."

"And how could you use a spear sideways?"

That was not quite so obvious. "You could if you went slowly, especially against a man on foot."

"He'd just dodge. And you'd be an easier target for him than he would be for you."

"You think you know everything."

"War is men's business."

The bickering was only habit; our hearts weren't in it. After a while we grinned at each other and concentrated on enjoying the ride.

We were following the Dardanian trail. Ahead of us the ruts crossed a rough meadow and entered the forest. I was sure that even Bienor would not risk going farther in that direction—if one of us was struck by a branch or the axle broke on a boulder, then he would have to explain what he had been doing so far beyond the limits of Lyrnessos.

The same thought must have occurred to him. He slowed the team to a walk. "Don't we turn off here somewhere?" Then he yelped shrilly. "Dardanians!"

I began to laugh before I realized that this was not make-believe. Another chariot came clattering out of the trees.

Bienor lashed the horses and turned us on one wheel. I hung grimly to the rail as we drove over the meadow, gath-

ering speed, our feet bouncing on the leather webbing. If he
tried to go all the way down the hill like this, he would break
all four of our necks. But that might not be a bad alternative,
because the strangers had whipped up their horses, too, and
were giving chase. I was being thrown about too hard to see
them properly.

The ground fell away as if we were plunging down a cliff.
I closed my eyes and hung on.

"Maybe they're slavers!"

"Lucky you!" my brother howled. "Slavers kill the men!"

Slavers took children, though, and I doubted he was eli-
gible for manhood just yet. I didn't say so. I opened my
eyelids for a moment and then closed them with a scream.
Oak trees went by us like thunderbolts. *No one* drove a
chariot down a hill this way! I reached a foot for the heels,
and Bienor yelled at me. "Leave them alone! I'm driving,
not you!"

"Please! I don't care if he's a slaver or King Menelaus
himself. Slow down . . . *Slow down!*"

"No! Hades! He's gaining on us."

There were two maniacs loose that day. Wind blew my
scalp lock out like a banner. The wheels hardly seemed to
touch the ground as the poor horses frantically tried to keep
ahead of the plunging vehicle. More trees dashed past us.
Our dogs had been left far behind.

We were almost into the first of the olives. I stole a look
behind me, but my eyes were watering so hard I could make
out nothing of the strangers except that there were two of
them and they were gaining. We were in the shade of the
olives. Then they were. Still Bienor flogged the horses'
backs, snaking them through the grove in suicidal curves
and bends and bounces. I clung hard and hunkered low and
wondered when the wheels would take wing from the axle.
Branches whistled by overhead.

We slowed for the final hill through the orchards. The
other chariot did not seem to—it was closing rapidly.

"We'll do it yet!" Bienor screamed, lashing the reins on
the foaming backs.

"Do what?" Then I realized that no slaver or brigand

would have followed us so near the palace. The gate was straight ahead. Men were coming running. "You mean this is just a race?"

No one had told me it was a race. No one had told Bienor, either. He may have seen it as a chase when it began, as I had, but he had a natural male instinct for such situations—two chariots in the same place going to the same destination meant a race.

Hooves thundered. With eyes wide and jaws foaming, the Dardanian team came alongside us on my right and drew past. I hardly had to look back at all to see the strangers. The driver flashed me a smile. His passenger was younger and not smiling. Then the two chariots were side by side, hurtling toward the gate.

"Bienor!" I screamed. "There isn't room! We can't both go through—"

"Yes there is!"

No there wasn't—the strangers' team edged over to the left, crowding us. Wheel rolled closer to wheel. A spoke hitting a hub would mean wreck and death for all of us. Bienor yelled and pulled our horses aside, and then we had a wall straight ahead. Howling with fury, he dragged on the reins and kicked out the heels. Men scattered as the Dardanian chariot shot through the gate. Our team followed a moment later, with Bienor spluttering curses as he reined in to a walk.

"There is so room for two! We could have come in together. He cut me off!"

"I hope Father cuts your fool head off!" I said.

We were at the paddocks. Grooms took charge of the strangers' horses, and the men jumped nimbly down to the ground. Other men caught hold of ours.

"Why would he do a fool thing like that?" Bienor snarled.

"Who?" I wiped my eyes clear of tears and dust and took a proper look at our visitors. Only then did I recognize the older man—as Bienor must have recognized him when he drew level with us or perhaps even earlier. It was Aeneas son of Anchises. He was family.

The queen of the Dardanians was always Hippodemia. The previous Hippodemia, Mother's second cousin, had died about three years ago, and I had last set eyes on Cousin Aeneas at his mother's funeral. His sister was the new Hippodemia, and his father, Anchises, was king emeritus, having been succeeded by his son-in-law, Alcathous. Aeneas, as he was to remind us several times during his visit, served his brother-in-law as leader of the Dardanian host.

He came strolling over to us with a glint of amusement showing even in his gait. The best word to describe him was *eagle*. He was tall and lean, clad in deerskin breeches and matching boots. Even dusty and with his tawny hair trailing in windswept ringlets from under his helmet, he was dazzling; he had golden eyes and a bronze glint in his close-cropped, pointed beard. As he approached, he slung a tasseled mantle of green and brown over his shoulders and fastened it with a golden pin. A sword with a silver-studded hilt dangled by his thigh.

"The royal twins, obviously. You have the makings of a driver, lad."

"I thank you, my lord." Bienor spoke as if speaking hurt.

"If you don't kill too many teams first. That was criminal folly, coming down that hill like that."

"But you came—"

"I know what I'm doing. You don't. Did you split any hooves? Have you looked at their feet?" Aeneas knew perfectly well that Bienor had not, because a murder-glaring groom had already led our heated team away. "And little Briseis! My, you've grown, haven't you!" He stroked fingertips over my fuzzy scalp and laughed as I twitched away.

Suddenly I was bubbling anger just as hard as Bienor was. "What news of our brother, my lord?"

I earned a glance of mocking reproach from the yellow eyes. He began to walk again, and of course we had to move with him. "News goes first to the king. So you're our latest oracle? Have you interpreted any more auguries, seeress?"

"No."

"It may have been a fluke," Aeneas said airily, "something to do with your time of life. Your mother's words must be taken seriously, of course."

I seethed in silence. He was a full-grown Bienor, an adult boor.

The charioteer had inspected his team carefully before letting the palace hands take it. Now he came stalking after us, carrying a bundle. He was tall and lanky and clad in the same sort of deerskin garments. His eyes inspected me casually, dismissed me as of no interest. Although he could be little older than Enops, he wore a sword and must have been in warrior training for several years to be a knight's charioteer.

As we reached the outer courtyard, Father himself emerged from the palace, running. By the time he and Aeneas had embraced, Mother also arrived, trailed by three or four of her women. There were more hugs and greetings and chatter of no consequence: How were the queen and the king, and poor, dear, Anchises . . . ? The charioteer waited patiently, evidently accustomed to being ignored.

"Come," said Father, "come, come! We must not keep you standing out here when you are wearied from your journey." He took Aeneas's hand to lead him in.

Bienor and I trailed behind the adults, exchanging angry glances. I was peeved that he had almost broken my neck; he was mad because he had lost a race.

Sphelos appeared in the vestibule and the whole welcoming procedure was repeated. I felt ready to scream, but the proprieties had to be observed. Eventually we trooped into the cool, dark megaron and Mother plopped down on the throne. Ornately carved chairs were brought forward and covered with fleeces; footstools followed. Stewards offered the visitors a silver bowl, tipped water over their hands, poured wine. Bienor and I hung back against the wall like part of the frescoes, afraid of being sent away if we were noticed. Finally the servants departed and we heard the news we wanted.

"My lord, I neglect my mission as a herald. My dear brother-in-law bade me address you in these words. 'Alcathous son of Aisyetes, king of the Dardanians, speaks to the noble Briseus son of Mydon, king of Lyrnessos, saying: May Zeus, the Father of Gods and Men, ever smile upon you and your house. I thank you for the gift of the wren and hope to send you a hawk in exchange before the hunting season opens.' "

Bienor and I hugged each other in glee as the others laughed.

"So he arrived safely?" Mother inquired.

Aeneas pursed his lips. "He arrived. He was somewhat footsore by the time he encountered one of our patrols. On hearing that he bore important words for the king's ear, they put him on a horse and rode through the night. He became sore in other places, but he did arrive in one piece." After a pause that was just a fraction too long, he added, "He shows promise. Certainly no one can fault his spirit."

Bienor and I exchanged glances of wonder. Traveling on horseback was a rare and dangerous feat, requiring horses larger and stronger than any we possessed, specially trained to tolerate riders. At night? Bouncing on a horse's back, legs dangling, all night? Oh, poor Enops!

Aeneas now opened the pack his charioteer had brought and produced a magnificently woven blanket, a gift from his sister, brilliantly decorated with a traditional lion-hunt scene. Mother called us forward to admire it and join in the choruses of praise. Then he remembered a little more of his manners and gestured at his lanky companion. "My charioteer, Akamas son of Antenor. You remember Antenor."

Sphelos cut into the exchange of greetings. "What news from Troy, my lord?"

Aeneas smiled, his eyes narrowing. "King Priam has welcomed his new daughter-in-law." He took a drink.

"Then it will be war?"

"We can certainly hope so."

"Sphelos!" Father rumbled. "There will be plenty of time to discuss such matters. Our guests are weary from their journey."

"Not at all!" Aeneas laughed. "I feel as sprightly as a mountain goat. If you care to try a little wrestling, son of Briseus, I'll be happy to give you a few falls." He turned his eagle gaze on Father. "As to war, my lord, that depends on Sparta and whatever allies it may be able to attract. Mycenae wields a very long spear."

He took another drink, while Sphelos sulked and the rest of us waited for an answer to the unasked question. Finally Bienor asked it.

"And which side will King Alcathous support?"

Our cousin beamed cryptically. "If it comes to war, he must consider what Dardania will gain or lose, depending on which side ultimately wins. And thus he must also consider the relative strengths of the two sides, to estimate which side will win. And for that, he depends on the advice of his host leader—me, in other words."

So justice and honor did not enter into it. That seemed wrong to me, but I was a naive child who had yet to learn the practicalities of life.

Mother frowned. "You have not yet made a decision?"

"No, my lady." Thus might an eagle smile if it could.

Sphelos pulled a sour face. "King Agamemnon may have a longer spear than King Priam does, but King Priam's is closer."

The raptor talons flashed. "And so are his treasure vaults! It isn't like you to forget the possibilities of loot, Cousin."

"Come, come!" Father heaved himself to his feet. "You must be eager to bathe and put on fresh raiment. I shall see you are both attended."

"That sounds promising. I was telling Akamas on the way here of the many exquisite maidens in King Briseus's palace."

Young Akamas flashed a smile like sunlight on bronze.

Father said, "I hope we can live up to your words, my lord."

"I am sure you can." Aeneas nodded respectfully to Mother and departed at Father's side. He seemed to saunter and Father to hurry, but they went out the door together, the charioteer eager at their heels.

"Mountain goat!" Bienor muttered resentfully.

"Oaf!" Sphelos agreed.

8

Having assigned two of the most winsome bath attendants to the honored guests, Mother plunged into preparations for the feast. With invocations to Potnia forgotten, I was free to go in search of Gorgon. I climbed all the way to the pastures, shouting and whistling, kicking the fallen leaves, trying to decide whether Cousin Aeneas was really handsome and if I really liked him.

Unsuccessful in my quest, I came home at last, tired and worried, to find her only a bowshot from the palace gate, still as a statue under a pear tree, staring upward. Realizing that she had probably been there the whole time, I strode over to her crossly. Her very immobility seemed to plead with me not to interfere. She had treed a squirrel and was waiting for it to come down and die in her jaws. Yes, that sounds very foolish, but she knew what she was doing. The tiny ball of brown fluff was already only shoulder height from the ground, slowly working its way down the trunk, chattering angrily but apparently unable to see the waiting Gorgon as long as she kept absolutely still.

I stopped and watched, fascinated. Downward, downward crept the prospective victim. Gorgon did not move a hair. Then the squirrel uttered a shriek and raced back up the trunk. Still the mighty huntress did not move. Her prey must have done that a dozen times already, and it would be back.

I laughed and went over to rub her ears and break the spell. "Are you giving me a lesson in patience, girl? Come along. We'll find you a less jumpy dinner."

Gorgon settled for that offer without resentment, and into the courtyard we went together. There the old folk were gathered under the olives as usual, no doubt discussing the visitors. As I was removing my shoes in the porch, Akamas appeared, resplendent in a red and blue tunic that I recognized as Anticleia's weaving. Now that he was clean, I could see that he combined boyishly rosy cheeks with a respectable fringe of whiskers. He had curly hair and dark gray eyes with very attractive lashes.

"Has our hospitality satisfied you, my lord?" I inquired in my sweetest and most ladylike tones. "Is there anything more you need?"

He looked down at me from the top of the five-year cliff that divided us. It occurred to me then, and perhaps to him also, that another two years or so would make that cliff vanish altogether. At the moment, though, I was too young for the sort of humor I had suggested, even if I had brought a touch of pink to the apple cheeks.

"For the moment, thank you, Princess, I am totally satisfied. I am seeking the bard, Demodokos."

I bit back a *why?* before it escaped. "I shall be happy to send for him." But I put my hands on my hips, as if planning to stay awhile. "Can you tell me any more news of my brother?"

This crude blackmail seemed to amuse the apprentice knight. "Not much. If he can survive the winter, I expect he'll live a few years yet."

"He really had to ride a horse all night?"

"Most of the night—until he'd fallen off enough times. He always got right back on, which is what matters."

"It was a test?"

"And also just our welcome for visitors." Akamas stepped closer, so close that I could smell the bath scent on him. He was trying to intimidate me a little, but the effort made him seem younger. "Enops is not very promising material, Princess. He has not been raised with warriors."

"Not tough like you?"

"I started tougher. He has further to go. But he is of noble birth, so I expect he will cope. Now, the bard?"

I pointed at the bench where the old men nodded. "The one with the hump."

"Thank you," said Akamas. "Then I need trouble you no further."

The feast that evening went off quite well. As always, the climax was the harper's performance. Demodokos came forth in his many-banded robe and sat by a pillar to sing of Prince Aeneas's exploits during the summer, when he had led an expedition against the Lykians. Given the geography and the names of the participants by Akamas, the old man adapted and combined some existing epics about Heracles. According to the information he had instructed his charioteer to pass on, Aeneas had personally sacked two cities, slain three knights plus an uncountable number of lesser warriors, and taken numerous beautiful maidens captive. Bienor, who had heard all the details months before, said the numbers were wildly exaggerated but admitted that Aeneas had won much glory. My nosy brother also whispered that the campaign had ended when Mother Troy threatened to send the Phrygians to the Lykians' rescue. This was not mentioned in the official version.

9

Aeneas prowled around Lyrnessos all the following day with my father at his heels. He inspected the militia, the stores, the water supply, and the walls. The walls would not have delayed him long, because they were very patchy. In many places invaders could just walk in. He sat up late that night, drinking with Father, Akamas, and Sphelos.

The following day they went hunting for boar, although they did not find any. I did not know they were back until I heard my name called as I was crossing the inner courtyard.

Aeneas was leaning on the balcony rail, eagle looking down from aerie.

"Come up here, Little Princess."

His tone annoyed me, so I took my time. Halfway up the stairs, I ran into Bienor.

"Ah, there you are," I said. "Aeneas wants us. Come along."

He asked, "Why?" of course, but he was too nosy not to follow me.

When we emerged on the balcony, our noble guest was sprawled in a chair with his feet on a stool and a goblet in his hand. There were no other chairs or goblets in sight. He had a relaxed, after-bath contentment about him.

I folded my hands demurely. "How may I serve you, noble son of Anchises?"

He looked quizzically at my companion, doubtless wondering whose idea *he* was, and promptly put me in my place.

"Have you started your bleeding yet?"

Bienor sniggered.

There is no harm in discussing sexual matters if all parties present are willing. I certainly quizzed the palace maidservants often enough. But I had not agreed to discuss mine with Aeneas. I was tempted to retaliate by asking my dear cousin why he had taken Chloris on her back and Pero on her hands and knees—was it because Chloris was plump and Pero was skinny? I was genuinely curious. I didn't, of course. I merely shook my head. I must have blushed, too, because he seemed amused.

"Your father wasn't sure. By the way, Helenus son of Priam agrees with your interpretation of the eagles. He's an expert on the significance of birds."

"I am sorry—sorry I am right, I mean."

He smiled lazily. "I'm not. Obviously you have a gift for interpretation." He continued to ignore Bienor. "What do you make of your mother's necromancy?"

"The warning seems straightforward enough."

"Is it? Who is the son of a goddess she was told to beware?"

There were dangerous answers to that question, as he well knew. "That is not for me to say, Cousin."

"Many men have claimed to be sons of gods, or been hailed as such. I am the son of Anchises son of Capys son of Assaracus son of Tros son of Erichthonius son of Dardanos son of Zeus."

"I do not question that so many great heroes—"

"No?" He smiled knowingly. "Some heroes turn out so much greater than their mothers' mortal consorts that only divine paternity can explain their prowess. A god may visit any woman in the privacy of her chamber, but a goddess is a different matter. The midwives can testify what womb they pull the child from, can't they?"

Bienor sniggered again. I shot him a moderate glare and then turned it on Aeneas.

"I do not think we should mock the Immortals, son of Anchises."

The golden eyes chilled. "I do not! If I mock, it is at the gullibility of the common herd. Your mother is priestess of Potnia here in Lyrnessos, and the vessel in whom the Mistress manifests herself on sacred occasions. Mine was priestess of Aphrodite, as my sister is now. Thus there are those who call me a son of Aphrodite, although they have learned not to do so in my hearing." He paused, waiting for us to tell him his own great exploits had made him seem more than human.

We didn't.

The familiar faint sneer returned. "So I suppose you are a son of Potnia, boy?"

Even Bienor looked alarmed now. "No, my lord. At least, Mother never . . ." He fell silent, red faced.

"Or your dear brother Sphelos, then?"

"He has never claimed to be such," I said angrily.

"He ought to be able to find *somebody* who would believe him, if he looks long enough."

I was furious now. "Nor do I claim to be the daughter of a goddess. Anyone who speaks thus risks the Immortals' anger."

The son of Anchises pouted and waved a hand. "Go tell your father I want him."

Bienor and I walked away without a word. For once we were in complete agreement—fuming at being treated like servants and hearing our father summoned like another.

As we went downstairs, I said, "Judging by his manners, Cousin Aeneas is the son of a pig herder."

"Ha!" My brother snorted. "And from what Chloris says about the length of his stabber, I don't think his mother was Aphrodite."

10

A little later that same evening, I was summoned to the king's balcony, where I found Father and Aeneas sharing an amphora of Rhodian wine, while Akamas sat stiff-backed on a stool nearby, learning how knights talked business. Westward, the sun was a pearly ball in the sea haze between the mainland and Lesbos, but the plaster walls still held enough of the day's heat to make the spot comfortable, and it was out of the wind. The sea was a sheet of burnished bronze.

I was told to sit down and narrate the story of the omen all over again, but Aeneas obviously knew it as well as I did. He nodded when I finished and held out his gold cup for my father to refill. After a few moments' reflection, he began to spew out conclusions. Not having been dismissed, I sat there and heard it all.

"We have time," he said. "Nothing will happen for a year or two. We are due for a big war—these little border skirmishes are only good for training. The last really big conflict was the Hittite affair around Miletus. Now the word is out, everyone will start preparing. Boys like your son, who couldn't see the point of all that effort and hardship in peacetime, suddenly catch the scent of glory. Normally it takes five years to make a knight, but we Dardanians can run them through in three if we have to. We lose more on the way, but there is never a shortage of highborn youths."

My father nodded, his face revealing nothing. "So even Lyrnessos must acquire defenders?"

"Not yet. May I speak frankly, my lord?" The golden raptor eyes made the question a challenge. Taking offense at anything Aeneas cared to say would be dangerous at the best of times.

"Please do," Father said with a sheepish smile. "What is the use of having a proven sacker of cities in the family if one cannot call on him for advice?"

Aeneas preened a few feathers at the compliment. "Those foresters and fishermen of yours are useless. Even if you could arm them decently, any Greek knight could unload his war band down there on the beach and roll up your rabble like a carpet. You know that! Stack your spears in a shed and start building a wall. No—" He raised a hand to forestall Father's objection. "I know you lack good building stone, masons, tools, and, and, and . . . ! I know you can't turn Lyrnessos into Troy. Troy's walls were built by Apollo and Poseidon, anyway. But you do have timber, which few cities have, and you do have time. Put all those husky sailors and woodchoppers to work over the next winter or two and build yourself a stockade to reckon with. Even a goatherd can defend a wall."

Father grabbed a chance to slip a word in. "We have no water on this hilltop."

"Build cisterns to catch rain. You need only hold out for two days, and I promise you I'll come over the hill with enough bronze to cut any insolent Greek into fish bait."

His words were an insult, or so a king might take them. They were also dishonest, because even I knew that the hill roads were closed for almost half the year. That might not matter in winter, when the seas were equally impassable, but ships began to travel in the spring long before the snows melted. My father did not mention that.

"You are most generous, Cousin," he said with obvious effort.

"It would be a pleasure. I don't think any of them will ever give me the chance, unfortunately. A man will bite on a grape, son of Mydon, but not a walnut in its shell."

"Even turtles are made into soup!" Father spoke mildly, but his hands were clenched into fists and young Akamas wore a sneer on his lip. It was not right for a child to hear her father insulted and ordered about like that. I wanted to jump up and leave but that would acknowledge the affront that Father was ignoring. "Three years, you say?"

"More or less. I expect them to start raiding the summer after next."

Father offered wine again. "Surely Menelaus can find all the men he can afford sooner than that?"

The sun was setting, turning red. Ida blushed like a giant nipple and a river of blood ran across the sea.

"Not if Agamemnon supports him. Mycenae has gold, it has treaties, it has vassals and royal kinships. Agamemnon can afford a major campaign, and I think he will, because Helen's a wonderful excuse. The Greeks' appetite for slaves is insatiable, and if they can break the power of Troy, the whole coast will be at their mercy, all the way to Rhodes."

"That is bad news," Father muttered.

"But put yourself in Idomeneus's position, or Nestor's. You have your lords of the exchequer, chancellery, and secretariat. You have your regional governors and counts palatine, your chamberlain and religious officers. You have scribes and surveyors and tax farmers. All these keep your kingdom running as smoothly as a potter's wheel. You also have knights to keep your neighbors respectful: your host leader and your personal followers, who are your biggest expense by far—except, of course, the alternative cost of being murdered by friends or neighbors. You also have your landgraves, who have their own followers. You have granted these mighty warriors estates and tribute, and keeping them from starting civil wars or dragging you into border disputes is probably your biggest headache.

"Suddenly Agamemnon starts demanding support for an attack on Troy. All the knights howl like watchdogs in moonlight. Your first reaction is that you would love to send those brawlers off and live in peace for a while. Then you think of neighbors who may not do the honorable thing and send their knights away too. You don't dare strip your defenses.

"So your next thought is to let Agamemnon do it all himself. But that raises other problems. He has the gold to hire and equip every free lance from Thrace to Egypt. The man is notoriously unpredictable, so you really don't want him commanding a force like that. Zeus knows what he might do with it after he has sacked Troy and emptied Priam's treasure rooms. Remember what happened when Knossos fell, back in Theseus's day? So what do you do?"

Father blinked uncertainly and glanced at Akamas, but he was staring at his mentor with an expression of bewildered hero worship. He was no help. Nor was I.

"I'd lend Agamemnon some men and keep some for myself."

Aeneas laughed scornfully. "You'd start a civil war in your realm! No, in the end you lead your army to Troy in person. That way you can keep an eye on the capricious king of Mycenae and share in the loot, and if trouble erupts while you're away, you can head home again with enough authority at your back to handle it." He stood up and turned to study the sunset. "If I'm right, then knights are going to be in very high demand."

"And it will be a very big war," Father growled.

"Very. A wonderful commotion!" Aeneas stepped over to the rail and leaned his hands on it, staring out at the setting sun like a captive eagle on a perch. "I'll be honest with you, Cousin—I welcome it dearly. Your news about the omen was like a trumpet call to me. I couldn't see how I was ever going to justify my existence as a warrior. Life on the banks of the Scamander seemed to promise nothing but breeding babies and wearisome old age. A warrior without war is a horse without grass. The sea is not my heritage, but I was seriously wondering if I ought to take a few stalwart followers

and set sail for the horizon . . . look behind the sunset . . .
seek glory in new lands. . . ."

The sun was a red wound in the haze, yet bright enough
to make my eyes water. I looked up. Enormously high in the
bowl of the heavens, a double line of birds was heading west
in an arrowhead formation. They glittered in the low rays
like a snail's track on a dewy rock, and they were right over
Aeneas's head as he spoke. I shivered.

"Briseis?" Father whispered.

"Nothing, my lord," I said quickly.

"So we shall see!" Aeneas strode back to his goblet. "In
a couple of years, Athena may have need of us under the
walls of Troy. I pray she will!" He peered down at his charioteer. "Akamas is almost ready for his tassels. He may yet
write his name among the immortal heroes. Right, son of
Antenor?"

The boy looked up, face wooden. "If I do, my lord, the
honor will be my father's for training me and yours for setting me so fine an example."

Aeneas laughed and clapped him on the shoulder. Then he
wheeled around and smirked at me. "Or defend Lyrnessos?
Briseis says she's not ripe for bedding yet, but a betrothal
could be considered. They'd be a pretty couple, yes?"

Obviously neither Akamas nor father had expected this
any more than I had. They both gaped. I suppose I blushed;
Akamas certainly did. Father went pale with fury. Our reactions amused Aeneas.

"Well, lad? What do you think?"

"You honor me, son of Anchises."

Antenor, not Aeneas, had been his teacher and the bard's
song had not mentioned him as Aeneas's charioteer last
summer. So why had Aeneas elected to bring him on this
visit? The answer lay somewhere in the mists of Dardanian
politics.

"Not unduly. Briseis, what do you think of our future
knight? I assure you he has great promise. You will not spurn
a son of the great Antenor, surely?"

"I am honored," I squeaked. "But the omens are inauspicious!"

Aeneas frowned. Had he been serious, he would have demanded specifics and my excuse would not have worked,
but apparently he was merely having fun at our expense, for
he dismissed the matter with a shrug. "Well, there is still
time, as I said."

It was not only fright that made me refuse, although a real
flesh-and-blood young man, a powerful, hairy person with
male organs and strong inclinations to use them, was much
more alarming than a husband in the abstract. It was not
even my memories of the eagles. No, I had remembered the
squirrel and realized in time that it was another portent. A
Trojan or Dardanian husband would not carry me off to a far
country, beyond the reach of the war. To escape from a tree
into the jaws of a dog, like the squirrel, was no escape at all.
I needed a different tree.

Soon Aeneas began dropping hints that he would enjoy a
bath and other luxuries. Father rose to escort him. As he left,
he shot me a smile of approval. Akamas started to follow
them, then turned and strode over to me with his chin high.
I rose to face him with what I hoped was adult poise. His
gaze was more heedful than before.

"My lady, the suddenness of the . . . I just want to tell you
that you are as fair a maiden as man may dream of. If my response lacked tact, it was only because I had been taken by
surprise!"

"No, the honor was mine, my lord." I was flattered at
being deemed worth flattering.

He grinned with a boyish shyness not befitting a warrior
of renown. "Nasty shock, wasn't it?"

"Just a shock."

"Well, please understand that if . . ." He took my hand in
thick, calloused fingers. "I mean when your father decides to
seek out a husband for you . . . I hope the omens will be better next time."

Even a very small kingdom is better than none. Was he regretting his hasty refusal? And was I? I might do much
worse than this handsome son of Antenor.

"I hope so too. And that we both survive the war."

His smile waned. "A knight's life is always at risk. If the

gods are kind, I will make my own name worthy of renown, so I may woo a lady without relying on my forebears."

"You would fight to support the theft of another man's wife?"

Annoyed, he puffed out his chest. "That's only an excuse! You mean do I want to fight? Course I do! I'm as good a man as most. I will fight unless my father tells me not to. I come of a long line of knights, Briseis. I will not be seen to be unworthy of them. When you marry, you won't want a husband who won't fight, will you?"

"Not when the cause is worthy."

"Defense of one's home and family is the worthiest of causes." He released my hand with a shrug. "And you won't tell me of these omens? When Aeneas was standing over there you went pale. Very suddenly."

"I do not recall."

He frowned skeptically but did not pursue the matter. In a sense, Akamas son of Antenor was my first suitor. The next day he drove Aeneas off in his chariot, heading to Pedasos to visit King Altes, and I never saw him again. From Pedasos they could easily cross back into Dardanian territory before the snows closed the hills.

It was a dark day indeed when I next met Cousin Aeneas.

BOOK FOUR

POLYDORUS

1

Father accepted Aeneas's insolent advice and set the men of Lyrnessos to building a stockade around the palace. That blistering labor was much more popular than military drill—because it showed results, I suppose, or because everyone would rather shelter from Greek raiders than try to fight them.

Time blurred the urgency of the gods' warning. Only the groaning of windlasses spoke of the war, while the men sang at their toil and axes beat in time. Enops's absence became less of an ache. Mother pursued my religious instruction without mercy. My hair grew long enough to fall over but not to curl, although I wanted to scream at it to grow faster.

Came the day I had so long awaited, when I could claim to be a woman. My coming-of-age celebration was staged as a state festival in the megaron with Our Lady Potnia manifest in Mother. I was impressed, but I distrusted my parents' motives—after that display, no one could doubt that I was the heir. No handsome suitor would be carrying me off to a distant land.

Everyone gave me gifts at the ensuing feast, but the grandest came from my parents: a chariot of my own, a carnelian sealstone engraved with two eagles, and a personal slave, Ctimene—a dainty nymph of about my own age with a heart-shaped face, a complexion of clear bronze, and heavy black hair. I had expected to have one of the palace girls assigned to me, but she had been bought specially. Deeply moved that my parents had been so thoughtful, I hugged Mother, who was all weepy at seeing her baby grown up, and kissed Father.

"You have adult possessions now, Briseis," he said gruffly. "Remember they bring adult responsibilities."

I assumed he meant I must not drive my chariot unwisely,

but I learned better very soon, when I took Ctimene out to the courtyard and a bench in the moonlight.

"Sit here beside me, girl," I said excitedly, "and tell me about yourself."

Her tale was very sad but not unusual. She was of noble birth, daughter of a Maeonian knight, and would have married well had the gods not decreed otherwise. One day a band of Mysian raiders slew her father when he opposed them and carried off all the women and children of his estate. Being a child, Ctimene was spared rape and reached the Thebe slave market still a virgin. Father had asked King Eëtion to look out for just such a well-mannered maiden, and she had been kept in his house until the appropriate time came, so she would be a complete surprise to me.

"The gods have been kind in giving you to me," I told her. "I intend to be a considerate mistress. You will live in a palace and eat well. Attend to your duties and you have nothing to fear."

"Well said!" remarked a male voice at my back.

I jumped and Ctimene cried out. Poias the smith had crept up behind us without a sound, which was a surprising feat for a man built like a storage jar. He stood there, breathing wine fumes down at us, one of the ugliest men in the kingdom, thick and squat, his hairy face, hands, and arms all pocked with bald white burn scars. Even sober, he was unpleasant. Drunk, he was a notorious boor.

"If she does her work diligently, you must reward her well, my lady!"

"That seems self-evident," I said coldly.

"That ring I gave you . . . Would you like a bracelet to match?"

The plain gold band that had been his gift to me had not impressed me much at all, especially as the gold must have come from Father. Most of the palace officials had been more generous.

Poias leered. "Girls pine without a man's attentions. You want good work out of her, you got to keep her happy. I'll make her happy for you."

Ctimene shivered, and I understood what Father meant

about responsibilities. I wrapped an arm around her. "As I was saying, you just attend to your duties and you have nothing to fear. Of course, if you are lazy, I shall have you soundly whipped. If you remain obdurate I shall have you branded. And if you are unspeakably, unthinkably perverse, I may give you to this man for an evening. But I don't think I could ever be so cruel, not for all the bracelets in the Troad."

Poias was not too drunk to work that out. He slunk off, muttering. By that time I was shaking with anger. "And that's a promise, may Potnia be my witness!"

Ctimene sobbed out her thanks.

"One day," I added, "you'll find some boy who pleases you. When that happens, you have only to ask, and I'll be happy to let you lie with him. But you will choose." I was being rashly extravagant, of course, because not only do a slave's duties include providing more slaves, but I was granting her a freedom of choice I did not possess myself.

Naturally, Ctimene was always eager to please a mistress so benevolent. I came to enjoy her company and confide in her. At times I found her almost too obliging, for I could never raise an argument with her when I needed one. Still, I had Bienor for that.

Winter passed in weaving, repairing, tallying accounts, preparing for spring. Father became crotchety, complaining of indigestion. The aunts grew smaller and deafer and louder. Boys grew more interesting, but I never let my eyes return the glint in theirs, no matter how much I appreciated a wide shoulder or bulging arm. Princesses can never submit to common porters or farmhands . . . almost never. Every year there was the feast of Dionysus. My plans for that I kept to myself.

Gradually talk turned to sowing and lambing, calves and foals began to arrive, and birds winged northward. Martins came, then the swallows, and after them the swifts. The women began the arduous work of shearing, hours of combing wool from the shaggy sheep. Suddenly there were flowers and warm days and the first ships, although the north winds started early that year, which was bad news for Lyrnessos.

The time for gathering saffron was upon us, an activity

even princesses were expected to engage in, for the season
is short and the labor arduous. It seems unkind of the gods
to have put something so precious on anything so tiny as the
stamen of a crocus. It takes thousands of them to fill a bowl,
so the whole population of Lyrnessos was sent out to crawl
over the countryside. It was then that I received my next
message from the gods.

One sunny afternoon, when I was breaking my back with
Ctimene and a dozen or so of the younger palace women, I
glanced up and saw four deer running westward across the
hillside, very far off. I straightened up to watch, fascinated
by their grace. Just as they were about to disappear from
sight, they wheeled together and went streaming back the
way they had come. I waited to see what had scared them,
but no wolves or lions appeared. The incident was odd
enough to make me take notice.

The next day, walking on the beach with Ctimene and
Gorgon, I observed a school of dolphins leaping in the bay.
In many lands dolphins are considered inauspicious, but
they were the symbol of Lyrnessos. Four of them headed
west, then reversed course, just as the deer had done. My
skin prickled. When they had returned to about the place I
first saw them, they dived and did not reappear. Each time,
Ctimene had seen what I saw—and noticed nothing. The
gods speak to those who will listen.

After some thought, I decided to wait for a third sign, and
the next day I saw four swallows going through the same
dance. I was less sure of them, I admit, because birds were
thick as gnats at that time of year. Without the deer and the
dolphins, I would certainly have failed to notice them, but
swallows do not normally fly in fours, so they were confirmation. Land, sea, and air—this was a message. Its meaning
was as obvious as a black cat on a rainy night.

I headed for the queen's hall. The aunts dozed in their
usual corner. Alcmene and Anticleia were weaving, standing
by a loom and passing the shuttle back and forth. Mother
was heaped on her favorite chair like dough left to rise,
munching cakes while Philona dressed her hair. She glanced
up as I marched in, then sighed dramatically.

"Yes, Briseis, what did you see this time?"

I felt as if she had kicked my feet out from under me. Mothers learn to be good at that. Her companions smirked.

"Am I so obvious?"

"Rain wouldn't wet you, dear. Another omen?"

"I think so!" I told her of the deer, the dolphins, the swallows.

She frowned, stared at the window for a moment, then bit her lip and said haughtily, "If you want to come with us, why didn't you just ask? You don't have to invent auguries."

"I didn't invent . . . Come with you where?"

"To Pedasos, dear. Your father and I are going to call on King Altes in a few days. I don't see why you shouldn't come with us, if you promise to behave yourself."

"I didn't know that!"

"No, dear. Of course not."

I truly had not heard of the proposed outing or I would certainly have demanded to be included—but with no great expectation of success. Annoyed at being doubted, I tested the limits of my seer's authority. "Why in a few days? I saw the deer two days ago, the dolphins yesterday, and the birds today, so surely we must travel tomorrow, the fourth day? There were four of them each time, too."

Out of the corner of my eye, I registered that Alcmene and Anticleia were exchanging impressed glances. Mother rubbed some chins fretfully. "Or perhaps it means you and Bienor to make four . . . ?" We all knew that taking me meant taking Bienor also, or provoking all-out war. "Tomorrow doesn't give us much time."

"I think it should be tomorrow," I insisted, trying not to show my excitement. I don't recall that I had any reason for interfering except stubbornness and a desire to seem important, but in the end I had my way. Triumphant, I was sent to inform Father of my latest divination and of Mother's agreement that we ought to leave the next day.

So we did, and that decision had many consequences.

2

The first to leave, before dawn, was a herald, running ahead to inform King Altes that my parents would be arriving sooner than planned because they had learned the day was propitious. Kreion marched out with our escort of a dozen spearmen. Mother and I made offerings at the shrine, asking Potnia to guard our home while we were gone, while Father promised a fine ewe to the Pathfinder if we all returned safely. The palace staff made their own vows to the gods on our behalf and cheered as we drove out the gates. I left Ctimene locked in near-mortal combat with Gorgon.

Father led the way, driven by Perimedes. I let Bienor drive my chariot, or he would have sulked the entire way. Mother drove her own, taking Anticleia as her attendant—the thick and the thin, Bienor called them. Even so, there were only four of us, as the augury had dictated, because Anticleia and Perimedes did not count.

We rattled down to the town and then headed westward along the coast, catching up with Kreion near the boundary stones between Lyrnessos and the territory of the Leleges. Of course we could travel no faster than our escort could trot, even when the terrain would have allowed us to race, and we had to stop at every shrine along the way to propitiate the local god. Most of the streams were high, which made crossings difficult. At some of them, Kreion's men had to carry the chariots. A wicker car by itself is no great burden for one man, but when loaded with Queen Nemertes and friend it was a challenge for six, especially in icy torrents.

We followed the coast all the way with the shore on our left and the long wall of Ida on the right, the trail varying from smooth beach to a random selection of holes and boulders. Everywhere herds and flocks grazed the rich grass. We saw sheep, cattle, pigs, and horses; vast groves of figs and

olives; hoers working amid crops Bienor confidently identified as flax, oats, wheat, barley, and lentils. I began to understand why King Altes' fighting men so outnumbered
Father's.

All day a solitary ship flanked our course, rowing westward against the wind. I noticed it several times but did not
think to comment, and when I mentioned it later to Bienor,
he said he had no memory of it. That seemed odd, but only
later did I realize its significance.

The palace of Pedasos stands on the summit of an isolated
hill in a saddle west of Mount Ida. I could see far more ships
drawn up on the shore than ever came near Lyrnessos, and
Bienor gave me an excited lecture on Pedasos's strategic location between the sea and the Satniois River. It had what
Lyrnessos lacked, good access to the interior.

"Good access can be bad access," I objected. "Depends
who's accessing."

He ignored my profound observation. When the winds
were unfavorable, he said, passengers or even cargo bound
for Troy could disembark at Pedasos and travel more
quickly overland.

As we drove up a fine, wide street to the palace gates, we
heard shouts and racket behind us. A caravan of chariots was
coming hot on our heels, traveling on this smoothed surface
much faster than Krcion's weary troop could manage. Bienor hastily pulled over, and the rest of our party cleared the
way also. Mother glared back at me furiously.

The newcomers went rushing by us at a fast trot, wheels
rumbling, dust swirling. I lost count at fifteen, but there were
at least thirty of them, all pulled by splendid high-stepping
horses. I caught glimpses of gold and silver and ivory on the
cars and trappings, but mostly I noticed the men—big, grim-
faced, armored men. Every passenger was a knight, and
many of the drivers also. They went by us in a blur of tassels, bronze corslets, and boar's tusk helmets.

"By the halls of Hades!" I said, although not loud enough
for Mother to hear. "Who were they? Priam and all his
sons?"

Bienor's cheeks were flushed under the day's grime. He licked his lips. "Some of them. What emblems did you see?"

"Just the first one," I admitted. "He was a Trojan." The knight in the front car had been holding out his mantle to display his identity to the palace lookouts.

"And Dardanians," Bienor said confidently. Several horses galloping symbolized Dardanians. One horse, standing woodenly by itself, meant Troy. Two griffins for Mycenae and so on. Everyone knew that much. "And I saw a pair of stars and—I think—a ship."

"Whose are those?"

The grand assembly was already entering the gates at the top of the hill. Father was barking orders for our disheartened company to move on. He sounded just as furious as Mother looked.

"What's chewing on his toes?" Bienor muttered, whipping up our team and ignoring my question because he did not know the answer.

"Prestige," I said sadly. The arrival of the royal family of Lyrnessos was going to be a very small sensation at the court of Pedasos after that army. It was my fault that we had come today, so once again my efforts at divination had brought public shame to my parents. "Don't count on being bathed and anointed by beautiful maidens this evening, Brother."

Judging by his look of horror, that possibility had not even occurred to him.

We made a dignified and leisurely journey up the hill, passing the cottages and vegetable patches of the Leleges, being watched curiously by men resting from their day's labor under the stretching shadows of blossom-bearing fruit trees. We rattled into a narrow passage between high walls from which defenders could shower missiles on any attackers approaching the gate, but today's problem was not enemies, it was too many friends.

Sure enough, the courtyard beyond was wild confusion, a welter of guests and staff, grooms and chariots, heralds, and hot-tempered knights amid a reek of horses. Shouts echoed clamorously from the walls. It took Kreion several minutes to corner a minor flunky and convince him that a second royal party had arrived and that King Briseus, guest friend of King Altes, must not be slighted.

I jumped down and went to hold the horses' heads. Bienor dived into the crowd like a hungry duck in a pond.

Mother's chariot was directly ahead of ours. Steadied by Anticleia, she stepped down heavily and found herself face-to-face with her least favorite daughter. She was definitely not at her best—eyes red, every wrinkle outlined in road dust, ringlets hanging like frayed rope.

Her temper was frayed, too. "I don't know why I ever listen to you—your omens are always evil! Queen Alcandre will be embarrassed. We will be embarrassed. You'll be lucky to catch one whiff of the roast ox tonight, my girl!"

Bienor appeared at her back, giving me a pelican grin over her shoulder. "Sparta!"

Mother spun around. "What?"

"The two stars mean Sparta. The king of Sparta—that's Menelaus himself, come to ask for his wife back, I expect. And the king of Ithaca, wherever that is. The rest are sons of Priam escorting them back to their ship."

Mother said, "Oh, no!" furiously.

My brother's glee grew even wider. "King Lethos of Larisa is here, with his son Hippothoös, leader of the Pelasgian host. Also the son of Aisyetes—Cousin Hippodemia's over there by the pillars."

Mother said, "Oh!" again, in quite a different tone. Then, "Truly?" And finally, "Where's your father?" She took off at a waddling run.

"That does help!" Anticleia chuckled, showing the gaps in her teeth. "If Alcathous and Hippodemia are here."

"A royal conference," Bienor agreed. "The cream of the Troad! Gracious of them to include Father, wasn't it?"

They smiled approvingly at me. Without my augury, we should have missed this. My relief was quelled by a stab of worry. "But not Helen?"

"No," Bienor said happily. "No sign of Helen."

3

As soon as the shipping season opened, King Menelaus had come to Troy to demand his wife back, being accompanied for unknown reasons by the king of somewhere called Ithaca. With the north winds so unseasonably early that year, the supplicants had chosen to disembark at Pedasos and proceed overland. Last night, Priam had denied their petition. Tomorrow they would sail for home. If what everyone said about Greek politics was correct, they would head straight to Agamemnon.

"How many days to Mycenae?" I asked.

Bienor never lacked for an answer, whether he knew the correct one or not. "Five or six by way of Chios and Tenos, if they have Boreas at their backs. Much longer if they have to go round by Crete." He shrugged wistfully. "You suppose the war will last long enough to let me fight?"

"I'm only an augur, not a goddess." The conversation was cut short by a shout from Father, and we went forward through the crowd to greet our hostess.

King Altes had never had the honor of meeting me, for he had given up traveling years before, but I knew Queen Alcandre, who was much younger than her husband—younger, in fact, than all her stepchildren. She had visited Lyrnessos the previous summer, buxom and beautiful and full of sparkle. Even surrounded by the current confusion, she was perfectly poised in an elegant gown of cool blues and greens. She greeted all of us in appropriate fashion, complimenting me on my recent accession to womanhood and Bienor on having grown so much. That latter remark was unjustified but still welcome to its recipient. My snigger was reasonably discreet.

At her side stood Elatos, Altes' oldest son and leader of the Lelegian host. He was a tall, grim man, clad in a white tunic and a scarlet mantle fringed with white tassels. As soon as he had paid his respects to these latest visitors, his attention began to wander, his eyes scanning the crowd, doubtless picking out boar's tusk helmets. With enough knights present to run a memorable war, he was right to be nervous. Alcandre took Mother's hand to lead her into the palace, apologizing for the poor choice of accommodation she had left to offer. Elatos conducted Father, but soon made his excuses and strode away.

Many layers of palace officials had been displaced to make room for the influx of nobility. Officially, the honored place for guests to sleep is the porch, at least in warm weather. Mother had told me once that the custom dated back to the time when even kings' houses only had two rooms and the family slept in the megaron. Father, more cynical, suggested that guests liked to be sure they were free to leave if they wanted to. To pack so many knights into one space would have been both discourteous and unwise, so I suppose they were distributed around the balconies of the palace. Lesser folk like us would have to sleep indoors.

Alcmene and I were shown to a dim, smelly chamber that was normally a dormitory for eight heralds—I did not learn that by augury, but from the number of sleeping shelves and the improbable female images scratched into the plaster. One of my guest gifts from Pedasos was to be a large assortment of heraldic fleas.

At Bienor's side I followed our parents into the megaron—already loud, crowded, and smelling most joyously of roast meat. It was little larger than ours, with the same central hearth between four massive pillars, the same encircling balcony, and an identical fog bank of white smoke floating overhead. I had no chance to inspect the murals until the following day, but they were very similar to Lyrnessos'. That is hardly surprising, because the same itinerant artists travel from palace to palace, replacing frescoes as they became smoke stained.

We worked our way toward the throne to pay our respects. Many of the guests present were merely palace officials and important local landowners, but the preponderance of large young men was noticeable. Even without swords and helmets, the knights could be recognized by their tassels and their arrogance. I tried not to gape too obviously at the Greeks, who were all clean-shaven and wore their hair much longer than the men I knew. Not one of them could have been mistaken for a woman, though—they were as slit-eyed and square-jawed an assortment of toughs as might be expected of a delegation sent to threaten Priam. I could see nothing exceptional about their clothing except the greaves of tooled leather on their shins.

Old King Altes seemed frail and faded on his throne, for his beard was white, his face had an unhealthy pallor, and his pie-shaped golden crown looked cruelly heavy for his scrawny neck to support. Yet his eyes shone brightly enough and he greeted us warmly as we were presented each in turn. Saturnine Elatos stood at his side like a pine tree. He spared me a brief nod to acknowledge that we had already met and at once went back to keeping a watchful eye on the guests. Bienor did not even get the nod.

"Wine, of course." Alcandre swept forward as soon as the welcoming ceremony ended. She had changed into a gown of innumerable colors and pleats, of flounces and patterns, and still seemed blithely unconcerned by the mass infestation of senior nobility that had taken over her house. Under the same circumstances, Mother would have been indulging in epic hysterics.

Wine appeared instantly, silver cups offered by a divinely handsome cupbearer. Another ladled a few drops into each from a great mixing bowl carried by a third, who had the most dazzling red curls I had ever seen. Father proclaimed a blessing and we tipped a libation. Then our cups were filled for us. It was a fine fruity-tasty vintage but well watered—a sensible precaution in this warlike company.

Two hefty Greeks were waiting to be presented. Queen Alcandre disposed of us Lyrnessians expertly. "You must meet Hippodemia and dear Alcathous. I think I saw them beside the bull leapers a few minutes ago. . . . Elatos?"

Her towering stepson extended an arm like a mossy

bough over the massed heads. "Under Artemis and the faun."

"Thank you." The queen led the way. "Bienor? Here's someone you ought to know." She detached my surprised brother as expertly as a wolf pack cutting out the weakling of the herd and more or less dropped him into the arms of a nervous-seeming girl. I had time to note only that she flaunted adornments I still lacked what my brother would describe to his friends as a nice pair of quinces.

A few more steps . . . "And, Briseis. Have you met Polydorus son of Priam? You two can have a long conversation about older brothers, I'm sure." The queen shepherded my parents away, leaving me staring up at a life-threatening case of acne.

He was tall and all bones. As a prince of Troy, he was dressed in fine fabrics and ornamented with treasure—several sealstones, a three-strand amethyst necklace, a gold-hilted dagger. Observing that the hand holding his wine cup was twice the size of mine and there were still only rumors of a mustache on his lip, I decided he was younger than he first seemed, a big boy on his way to being enormous. He eyed me with suspicion and traditional Trojan hauteur.

"Briseis? Lyrnessos?"

"Correct. You get to roll again."

He blinked, then glanced surreptitiously at my bodice—a closed bodice, whose bulges were regrettably hard to detect in that light.

"What did Altes' wife mean about brothers?"

"I have three older brothers."

"You're lucky. I have forty-nine. And a dozen sisters." He drank and scanned the crowd in search of more interesting company.

"Being fiftieth in line to a throne must seem depressing! I suppose I'm lucky not to have any sisters."

Interest flashed behind his eyes like sunlight catching a trout in a tree-shaded pool. "Old ways?"

"Certainly."

A scarlet blush crept over his cheekbones, between the zits, under the fuzz, and came to a halt on his stringy neck. "I'm not very subtle, am I?"

"I think subtlety would be quickly fatal in anyone with forty-nine older brothers."

"Probably. How did . . . You're the girl who prophesied a war?"

"I interpreted an omen." *Was I to carry those two wretched eagles around my neck for the rest of my life?*

"Correctly, I think." He glanced around. "Helenus is here somewhere. You must meet him. He's brother number twenty-something, Cassandra's twin . . . an augur, too, a very good one. And a fine fighter—not as good as Aen—not like Hector, of course, but better than most."

"I expect knowing the future would help in that."

My gangling companion pulled a face. "Not necessarily!"

"No, I suppose not necessarily. Does he think there will be a war too?"

"Oh, yes. And it will end— Aren't we distant cousins, you and I?"

Not altogether lacking in subtlety, this gawky Polydorus had made a slip and diverted me away from it without drawing breath. I ran after the stick he had thrown.

"Probably. I think I'm related to every noble in the Troad. Let's see. Hippodemia and Aeneas are my third cousins through their mother. Does that help?"

Evidently not, for he frowned narrowly. "They're mine too, through my father—we have the same great-grandfather. Family doesn't always stretch that far. Can we find a closer link? My mother is Altes' daughter."

That explained why he had been sent along on the Pedasos jaunt, but not his reaction to my mention of Aeneas. "No connection."

"So it's safe to kiss you."

"Not unless you can think of a good excuse."

"I could probably think of several if I tried."

"Work on it." I saw his gaze flicker downward again and wished I had real quinces there to inspire him.

"I'm very fond of plums," he remarked casually.

"*What!?* I mean, what happened in Troy?"

The prominent bulge in his neck jiggled. "A council. I wasn't there, of course. You'd have to ask Mestor. He's brother number thirty, and I'm his charioteer now. He's around somewhere."

If I couldn't even worm details of the Menelaus negotiations out of my lanky new friend, he would not wish to tell me what his augur brother Helenus had foretold about the outcome of the war, but he had already done so unwittingly. If the family seers were predicting a Trojan victory, that information would not be kept secret.

"What did Aeneas say at the meeting?"

I had scored. He bared his teeth in anger. "Oh, you are a soothsayer, aren't you!"

"Not at the moment. I'm using feminine guile to entrap a valorous but innocent warrior. Mostly, I just know our mutual cousin. He wouldn't be against the war . . . ?"

Polydorus said, "I'm much more devious than I look. Why don't I introduce you to a dozen or so brothers for you to practice on? A game bag full of sons of Priam."

"Only married ones, of course?"

"Goes without saying." This time he did not blush. He smiled. A little more meat and a lot less acne and Polydorus would be quite a cute Titan.

"The person I really want to meet is Menelaus."

"I'm not allowed up in those circles, but I'll point him out for you. Here's my brother, Lykaon, to start with, my only full brother." He raised his voice. "No, I can't let you near him. He's too unmarried."

Lykaon turned around. He was not many years older and his resemblance to Polydorus was obvious. Priam had several wives; and the half brothers I met soon after were different in various ways, although almost all of them were tall. Royal brats eat well.

Polydorus wrapped a long arm around me possessively. "Briseis of Lyrnessos."

"Want one!" Lykaon said graciously. "Watch this kid, Princess, he's not as simple as he looks. Have you met Helenus? He's an augur, too." He did not introduce me to the Greek at his side.

Nor did Brother Isos (number twenty-two) when we reached his group. Nor did Helenus, and he said nothing

about auguries either. As Polydorus moved me around the
hall from brother to brother, Iris whispered a truth in my ear
so I would understand what game was afoot. Paris had won,
obviously, and Menelaus was being thrown out with mud in
his ears. Priam had spurned his threats, but here in Pedasos
were Altes and Elatos of the Leleges, Lethos and Hippothoös of the Pelasgians, Alcathous of the Dardanians, and
even Briseus of Lyrnessos, although that happenstance was
not by mortal design. All of these men were Trojan allies
while the sun shone, but there was stormy weather ahead.
Thus every Greek had been provided with a Trojan prince as
chaperon. There would be no secret negotiating in Pedasos
if those men could help it.

All of which made me even more curious to know why
Aeneas was not there to back up his father-in-law.

The party grew louder. I was famished, but no one was
eating yet. We obtained more wine from another cupbearer
playing truant from Olympus.

Polydorus pointed. "That's Mestor. Ginger hair is
Menelaus."

Obviously we were not about to intrude on the king
of Sparta and his companions, just look. I looked. Indeed, I surveyed the group with considerable surprise
and then amusement.

I could have spent the rest of the evening admiring
Mestor, Polydorus's knight. Perhaps their brother Paris was
better looking, but it would have been a close call. Mestor
had a harder look to him, which was not unbecoming, an impression of having been carved instead of molded. Men had
become more interesting since the previous summer, and
that one would be the prize in any collection. His attention
to Menelaus was the concentration of a leopard watching its
prey.

The rest of the audience comprised Mother and Hippodemia, nodding attentively as the king droned on in his
peculiar accent. Set alongside her young cousin, Mother
looked old and stooped and saggy. Hippodemia had always
been lovely: had always known how to dress well, how to
mix colors and patterns in her weaving, how to add just

enough jewelry and not too much. As a child, I had believed
that the goddesses of Olympus must be very much like Hippodemia, only not so pretty. Tonight she was lovelier than
ever, for she was in the early stages of childbearing. Her
breasts thrust forward proudly from her bodice and her face
glowed, framed by her dangling locks. She was hanging on
every word Menelaus said, and yet he barely seemed to notice her.

After Bienor's coaching, I could have identified Helen's
husband by the twin-star emblem on his mantle. He was a
thick, beefy man, clad in a patterned wool tunic and Greek
greaves. His face and hair were both red, his bulky arms
speckled with sandy freckles under a haze of pink fluff. He
had too much gold on him—on his hands and arms and belt,
a lion-and-stars pendant at his throat, a diadem that drew attention to his thinning hair. He stood there with his feet
apart, clutching a silver cup and blathering.

". . . many women as she could possibly want. Used to ask
her if she had a separate girl to cut every fingernail. And
toenail, too, shouldn't doubt. Had the whole of her quarters
replastered every spring, brought in new furniture for her
from Mycenae, the best workmanship and design in all
Greece, inlays of ivory and gold and that blue stuff. Oak and
ebony and olive. Perfumes imported from Crete and Egypt.
No wife was ever so pampered. She could sacrifice to the
gods every day and I never questioned the cost, never questioned the cost of anything—or almost never. Nor did she
have any complaints about me, I can tell you. I was a faithful, ardent husband. More ardent than most, I'm sure, and well
qualified in every way. I never amused myself elsewhere—not
while I was in the palace, I mean. Off campaigning or on
hunting trips, well, you understand that's different. Or a boy,
once in a while. No harm in that. She had harpists and
dancers and jugglers galore to amuse her. And clothes! Let
me tell you about her clothes. . . ."

I looked up at my escort. He rolled his eyes. We faded off
into the smoke and clamor.

"Does he honk like that all the time?" I asked.

"I don't know—he was only at Troy for three days." Polydorus grinned through his acne. "Any man who lost Helen might feel that the gods had a grudge against him."

"He ought to be grateful he ever had her to lose. She told me he was dull." I followed my guide between the shouting knots of people.

He stopped. "She must know. There's brother Pammon, but I'm not letting you near him."

Pammon was a tall youth, lacking both tassels and acne. He was laughing uproariously at something.

"Oh, but I must meet him! He's just like Paris."

"He is not! And don't you dare tell him so. That Greek with him is only a herald." Polydorus took a firm grip on my elbow. "Over here . . ." He stopped, frowning.

Over there was my father beside the king of the Dardanians and a Greek. There was no son of Priam in attendance.

"Who's he?" I asked.

"Alcathous son of Aisyetes. I don't know the old man. The Greek is the king of Ithaca: Odysseus son of Laertes. I haven't met him, but that's who he is."

"He seems to have escaped from his keeper."

Polydorus scowled down at me in exasperation. "The gods do chatter to you, don't they?"

"Sometimes. The old man is my father. Come and I'll present you."

I eased forward to the edge of the group. Seen from the back, Odysseus was massive, all width and bulk with dark hair hanging to his wrestler's shoulders. His dull brown tunic had given long service, but the purple mantle was the finest piece of weaving I had yet seen in the hall, bearing an emblem of a solitary ship; it was clasped by a gold pin in the shape of a hound catching a fawn. He was listening intently to the other two kings, his gaze switching from one to the other, studying each speaker in turn.

". . . for a hundred amphorae of the first pressing," my father said.

"Or two hundred bales of wool," Alcathous added.

They were talking trade! That was not unexpected for my father or even Alcathous, who was an easygoing but earthily practical rancher. He left the romantic glory hunting to Aeneas and concentrated on the welfare of his people and his herds. Aeneas swore his brother-in-law knew every horse in Dardania by name and could call any one of them to him. I liked Alcathous, his booming laugh and weather-beaten smile, even if he was starting to go bald already. I could understand his talking trade rather than war, but why was the Greek finding that topic so interesting? Knights are supposed to spurn such matters as unbefitting a warrior's honor—although Father maintained that most of them could glance at a suit of armor and tell you right away how many oxen it was worth.

"What about horses?" Odysseus said. "We shall want many horses."

Aha! Again the goddess whispered a truth in my ear. Earlier I had wondered why Menelaus had brought the king of Ithaca with him on his mission to Troy. Now I knew. Menelaus was still picking his scab in public, but the king of Ithaca was already planning the war—and trying to enlist allies right on Priam's doorstep, too.

My father saw me. Odysseus noticed and spun around. "Prince Polydorus! Do you know these royal knights? And who is the goddess?"

"My daughter, my lord," Father said, frowning.

I bent my knee to the king.

He did not smile, but his glower faded to courteous attention. "My lady Briseis, I would be honored to meet so famed an augur no matter what she looked like. Seeing you, I cannot imagine why Paris needed to come all the way to Greece in search of beauty." His voice was gruff but compelling, and he mouthed the perfumed compliments so seriously that they did not sound like an adult mocking a child—not to me, anyway. "My lords, have you met Polydorus son of Priam? The youngest of them all but destined not to be the least, I think. This is King Briseus of Lyrnessos, Prince, and I'm sure you know the son of Aisyetes. I asked your father which of all his sons was his favorite and he named you at once."

It was very slickly done. The negotiations had been suspended for the time being, and Polydorus was so flattered that he might not register what had been going on. The king

of Ithaca was by no means handsome in the way the best of
Priam's sons were, but I suddenly decided that he was the
most interesting man in the hall, an imposing combination
of brawn and brains. I wondered if he was married.

Doubtless he would have soon disposed of the two un-
wanted juveniles, but then the heralds began sheep dogging
the guests to start the meal. To cater to such a throng, stewards had set up what are often called nine-legged tables—
big triangular shapes with a regular small table supporting
each corner, able to serve a dozen people. Doubtless some
seating plan in proper order of precedence had been agreed
upon beforehand, but the king of Ithaca had his own notions.
Before anyone could direct him, he took a corner stool, with
Alcathous on one side of him and Father on the other. Then
he gestured for me to sit beside Father and Polydorus next to
Alcathous. Other people eventually took the rest of the
places. Odysseus had his back to the throne, which was certainly a breach of etiquette, but in that din only Polydorus
and I had any hope of overhearing what the three kings were
saying, and even we would have to strain. I was willing to
strain.

Elatos offered choice portions to the gods, then stewards
began serving the feast: roasted meat, bread decorated with
sesame, lumps of cheese, bowls of beans and chickpeas in a
fragrant coriander sauce. Tearing off a hunk of bread and
scooping a load into his mouth, Odysseus went right on talking as if he knew his little tête-à-tête would not be left undis-
turbed for very long.

"From what you tell me, my lords, you will support the
same side in the war, whichever it may turn out to be?"

Father glanced uneasily at me, who should not be privy to
such momentous discussions. "I shall be guided by the son
of Aisyetes."

"And you, my lord?" Odysseus refilled his mouth.

Alcathous laughed. "Can you see me resisting Aeneas?"

"You are afraid to oppose him?"

"Afraid? No, son of Laertes, I am not afraid of my
brother-in-law!"

"But if he persists in his present mood, you will defy

Troy?" The king of Ithaca could be subtle like a stalking cat or boisterous as a winter storm.

Alcathous set his jaw stubbornly. "Great decisions are not made between mouthfuls at a banquet."

"They may as well be when the question is as simple as this one. Priam is an old fool. That wayward son of his has angered half the gods on Olympus. They will support our cause, and the towers of Troy will surely burn. Why call down the wrath of the Immortals upon your own people?" Odysseus wiped his bowl with a last piece of bread and held it up to attract a steward. I had never seen anyone eat so much so fast.

Father was listening in worried silence to the two younger men, barely touching his food. Alcathous chewed leisurely before he replied. He must see that this quick-eyed Greek outmatched him in debate.

"The gods make their own decisions, my lord of Ithaca. Priam honors them with rich hecatombs, just as the Greeks do. You seek to direct them?"

Not a bad effort, I thought.

Odysseus laughed and started on his second bowlful. "If Priam were less of a fool, he would have made your brother-in-law leader of his host. Hector has no experience and deceives himself."

Polydorus had been catching some of this, although probably not as much as I did, for a strikingly beautiful woman had taken the stool next to him. Now, looking worried, he tried to whisper something across to me, so I missed what came next. I leaned over to him.

"If there is to be a war," I asked, "then who leads the Trojans?"

"Hector, of course!"

"Aeneas has more experience, surely?"

He scowled as he licked his fingers. "Hector!"

Ha! Dear Cousin Aeneas would never be satisfied with anything less than supreme command, so there was already a split between the Trojans and the Dardanians. The wily king of Ithaca was trying to hammer a wedge into it. I turned my head to pick up the conversation again. He was signaling for a third helping and becoming even more bullish. He seemed much larger sitting than he did standing.

"I confess I am puzzled by the relationship between the Trojans and the Dardanians. Explain it to me, son of Mydon."

My father hesitated as if fearing that a hasty word in this company might topple him into a pit of spikes. "They are close kin. You could say that those that live at the mouth of the Scamander are Trojans and those up in the headwaters are Dardanians."

"Except that we move about a lot," Alcathous added cheerfully. "I own a house in Troy; Priam has some grazing rights on Mount Ida."

Odysseus sprang the trap. "Why does one people need two kings? Your wife has as good a claim to the throne of Troy as Priam has, son of Aisyetes. Suppose Agamemnon offers to make you king of Troy?"

"As his vassal? I would rather sleep under the stars with my honor intact than have men say I had been bribed by the Greeks."

"Priam is a stiff-necked dotard who brings destruction on his people for the sake of a harlot. Yet you say they are your people also."

Alcathous stopped eating, his face dark in the shifty light of the fire and the lamps. The surrounding ruckus was becoming deafening as the wine worked on a roomful of unruly young men. They had left their swords outside, but every one of them had a dagger, and the stench of impending war was as pervasive as the eye-stinging smoke. The bragging was starting now, and even my temper was rising. I was angry at the stubborn Trojans for supporting Paris, at the predatory Greeks for exploiting a minor crime to ignite a full-scale war, at all these warriors spoiling for violence. If they would confine their slaughter to one another, I would not care, but that could never be. Like millstones, they would grind the innocent.

My father tried to calm the local waves. "Is there not a proverb about killing the game before warming the pot? The Greeks will have to take Troy before they can give—"

Mestor son of Priam arrived, intent on breaking up this

conspiracy. Before he could say a word, Odysseus spoke to me around Alcathous.

"I'm not surprised you've never heard of it, my lady. Ithaca is a very small island off the west coast of Greece."

"And what brings you so far from home, son of Laertes?" I retorted.

Father and Alcathous were nonplussed, but a flash of amusement lit Odysseus's eyes, the first I had seen there.

"A favor for a friend, a matter of honor. Troy is impressive, but I am eager to return home to my humble Ithaca, to my dear wife and parents."

Alas, he was married! But he was being slick again. If his parents were both alive, then he ruled as king consort. He had just informed his audience that Ithaca followed the old ways, as Lyrnessos and the Dardanians did, as Troy did not.

"No children?" I asked, in case he had overlooked a source of pathos.

"Not yet. But soon."

"And when you do return, will you stay there and dwell in peace?" I sucked my fingers with ladylike delicacy.

"Unless I come back here to fight a war."

A burst of jeering laughter at the far side of the hall coincided with angry yells nearer to hand. In that roiling, choking megaron, I was moved to an indiscretion.

"You, my lord? What reason have you to make war on Troy—just loot, common larceny?"

Imagine a large bull, standing at the front of its herd. Imagine frail little me going up to it and kicking it on its soft, tender, black nose. A bubble of shocked silence seemed to close off our group from the rest of the crowd.

Most of the bulls in that hall would have charged, but Odysseus turned the situation to his advantage as usual. "Loot is important to a warrior as a measure of his success, and it repays the cost of raising an army. But a king's first duty is to keep his kingdom safe from oppressors, and a kingdom's first defense is the reputation of its warriors. How can they prove their worth except in war? When a just cause like this presents itself, I am duty bound to support it, so that Ithaca's enemies will know that she is well guarded and

Ithaca herself will appreciate her king. I am surprised your noble father has not instructed you in these matters."

Father's face twisted in shame. My impudence was bad enough—no woman, even a reigning queen, should ever speak to a knight as I had—but my heresy against the code was a thousand times worse. He opened his mouth to denounce me. I hastened to repair the damage.

"Indeed he has instructed me, my lord. He taught me that a knight's paramount duty is to his parents and children. I assumed that a king would therefore remain at home to defend his realm, for troublemakers may arise in his absence. If my words have given offense, I must humbly beg pardon. I was merely thinking of your dear wife and how she will worry if you embark on foreign adventures. Surely no material riches can ever compensate her for your absence or the dangers you will face."

The king of Ithaca pursed his lips and nodded as if acknowledging a nice piece of footwork. "The Lady Penelope is a warrior's daughter and understands the need."

"And I am sure," Father said, "that she knows how to remain silent in the presence of her betters, as my daughter evidently does not."

"Your daughter displays a truly martial spirit," Odysseus countered smugly, perhaps implying that my father had not. "You must find her a husband worthy of her mettle, one who can tame her."

To my unbounded relief, I was saved from further desolation by Mestor, who remarked that the music would be starting soon and King Altes wished to talk with his distinguished guest. As the two of them departed, Alcathous completed my rescue. He slapped his thigh loudly.

"By the beard of Zeus, son of Mydon, she pricked that mealymouthed scoundrel better than we did! He tried to stroke a kitten and found he had grabbed a wildcat. Well done, Briseis, lioness of Lyrnessos! That was the best brawl I have heard in years!"

Mollified, my father gave me a look that threatened a mere thousand lashes instead of whatever he had been planning earlier.

4

I had not finished with the king of Ithaca. I watched the dancing and other entertainment in the company of Polydorus, Lykaon, and a young lady Lykaon was squiring. Afterward the men excused themselves rather abruptly. She remarked how hot the megaron was. She suggested that the two of us take a stroll out to the courtyard.

"Would that be proper?" I inquired.

"Absolutely. To go alone or with a man would be scandalous, but we two can chaperone each other."

Hand in hand, we went outdoors to blissfully cool fresh air. Moonlight silvered the sea, with Lesbos basking along the horizon like a vast stone whale. Over the treetops hung a web of stars. Wine and excitement twirled my head like a spindle.

"There's a secluded bench under this apple tree." Polydorus slid a strong arm around me and eased me away from my companion, who had been similarly ambushed by Lykaon.

"What a wonderful night!" I remarked sagaciously.

"Yes."

"Why do those hateful Greeks have to spoil it by threatening war?"

"Forget the Greeks. I have discovered those other reasons." We had not even reached the bench.

"Reasons for what?"

"This."

I expected his kiss to be a gentle compliment to a child trying to be a woman, but it was a lot more serious than that. So was the next one, and the fingers sliding into my bodice even more so. He became genuinely enthusiastic, while I discovered that a man's touch on my breasts produced effects I had never anticipated. My nails dug into his bony back of their own accord. The grape festival began to seem a very long time away. Annoyingly, I found myself thinking of Odysseus.

At last I broke loose and said, "Enough!"

"Why?" He was panting. We both were.

"Because my brother is behind that bush."

"You are mistaken."

"No, she isn't," Bienor said, emerging. "Go indoors, Briseis."

"Alas!" I cried. "Son of Priam, your company this evening has been a great joy to a lonely, friendless maiden. In the absence of my father I must be obedient to my brother."

"If you can wait a moment, I will break his neck," Polydorus responded glumly. "I'll see you in there."

"As you wish, of course, my lord."

Brothers can be useful sometimes, and I made a note to congratulate mine on his tact in not appearing until I summoned him. I had tasted romance and been satisfied. With my heart gossamer on the night breeze, I headed back toward the party, hearing the youngest son of Briseus introduce himself to the youngest son of Priam. As I neared the marble lions in front of the porch, a gruff voice spoke from the shadow of a pillar.

"Behold the Amazon queen!"

I stopped. "Not I, son of Laertes. If I offended this evening—"

"Not at all." Odysseus stepped forward into the moonlight, a silver statue of a god, draped in that beautifully crafted mantle. I assumed his wife had woven it. I knew nothing about her except that I hated her. "You held the field, Amazon. Let experience temper your courage with discretion but never blunt it. I find sweet words work better than sour, and this must be doubly true for a woman."

"I shall take your advice to heart, my lord."

"Give me some of yours in exchange. Tell me what future the gods have revealed to you."

"Only that our paths will cross again." Lubricated by wine, the prophecy slipped out before I realized, but it felt true.

He nodded as if he believed me. "Tell me how you know this."

"That emblem you bear. A solitary ship tracked our course today, and no one seemed to notice it but I."

"I hope we meet in peace, then. Polydorus is a promising lad, but for your father to unite you with a son of Priam would not be prudent politics just now."

"My father has no present plans for my marriage, my lord."

He held me with his deadly, all-seeing stare. "And what are your wishes in the matter?"

"To be a dutiful daughter, of course."

"If he asked you?"

The night seemed to close in menacingly. With a murmur of protest I turned away, but I did not leave. The son of Laertes came another pace closer, speaking at my shoulder.

"Pretend that I am Aphrodite, come down from Olympus. What prayer do you make to the goddess?"

"What any highborn maiden asks—a valorous knight to cherish and protect me in these troubled times."

"Times are always troubled."

"They will soon be more troubled than usual in the Troad."

He sighed. "This is true. If you were my sister, I should want to see you settled far from here."

To have agreed aloud would have been disloyal, but I nodded.

"You deserve a man of excellence, Briseis, and those are rare. You need one who lives far off, but your chances of finding such a man in Lyrnessos are remote."

What was this honey-spoken Greek after? My heart thundered like a war drum. "You are kind to take thought to my problems, son of Laertes."

"I know a young Cretan at the court of Mycenae, a man of noble ancestry and exemplary character. He is like unto Apollo in appearance, but the gods so blessed his parents that he has nine older brothers and will inherit little of value. A portable dowry—some silver bars, for example—would have great appeal to him, as would your noble self, of course. I could recommend him most highly to your father."

I did not know what to say, and I still do not know if the answer I eventually gave was wrong. "By all means mention your candidate to my parents. I am sure that they will invite the noble lord to visit Lyrnessos."

Odysseus laid a powerful hand on my shoulder and turned me to face him. His dark eyes glittered in the moonlight.

"But would his suit prosper? You are the heir, so your departure would be a grave upset to the kingdom. Can I honestly tell my young friend that his journey might be worthwhile?"

"Surely you should put that question to my father?"

"Properly speaking, yes." He smiled. "But what is the real answer?"

I could have lied, I suppose, and then my entire life might have been changed; but I knew Mother would never bring herself to part with her youngest kitten, and Father would rather cut off his feet than pay out a dowry. Why bother lying?

"Would he have a chance?" Odysseus persisted.

"If he brings the tail of the Sphinx with him, certainly."

He uttered a single rasp of laughter and shook his big head, making the dark locks shimmer. "Oh, you are a rare one! I doubt that even my Cretan is worthy of you, Briseis. If I ever meet a man who is, I shall tell him of you."

At that moment Bienor and Polydorus came hurrying across the courtyard to see what trouble I was in now. I presented my brother to my friend the king of Ithaca, and the four of us went in together.

5

"Monstrous!" Mother shrieked. "Depravity! Shame! I shall disown you. I shall have you chained to the . . ."

But I am getting ahead of my story.

Menelaus and his embassy sailed away. We remained at Pedasos for three days and were presented with lavish gifts when we departed. Mine included a string of blue glass beads, which I wore often during the rest of my life in Lyrnessos. Bienor received a gold bracelet.

Spring warmed to summer and the portents of war shriveled in the heat, just as memories of nightmares fade in noontime glare. Rumors buzzed around like bumblebees in a meadow, but they proved as unprofitable.

To his unspeakable joy, Bienor was at last growing taller. I was growing womanly and could feel men's eyes tracking me as they never had before. If I was going to be a beauty, as Helen had predicted, then I would be a strikingly tall beauty.

Summer relented into fall, and fall brought the grape harvest, which ended every year with the festival of Bakkhos, whom the Greeks call Dionysus. Then the youth of Lyrnessos donned masks and fawn-skin garments to honor the god who gave wine to mankind. Men and women danced together in nightlong revelry. Often, then, the god would reward his worshippers with his holy madness and there could be no shame for what happened at a Dionysia. The masks helped too. Since childhood I had listened to the merriment from afar, but this year I was qualified to attend. I would mingle unrecognized with the common folk, experience their ways, and perhaps even enjoy my first romance. That was my plan, but not everyone shared my enthusiasm for it.

Ctimene was reluctant to express her doubts, but I finally bullied them out of her. "My lady, there are few young women in the kingdom of your stature—or with your wonderful figure, my lady. You cannot hide those behind a fur mask."

"What does it matter if some of them guess who I probably am? They can't prove it. Everyone is equal at the grape festival."

Her jewel lips pouted sorrowfully. After a little more harrying she said, "I fear there may be evil men who might line up to *share* a princess, my lady."

Hades! I hadn't thought of that. "They wouldn't dare! Father would kill them!"

She stared at me like a dead owl.

"Except they would be masked too, wouldn't they? Do men really treat women so?"

I consulted Bienor, my resident expert on everything. In matters of sex and depravity, however, my twin was as ignorant as I, although never willing to admit it. The best he could manage was, "Anything can happen at the Dionysia." He sighed.

"Such as?"

"Don't even ask."

"You don't know, you mean. I suppose you're hoping to find out?"

He leered. "Course."

"You're only a boy!"

"Am not!"

"Show me."

Thus cornered, he proved strangely reluctant to display whatever adult plumage might be sprouting under his loincloth. He even confessed to misgivings, which was most unlike him. "Easy for you women! All you need do is submit. We men must deliver! It stands up all the time by itself, when I don't want it to. Suppose it won't when I do? Suppose it gets *shy*?"

"Take a parsnip along," I suggested. "She won't know the difference in the dark."

That did not comfort him—he was not even sure she *would* know it from a parsnip, whoever she was.

As the fateful night drew closer, my resolution began to soften like salt on a rainy day. The palace girls all whispered excitedly of the men who would take them to the revelry or the ones they hoped to snare on the spot. It was easy for them, because proof of fertility brought a free girl quick marriage and earned slaves favored treatment, but princesses were a breed apart. I could not imagine myself maintaining through storm and high water that Zeus or Apollo had visited my chamber in a blaze of light. Mother would not shell those beans.

Everyone, it seemed, was working on a mask. These were flimsy things of wicker and scraps of fur and cloth, supposed to resemble an animal's head. The fawn-skin costumes resided year-round in the palace storeroom. A few days before the feast, they were handed out to anyone who wanted them, slave or free. Ctimene collected two, one for herself and one for me. Sphelos noticed and told Mother.

She began stern, wagging a finger. "Absolutely out of the question. You are only a child."

I offered to display evidence to the contrary. At that point she sent everyone else out of the hall—the maids, Alcmene, Anticleia, even the aunts—so that the two of us could enjoy a quiet talk.

She tried motherly, patting my knee. "Sex is not something to indulge in lightly, my dear. It takes a lot of handling. Men may stand up and shrug and walk away, but we poor women usually find that our emotions have entangled us like sheep in a thorn patch. When you are older, you will be better able to cope."

"I'm sure one improves with practice."

She waxed regal, looking down her nose at me, although she had to stand up to do so. "You are of royal blood, heir to the realm! You cannot go consorting with commoners and slaves! Whatever would people say?"

"I shall be masked. Did I tell you I'm making a vixen face, with—"

She became practical, folding her arms. "You are the tallest girl in the kingdom—everyone will recognize you. They'll know you at a glance."

Now we had come to the nub of the problem. Had I been able to disguise myself as other people could, she would merely have told me to keep my mask on and have a nice time.

"They won't be able to prove it."

"Scandal does not require proof!"

Having no direct response to that, I went on the offensive. "How old were you when you attended your first grape festival?"

"Older than you, certainly. I don't remember exactly."

"I expect I'll tell my daughters that one day."

"You may have daughters by next year!" Mother yelped, and from then on the meeting became markedly less ruly. But it was not the thought of progeny that bothered her, it was gossip.

"You are crazy!" she screamed. "The god has stolen your wits already!" Flushed and heated, she stormed back and forth across the room, weaving between the looms, waving her hands, endlessly repeating the same arguments. "What will the court say? What will the Dardanians and Thebe and Pedasos and Troy say?" For a woman who rarely moved at all unless she had to, this was a rare display of exuberance. "My daughter, my heir, a princess, coupling in the woods like a cat! With *slaves*? I forbid it! I will not have it!" Half the palace must be able to hear her.

When she paused to catch her breath, I said, "You blaspheme! To stop me attending the festival would be an insult to the god."

Off she went again, striding up and down the hall with her flounces flouncing and her bosom heaving like twin dolphins breasting a heavy sea. She told harrowing tales of women being raped, crippled, sodomized, or murdered, of frenzied people jumping off cliffs or choking to death on their own vomit. She could not admit that I was no longer a child and therefore she was growing old—that was another problem. Waving her baggy arms overhead, she repeated everything another four or five times, even threatening to have me chained up.

"Now that *will* make the tongues wag!" I said.

She came to a sudden halt, thrusting her inflamed face close to mine, a gesture spoiled by the fact that I was now half a head taller than she. "You are playing with fire, child! You will get burned!"

It was an admission that she could not physically prevent me from going. That was all the permission I needed.

6

I knew the game was not over. Mother ransacked my room,
but Ctimene had hidden our masks and costumes elsewhere.

She brought Father into the battle. He told me my mother
would be very unhappy if I went to the grape festival. I told
him his daughter would be very unhappy if she didn't. And
what about my twin brother, who was still bald from the ears
down? Was he to be allowed to go? Father sighed in a nos-
talgic sort of way and changed the subject.

One morning just before the grape festival, I met Bienor
strutting like a peacock and demanded to know what he had
been up to.

He shrugged. "The usual. I do hope you manage to come
to the Dionysia. You'll find sex is quite enjoyable once you
get used to it."

Discreet inquiries led me to the kitchens, where Pero was
shirking the duties awaiting her elsewhere and gossiping
with the cooks. I asked her sweetly if it was true she had a
new lover.

"A noble lover, my lady!" Smirking shamelessly, she rummaged in a basket of parsnips and found a very small one.
"More noble than Lord Aeneas, as I recall." The audience
sniggered. She chose another. "A little slender, perhaps?"
Another, short and thick. "Not quite up to his manly brother
yet." Guffaws and shouts of agreement. One with a bend. "A
most *enjoyable* curve to it . . ." She opened her mouth wide,
and I beat a hasty retreat from the howls of mirth.

Bienor, curse him, was now ahead of me in the growing-
up game.

Later that same day, a herald arrived at the palace, all dusty
and sweaty, having just run in from Thebe. He announced

that Prince Helenus begged my mother's pardon for giving such short notice, but he and his brother Mestor would arrive next day—just the two of them and their charioteers, an informal visit, and please not to make a state occasion of it.

Guests always provoked Mother to fuss like a swarm of bees. The prospect of entertaining sons of Priam drove her to sheer panic, but that did not matter because everyone else did what was required in spite of her.

When I heard who was coming I panicked, too, and forgot all about the Dionysia. That was romance, but marriage was permanent.

"Your new gown with the open bodice," Mother said when she got to me in her mental list of Things To Be Attended To. "You can have it finished by tomorrow."

"I'm sure the old one will be adequate!"

Her eyebrows rose very high, yet somehow managed to convey intense satisfaction at the same time. "You are bursting out of it. You keep insisting you're an adult—"

"Mestor's charioteer is Polydorus!"

"So?"

"He kissed me!"

Mother blanched.

Two chariots swept in through the gates at noon. Helenus's charioteer was nobody special, but Mestor was still being driven by Polydorus. He had more beard and less acne, his shoulders were broader, but he was still a boy standing on a stool.

The family assembled in the portico to welcome the honored guests. I did not take in a word of what was said. Utterly tongue-tied, I tried not to stare at Polydorus but also not to ignore him, in case anyone noticed. He was Priam's favorite, and Priam ranked next to Apollo in the Troad. I had not slept all night.

Some hint was dropped. When the princes were led into the megaron to drink honeyed wine, the rest of us were excluded. Sphelos stalked away looking as pleased as a cat with a bowl of cream. I found myself alone with Bienor. For

once my pestilential twin was regarding me with something
akin to respect.

"You have a suitor!"

"Rubbish! Absolute nonsense. I cannot imagine where
you get such ideas." I left.

He followed. "And what a suitor! Didn't you see how
he looked at you? He's handsome! And rich! What's the
matter?"

"Leave me alone!" I wanted to jump on a winged horse
and fly away to the land of the Ethiops.

After what seemed like days, the little reception broke up.
The participants emerged into the vestibule, Polydorus giving me an excited grin. The moment the visitors were taken
away to be bathed and oiled and so on, Mother enveloped
me in a suffocating hug and snuffled in my ear.

Father said, "A word with you, Princess. Go away, Bienor." He led the way back inside. Mother kept a cushioned
arm firmly around me. She was growing more snuffly by the
minute. Father was troubled, chewing his beard. Rulers like
to think they obey only the gods, but now the long, chill
shadow of Troy lay over Lyrnessos.

Father said, "It's not a formal offer, you realize."

I licked my lips. "No, my lord."

"Just an elbow in the water, reconnaissance. Helenus
explained—it's between us and Mestor, nothing to do with
him, even. Not official."

"No, my lord."

"Just Mestor, as a favor to his charioteer brother. You must
have made quite an impression on that young man!"

He was trying not to blame me, I thought. Then I realized
that he was not nearly as upset as Mother was—why not?

She made a bubbly noise. "Bah! It's not Briseis he's interested in. He's the youngest of fifty. Lyrnessos is the best
he's ever likely to get. That's all."

"Now, now, Nemertes! He denied that, and I believe him.
He could force our hand, you know. He's leaving us the op-
tion of declining. If we indicate interest, then obviously the
formal proposal will be forthcoming. Mestor wouldn't go
even this far without Priam's knowledge and at least tacit

approval. And Altes' too. A union with both Troy and Pedasos would have expansive advantages."

"Aeneas won't approve at all!"

"He can't defy Priam on something like this." Why *was*
Father so pleased? "It is not a war matter, so it would be up
to Alcathous. He certainly wants no more trouble with Priam
than he has already."

"She's far too young!"

"That's not true, and you know it." He turned to me.
"They would want you both to live in Troy until such time
as you are called upon to serve the goddess here, long may
that day be withheld. The boy still has to complete his training, and so on. Because you are your mother's heir, Mestor
implied that a purely token dowry would—"

"That's what appeals to you!" Mother roared. "You won't
have to provide a dowry! Why don't you ask her what she
wants, instead of thinking of land and herds all the time?"

I pulled loose from her, fell down before Father and
hugged his knees. Words spilled out. "My lord, I beseech
you—don't send me to live in Troy! Troy is going to
burn. The towers will fall. Its men will die, its women be
carried off."

Mother wailed.

Father was silent a moment, then barked: "Oh, nonsense!
Briseis, don't be ridiculous. Stand up, for gods' sake! What
omens have you been imagining now?"

I had no answer to that, for I had not known what I was
going to say until I said it. All I knew was that the prospect
of going to live in Troy was absolutely terrifying. I stammered and sobbed, insisting that Troy was the problem, not
Polydorus.

"You must be guided by me," Father said firmly.

"Oh, must she?" Mother took my arm and pulled me up.
"If I had been guided by my father, Briseus, then I'd have
married Euneus, not you. I shrieked a lot louder and longer
than she has. There's plenty of time yet to think of marriage.
You tell the prince that, or I'll disinherit Briseis, and then
we'll see what happens to all his heartfelt affection."

Father groaned. "Is this what you want, child?"

"Oh, yes! Yes, please."

He grumbled some more, but he would never resist Mother when she was in that sort of mood, and just then she was a lioness defending her cub. Before evening, the informal proposal had been informally declined. At the feast we talked about the war and the harvest.

Of course I could not evade my would-be suitor—Polydorus was not the sort of young man to be discouraged by anything less than a ten-cubit spear. After Demodokos had sung for the court that evening, when everyone rose to stretch, move around, seek out new conversations, he headed in my direction. I was terrified that he would talk me into admitting that I liked him. Given even that little encouragement, he might go smoking back to Troy and have Priam's consent converted to a command. I resolved to be cool and distant—flattered but unmoved. Feeling as if I were being pursued through shrubbery by a tall tree, I retreated into the shadows, and there he cornered me.

He folded his arms and gazed at me until I began to tremble. Then he said, "You make Helen look like an old frump. I can't imagine what Paris sees in that Spartan hag."

"Er, thank you!" No one had ever spoken to me like that before. "And you . . . Polydorus, it isn't you! You mustn't think it's personal. There is no man I'd rather—"

"Personal? *Personal?* My lady, I am a son of Priam. We have no personal shortcomings."

I thought he was serious and I had offended, but then he waxed even more outrageous. "Of course we are required to find equally perfect people to marry, which is usually impossible, but you are the most perfect woman I have ever seen. I haven't slept since I first set—"

"Stop! You mustn't!"

"Why? Mestor says it never fails."

I had expected threats from a Trojan, possibly pleas or logic, not banter. Knowing no young men of my own rank, I did not know how to respond. "It's not you. It's Troy. Come back with a ship and carry me off to the wilds of Thrace and I will go with you gladly. Offer me a hovel in the desert and a life of penury and I will accept without hesitation." Alas, this was not being cool and distant. "But not Troy! All its famous horses could not drag me there to live now."

"And they could not drag me away now."

"Truly?" I said, unwilling to mention the awful prophecy I had pronounced earlier. "Even if . . . if . . . Say your sister Cassandra foretold that Troy must fall and all her defenders die? Is there no way that even one of the sons of Priam can honorably escape that destruction so that his line . . ."

He stared at me as if I was raving. "The youngest of fifty? To be known as the one who wouldn't fight? The runt of the litter? My lady, you shame me even to suggest it."

I had hurt him. "I'm sorry. Really, I am. Of course it was an unworthy suggestion. I just cannot see why your father must persevere along so terrible a road."

Polydorus shrugged. "Reasons? If you really want to know . . . First, Helen is only a symbol, he says. The Lycians and the Rhodians have been hacking at each other for years, with Greeks supporting Rhodes and Troy aiding the Lycians. Agamemnon has been looking for an excuse to enlarge the war."

He stuck out his big jaw, trying to look manly. "Secondly, we Trojans don't like yielding to threats. Today they tell us to surrender a woman. That's easy enough to do; but if we agree to that, then tomorrow they will say we must abandon the Lycians, and so it would go—demand after demand after demand, until we surrender our spears and they seize our women and children. Accede to one threat and another must follow as night follows day. The only place to stand is here. The only time to refuse is now. Always."

I could almost hear the old warrior saying it.

I sighed. "It makes sense, I suppose."

Polydorus edged a little closer. "So dreams must end?"

"Or at least await the gods' decision." I tried to move back and encountered a wall. He slid closer yet. I caught a whiff of bath scent and an intriguing whiff of man scent as well.

"And we may both be grandparents by then. I am glad

your objection isn't to me personal, though. Tell me that
again to ease the pain."

"It's Troy. And with you—is it Lyrnessos?"

"I do not wish to insult your lovely home, my lady, but it
is you in spite of Lyrnessos."

If he kept this up much longer, he was going to mold me
like clay.

"People are looking," I said hastily and squeezed by him,
trying not to touch him. He moved just enough that we
brushed against each other, and my heart jumped almost
hard enough to stun me.

"We could go outside?" he said.

"*No*! I mean, that would be frowned upon. Let us rejoin
the others. How long shall we have the pleasure of your
company?"

"A few days," Polydorus said happily. "I hear your Dionysia
is coming up."

7

Next morning I had a stabbing headache, not helped by the
prospect of trying to stay out of Polydorus's way all day. I
did not trust myself in his company. Being wooed is a se-
ductive experience.

Fortunately, his brother Helenus had his own plans for
me, nothing to do with marriage. When I had met him in the
fire-lit megaron of Pedasos, I had taken Helenus for elderly.
In daylight he was quite young, with hair prematurely white.
He was tall, slightly stooped, lantern-jawed, his manner
aloof and preoccupied. His habit of staring off into the distance when he spoke made him seem intimidating, but augurs bear burdens of their own and learn to keep passion at
a distance.

He sent Xanthus to find me and bring me to him out in the

courtyard. There, under a tree, we two remained half the day, listening to the distant thump of grain being winnowed, of men chopping wood, of potters' wheels squeaking. Ctimene watched from a respectful distance, sitting cross-legged on the paving and holding Gorgon's collar. Passersby gave us a wide berth.

He wanted to hear of all the omens I had seen and what meanings I had found in them. I obeyed, not daring to argue with his godlike calm, and he sat like a rock while I spoke, except sometimes nodding encouragement. When at last I dried up like a summer rivulet, he pursed his lips a few times.

"You have done well. Everyone has eyes, but very few can use them. You are indeed a seer and learning to understand what you see, too. Without any proper instruction that is re-markable."

I was flattered, of course, but then he alarmed me.

"You must never *try* to prophesy. The gods send auguries as they choose. Try *not* to try, not at all. A soothsayer is the voice of Iris. Let her speak through you when she is ready; you cannot coerce her. Remember that we usually prophesy for others, rarely for ourselves. Trust your sight. Do not measure your tread but go and let the gods guide. Do not say, 'Ah! A hawk carrying a snake means this' or, 'An owl crying by daylight portends that.' Learn to see without noticing."

He glanced at me briefly, then away again. "Of course, speak always the truth and only the truth. Forswear the gods and they will desert you! If you try to deceive others, you will deceive yourself, and your power will be lost. Speak the truth, even if it hurts. Yes, it will hurt! Oh, how it can hurt! But you must speak honestly, as the gods have spoken to you. Sometimes you may find yourself speaking truths you have not yet grasped yourself."

"Yesterday, I—" I stopped, horrified, as I remembered what I had told my parents.

"The truth!"

"My lord, I said . . . I said that Troy would be burned, its men slain, its women borne off in slavery." I dug nails into my palms until they hurt.

He sighed and went back to staring at the leafy canopy. "I have said the same. So did poor Aesacus, long years ago."

"I am sorry!"

"Why? I said it at the council when we turned Menelaus away. My words did little to increase my popularity, I assure you. My father struck me and banished me from his presence. Being an augur is not without its drawbacks."

I shivered, although the day was hot. I noticed Polydorus standing in the porch, staring moodily at us but not daring to interrupt. Would he be one of the dead? Could any son of Priam hope to escape?

"My lord?" I whispered.

"Mm?"

"What of yourself? If the fate of the city is determined, will you fight for a doomed cause?"

I shall never forget the pain in his eyes then.

"What sort of augur disbelieves his own auguries? I see all my brothers fallen and myself fated to live. Yet I shall slay not a few Greeks in battle. Others will hate them for what they have done, but I can hate them for what they will do."

"Is there no chance that the Lord of Storms will relent? If you fight bravely and make many rich offerings, may not great Zeus deem Troy worthy of reprieve?"

"Can even he turn fate aside?" Helenus sighed deeply. "Now it is my turn to talk. I was taught divination by my brother Aesacus. He was a great augur, although little good it did him in the end. In the short time we have, you and I, I cannot hope to teach you everything he taught me, or even a fraction of it, but I can give you some hints. Are you willing to learn, or would you rather be blind like other mortals?"

I took the question seriously, as he intended. "I might be happier being blind, my lord, had I always been blind. But to lose the sight now that I have already had a glimmer of it would be like tearing out my eyes."

He nodded, understanding and sympathetic. "Remember that prophecy almost never makes any difference. I warned my father to send Helen back, but he would not, and I knew he would not."

Old Maera had said much the same. "People will not believe?"

"Will not believe or will not obey. Our fates are fixed for us whether we know of them or not. The gift brings no happiness, neither to the speaker nor to the listeners. Well, I told you how to lose it. Let us see if I can tell you how to gain it." He paused. "Where to begin?"

Thereupon he began to enlighten me. He spoke of birds, of snakes, of fish, of thunder, of the dreaded rainbow, the sculptured clouds, and of other things I will not mention—no, not even now. He explained the interpretation of dreams, the significance of the signs in the heavens—eclipses, comets, falling stars—quoting famous examples and how they had been interpreted or misinterpreted. He went on to talk of minor portents, such as spiderwebs and the cries of wild animals. I struggled to commit everything to memory, wishing I had a dozen scribes from the record office writing it all down for me. Eventually we sent Ctimene for wine and fruit, and even as we refreshed ourselves, Helenus continued to instruct.

From that day onward, I could believe in myself as a seer.

8

Helenus departed the next morning, carrying gifts from Father—an ancient ring of amber for him, a silver rhyton for his charioteer.

Mestor and Polydorus remained, and Polydorus clung to me like a limpet, although a most desirable limpet. He pursued me with sighs and vows, with lover's poetry and warrior's bombast, plus humor so bawdy it shocked even Bienor. All of it being new to me, I melted like wax before his flame. Soon he had me sewing a mask for him to wear to the Dionysia, the one night of the year when anything might happen and in this case certainly would.

When the morning of the great day dawned, I fled in panic to Mother's embrace.

"Help!" I cried. "Three days of being wooed have turned my wits! Last night he kissed me and I lay awake all night. If I let him take me to the festival, I will be betrothed by morning!"

"Nonsense, my dear. I have complete faith in your judgment. He is a wonderful escort for you. You will have a marvelous time. How well I remember my first grape festival! I was even younger than you, I believe. I look back on it as one of my happiest memories." With a happy sigh she heaved herself off her chair and waddled over to her current weaving, which she had not touched in a month.

I stared at her fat back in dismay. Betrayed! What had happened to change her mind?

"By the way, dearest," she told the loom, "do remember that vigorous dancing can be very beneficial for the figure."

I knew that tone and distrusted it. "In what way exactly?"

"In shaking out any seeds he may have planted, dear."

As soon as I left the queen's hall, Polydorus pounced, suggesting we sneak off to the stables for a rehearsal. I blushed, laughed, and refused, but he stole a few kisses and fondlings right there in the corridor, making my knees so soft that I could barely walk.

For any boy or girl in any land or time, the first lovemaking must be a memorable experience, but it is a very personal one and of little interest to other people. The same things happen and I expect are always followed by the same vague sense of disappointment, the sense that something quite natural has been treated with a lot of unnecessary fuss. In my case, the most memorable part of it was the brawl that followed.

Our fawn-skin garments were simple chitons, pinned at the shoulder, most of them ancient, stained, and smelly. Ctimene looked very enticing in hers, but mine exposed far too much thigh. It was also tight over my newly sprouted breasts and scratchy on the nipples, a sensation I found disconcertingly erotic.

Taking no chances that I might partner the wrong man by mistake, Polydorus was at my side before I even reached the stairs, but I would have known him by his height and leanness even if I had not made his mask myself. He was wearing nothing else except a skimpy loincloth, very tight because he had hips like a snake. It had a furry tail hanging down behind and an odd little bump in the front.

"Will you dance with a stranger, lady?" he demanded, wrapping a ropy arm around my neck.

"I will drink with you, my lord."

Glued together, we went down the stairs and out through the portico into a night full of flaming torches and staring eyes. Everyone knew me, even Mother and her cronies beaming down from the balcony. Had I been on my own, I might have fled back indoors or at least slunk along at the tail end of the procession, but Polydorus propelled me to the front so we could lead the way out through the gates to join the twinkle of lights coming from the town.

The priest of Dionysus was Titios, master of the king's vineyards. He performed the sacrifice to the god and emptied the first amphora into the great krater while the last rose glow of sunset faded and the bonfires grew bright. I remember the burning anticipation in Polydorus's eyes as we shared our first bowl of wine and honey. However nervous I may have been, I was flattered to be the cause of so much desire, and Dionysus soon washed away any scruples I had not lost already.

Things became fuzzy after the second bowl and positively discontinuous after the third. Polydorus made sure I drank much more than my share, but I did not care. We sang and we danced. He was agile and spirited, more forceful than graceful, all long limbs, whirling me around like a banner. He had very large hands—and that evening at least six of them. They were everywhere, but the same pawings and fondlings were going on all around us. The night was full of wine and laughter and prying fingers. When at last he scooped me up in his arms, both of us panting and slickly wet from our exertions, I made absolutely no protest at all. I put a hand in his sweaty hair and pulled his head down to kiss. This dislodged his mask so that he almost rammed me into a tree. He was not nearly as drunk as I was.

He stretched me out on the grass in the shadows, and I pulled him on top of me, where he belonged. His mouth tasted of wine. At sixteen a prince knows what he is doing. Only impatience made him clumsy, and that mattered little, because I was just as eager. He had me stripped before the first kiss ended, so I pushed down his loincloth to discover what had been causing that eye-catching bulge all evening. It *did* feel like a parsnip, a very large parsnip, hot from a stew pot but definitely not softened by long boiling. He moaned and took my action as a signal to make haste. By the time I had located some unspun hemp and a couple of onions down there, he was wriggling himself between my legs and I had to let go. I spread my knees, he entered me in one long push, and that was that. Well, after a few minutes' strenuous thrusting and some low wails, that was that. Nothing much to it. It says a lot for my own eagerness that his entry caused me no discomfort. Many men in future years were to put a wick in my lamp, but I don't think any of them ever used me faster than Polydorus did that first time.

"I wish we'd found a bed to do this in," I grumbled, trying to hide my disappointment. "I'm going to be picking twigs out of my back for months."

He just lay on top of me, panting. He was much heavier than he looked.

"Dancing!" I twisted violently as I recalled Mother's words. "We must go and dance!"

I think Polydorus knew my reasons, because he struggled to his knees and fumbled around in the grass to find our discarded rags and masks. Soon we were back in the noise and the crowd by the bonfires, bounding and leaping again. I felt a cold trickle of relief run down my thighs.

So it went: drinking, dancing, singing, kissing. The second time he bore me off to the darkness, he was more deliberate and showed off tricks he had learned to pleasure a woman. For his age, he was extremely skilled. With lips and teeth and tongue, he worked me over from mouth and ears to breasts and thighs and then to regions I had never expected him to explore so closely. Eventually he arrived at the gem Ctimene referred to as my sealstone, for it was not unlike the carved carnelian of my ring. Playing his tongue on that, he raised me to new heights of rapture, soaring higher than Olympus, only to be struck down by thunderbolts of ecstasy. I writhed and moaned in delight.

When the storms had passed, I was lying in the weeds of the royal vineyard, soaked in sweat, half dead and yet convinced that there was something to this mating business after all. The kind young man still working busily between my legs deserved some reward. I stroked his hair.

"That was very nice. Thank you."

He stopped what he was doing and slithered up me to kiss my lips. "You want to try?" he asked hopefully.

"Show me how!" Drunk as I was, I would have tried anything that night. Polydorus instructed me in the best way to peel a parsnip and made very encouraging noises as I practiced. Then I grew venturesome and learned that one must not be too rough with the onions. When he had recovered, he said he forgave me, but he went back on top after that.

The third time, close to dawn, we were filled with the madness of the god and roamed no farther than the edge of the firelight, in among all the other writhing or sleeping couples. We experimented on each other and tried many of the things we could see others doing. At the end, as I crouched with my face in the grass and Polydorus straining on my back, I remembered Mother's words about a cat. Well, cats are smart and know what they're about. That position is not dignified, but no position is dignified, and it does have advantages—Polydorus's hands had free rein to fondle my breasts and groin, and his parsnip thrust deeper inside me than ever. I also liked the way those onions of his swung against me with every stroke.

I climaxed first, then he did. We tumbled to the ground and rolled into each other's arms, exhausted and replete. "Wonderful," I whispered. "More?"

"Impossible!"

A harsh voice said, "Move over, boy, and let the men try."

I squealed, shocked suddenly almost sober. There were three of them standing there looking at us with their spears of manhood raised—big and hairy and utterly in the madness of the god. Polydorus went from limp rope to raging lion in an instant. Uttering a war cry that must have been audible in Thebe, he sprang to his feet and attacked. They were all shorter than he, but older and thicker   sailors or woodsmen. Yes, they were drunk, but they must have had experience of brawling, and at those odds he should have had no chance, a willow against three oaks. He won by sheer ferocity. He smashed one in the face with a rock, kicked a second in the phallus, and jabbed fingers in the third one's eyes. Knocking that one's legs from under him, Polydorus went down on top—still screaming—and proceeded to hammer the ground with the man's head. I am sure he would have killed him had other men not hauled him off his victim.

That concluded the night's festivities. The three crippled assailants were carried away, and Polydorus escorted me back to the palace. We had lost our masks, so that everyone knew who we were and the story would spread everywhere. Ashamed and subdued, I would not even let him hold my hand, but he hugged me to him with a sweaty arm I could not shake off. Worst of all, he kept laughing at what he had done and rehearsing aloud how he would boast of it to his brothers.

He had taught me what a man did with a woman, and that I had enjoyed greatly, but he had also given me my first lesson in the distinction Father had tried to explain to Enops—the difference between an ordinary man and a trained killer.

9

Father had been right, Mother had been right, and I had been most horribly wrong.

I never felt worse in my life than I did that morning. The outside of my body was a disaster of scratches, bite marks, and nettle rash; but the inside of my head was worse, a festering midden pit. No matter how much paint Ctimene's trembling hands spread on my face, it remained stubbornly green. Swathed in the most all-enveloping winter gown I possessed, I tottered down to attend the farewell gift giving. Mother glanced at me briefly, then looked away—hiding smiles, I am sure.

I stood alongside my parents in the shadowy megaron, very glad I did not have to sit on anything, registering little of what was happening. A skeleton court had assembled around the walls, a few lesser folk on the balcony. The sons of Priam stood before the throne, strong warriors completely undiminished by their exertions in the night. Grinning, both of them!

The only thing I could see was Polydorus's blazing satisfaction. Even standing still, he was strutting. Mestor kept smirking proudly at his lion cub protégé. A victory over commoners would not normally be a source of pride—would be beneath mention, in fact—but one boy defeating three men and emerging unscathed was laudable. Even to me it seemed so by then. Sometime in the brief interval since I had returned to the palace and collapsed on my bed, I had forgiven Polydorus his homicidal defense of me. He was exactly what Maera had told me I needed, a powerful defender.

Worse still. Battered and sore as I was, I wanted more, much more. I wanted as much of Polydorus as I could get, but now he was leaving. Mother had warned me that I would get burned. I stared at him in silent appeal: *Ask me again!* I thought. *Ask me just once and I will accept. Gladly will I let you carry me off to Troy—right now if you want. I will risk the worst the Greeks can do if I can just be with you always.*

He wasn't going to ask. Polydorus was having second

thoughts. Mother had summed him up perfectly—that was why she had encouraged me to go with him to the Dionysia. Having satisfied his curiosity about the Amazon princess, he had lost all interest in a betrothal.

Father presented Mestor with a truly royal treasure, a gold drinking cup of Cretan make, embossed with octopuses.

"And for your honored brother, my lord," he continued, "because we had to disappoint him in his quest, much as we were ennobled by it, I have here a bronze dagger." It didn't look like much of a gift to me, and Polydorus raised his beautiful eyebrows in surprise. "This, my lords, was won by your great ancestor Tros in battle against the Amazons and given by him . . ."

He went on to explain at great length how it had come to be in Lyrnessos. It looked to me extraordinarily like the dagger he wore when he went hunting, a battered old thing that he would not much mind losing, but Mestor and Polydorus had already become very excited at being given a relic so sacred. I tried to catch Mother's eye; it was elusive.

I awoke from my daze only briefly, looking up with a wild wrench of hope when Polydorus came striding forward and stood before me. He said something about guests not normally giving gifts to hosts but wanting me to have this. He held out a spindle of solid gold. It felt a little smaller than the spindle he had given me in the night, the one I wanted more of, but much heavier and ice-cold in my hand. I suppose he had brought it along as a betrothal present and felt I had earned it anyway. I gasped suitable thanks. He smiled politely and went back to Mestor's side. A month or so later I dropped it and it shattered, because it was only gilded pottery. He probably didn't know that, though.

We had no private farewells. As I watched him drive his brother's chariot out the gate, I remembered Helenus's dread prophecy about the sons of Priam, and my eyes flooded with tears.

BOOK FIVE

HECTOR

1

The dust from Mestor's chariot had barely settled before Bienor began demanding his coming-of-age celebration. Mother fussed for a few days and yielded when he threatened to call witnesses. He was presented with a chariot and the usual jewelry, and also a sword, which he wore from then on everywhere except in bath or bed—and I had my suspicions about the bed. Father made some vague remarks about warrior training in a year or two, but the truth was that we had no use for a juvenile third son. He was too young to be a fighter and showed none of Sphelos's fig-counting skills.

My fatally shattered heart healed. The Dionysia, far from creating scandal, had enhanced my stature. A son of Priam had wooed me; another had confirmed my status as an oracle; and then a god, probably Hermes, had rescued me from would-be rapists. Such at least was the popular belief and it seemed logical enough, although Polydorus would have been hurt at losing the credit. In sleepy little Lyrnessos, people tended to forget that royalty were a breed apart, but that incident reminded them I was the chosen of Potnia.

The olive harvest was soon upon us, and Mother, always willing to delegate anything requiring effort, graciously allowed me to make the offerings to the Lady. I enjoyed doing so, but that was as far as I was prepared to go. As a child I had scrambled around in the boughs like a squirrel, whacking away with a stick to dislodge the fruit, but this now seemed beneath my dignity as princess and seer. Bienor wanted to agree with me, but the sight and sound of all the youngsters in the kingdom rollicking aloft were too much for his monkey instincts. Would anyone but my idiot brother have tried to harvest olives while wearing a baldric and sword? On the third day he tangled himself in the branches, lost his footing, and pitched headlong to the ground. According to the witnesses, he should have broken half the bones in his body, but he escaped without as much as a bruise.

Anticleia had dragged me down to the town before dawn to witness a birth, so I knew nothing about this miracle until after it was all over, including the thanksgiving ceremony in the grove. Some small boys brought the story to us just about the time the baby appeared, and I knew at once that this was *ominous*. At least it kept my mind off the bawling bloody birthing business. Feeling a niggling uncertainty, I went back to the palace and wandered around with Ctimene and Gorgon trailing behind. I arrived eventually at the stables, and there I ran into Bienor himself, now with a spear over his shoulder and dog at heel. He was wearing a predictable smug smirk, but sudden insight darkened the day as if the sun had dropped from the sky.

"Where are you going?" I yelled.

"Hunting." He sounded a little guilty as he said it, for although he could do very much as he pleased, he would undoubtedly want to take a friend or two along and their labor would be missed. He looked at me oddly. "What's troubling you?"

"An omen!"

"What omen?"

"You!" Everything slid into place, like the parts of a chariot being assembled. It was a year since I has seen the eagles, and I felt the same overweening apprehension I had sensed then, but now I had the experience and training to interpret the song the gods were singing. "Oh, Bienor!"

"Hades!" He was alarmed by whatever he saw in my face. "What's wrong? The goddess was kind to me this—"

"I heard. I'll show you. Ctimene, fetch food and wine!"

"Food, my lady?"

"Yes, food! Fruit, bread, cheese . . . Enough for three. Better make it four. And wine. Hurry! Come, Bienor."

I dashed into the shadowy carriage house, where the cars stood along the wall with their poles in the air. I grabbed the first wheel I could find and rolled it over to my own chariot.

Fortunately, it fitted quite well. I had never assembled a chariot before and would have made a complete mess of the job without Bienor's help. We slid the wheels on the axle, pinned them, tipped the shafts down, and attached neck straps to the yoke. I began to haul the rig to the door as he went to pick up his spear.

"Briseis? Are you going to pull that along the beach by yourself, or do you want horses?"

"We've got to go and meet someone and there isn't a moment to waste! Yes, of course we need horses!"

Even Bienor did not question my auguries now. He ran outside and bellowed for help. By the time Ctimene came panting back from the kitchens, carrying a hamper and accompanied by a boy bearing a jar, stable hands were harnessing Dancer and Whitefoot. The supplies went aboard and I jumped in. Hampered by his spear, Bienor was a fraction too late reaching for the reins.

"Off we go!" I shouted. "Ctimene, tell Mother to have a fat calf made ready for sacrifice."

Leaving the onlookers openmouthed, I set the team dashing for the gates. Gorgon and Griffin romped after us, barking excitedly. Half a dozen other dogs followed in noisy pursuit, but before long they all gave up and went home.

Bienor clutched his spear with one hand and the rail with the other, bouncing up and down on the webbing. "You going to tell me now?" He still was not as tall as I.

"No."

"Tell me what you saw, then."

"I saw you." I would tell him no more, for he would not understand. I had to show him. Bienor falling from a tree, Bienor with a spear.

The trip up the mountain was a strange echo of the previous year's journey when the two of us met Aeneas. With a little time in hand, we made the place I wanted—the high pasture at the edge of the forest. The highest ridge of Mount Ida wore the warm tints of autumn under a cloudless blue sky; here and there on its lower slopes, gold trees showed in among the pines. Perfect. I reined in.

"There! I'll set out the food and you hobble the horses."

"When horses are steaming like that they have to be walked."

Man stuff. "Walk them, then. That boulder will be our table. Er, lift out the wine for me, will you? Your arms are *much* stronger than mine."

"So are my wits."

By the time Bienor had seen to the horses, I had set out the meal on the boulder, tipped wine into a goblet, and arranged myself artistically on the grass with my skirts around me, wishing I had taken time to change into a more imposing dress. A year ago Daos had accompanied me to this meadow, and already I had almost forgotten what he looked like. The sun rolled on without noticing the absence of a mere slave. I don't suppose it will miss many of us when our turns come.

"This is very nice," my brother said sarcastically as he flopped down beside me. "Now tell me who." He reached for a handful of olives.

"It's bad manners not to wait for company."

He pouted, impressed by my self-confidence but not quite totally, finally, absolutely certain I was not having fun at his expense. "It can't be a lover or you'd come alone. A suitor? A party of woodcutters dragging logs down to the jetty?"

"Ah, you guessed. Six beautiful strong woodcutters."

He fingered his sword hilt uneasily. "Then who *are* we here to meet?"

"Fate."

"Real soothsayers don't drop mysterious hints! If you won't make a real prophecy, then how . . ." He lifted his head and listened. His eyes widened. "Not Aeneas again?"

"No, not Aeneas. Well, Aeneas may be with him."

Aeneas was not. The chariot that came rolling out of the trees carried only the one man I expected. He had grown so much that I hardly recognized him, but Bienor did, right away. With a yell, he was on his feet and running. Realizing that my artistic wood-nymph pose was not going to be noticed, I jumped up also and ran to join the melee.

So Enops returned to Lyrnessos and was understandably surprised to find us waiting for him. For several minutes there was much excited, three-way hugging, while we all told one another how much we had grown. Bienor explained airily how proficient I had become as a seer, as if he deserved the credit himself. When we all calmed down and the boys had attended to the horses, we settled ourselves around the repast on the boulder, but at first we talked much more than we ate.

Enops had grown not only taller but also broader, thicker, and hairier. He sported a real beard and a hard, weathered look. His nose had been broken; he had scars. He was not quite the brother I remembered—we had a warrior in the family.

"I'm home for a couple of days," he said. "I must be back before the snows come." With no visible effort to appear modest, he added, "I'm doing very well."

Bienor and I made admiring noises.

He flexed an arm to show us the muscle. "I can handle an eight-cubit spear and run the track in full armor. I came second in a chariot race last month and threw four men in succession in wrestling, most of them bigger than me." For a moment the old Enops grinned out at us. "The fifth one spread me like dung, but he's big as a cyclops! I can throw a javelin eight-two paces. That's very good."

Bienor was looking appropriately impressed.

"And hit the target, of course. Doesn't count if you miss. I was in Troy last month—"

"Troy!" I exclaimed. "What is Troy like?"

He shrugged. "Crowded. Too many people squashed into too little space. But rich . . . impressive in its way, I suppose. Akamas son of Antenor won his tassels, and we all went to the shrine of Athena so he could swear his oath. Then he—"

I insisted on hearing more about Troy.

Impatiently Enops said, "The town is nothing, just a lot of shacks like Lyrnessos, only more of them, but the citadel . . . that's splendid—smooth stone walls, bottom half cambered and top half straight up and down . . . the palace at the top . . . When you reach the Scaian Gate there's the Great Tower of Ilium on your left with the gods displayed before it—Apollo and Athena, Zeus, Poseidon, and, um, a couple of others. And on the right is the house of sacrifice—"

"Outside the walls?"

"Of course! Gods needn't hide behind walls. Akamas sacrificed a white heifer there, but he swore his oath before the Palladium in the palace. . . . He's a knight now." He paused meaningfully. "That's why I had to come back."

I could rely on Bienor to ask the required question.

"Why?"

"Because," Enops explained offhandedly, "Aeneas needs a new charioteer. He takes whoever's best."

"*You*?" Bienor squealed.

"I'm his first choice, he says. It depends on the gifts I offer, but I'm sure Father has enough in his treasure room to satisfy even the son of Anchises."

"That's a tremendous honor!" Bienor's eyes grew big as sea urchins at the thought of being brother of the charioteer of the leader of the Dardanian host.

Clearly Enops did not disagree. "Yes, it is. The others were so jealous I thought they were going to strangle me; but Aeneas said I'd done much better than anyone expected of me, better even than the Dardanians of my age—and they cut their milk teeth on swords. When I first got there, a lot of them tried picking on me, until I taught them to do it in pairs. He says he'll make a knight of me in another year. That's very fast."

Strangely, the real Enops, the one I loved, was still faintly visible inside the hulking braggart. This was the sort of brother I needed now. I waited for Bienor to see the door opening for him, but he just sat and stared with the dumb longing of a starving dog.

Enops glowed when he talked about the war. "There's no doubt now! Agamemnon's been recruiting all over the Aegean. He's offering gold, making threats, calling in favors, whipping his vassals into line. Every free lance in Greece has found a lord. They'll gather next summer at Aulis and sail from there for Troy. It's going to be a big, big war!"

"What about Aeneas?" I asked. "Will he fight?"

The pot went off the boil. "Pass the wine. He still hasn't committed us—the Dardanians, I mean."

"He wants to be Trojan host leader, doesn't he?"

"And so he should be! He has far more experience than Hector."

Bienor looked horrified. "He won't fight for the Greeks, surely?"

"He says," Enops explained with care, "that he will wait and see what the Greeks do. He says he may not fight at all, as long as no one attacks us—Dardania, I mean."

Good for him, I thought, but I had the sense not to say it.

"But I think he's just bluffing. He's a fighter. He'll fight!"

Then Bienor demanded to know more of what Enops had been doing, and was given a long list of what I considered horrible experiences—sleeping on the ground and drinking out of ditches, pitching tents and tending horses, running for days and nights on end. Broken bones were involved, too, and scars displayed. There was also much talk of weapons and horses and chariots, none of which interested me at all, and of men being killed in training.

"That's awful!" I wailed.

"Women!" Bienor said scornfully, although he was looking queasy himself.

Enops displayed a manly tolerance. "Dear little sister! When a warrior goes into battle, he must be able to trust his comrades. He can't depend on some ninny who'll faint at the sight of blood or run away from a war cry. Facing danger is a necessary part of the learning. Real danger—there isn't any other kind."

"I'd rather hear about Troy! What does Athena look like? And what oath did Akamas swear?"

"The oath all knights take, of course. A knight's daughter should know that."

I did not ask if he had known it before he left. "Then you'd better tell me quickly."

"He swears to be hungry for glory and be always at the front in battle. He swears to respect the honor of his leader and his own followers, and to grant his foes the proper rites, not just leave them for the dogs."

It sounded like nonsense to me, because who was to say where honor became arrogance or stupidity? But Bienor sucked it all up like a calf at a cow's teat, growing more and more wistful. Finally, when Enops set to work on the food, he asked the question I had been waiting for.

"Can I come back with you?"

Enops shrugged and looked him over critically, chewing.

"The war's coming!" Bienor protested. "I know it'll be over before I'm old enough to be even a charioteer like you, but I ought to learn something! I can at least be a spearman."

"You're growing fast," Enops conceded, clearly tempted by the thought of having a minion of his own to boss around. "Will Father allow it?"

"Maybe. He did mention something about—"

"No, he won't," I said, "because Mother will scream like a branded cat."

Bienor groaned, not disputing my analysis.

I said what the gods required of me. "Don't ask."

"What?"

"Don't even mention it. When Enops leaves, I'll cover your tracks for an hour or two. By then you'll be gone over Mount Ida."

Enops laughed. Bienor lunged over to hug me. Thus we hatched our conspiracy before our parents even knew that their warrior son had returned. When he left, two days later, bearing many rich gifts for Aeneas, Bienor was driving. Our fates are spun when we are born.

2

That winter the Archer sent a sickness. To most it brought no more trouble than a brief fever, but many children died, as children always do, and many of the elderly perished also. Great-Aunt Melite was one of the first to go. Klymene, although she showed no symptoms, took to her bed and pined, refusing all comfort, and her shade soon followed her sister's. We gave them lavish funeral rites to help them find their way through the baleful realm of Chthonia to the Fortunate Land beyond. Enops and Bienor and now the aunts— the family was shrinking fast.

Mother was not. She complained all the time how difficult it was for her to get into her gowns. Father was perniniently short of breath.

And I? I stood in for Mother at many of the festivals, excluding the major rituals in which Potnia was manifest, of course. I suppose I was growing more mature. I had outgrown my childish dreams of being snatched away by some wealthy, handsome knight to some haven beyond the seas. If the gods intended me to be booty for a Greek slaver, then that was how it would be. My only comfort was that so far they had not told me so—I had not found my own name in the portents.

Waiting for trouble is usually worse than dealing with it. Ares' dread shadow hung over the Troad like the smoke of a forest fire. No more news could arrive until spring opened the highways of the sea, and we all feared that then reality might outrun it. In even the worst weather, Sphelos pushed work on the rampart, which was becoming quite imposing.

War did not come winging in with the butterflies, but it did send an unexpected inactivity, the sort of uneasy hush that precedes a storm. The Aegean had been stripped of shipping, so our beach lay empty. Sphelos fretted like a new mother. How could we survive without tin and copper to make bronze? The Dardanians' hides had all gone to make armor. What could we offer when ships did come?

If the beaches were unused, the roads were not. The nobility of the Troad had sat uneasy by their hearths all winter. At the first sign of better weather, the leaders of the cities and tribes succumbed to an urge to consult one another, and the first to announce that he would be arriving at our gates was Pollis son of Eëtion, bound for Pedasos.

When I heard the news, I felt a stab of excitement. I found

Mother enthroned in the bathtub like a gigantic heap of white cheese, her hair wrapped in a red cloth.

"My lady," I said, on my best behavior, "I suspect we are about to have noble visitors in the near future."

"Omens?" she demanded nervously.

"No omens. But don't you think it's time you appointed some new bath attendants?"

They were a vital part of the household, chosen from the youngest and loveliest of the slaves. Ctimene bathed me now, but no person of any importance at all ever bathed without an attendant. Mother was being sponged by Philona and Pero was waiting to oil her.

She bounced her chins in approval. "Meaning you, of course?" Her eyes twinkled knowingly.

"Among others."

"Yes, it is a necessary part of your education, and I suppose you are almost old enough now. Amphitrite is getting past it, and some of the others are attending to other duties."

The remark certainly included Pero, who was visibly pregnant, by unknown means. I don't mean a god had visited her. Pero was very popular and just sighed vaguely when asked to name the father.

"Whom do you suggest?" Mother chuckled. "A pity we can't ask Bienor. He displayed an eye for beauty."

My, but she was in a good mood, today! I had not realized she had been so nosy about my brother's philandering.

"He would probably suggest Polydamma and Amphidora. He entertained Kopi seven or eight times."

"Kopi? Oh, yes. Poor teeth, nice figure! Yes, well I shall demonstrate the necessary techniques." She meant in a month or two, when she got around to it.

"I don't need to be shown how— Demonstrate on a real *man*, you mean?"

"You would prefer a yearling calf?"

I felt mildly disgusted by the prospect. Performing a holy ritual with a nobly born stranger was an intriguing prospect, but playing body servant for some gossipy palace menial had much less appeal, especially if it had to be done under her watchful eye. "I believe I can manage without . . . Whom could we use as a subject?"

"Your brother, of course."

I think I managed to keep my face straight as I said, "Oh, of course." Sphelos would be outraged! It would have been more fun to torment Bienor, though. I missed him.

"Soon, Mother! Very soon."

Panic flared in her eyes. "Visitors? Who?"

I told her the news about Pollis, and she exploded out of tub like a surfacing whale.

Later that very same day, I was instructed in ritual bathing.

The royal bathroom was a bright and spacious place, richly decorated with frescoes of a slightly mildewed Potnia accepting offerings from a line of diminutive worshipers. As well as the great terra-cotta tub, it contained jars, stools, shelves, and a wide, low bench in the center.

Sphelos did not approve of his new assignment at all, and it took a thunderbolt from Father to bring him. When he arrived, Mother was fussing with towels, scents, bottles of oil, freshly aired garments, humming cheerfully as if this rehearsal was to be a treat she had not enjoyed since childhood. I smiled a welcome. He stood with his back to the wall and glared. Kopi, Polydamma, and Amphidora were still hurrying in and out with jars of hot water, making the place steamy. They were all about my age, all very pretty, and not one of them came up to my shoulders.

"Just about ready, dear." Mother sniffed doubtfully at a flask.

He glowered harder. "If I must be shamed before my sister, I must, but you don't need these slaves present, do you?"

"We don't, dear," she said brightly, "but you do. If your member becomes febrific, you want to be able to blame that on someone other than Briseis, don't you?"

Sphelos's face became somewhat febrific and I suffered an unfortunate paroxysm of coughing.

At length Mother professed herself satisfied with the depth and temperature of the water. She folded her fat hands and assumed her most queenly expression.

"Close the door, child," she told Kopi. "Now, you all understand that we are not concerned with ordinary bathing but a holy ritual of welcome? This is much more than a wash. It is a consecration, an offer of unstinted hospitality, symbolizing the guest's acceptance by the goddess of the house."

We all nodded. When the visitor was of high rank and the house included a nubile and unmarried daughter, that was her honor and duty. I was looking forward to serving Potnia in this enjoyable way.

"You have arrangements to make before the subject arrives," Mother continued, ignoring Sphelos. "Fill the bath, of course, and check that the water is hot. Have spare hot and cold on hand. And the usual supplies: oil, towels, and so on. Clean fleeces on the bench, at least a double layer. Prepare yourselves properly. Wash all the important parts. Rinse your mouth with mint, to freshen the breath. We have some here." She took down a bottle and passed it around. "And perfume—a little in the armpits helps, but nowhere else. When a man has his eyes shut, he likes to know he's nuzzling a woman, not a rosebush."

I may have blushed a little. Sphelos coughed harshly.

"Some men prefer to remove their own clothes, others enjoy assistance, so be attentive to his wants. Briseis, undress your brother. Don't leer!"

"Let's see how big the problem is," I said, reaching for the hem of Sphelos's tunic.

"*Briseis!* We are rehearsing a holy ritual. You are a servant of the goddess. You do not make vulgar jokes. You do not speak at all unless the subject indicates he wishes to make conversation with you."

Sphelos sneered agreement.

She waited until he had climbed into the tub. "Now you change into one of these. Turn your back modestly, but stand where he can see you without having to crane his neck. One at a time, so I can watch how you move."

She gave me the first girdle, a golden cord embellished with many dangling strings. The tassels swayed suggestively with every move I made, slithering against my thighs. It made me slink, and I felt a thousand times more naked than

I did in nothing at all. The girls tried not to snigger as they watched me, but I sniggered at them in turn, when I saw the belts affecting them in the same way.

"Very good," Mother said. "Move proudly. Men usually find a garment like that stimulating. Now, begin by sponging the subject's back."

Wishing I had a really coarse brush handy, I approached the subject.

"You look like a wood nymph," Sphelos said sarcastically, no doubt implying that I was built like an oak.

Oak or not, he did not raise his ax to me during the demonstration nor to any of the others, not even when he was flat on the bench and Mother was instructing us in the tricky maneuver of Oiling the Thighs. Girls did not have that effect on him.

"And that's all." Mother sighed, when we reached his toes. "Except for dressing him. If you get to that stage without being interrupted, then you have failed completely."

I could have done worse than Pollis of Thebe for my first essay in ritual bathing, but I could have done better, too. Youngest of Eëtion's seven sons, he was not very much older or more experienced than I was—plumpish in spite of his youth, a fair-skinned blond with a scant ginger beard and copper-colored pubic hair. His reactions were more conventional than Sphelos's. The heat of the water turned his smooth body bright pink and made even his nipples stand up. I had hardly started drying him, let alone begun oiling, when he moaned that he could wait no longer and took charge of proceedings.

I struggled at first, protesting that he was in too much of a hurry; but he was insistent, pressing me down on the bench and prying my legs apart. I winced at his entry, but once the initial discomfort passed, I quite enjoyed the absurd romp. When I sensed that he was going as fast as possible, I let out a few discreet gasps and raked my nails along his back— techniques Mother had suggested. Instantly he went into spasms of joy and squirted his holy offering into me under Potnia's stony gaze. When we had recovered, we went back to the tub and began all over again, but even his second venture did not raise me to the giddy heights of pleasure I had known with Polydorus.

On being formally introduced at the feast that evening, Pollis and I both blushed hotter than Helios, but nobody paid any attention. Mother had warned me that that might happen the first few times.

Poor Pollis! A few months after that he married the obnoxious Chryseis. He died when Achilles sacked Thebe.

I had a few anxious days of waiting after this initiation, for I had no wish to become a mother yet, although a child of Eëtion's noble line would have been a welcome and honored addition to the family. Many children conceived in such couplings have been confidently attributed to Hermes, most mischievous of the Olympians and much given to taking on the guise of a mortal traveler. I was confident that the god had not so honored me, though, for his technique would surely have been more polished than Pollis's.

Soon after, Elatos of Pedasos paid a return call on Thebe and came by way of Lyrnessos. He was accompanied by, and a little too attentive to, his charming young stepmother, Queen Alcandre.

I had found that towering, melancholy man intimidating even at a public banquet; he also seemed old to me, although he could not have been much over thirty. I was apprehensive when he closed the door and the two of us were alone in the steamy bathroom. He did not smile or speak, just stood and looked at me expectantly with his deep-set black eyes until I realized he expected me to undress him. He was heavily muscled and excessively hairy; but my worries eased slightly when I observed that his manhood was as small as a toddler's, a ludicrously small decoration on a man of his size, almost completely hidden in his black pubic jungle. I had little to fear from that, I decided.

He spoke not a word during the bathing and drying, and it showed no signs of interest either, although I toweled him vigorously, as Mother had recommended. He lay down so I could oil his furry back. When he rolled over, I was astonished to see he now possessed a completely adequate tumescent phallus. He must have been watching for my reaction, because he chuckled and spoke for the first time.

"You were disappointed, weren't you?" His hand stroked the back of my thigh.

I was thrown into confusion. "Oh no, my— I mean, I don't know what you mean, my lord." I tipped oil into the forest on his chest and began to spread it, not meeting his eye.

"You can't judge a warrior in peacetime."

"My lord?"

"Nor a sword until it's drawn. However much men's weapons vary in size normally, they're usually much the same when they're excited." His fingers untied my girdle and explored the small of my back. "You will let me couple with you later?"

"I shall be honored to please you." I was being brave, although Aphrodite was starting to whisper encouragement in my ear.

He chuckled again. "We'll see what an old man can do, then. Don't stop. You're doing splendidly. Beat me as hard as you like, I won't break."

While I kneaded his pectorals, his hand cupped my breast. When I rubbed his nipples, he rubbed one of mine. He let me complete the oiling, all the way to his feet—even his toes had hairs on them. By then he was sitting up, so he could stroke me as I worked on his legs.

"I am ready," he said. "Are you willing?"

I lowered my eyes humbly, a pose which let me admire his warrior, which was definitely full-grown now and poised for battle, with its purplish blade peering out from the sheath. "Very willing, my lord."

"Bring a comb."

Surprised, I fetched a tortoiseshell comb. He pulled me onto his lap and began to comb out my hair, a procedure I found to be astonishingly sensual under those circumstances. He kissed my ears and nibbled my neck. He tickled and teased me all over, one minute enthusing about the size and firmness of my breasts and the next sucking daintily on my toes. He made me feel desirable and beautiful and not at all overgrown, for he was a big man. He taught me many things—I learned more in two hours from Elatos than I had in a night under Polydorus. He taught me how men's body hair can excite women's nipples. He taught me to restrain my own joy, keeping some of it for later so that I could find rapture a dozen times in a single night, if I had a partner with enough stamina. Elatos himself had amazing stamina. He worked me long and hard on that bench, leaving me weary and tender, but enormously satisfied with my new ability to inspire a partner. When I slipped the tunic on him at the end, I saw that his warrior had fled back into the jungle, tinier than ever.

We met formally that evening in the megaron. This time I was confident I was not blushing and felt rather smug in consequence. Alas, only moments later I sat down a little faster than was prudent and could not restrain a wince. Queen Alcandre raised her eyebrows very high, causing my cheeks to burst into flame.

"My stepson speaks highly of you, child."

I took a quick glance around, but no one seemed to be listening. "He is an upstanding warrior. I have never met a man who impressed me so deeply."

She regarded me over the rim of her wine goblet with eyes of ice. "Neither have I."

She couldn't possibly mean that, could she?

"He's a human ram, but he does have his limits, and you have ruined my plans for the evening." Alcandre's smile had the slow menace of a cat unwinding. "I tried him a little while ago, and he's as limp as kelp on a beach."

"But he's your stepson!"

"And more."

I took a very long drink of wine. It didn't help. When I finished, she was still as smug and I felt like a snubbed child.

"What if your husband finds out?"

"He can't do anything about it." She smirked. "Or instead of. If he makes trouble, the host will back Elatos."

I found this incredible. "Cuckolded by his own son?"

Amused, she shrugged. "Why not? If anything comes of it, then better a grandchild than some stranger's spawn."

I had no more answer than King Altes had.

Alcandre chuckled and patted my hand. "I don't see why men should have all the fun. Did you enjoy tussling with my big hairy stallion?"

"Very much," I admitted.

"I look forward to tomorrow." She smiled. "I don't expect Thebe will match you, dear."

"Kind of you to say so," I replied stiffly.

Elatos departed the following morning. I never met him again, but I did have dealings with Alcandre.

Our third visitor that spring was old Anchises, son of Capys, father of Aeneas and Hippodemia, king emeritus of the Dardanians, who arrived as soon as the snow cleared from the high country. He was a spry old rascal yet, although his eyesight was failing badly. Mother refused to let me attend him, and I had to agree that it might not be quite proper, for I had known him as an honorary uncle all my life. She assigned Kopi to him, and Kopi told me later that he acquitted himself with distinction, in spite of his age.

Ever since Father came to the Troad as a penniless free lance, Anchises had been his closest friend. In the days that followed, the two of them slaughtered many a jar of wine together, doubtless reliving old times and scorning the new. They did not deign to tell me what conclusions they reached.

I had no forewarning of those visits. Do not think that my life was an unending torrent of omens. I might not see anything portentous for months or think of the impending war for days on end. At those times I was merely a rather lonely fifteen year old, ruefully watching the girls I had played with in my childhood bearing children to husbands not much older.

The summer heat came; ships did not. Rumors flew thicker than midges, and the only one of them that was true was that the Greeks were assembling a fleet.

During the barley harvest, the Pelasgian host leader, Hippothoös son of Lethos, came through Lyrnessos and was granted the welcome due his rank. He was impressive in a bullnecked, barrel-chested way, but curt and seriously lacking in finesse. He seemed to tackle every assignment with the same frenzied zest he would have applied to storming a city, and that included me.

No sooner had he returned to Larisa, though, than his young brother Pylaios decided to make offerings to Smintheus at Killa and call in at Lyrnessos on the way. He had dazzling charm and a lot of ripply bronze muscle. I persuaded him to stay on for a few more days, and I am sure he would have tarried even longer had Mother not intervened to chase him away. She told me afterward that she did not like Pelasgians, but she really meant bachelors.

3

Our last and most important royal guest that summer arrived soon after Pylaios's departure. After visiting his father-in-law in Thebe, he called at Lyrnessos bringing twenty-one brothers with him. In all, his train comprised forty-four knights and charioteers plus two hundred armed nobodies who camped in the orchards. Many of the brothers or half brothers I had met at Pedasos were included, although not Helenus, to my regret. For three days, the palace swarmed with warriors. I could not turn a corner without meeting appreciative male stares, a situation I found very tolerable.

I intended to hate Hector for usurping Aeneas's rightful place as Trojan host leader. I could even blame him for the war itself, because Priam would certainly have had to send Helen packing if Hector had not taken her side in the debate. I discovered that the prince was a difficult man to hate. He was not an easy man to like, either. Admire, possibly.

Hector was a very different brother. That he was big went

without saying. Whether he was handsome or not was a matter of taste—most women thought he was. He was certainly well built, meaty and powerful with a curly black beard and hirsute limbs and chest, which I ritually washed for him. He had conventional male reactions. Indeed he raised his spear in salute to me twice—first when I was bathing him and then while he lay on the bench being rubbed, pummeled, and anointed. I was very eager for the honor by then. Women's responses are less conspicuous than men's, but more than the steamy air was dampening my thighs.

He spoke not a word until I inquired demurely which tunic appealed to him. He said, "This one!" and quickly draped it across his lap, as if I might not have noticed his arousal yet. Then he thanked me for my ministrations and said he would attend to his own dressing.

Dismissed! Spurned! He did not even seem to realize how greatly he was insulting me—and not only me, but Lyrnessos and its goddess also. I wrapped my chiton around me and departed, slamming the door. One of his brothers told me later that Hector was fanatically loyal to his wife and never slept with another woman, even slaves. I cannot imagine how any woman could be selfish enough to find such unnatural restraint commendable.

I went striding back to my room and snapped at Ctimene all the time she was helping me prepare for dinner.

I observed Hector throughout the three days of his visit and still did not feel I knew him when he left. He was kingly, yes, but royal demeanor did not come easily to him. He wore his rank like a mantle, hiding his own skin. It became a game for me to watch for glimpses of the real Hector behind the clouds, but I doubt I ever saw it. That his followers adored him was obvious, although they were strangely inclined to talk back to him. A couple of times someone in his retinue provoked a blaze of temper from him, and the culprit would flinch like a child before a father's wrath; yet when he spoke of his wife and her new baby, hard bronze melted to soft gold. He also said a few things that seemed out of place in the mouth of a warlord, hints of modesty and compassion that did not belong there, defects he tried to suppress.

I was formally presented in the megaron before the feasting began. Mother had cautioned me repeatedly that I was no longer a stubble-headed child who could get away with cuteness, so I was determined to be on my very best behavior.

But Hector did not play fair. Amid an audience of brothers, he clasped my hands in his and proclaimed, "The famous Briseis? Oh, I have heard much of you, my lady! Paris claimed that you were terrible as Hera. Helenus said you were as wise as Athena. Polydorus compared you to Aphrodite. But now I see the maiden Artemis."

His followers whooped at such wit. Father swelled with pride and Mother stared at me anxiously. I blushed, but mainly with annoyance, for I had already sensed that Hector was a humorless man. He had prepared that speech in advance, and the reference to the virgin goddess might be a sneering reminder that he had scorned my charms in the bathroom.

"You are too kind, my lord," I replied. "But the sons of Priam are outshone only by the sons of Zeus. I saw the noble Paris ride in on storm waves like Lord Poseidon. Helenus has the wisdom of Apollo, while Polydorus is as nimble as Hermes himself. And now I behold Ares."

Hector thought that over. "Poseidon is not a son of great Zeus," he objected, but then he thanked me for the compliment. My parents relaxed; the formalities were resumed.

While the food was being brought around, I overheard him lecturing Father on strategy, although many of the palace officials were listening: "There are only two places the Greeks can land at Troy: they must either round Cape Sigeum to enter the bay or come ashore at Besik and save themselves a long, hard row. It doesn't matter which beach they choose, because I have stationed signal beacons at every lookout. Wherever Agamemnon decides to land, we shall be there, waiting for him. We have chariots by the hundred, plus cavalry, and if he manages to bring more than a dozen pairs of horses with him, I shall eat them raw. He can't possibly beach every ship at the same moment, so we can concentrate our attack. I tell you, son of Mydon, that I shall be astonished if one solitary Greek walks out of the surf alive."

Father replied blandly that this was very encouraging news.

After the meal came the informal pause when people rose and walked about, when the servants cleared away the big tables and guests slipped out to relieve themselves. Then Hector harangued Mother on the subject of Aeneas. "It is true that he is a mighty fighter, but we are both of the line of Dardanos, and I excel in such arts myself. I would cheerfully stake my life in single combat against the son of Anchises."

A couple of lesser Trojans growled agreement.

The feast was going well, and Mother had drunk more wine than she normally did. She was in an unexpectedly relaxed and benevolent mood, pinker than usual all the way from the oiled curls peeking out under her crown down to her painted nipples. She beamed. "Oh, surely that won't be necessary?"

"I hope not, for his sake." Hector could be absurdly pompous at times. "Trojans and Dardanians are a single people, or nearly so. With his stubborn posturing, Aeneas puts his own glory ahead of the welfare of his people. He is either a coward or a traitor or both."

"Woe, woe!" Mother said politely. "He did explain all his reasoning to me, but I'm afraid that most of it went right over my foolish woman's head. I have the feeling he intimated his belief that a decision pro or con at the present time might possibly be premature."

"He need only choose between honor and cowardice."

"Surely the experienced warrior never reveals his intentions prematurely? Is not circumspection a virtue?"

Finding himself backed into an indefensible corner, Hector changed the subject.

Later still at that same banquet, he made another speech, an official Oration From the Leader for everyone to hear. He had probably said the same in Thebe and would again in Pedasos, Larisa, and wherever else he was to visit on his tour.

"So the Greeks are coming? Let them come! We have firewood in abundance for their pyres. We do not ask for war, nor do we fear it. Our shoulders are as strong as theirs, our spears as sharp, our hearts as brave. Justice and honor are ours. They come as pirates, seeking loot and booty, but we fight to defend our hearths and those dear to our hearts. We ply the Immortals with offerings as rich as any. For every chariot the Greeks can ship across the roaring seas, we can field a score. For every horse they bring, we have a hundred grazing on the hills. We have allies aplenty: Lycians, Lykians, Thracians, Mysians, Kikones, Carians, Kilikes, Leleges, Phrygians, and dozens more. If the Greeks expect an easy victory, they will be sadly disappointed! If they come for land, we shall give them graves. If they crave glory, we shall give them shame. If they long for everlasting fame, we shall carve their names on steles."

The megaron rocked with acclaim, although his companions must have heard it all before. Watching him sit down and take a drink, I concluded he was relieved to have got it over this time. I wondered who had composed the oration for him and how much of it he truly believed himself. Hector, I was beginning to think, always thought whatever he thought he ought to be thinking.

Later that evening, after the bard had sung his first couple of songs, I went outside briefly. Returning, I was waylaid in the portico by Lykaon. He was an older, thicker version of Polydorus, with a deep chest and a trim beard that was gold in some lights, bronze in others—an interesting instance of young royal Trojan.

"My lady Briseis!" He also had extraordinarily long lashes and knew how to use them.

"Prince Lykaon? I trust your quarters are satisfactory?" I retreated two paces.

Shaking his head, he advanced three. "No."

"No? Oh, well, the palace is very crowded and—" My back came into contact with a pillar. I had met this technique before somewhere.

He favored me with a steamy look that would have made

a fresco goddess climb higher up the wall. "Sharing with two of my brothers? How could your mother have inflicted such torment upon me, when there are vastly more appealing chambers available?"

"I cannot imagine what chambers you mean, my lord." He couldn't possibly expect . . . Of course he did; he was a son of Priam.

"Yours. I have already ascertained which is your door, so all I need to know is the secret knock required to gain admittance."

He was practically leaning on me by this time, and I could feel the heat from him. Rosewater and lavender . . . I stared up at his handsome leer in maidenly shock. "But that would be highly improper! I don't know what you are dreaming of!"

"I hope there is no misunderstanding, my lady? I am dreaming of removing your clothes, slowly and deliberately and completely. Of smothering you with kisses from your lips to your toes. Of sucking on these splendid nipples, at first gently, and then, as they rise under my caress, with increasing fervor and judicious nibbling. Of running my fingertips and mouth over every inch of your body without exception. Of easing my head into the fragrant bower between your thighs and applying my tongue there in skillful stimulation of your most sensitive organs until you cry out and thrash about in unbearable pleasure, enslaved and helpless before my lust. When I have raised you to a madness of passion, I shall mount you and manfully massage your deepest internal reaches with an appendage I brought along especially for that purpose. Furthermore, I shall continue to torment you in this fashion at frequent intervals throughout the entire night, without mercy."

"How lewd of you! You are just like your dear brother Polydorus."

"I taught him everything he knows, just as Hippothoös taught me. Polydorus, poor lad, is the last of us and has no one left to instruct—fortunately, because he never acquired much skill. Not by my standards."

Between the pillar at my back, his hands grasping my

shoulders, and the linen of his tunic against my nipples, I was somewhat short of room to breathe.

"Your interest is flattering, my lord, but there is no secret knock. I rarely bolt my door, because the bolt is so stiff."

"Very foolish! I'm sure I can thrust it home for you." His lips lightly brushed my cheek.

Obviously I must revise my plans. If I stayed around to supervise the bard, this son of Priam would rape me in public. "That might be advisable, with the palace so full of dangerous men. Are you sure you know the right door?"

"Fourth on the right?"

"No, no! That is Sphelos's room and best avoided. Why don't I show you, to avoid misunderstandings?"

"That may be safest," he said. We hurried upstairs. He slid the bolt very easily, but by then we were both on the inside and I was helpless. He did everything he had threatened to do and more. I suspected he was faking his fourth climax, but I had lost count of my own long before that, so I had no complaints. Lykaon more than made up for Hector's rudeness.

The following night I discovered that Priam's son number forty-five, the gangly Pammon, was even more talented. I met so few young men of my own rank that I had a lot of catching up to do.

I had only one private conversation with Hector, and that was on the last evening, just as the sun was setting. I had endured a miserable day. It had begun quite normally, but the heat soon became sultry and I was oppressed by omens. Twice I saw owls in broad daylight with the smaller birds ignoring them, which was bizarre. A crow mewed at me like a cat. Looking down at the shore, I became convinced that I could see bones washed up by the waves. I even sent a boy down to look, but he came back to report that he had found nothing except driftwood. I cursed him and slapped his face.

There was nowhere in the palace to be alone. Food tasted of ashes and wine of lye. I had rejected advances from no less than five sons of Priam, which shows how upset I was. Men do gossip.

By sunset, I had a pounding headache. I slipped out to the balcony and stared at the sea. There was no wind, just crushing, nauseating heat and a fluffy white squall to the east. Its trailing gray tendrils were ominous symbols of the Lord of Storm, its crest was red as blood. That was it, I decided—that was the culmination of the whole miserable day. If I could understand that storm, then I would know what the gods were telling me.

I heard footsteps but did not turn. Two hands joined mine on the railing, large, hairy hands. I tried to smile, but I expect the throb of pain in my head made the result grotesque. He did not seem to notice my distress. He mouthed a few platitudes about our hospitality before he got down to business.

"Last year I thought Polydorus was exaggerating, just a sprightly yearling feeling his first spring. Having met you, I think he is a better judge of women than even Paris."

I thanked him and went back to studying the storm.

"He seemed quite smitten with you. I do not wish to pry, my lady—" That meant he was about to pry. "—but I do wish both you and my father's youngest to find happiness. If the choice was yours, of course . . . What I mean is, I do have some influence, and if there is any way I can be of help, then you have only to ask."

Oh, the silly man! I forced my aching brain to concentrate on his maundering. He had not been told the whole story, obviously. He did not realize that Polydorus had obtained everything he wanted of me. This bumbling interference was Hector's idea of how an elder brother should try to help.

"My lord, will you forgive me if I speak plainly?"

"Please do. I despise people who tangle words to trip others."

"While I was enormously flattered by your brother's interest, it was I who persuaded my father to reject his suit. I have foretold the destruction of your holy city."

"Helenus told me. So has he. It makes no difference."

"Courage must be a burden at times."

"You jest, surely?"

Talking with Hector would always be a strain, and at that

moment my head was about to split open. "No. But call it duty if you prefer." I knew he would understand duty—he was obsessed by it. "If Polydorus and I were not constrained by duty, then we might run away together and rely on love alone to bring us happiness."

"And be miserable all your days. You are not Helen, Briseis. And Polydorus is not another Paris, thanks be to the Immortals."

"Exactly," I said and hoped the conversation was now over.

As the sun clasped the horizon, its low beams were painting the storm towers bloody over the dark landscape. It would be raining in Thebe, I thought. No, south of Thebe. Was that a distant murmur of thunder? The enemy lay somewhere over the sea, so the storm was to the left. . . .

But Hector had not done. "I trust you did not take offence when I . . . that we . . . I do not wish to belittle your hospitality, I mean."

What was I supposed to say to that? *Yes, I wanted you to service me, you big bull?*

"It was entirely a matter of duty," I mumbled.

"I am glad you see it that way." His big hands had closed into fists. "You comprehend the burdens of royalty. I, for example, do not want to fight a war. I want to cherish my dear wife, to watch my son grow to be a warrior. I hope in the gods' good time to succeed my father as shepherd of our people. Such ambitions become a man better than mindless thirst for blood and glory; but fight I must, because otherwise Andromache will be raped and enslaved, my son condemned to poverty, my father cut down and shamed, the people slain and scattered. Even if I believed with all the doomsayers and croakers of ill omens that such is the will of Father Zeus—which with respect I do not, my lady—I would still fight, because only thus can I hope to die with honor and not have to witness such horrors."

Was he saying all this just to impress a woman? I did not think so; it was duty again. Was the real Hector showing through the clouds? No, not that either. He was too mighty a man not to revel in battle and the power of command. I could not like him, but I could not hate him either.

"I am certain you will acquit yourself with great distinction, my lord."

"Indeed I shall! I will send a multitude of Greeks down into the shadows before me. My spear will make the surf run red and bloat the fish with the kidneys and entrails of corpses."

"Soon!" I muttered. Of course! How could I have been so stupid?

He realized at last that I was preoccupied. "Helenus spoke highly of your gift for augury." It was a question.

I pointed to that vast brightness, the darkness below it, and now the awesome glint of colors within that rumbling murk.

"Surely you do not need a seer to understand that!"

"I see some welcome rain, sent to ripen the crops."

"Listen to the thunder, Prince Hector. Look at the *rainbow*! Don't you know that a rainbow is the surest sign of war? Your brother taught me that."

"We all know that war is coming."

"Then now you know that it has begun," I said. "Somewhere south of Thebe. I tell you it has started."

I looked up and saw cold fury in his onyx eyes. His glossy beard seemed to bristle and spark.

"We shall see. Anyone can claim to be an augur." He turned on his heel and stalked away.

I leaned over the rail and wept.

4

I made no secret of the portents I had seen and their implications—why should I? Hector continued his stubborn disbelief; and his followers pretended they supported him, although I know that at least one runner was dispatched in the night, hotfoot to Troy. When the royal procession departed next morning, it continued on its original course to Pedasos.

The moment it was out of sight and hearing, Father had the war gongs beaten. He sent couriers to Thebe and Dardania. He posted a day-and-night watch on the coast. There had been no visible gaps in our stockade since last winter, but in many places it was largely bluff and in need of reinforcement. Women and children of the town trooped into the palace compound. By noon, shacks covered the pasture like seaweed draping the shore after a storm, and by dusk they were spreading into the courtyard. All day, a line of bearers, oxen, mules, and horses carried water up from the spring to charge the cisterns, dried out by the summer heat.

All this because I had seen a storm.

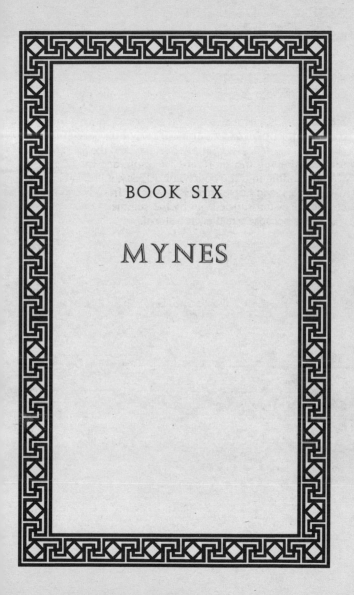

BOOK SIX

MYNES

1

Agamemnon, the Great King, had set a firm date for the great muster at Aulis and been forced to postpone it twice. Even so, barely half his forces had arrived by the time of the midsummer sacrifice. It was a noble assembly of hundreds of tents ranging from grand pavilions of painted leather to makeshift kennels of oiled linen. The long white sand was crosshatched with scores of black ships, all rigged with new hemp and canvas and oars of fresh-cut fir. Before them lay the azure sea and the sun-baked hills of Euboea, behind them the rocks of Boeotia.

The host strained on its leash like a pack of dogs scenting quarry—thousands of armed youths, all thirsty for loot and blood, every one eager to prove himself, scorching on a beach with no enemy at hand and no women at all. Most contingents were loudly distrustful of their neighbors, who spoke with strange accents, let their horses stray in the night, and crowded their latrines too close to the boundary. On this human tinder fell a constant shower of sparks: thefts and insults and age-old feuds erupting anew. The risk of ignition grew by the hour, and the sheer cost of feeding an idle army was unbearable.

Should the Great King launch his attack with the resources available or wait for the rest to arrive? Agamemnon vacillated for days before deciding to call a council, and he needed even longer to decide whom to invite. Some of the self-proclaimed kings ruled insignificant hilltops or islands, while others had brought fleets almost as great as Mycenae's. Some were vassals, some truly independent. One or two landgraves led more men than monarchs. The only distinction that could be made without argument was between the nobility and the lowborn, between knight and rabble. Agamemnon summoned all the knights to his council. That was not the way the Hittite emperor waged war, nor the Great King of the Assyrians. Pharaoh did not tolerate such nonsense in Egypt, and the king of Babylon would have howled with scorn; but these men were Greeks, stubbornly loyal only to their own leaders.

While bowing to the inevitable, the king of Mycenae could at least try to keep the discussion as brief as possible. He ordered benches set up on the sun-drenched sand and called the council for noon, when the heat was greatest. He began by requiring every knight to swear to follow his leadership until Troy fell, and only after that long ceremony was over did he pose the question and ask for advice. The senior kings spoke in turn, some favoring delay and others attack. In the blazing white sunlight, tempers began to fray.

Then Odysseus of Ithaca rose to take the speaker's staff. Even in those days he had a reputation as a strategist, but his greatest asset was his skill in debate. He spurned oratorical tricks and flourishes. Indeed he stood for a long moment in silence, leaning on the staff like a serf resting from hoeing an onion patch, staring at the sand. His pose was so gauche that the rabble in the background began to chuckle, but when he raised his big head and scanned the crowd, Athena silenced them all for him. His voice boomed out over the crowd, words thudding like arrows in their target.

He began by rejecting both alternatives. Granted, he said, a premature attack with inadequate forces might possibly succeed, and such a feat would bring the victors great glory and loot that need not be shared among many. But failure would mean total disaster. Yet an inactive army must soon lose its edge. An egg unhatched will rot.

"Son of Atreus, we know that you are a warrior well seasoned in war, else we should not follow you. I see many other famous men of valor among us, but I also see youths who have never shed blood and a few who do not shave yet. Without doubting their courage, we may reserve judgment on their abilities. The fleet must sail, but must it sail against Troy? Let us first try our mettle on lesser game. We have no lack of foes. From Rhodes north to the Troad itself, the whole coast is hostile to our cause: Lycians, Carians, Maeonians, Mysians, Kilikes, and others. When we land at Troy, they will send their hosts to oppose us—so they have sworn to Priam—and there we shall face them all assembled. Why should we let our enemies combine against us when we can smite them separately? If, with the help of Athena and Almighty Zeus, we can chasten some of them, the others may hesitate to send their young men to fight on the windswept plains of Troy."

This suggestion was greeted with roars of approval. Odysseus waited for the hubbub to die away, leaning on the staff and showing no sign of satisfaction or impatience. Then he added, "Besides, they can help to pay for the war." That won an even louder roar.

Agamemnon accepted the assembly's counsel. He ordered sacrifices made and commanded that the ships be launched at dawn the next day.

Almost nothing went right. Slow vessels were left behind, others scattered by the wind. Few beaches could hold such a fleet, so ships fouled one another at every evening's landing and every morning's launch. Food and firewood ran short; horses panicked or balked; men quarreled. It was a reduced and disheartened army that landed at the mouth of the Caïcus River in the area known as Asia, which the Hittites call Assuwa.

King Telephus of the Mysians must have been forewarned by portents, for a multitude of roaring spearmen swept out onto the shore before half the raiders had disembarked. The Greek vanguard was swiftly driven back into the surf, where many an armor-laden warrior drowned among the feet of friends too busy defending themselves to notice. Archers in the background lobbed a steady hail of arrows onto the invaders, and in minutes they faced disaster.

Reefs and overcrowding had forced the five ships sent by King Peleus of Thessaly to beach some distance along the shore. Spurning knightly armor, their leader took up shield and spear and led his well-trained, hard-fighting Myrmidons in a massed charge upon the Mysians' rear. That he was the last man to disembark and the first one to reach the enemy established his reputation forevermore as the fastest runner in the army. In minutes, he turned the battle from a Greek rout into a Mysian one. King Telephus tried to rally his troops, but fled when he saw Achilles and Patroclus converging on him. He tripped on a vine and was speared where he fell.

The invaders looted city and countryside, then loaded the women and booty into the ships and set sail back to Aulis, triumphant but humbler than before. The expedition had taught them many lessons. The most important lesson by far—or so my informant insisted—was that now they knew who their best warrior was. Few of them had ever heard Achilles' name before Mysia, Patroclus said, but from then on they had no chance to forget it.

2

No news came to Lyrnessos in the three days after the Trojans' departure, but this meant nothing because nothing traveled faster than a ship. If the Greeks were coming, they would announce themselves. Father kept us on war alert.

On the third evening, Bienor and two Dardanian horsemen rode in through the gates. The palace was in such chaos that I did not hear the news for some time and when I tracked him down in the queen's hall, his fuzzy cheeks were already well daubed with Mother's face paint. Tall and shaggy haired in his dusty, sweat-stained Dardanian leathers, he was barely recognizable as my twin.

Father was mixing wine and beaming like Helios on a summer morning. Mother had subsided into her favorite chair to dab at her eyes, smiling bravely. The way was clear for me to hurl myself upon the hero, although less than a year earlier I would not have kissed Bienor for all the bronze in Troy. We were still entangled in fond sibling embrace when Sphelos walked in.

"What is this—Ares and Aphrodite? Now we can sleep soundly."

Bienor set me aside with surprising firmness to meet the challenge. "Are you mocking me, son of Briseus?"

Sphelos's sneer wavered uncertainly. "I assume Aeneas sent you to defend us from the Greeks?"

"He heard there was a shortage of fighters in Lyrnessos."

"Boys, boys!" Father growled. "Let us make offerings."

He passed out goblets and, when we had all thanked the gods, ordered us to sit. Bienor leaned back gingerly, sighing with content, a warrior at his ease among the looms and the baskets of deep-dyed wools.

"Where is Aeneas?" I demanded. "He promised to defend us."

"In Troy. Even if you— I mean whatever you foresaw is not enough to move an army south."

"He doesn't believe me?"

Bienor squirmed, avoiding my eye. "It could be a feint, you understand. He'll be seeing Priam again, and there are new knights to be sworn, and—"

"Enops!" Mother told me, unsure whether to smile or weep. "He's won his tassels." I had not thought to ask.

Bienor nodded eagerly. "I came to fetch a helmet for him. Boar's tusk are scarce as griffin feathers now."

We all spoke at once.

Father said, "He shall have his grandfather's. It's waiting for him. I had the plates mounted on new felt and leather."

"A knight already?" I exclaimed. "That's—"

"And I have a mantle ready." Mother peered around vaguely. "Now, where did I put it?"

Sphelos was sneering again. "I thought it took five years to train a knight. The Greeks have done him a favor, I suppose. Is he any good?"

Bienor considered him for a moment before replying. "Aeneas hails him as the best since Akamas."

"Aeneas! How much does he expect this time? Did you just come for a helmet, or will you empty the treasure room as Enops did last year?"

Bienor rose. Goblet in hand, he paced across to Sphelos

and looked down on him with obvious menace. "I say Enops is worthy. Do you question my word?"

"I say you're biased and—*arrgh!*" Sphelos howled as wine poured down on him, soaking his face and robe, spattering like blood on the plaster floor. Mother and I joined in the yells. He leaped to his feet and balled a fist. Then he looked up at Bienor's tight smile and hesitated.

"Father! Control this hooligan!"

Father sighed but did not seem greatly displeased. "Sit down, Bienor. You should respect Sphelos as your senior and as a valuable officer of the realm. Sphelos, if you taunt a warrior, what do you expect but violence? Next time it may be worse than wine."

"Much worse," Bienor said. He strolled back to his seat, not exactly grinning but conveying the satisfaction of having just scratched a long-suffered itch.

"Who will be Enops's charioteer?" Father asked.

That brought the shiny-eyed smile I remembered. "Me! And he wasn't the first to ask me, either!"

There was cause to refill the goblets and thanks to the gods again. Father remarked gruffly that his sons were proving worthy of their great ancestors, although I could not recall ever hearing much about them. Sphelos glowered in silence, still wiping his face with a hairy wrist.

"I was not greatly impressed by Hector," I said.

Bienor pulled a face. "Who is? He'll make a dung heap of the war, and then Priam will have to call on Aeneas, but by then it may be too late."

"Suppose," Sphelos remarked, "just suppose that they land here, sack Lyrnessos, and then attack the Dardanians from the rear?"

"Suppose horses can fly! No warrior would even consider such a stupid idea. The first principle of war is to aim your spear at your enemy's heart, not tweak his nose. Why would they march over a mountain and down a river when they can sail into the front door? They'll attack Troy from the sea."

"I prostrate myself before your wide experience. I daresay the Mysians wouldn't agree, but—"

"Silence!" Father roared. "Sit down, Bienor! Aeneas is

deceiving himself. When the fighting starts, his Dardanians will decide they're Trojans after all and he will be a leader without a host. That's what his father says. Tomorrow, charioteer, you will inspect our defenses and give us the benefit of your skills."

Greatly flattered, the warrior sighed and squared his narrow shoulders under the burden of duty. "I'd better do it now, my lord. I'm under orders and must leave at dawn."

But tomorrow the war came to Lyrnessos.

3

In fair weather I slept on my balcony and Ctimene on a rug just inside the door. At dawn the clamor of the war alarm wakened me. Suddenly every metal pot in Lyrnessos rang, conches wailed, children were screaming, geese cackling, horses neighing. I reeled to my feet, clutching a sheet around me. The first thing I saw was the gates being closed behind a horseman. He headed inland at a gallop, one of the Dardanians going to summon help. Help against what? Beyond him, the sun-parched hills were empty. Within the palace compound, though, men with spears and shields were running, some of them stark naked, as if just roused from sleep.

I spun around and headed for the door. Ctimene neatly intercepted me and swept a gown over my head. Hair streaming, I rushed through my room and out into the passage. Rounding the corner by grabbing the wall, I reached Father's chamber and found it deserted, the door standing open. I dashed to the seaward window and saw the foe—a solitary black ship approaching the beach, trailing ripples on water mirror calm.

How could a thing of so much beauty portend such evil? Her prow curved up and forward, questing like a swan's neck. The sail was furled on the yard, and banked oars spread winglike on either side. The bards sing of "black" ships, but the oak weathers more to a dark brown than true black, and the outside of the hull was smeared red with cinnabar to protect against rot. She had been sailing by night, taking advantage of the full moon, so her captain was no ordinary seaman. I registered the innumerable men aboard, the glitter of bronze.

"Idiots!" I screamed. "The sentries! Why didn't they see that an hour ago?"

"Mmf, my lady." Ctimene was fumbling with the laces on my robe and holding an ivory comb in her mouth.

"Never mind that! Come on. I'm going to kill a sentry if Father hasn't already."

I fled back along the passage and started down the stairs. Mother was trudging up. She paused to catch her breath and frown at me, blocking my way.

"I trust you are not going to appear in public in that condition," she puffed. "Your gown is untied."

I groped for the laces, wondering why this should matter when I was expected to expose my breasts completely on formal occasions. My hands shook, my heart flapped like a bird in quicklime, and yet Mother seemed completely composed. If she was not quite her usual well-groomed self, at least her hair had been combed and her face painted. She had an Olympian ability to ignore unpleasantness, but never had I seen it better displayed.

"What's happening? Where's Father?"

"There is a raider down at the beach." She began to climb again, driving me backward up the stairs, Ctimene behind me. "You will help with the sacrifice to Potnia."

"Where's Father?" I repeated.

"Putting on his armor. I shall want—"

"Armor? But he can't go out and fight!"

"That's what kings are for, dear."

"He's too old! He can't even climb the stairs without needing to sit down after." He would die before he as much as saw the enemy.

Mother reached the top step and speeded up, still herding Ctimene and me before her along the narrow corridor. She spoke with a confidence she could not possibly be feeling. "Well, I doubt that he will be required to fight. There's only one ship out there—fifty men at the most. We have three hundred or more and, thanks to Aeneas's advice, our walls are in excellent shape now. But he must show an example. Bienor has gone to fetch his chariot."

"Walls?" I could not imagine that paltry palisade delaying a horde of bloodthirsty Greeks for very long. I also remembered what Aeneas had said about knights—one would be enough to grind the entire host of Lyrnessos into meal. Even one ship might . . .

Some god took pity on me then. *One ship!* I spun around, pushed past Ctimene, and tore back along the corridor. Aeneas and all the Dardanian knights were in Troy, which meant at least four days before help could arrive. I rounded the corner and plunged into the nearest room. Throwing the net aside, I hurtled out on the balcony.

The ship was already backing away from the beach. One man had disembarked and was plodding toward the town, still too far away to recognize. There was only one man it could be—I had seen the omen the previous year. I must tell Father. . . . Ctimene jumped out of my way again.

I shot down the stairs like a rock slide, along the passage, across the inner courtyard, and reached the porch just as Bienor came rattling up to the steps in Father's chariot. His face was hidden in a helmet of bronze-scaled leather. Apart from that, he was wearing only ugly Dardanian breeches, but a heap of metal at his feet must be some sort of charioteer's corselet. A group of spearmen came running after him, and another man took hold of the horses.

The watching women started a feeble cheer as Father came clanking out from the guard room, holding himself very erect inside a casing of bronze plates hooped around him. Little more than his eyes could be seen, peering out over a high collar, and sweat had plastered his wispy white hair to his scalp already. Behind him came a man bearing his spear, shield, and a bronze war helm.

I went to him. "One man has come ashore, Father. The ship has pulled back. It's Odysseus."

He stopped, swaying a little to catch his balance. He peered at me vaguely, as if bewildered. "The son of Laertes?"

"The king of Ithaca?" Bienor shouted. "Are you sure?"

The listeners moaned at this mention of a Greek, although none of them could have heard of the dread son of Laertes in those days.

"Quite sure."

"Think, Briseis!" Father's voice was muffled by the neck of his metal barrel. "This could be disastrous if you're wrong."

I hesitated, but I could find no doubts. Helenus had confirmed my reading of that omen. "I'm quite certain, my lord. He's not close enough to recognize, but I know it's him."

Father turned his head and strained to see over his collar. "Ponteus—find out what's happening now."

The porter pushed out of the gathering crowd and raced to the stockade that cut off the courtyard's former view of the beach. He shouted ahead to one of the watchers on the rampart, then turned and hared back with the reply.

"He says one man's coming, my lord. He has a spear, but no armor. The ship's lying a bow shot offshore."

"A herald's staff!" Bienor declaimed unnecessarily. "Not a spear if he has no shield. Can I go, Father, please? Oh, please?"

"Go, then. But be careful—it may be a trap."

Bienor slapped the reins and yelled at the horses, sending the chariot plunging dangerously through the spearmen, most of whom were now making for the stockade to see for themselves. In a shower of dust and curses, he wheeled around, heading for the gates through the muddle of shacks and tents. Father began the difficult maneuver of turning himself about without overbalancing, for his old bones were not fit to bear the load of his armor.

"It won't be a trap," I called after him. "He's slyer than an earth of foxes, but he wouldn't—"

Why would Odysseus have come here alone? My mouth went dry.

*   *   *

That was Bienor's moment of glory, being Father's emissary to another king. His worst problem, he said afterward, was the pig-stinking, dog-faced helmet, which had a rough seam that cut into his right ear at every bounce, but he sent the chariot whirling down the road to the town. Birds flew up; stray dogs ran out, their shrill barking unnerving the horses. The hovels were deserted now, doors hanging open. The solitary figure marching up the trail from the beach stepped aside to wait for him. Bienor reined in, kicked out the heels, and brought the chariot rattling to a halt right alongside Odysseus. Aeneas himself couldn't have done it better. The two regarded each other warily, Bienor squinting into the sun. Dust settled.

"By Sisyphus's pebble, it's the son of Briseus!" The Greek was clad in sandals, leather greaves, and a plain linen tunic, already sweat soaked in the morning glare. A small knife hung at his belt. Only the ash-wood staff proclaimed his status, but his massive limbs were authority enough. He needed no tassels or boar's tusk—give him a lion skin and he would be Heracles himself.

"My lord . . . do I address you as *herald* or give you your royal title?"

"You have put the last year to good use, charioteer—a good two hands taller or I'm a Cretan!"

"You flatter me, my lord."

Odysseus wiped a thick arm across his forehead. "It's a bad habit of mine. You'd better stick with *herald*, Prince. And we may not need prolonged negotiations here, if you'll just answer a simple question for me: Is Lyrnessos with Troy or with the Greeks?"

Bienor felt his skin go cold. "I am only my father's driver, herald. I cannot answer that question."

"You mean Aeneas still hasn't chosen which bed he'll lie in?"

"Nor speak for the son of Anchises either."

The king of Ithaca glowered at him. "Don't be pompous, boy. If my crew sees me throw down this stick, they will come ashore at once. After that, there will be no more talking, only screams. What knights do you have up there in that sheepfold?"

Fortunately, Bienor then lost his temper, or at least when he opened his mouth his words came out angry and not scared, which was what he had expected. "You think me such a fool as to answer that? I was sent to drive you to the palace, herald, not to negotiate. Stop trying to trick me. Climb aboard and ride with me or walk by yourself—or swim, for all I care." This was not how kings should be addressed, especially when they had a shipload of warriors at their backs.

Odysseus uttered a harsh, grinding laugh. "It has teeth! I just want to be sure that I will not find myself in the company of Aeneas and Elatos if I come with you. What safeguard do you offer me if I jump into the snake pit?"

"My father's honor! If you come as herald, you will be treated as one." That, Bienor thought, was a worthy response. He was proud of his words, but then Odysseus deflated him.

"And will you offer yourself as hostage for my safety, Prince? Give me the chariot, and you go to my ship."

"Me?" To refuse would seem like cowardice. He was about to accept when he saw that the question was insulting. "No, herald, I will not. That is not how we do things in the Troad." He yanked the cord to pull up the heels. "Are you coming or not?"

The king chuckled. "Answer me this, then—is that glorious sister of yours married yet?"

"Briseis? Well, no, my lord! Married?"

Odysseus took two quick strides and swung himself up into the car, which rocked violently and was suddenly crowded. "It's something that happens to beautiful maidens. Drive on, charioteer."

Bienor slapped the horses. He let them pick up speed so he could swing the chariot around on one wheel, then he headed back to the town and the hill. Surprisingly for such a big man, Odysseus was no taller than he was. Blinkered by his helmet, Bienor stared at the huge hand clutching the rail, then let his gaze track up the thick-thewed arm to his passenger's eyes.

They twinkled at him. "You did well, boy."

Such praise, he admitted later, felt worth having.

4

As Bienor drove Odysseus in through the palace gates, I was crossing the cool, dim megaron, still puffing from a very fast toilet. I had chosen the most unassuming garment I possessed, a robe of fine blue linen, and Ctimene had worked a miracle to turn my hair from a bush into dangling ringlets so quickly. The hearth lay bright and summer bare under the sunlight laddering down from the clerestory. On the throne in the shadows sat Father, attended by Sphelos, Captain Kreion, and four or five palace officials—all men, all stooped and urgently whispering. I approached with humble grace, knowing I would meet resistance.

He had replaced his armor with a simple robe and his knight's helmet. He looked exhausted already—face flushed and puffy, dark around the eyes, expression stormy.

"This is no place for a woman, Briseis. Go and assist your mother in her prayers."

I bent a knee. "My lord, I come as your augur, not your daughter."

He clawed at his beard. "What do you foresee?"

"I think the son of Laertes comes in peace." How much of that was a seer's vision and how much the wishful guesswork of a woman's heart? "He is dangerous, yes, but I don't think he came to sack the town."

"If he had," old Kreion growled, "he'd have done it by now."

"Silence, fool!" Father swung the scepter at him, but the old man dodged in time. "What sort of cowards' talk is that? You are supposed to set an example! Stand here, Briseis, next to me. If the gods advise you, then touch my shoulder." He leaned his head back with a sigh.

Shadows darkened the brightness of the doorway. Odysseus came padding across the patterned floor with Bienor at his heels. He stopped before the throne, and the two kings studied each other in silence, as if each were daring the other to speak first. Bienor hid himself behind the advisers. In the lengthening pause, I realized that Mother and some of her harpies were watching from the balcony, although they were all supposed to be down in the shrine placating the gods.

Finally Father said, "Will you take wine with us, stranger?"

"I cannot accept your hospitality, my lord. Not yet, anyway. Must I keep up the herald mummery?"

"Kings should negotiate on neutral ground."

"It was respect for your years, my lord, that led me to wait upon you here. If I speak in my own name, do you give me safe conduct back to my ship?"

Father wheezed cautiously a few times. "I do. Your oath that your crew will stay aboard while we talk for mine that I shall not harm or detain you. As Athena is my witness."

"You have my oath, likewise."

"Bring a seat for the son of Laertes!"

Odysseus turned his quick, dark eyes on me—measuring, assessing—and I felt heat rise into my face under that intense inspection. His strength glowed like a dark god against the brightness of the sunlit hearth behind him. Was it possible, just possible, that his wife had died, perhaps in childbirth? That he had remembered the saucy maiden he met in Pedasos and decided to rescue her from the coming devastation—take her back to Ithaca, wherever that was? Was I being a romantic fool? Would I abandon my family if he asked me to?

A steward brought a stool for him. Now the negotiations would start. Now the trade goods would be laid out on the shore for the barbarians to inspect.

"You have met our royal soothsayer," Father said.

"No man could forget such beauty. Son of Mydon, have you heard what happened to the Mysians?"

"No man could forget such atrocity."

"What atrocity? We despoiled no altars. Have you decided . . . No, let me pose the question otherwise." He

rubbed his big chin and stared at the floor for a moment. We
all knew the question and the penalty for a wrong answer.
But both answers carried the same penalty, because Thebe
and Pedasos would not tolerate a Greek stronghold between
them any more than the son of Laertes could resist the
chance to sack a helpless Trojan town. We had a choice of
mourners, that was all.

"Take your time," Father said. "My men are in the shade."

I decided he was doing quite well for a has-been, and
Odysseus's smoldering glance confirmed my opinion.

"Harken, then. Aboard my ship I have two very remarkable young warriors, of royal breeding—brothers—and
greatly skilled in war. I do not use the sly words of traders
when I say this, son of Mydon, but speak as knight to knight.
The elder's spear slew eight men in the battle at the River
Caïcus, and the younger's five. They may not quite rank
with the son of Peleus, but they put the rest of us to shame.
They at present owe loyalty only to their father, but he in
turn holds his kingdom as a grant from Agamemnon. Being
too old for warfare himself, he was commanded to send
these stalwart sons of his to fight in his stead. This edict
posed a problem of honor for him, because in his own youth
he visited Troy and became a guest friend of Priam. Their
sons should not meet in battle."

He paused, appraising the effect of his words with his
blood-chilling stare. Father did not comment.

"Having sought advice from a soothsayer, he resolved to
send them both to Aulis with a gift of fine horses for the
Great King and a prayer that they might thereby be relieved
of their duty. I doubt that Agamemnon would have consented to this plea had he set eyes on them, for they are
mighty men, both of them. As it happened, Hermes or some
other god delayed them on their journey, and they arrived
just after the Great King's ship had sailed."

"To their undying chagrin, I suppose?"

Odysseus did not smile. "They bore their grief with true
warriors' courage. But then Athena or some other god
caused them to fall in with me as I prepared to embark. They
learned that I was not bound for Troy itself. One thing led to

another. I offered them passage in return for their assistance when we reached Mysia, and there they acquitted themselves with distinction, as I have said."

He stared down at the staff lying across his lap and rolled it back and forth a few times with his big spearman's hands before looking up again.

"You entertained Paris in this hall and are therefore his guest friend, my lord. It occurred to me that you have something in common with these young men."

Father was guest friend of half the Trojan royal family.

"You have no host leader," Odysseus said bluntly.

"My son Enops has come to knight's estate and will serve me in that capacity."

The son of Laertes peered around the hall in search of this invisible warrior and then looked at Father again inquiringly. "He is presently attending to more important matters? You understand my proposal? They should not fight against Troy, and neither should you. Equally, they must not bear arms against their father's liege, Agamemnon. But any man has the right to defend himself and his home. If Lyrnessos could field those two knights—plus your noble son, of course— then it would no longer be the tempting morsel it is at present." He folded his arms, hugging the staff across his great chest.

He did not need to mention the alternative, which was Father and his ragtag militia against three knights and fifty spearmen. Aeneas could not possibly arrive before Lyrnessos was sacked and burned. The Greek had laid out his trade goods. Now it was Father's turn to offer his daughter and the succession to his throne. Curiously, I did not even consider the implications for myself. I could think only of the town and palace. How could we possibly refuse? Potnia had heard our prayers.

Father cleared his throat. "You say these two young knights are of warlike disposition?"

"Like hungry lions, my lord."

He was playing for time to think, or else he suspected an unseen trap. Was it possible that Odysseus was hiding something? He was a superbly crafty negotiator, as I had known from the first. Had Father sensed trickery, or was he floundering as I was? He looked to his advisers in a silent appeal for help, but the megaron remained as hushed as a tomb. Ares had stolen the courtiers' wits. At last Sphelos spoke up, his voice shriller than usual.

"You think to make this town into a Greek ally, son of Laertes? You think Troy will stand for that? Or Thebe? Or Pedasos?"

Odysseus studied him for a moment, and his gaze somehow became contemptuous—no warrior, this. "Inform them you are adopting a position of armed neutrality. The cities of the Troad will soon have too much war on their hands to go seeking more."

"And what is your own interest in this, my lord?" Father asked.

That, said the king of Ithaca's smile, was always the shrewd man's question. "A neutral port on a hostile shore, where ships may overnight in safety or obtain food and water without fighting for them. Wait. There is more to it than that. When I met your lovely daughter last year, son of Mydon, I told her she needed a valorous protector, a stalwart husband. I promised her that if I encountered a young man suited for that role, I would inform him of her plight. I spoke mainly in jest, I admit, but the gods hear our jests and may turn them to their purposes. They answered her prayer—I did meet such a man. I have him with me. Accept the noble Mynes as your host leader, my lord. Name him as your successor in the old ways by marrying him to your daughter. Epistrophos will stay to aid his brother until the war is over. Such is my advice, and if I cannot speak as a friend, I say truthfully that this is not an offer you would receive from an enemy."

Father nodded wearily. "The prospect has merit, I admit. But I cannot betroth my daughter and assign my kingdom to a man I have never met. Summon this Mynes to—"

"Time grows short." Odysseus laid the point of his staff on the floor as if he was about to rise. "I will hazard my ship no longer in enemy waters on a mission that offers so little profit. If you do not accept, my lord, then I assume that you refuse. I must be about my business."

We knew what his business was—he was a sacker of cities. Father began to expostulate about needing time to consult his advisers and his family, and it was then that a god whispered in my ear. Oh, how obvious! I spoke a silent word of thanks. Something was missing, and it must be important, although I could not imagine why it should be. I touched Father's shoulder.

He started as if he had forgotten I was there. "Yes, Briseis?"

"My lord, have these young nobles no homeland, no patronymic? Ask the son of Laertes to name the king their father and his fair realm."

"What does that— Yes, that seems a reasonable request."

Odysseus shrugged. "They are the sons of Euneus, king of Hire, whose meadows—"

Father jerked upright. "Euneus son of Selepus?"

"I believe so."

Father's bellow of laughter made everyone jump, even Odysseus. Courtiers stared at one another in bewildered dismay.

"You threaten me with the sons of Euneus? He dwelt in this house for many months after his brief visit to Troy. If honor bars his sons from making war on Priam, they will certainly not raise their spears against Lyrnessos. My wife will welcome them at our hearth with tears of joy. I shall send a herald down to the shore to fetch them immediately."

The Greek's threats had just dissolved like dew. He rose, his face dark. "I did not know! They never mentioned such a matter to me."

To accuse him of lying would be suicidal, but Father's laugh was hoarse with skepticism. "I suppose Euneus would have seen no need to warn them if he sent them only as far as Aulis. You said yourself, son of Laertes, that the gods directed you to bring these young men here. Will you have wine with me now while we await them?"

"Not yet. I must accompany the chariots you send down to the ships, or my men will assume evil has befallen me."

"Let it be so, then! A young bullock for your crew? You will fill your water jugs?"

The two kings headed for the door, leaving the courtiers in excited jackdaw jabber. Mother was beckoning urgently from the balcony.

Bienor caught up with me and stalked along at my side. "Congratulations on your betrothal, Sister."

"Oh, don't cook fish till you've caught them. You mustn't assume—"

"Nothing can stop it now." Bienor had never sounded more confident than he did then. "It is fate, truly. The sons of Euneus have a hearth friendship with Lyrnessos, so no one can object to them coming here to help with its defense. Even Troy can't."

"Oh!" At that moment I emerged into bright light—in more senses than one. Betrothed? To a man even Father had never met? "But what about Enops? He expects to be leader of the Lyrnessian host."

"He may be peeved at first. He'll come around, because the thought of defending Lyrnessos worries him. He'd much rather go off and find a good fight out in the open somewhere. So would I! I'm sure we'll soon find someone ready to oblige us."

Odysseus was already driving off in the chariot. Father was shouting for two more teams to be made ready and telling the guard to stand down. I smiled at the wild cheers of relief and turned again to my unbelievably tall, manly, self-assured twin.

"You've grown up!"

He smiled wistfully. "So have you."

That was going to take some getting used to. "You're leaving already?"

"There won't be any bloodshed here today, so I must follow orders. May Aphrodite bless your marriage with many

glorious sons, Sister." He kissed me, then strode off toward
the stables.

Marriage? Sons? I ran as fast as I could, but Panic was
faster. I hurtled up the stairs and flew along the corridor, past
all the birds, flowers, hunters, dancers, diamonds, chevrons,
and spirals, until I reached Mother's chamber and could
throw myself into her arms.

Busy hands worked on me all together as if I were a goddess—
Mother, Maera, Alcmene, Anticleia, and Ctimene washing,
oiling, perfuming, and dressing me. They loaded me down
with gold and jewels until I could barely stand. Other
women flitted in and out to help or get in the way or fetch.
Mother prattled constantly—how wonderful that the gods
had sent the sons of Euneus to aid us in our time of need,
how marvelous that her old suitor had found himself such a
wonderful kingdom, and where was Hire anyway?

Then came the waiting. We saw from the window that
Odysseus had sailed away already, but that was mere pru-
dence. Ctimene, sent to scout, returned to report that Father
and Sphelos were in conference in the megaron with two
young men.

"What does he look like?" I yelped.

She rolled her eyes. "Oh, my lady! Like a god!"

"Which? Do you know which is which?"

"No, my lady. They both do!"

And more waiting. I felt sick. When the summons came,
it was not for me but for Mother. She departed with Alcmene
and Anticleia at her heels. More waiting. I sat on the edge of
the bed and died a thousand times. Maera huddled in a chair
and grinned toothlessly. Ctimene, bless her, worried along
with me, holding my hand. At last Mother returned, bubbling with happiness to conduct me downstairs to meet my
future husband, the new host leader.

She remarked afterward that my behavior was absolutely
perfect. Both she and Father were proud of me. Mynes son
of Euneus was obviously very impressed. I was poised and
graceful, as gracious and lovely as a goddess. Of course! It
was a goddess they saw—Potnia herself, I expect. Our Lady

had taken pity on Briseis and taken her place. I wasn't there.
I remember absolutely nothing about it.

We had promised many offerings to the gods if they would
spare the town, so there was an epic feast in the megaron
that night. Even the slaves ate meat. I sat between Father and
Mynes. Officials and priests came to pay their respects to the
new host leader, most of them having trouble expressing the
extent of their approval and relief without insulting the king.
Women brought me smiles and flowers and congratulations.
Clearly Lyrnessos would sleep more soundly with these new
warriors to guard it.

The sons of Euneus were indeed mighty men, in their
middle twenties and very much alike, even for brothers. They
had clear gray eyes and trailing manes of honey-colored hair,
and they shaved their faces in the current Greek fashion. I
supposed I could get used to that. Mynes was relatively
thicker and broader, Epistrophos taller and leaner, but the
differences were slight—either of them could fill a doorway.
Mynes was quiet, while Epistrophos talked a lot and smiled
all the time. I was not offered a choice.

My fiancé had been fitted out in a faded blue tunic that must
have belonged to Father at some time, for it had a tasseled
hem. I could not but notice how it strained to contain his
mighty chest, how taut the sleeves were around his upper arms.
The wedding would not be celebrated for at least another two
months, which had seemed a frantically short time when I was
told of it, but began to feel unendurably long as the evening
progressed and the wine flowed. Mighty man, mighty man.

I wondered who had been assigned to bathe these guests
and was racked with jealousy. One of those sluts cavorting
with my fiancé? He wouldn't have, would he? I wanted to
marry a man who would, didn't I?

Mother kept asking about Euneus. He was well, both sons
insisted, but feeling his years now. Epistrophos assured her
that he often spoke wistfully of the beautiful Nemertes he
had wooed in his youth. Even in my bemused and rhapsodic
condition, I found this statement suspect. Most husbands
have more sense than that.

"Hire still follows the old ways?" Father said. Was he piqued that his old rival had found himself a kingdom after all?

"Hire does what Mycenae tells it," Mynes growled.

"Adrestos lost all his sons in battle," Epistrophos explained, "and Mother was his only daughter, making Father his obvious successor. Mycenae approved, but that was back in Atreus's time. Agamemnon has a nasty habit of promoting his own favorites, and we're not in favor now. Not that Mynes need worry any more—he has found a better realm."

"Is it better?" I asked eagerly. "Are you happy with the exchange?"

Mynes' eyes were the color of iron. "Lyrnessos has one big advantage that Hire has not."

"Yes? Yes?"

He took a drink. "It is close to a war."

Oh. "Of course."

"It was strange that Odysseus did not know of your father's friendship with Lyrnessos," Sphelos remarked loudly. Sphelos had been drinking much more than usual.

Epistrophos's eyes caught the firelight like a cat's. "I am sure we mentioned it to him. It may have slipped his mind, but I think he lied about it. He enjoys lying and cheating."

Mother gasped.

Father said, "My lords?" heavily.

"The king of Ithaca omitted to unload our armor before he departed."

"And that's not all he forgot to unload." Epistrophos had not matched Sphelos goblet for goblet, but his face was flushed. "Twelve helmets; ten spears; eight swords; two bronze cuirasses; nine corslets of leather with bronze scales and two of linen; eleven daggers; thirteen shields, seven of them with metal bosses—this is what we two won at Mysia! What we retrieved, at least. Some things we didn't manage to strip and the rest was stolen before we got it aboard. That's without our share of the loot from the town."

"But that's a fortune!" Sphelos said in amazement. "That would buy a thousand cattle! And you won all that in one day?"

"In less than an hour. And now it's on its way to Ithaca."

There was an awkward pause then.

"We look forward to meeting the son of Laertes again one day." Epistrophos drank a personal toast to it.

I shivered and addressed my fiancé. "Perhaps he considered it a fair fee for finding you a kingdom, my lord."

"Lyrnessos isn't worth that much."

"It isn't?"

"But you, my lady . . . all the bronze under the sun! Did I do better that time?" He produced a smile—a cynical and somewhat inebriated smile, perhaps, but a smile.

It was an appropriate moment to blush. "Much better!"

Unfortunately the effect was spoiled by a spluttering noise and then great blasts of laughter that Father could contain no longer and was unable to stop until his face was purple.

He apparently approved of Odysseus's banditry.

It was very embarrassing. The sons of Euneus were not pleased.

In the ensuing silence, old Demodokos came forward with his kithara to take his customary seat by the pillar. Father waved him away.

"My lords, we are eager to hear tell of the battle against the Mysians and your great deeds, which the king of Ithaca praised highly."

Mynes shook his head, setting his golden locks a-flashing in the firelight. "Ask not me, my lord. I am a man of grunts and gestures, as your daughter has been discovering. Fortunately Apollo gave my brother a tongue of silver."

Epistrophos rose. "Such modesty is most unlike him. It must be an insidious premonition of his forthcoming marriage. I cannot sing as your bard would, my lord, but I shall do the best I can." He strolled forward into the firelight, where everyone could see him, then turned to bow to the throne, like a juggler about to perform.

The hall was hushed. "Where to begin?" he declaimed. "Back in Hire, of course, nigh twelve years ago, whither came the outlaw Eumaeus, a most monstrous man, tall as a ship's mast and cruel as a rabid wolf." He had the audience shivering already. "This ogre, fresh from despoiling some lonely shepherd's household, descried a herd of the royal cattle tended only by a boy and thought to drive them off and perchance take the boy also. 'The gods have been kind to me this day!' he cried, promising a calf to Hermes. But the tender lad, being the eldest son of the king, and armed only with the slingshot that he used to slaughter vermin, waited coolly until the scoundrel was almost upon him and then contrived to stun him with a well-placed pebble between the eyes, ran up to him before he had collected his wits, and cut off his head with his own sword. . . ."

Thus Mynes made his first kill at thirteen. Numerous other fatalities followed, provoked by duels, vendettas, and raids into adjoining realms. The neighboring kings were forced to appeal to Agamemnon, who duly warned Euneus to control his son, which was a tremendous compliment but forced Mynes to venture farther afield. Epistrophos himself began to appear in the later incidents, fighting at his brother's side against Lycians, Thracians, and assorted barbarians. How many of these tales were authentic was anybody's guess, but the audience cheered them all. At last the story arrived at the current war, the summons to Aulis, the conflict of honor, and the battle against the Mysians, with men being speared in the surf like fish. Mynes listened with tolerant approval, nodding from time to time. I sat and stared at those great fists resting on his knees, wondering how it would feel to be fondled by hands that had slain so many men.

When the tale was over and the cheers had ended, Sphelos reeled upright to explain again how these mighty knights had undertaken the defense of the realm, and that the landholders of the kingdom, both secular and religious, and indeed all freemen, would certainly wish to show their appreciation by presenting the newcomers with suitable gifts.

That evening was the first time I heard Achilles' name mentioned.

6

Next morning, after a meticulous toilet, I appeared as a picture of radiant maidenhood. I learned that my fiancé was already far afield in a chariot, inspecting the borders of the kingdom with Father as his guide. Epistrophos had likewise commandeered Sphelos to take him on a survey—but of the crops and orchards in his case, surprisingly. Prior to that, the brothers had examined Father's plate armor, dismissed it as a hundred years out of date, and dragged the smiths out of bed.

Mother, supported by an unusually large plague of cronies, was very much available. Wool baskets were pushed aside and stools brought into a circle.

"You must make suitable offerings to Potnia to thank her for bringing you such a marvelous husband!" She clasped her fat hands. "How extraordinarily like his father he is. Don't you think so, Anticleia?"

"I think the noble Epistrophos is even more like, my lady."

"They both are! So strong and handsome—you agree, Briseis?"

"Possibly. Why do we have to wait two months for the wedding?"

"Yesterday you wanted to put it off for twenty years. What has changed your mind?" Her smirk irked me.

"Because I suspect I am already carrying another man's child."

"Anticleia can solve that problem for you—can't you, Anticleia?"

"Of course." The old crone bared tooth stumps in a leer. "With my trusty willow twig."

I shuddered. We declared a truce and got down to serious planning.

"Of course we must invite Hippodemia and the rest of them," Mother said, "and Alcandre and—"

"They can't come," I pointed out. "The men won't let them. Not before winter stops sailing, and by that time the passes will be closed."

She pouted her plump lips. "This war is very annoying!"

"The procession?" I asked. "How do we arrange that when Mynes is living in the palace?" A wedding would be nothing without a torchlight parade from the bride's house to the groom's. When townsfolk were married, Father always lent the bride and groom a chariot team. It didn't cost him anything.

Mother chuckled. "You could go 'round and 'round the courtyard."

"Don't be ridiculous."

"No, dear. When your Father and I were married, we paraded down to the town, and all the townsfolk showered us with nuts and fruits and flowers."

"That sounds acceptable."

"Ripe figs?" Alcmene suggested archly.

I silenced her with a glare. "I shall need a new dress."

"Oh, of course, dear. You must start on it immediately. But let's begin at the beginning. The day before the wedding, Father will sacrifice a white ewe to Our Lady Dictynna . . ."

We discussed the feast, who should attend, what singing and dancing there would be. When we reached the part where the groom led the bride off to the wedding chamber, I went back to discussing the dress again.

I managed to corner Mynes at dusk in the vestibule to outline our plans. I admit I chose a bad moment. He had just come from examining the smiths' first attempts at plate mail and was explaining to his brother how bad they were. He had probably not eaten or been off his feet all day. Plastered with road dust, he looked at me as if he could not remember who I was.

"Two months? No, that's much too soon."

"Too soon? Too soon! Don't you want to marry me?"

He groaned. "Of course I do, but the war's more import— Oh, Hades! 'Strophos, help!"

The family spokesman came to the rescue. "What he means, Briseis, is that his duties will not let him relax for a moment. If you want his full attention after your wedding, you will have to contain your impatience and put it off until winter shuts down the shipping season, understand? Then you can have him all to yourself all day long, and all night long too. Now kiss her, you great oaf."

With the emergency over, Lyrnessos tried to return to normal, but the arrival of the sons of Euneus ensured that there would never be a real return to normal. Those two young men changed the kingdom forever, and Father could do nothing about it, for no king overrules his host leader in time of war. Mynes scorned the stockade, pointing out a dozen places where it must—and would—be improved. He ordered all the townsfolk's shanties removed, except those of able-bodied archers or spearmen. That decree gave him all the young men he needed under arms and turned the palace into an armed camp. With all the smiths and leather workers making armor and weapons, bronze was soon in very short supply. Epistrophos sent collectors of taxes to search every house and seize any they could find, even holy vessels.

Old Captain Kreion vanished faster than the blush of Dawn. Father appointed him priest of Enualios and deeded some herds to the god so the god's servant might eat.

In rearranging the sleeping quarters, Mother had assigned the newcomers rooms on either side of mine. I considered that most thoughtful of her, because although the balconies were separated by walls, an active man could climb around them without trouble or even come over the top if he was reasonably motivated. I retired early, telling Ctimene to find somewhere else to sleep.

I lay awake under the stars for a long time, but no visitors came calling. I did hear voices from Epistrophos's side, eventually followed by gasps and greatly exaggerated moans of pleasure, which grew louder and louder until he said something sharply. After that he was allowed to finish whatever he was doing in silence. I decided his companion was Polydamma, a lithesome wench, if somewhat dramatic, so I could not fault his taste. The rumbles from Mynes' balcony were definitely both male, though, and that I had not expected.

Next day I learned that my fiancé had appointed a boy from the town to be his herald and apparently bedmate also. Philaios was comely, admittedly—slender and doe-eyed— but I resented the impudent airs he soon developed and the smirks he directed at me. When I took my wounded pride to Mother, I received no sympathy at all. She looked at me as if I were a simpleton.

"I fail to see why you are troubled, young lady. Would you rather he chose women? Or, even worse, one woman? I think he is behaving very correctly. If he preferred to sleep alone, I should suspect that he was not at all normal."

With that I had to be content. Ctimene returned to her mat.

A day or two later, when the sun had just set and the stars of autumn were making their entries, I went in search of Sphelos, who had not appeared for the evening meal. I found my brother on his balcony, sprawled on his bedding with a jar of wine, no clothes on, and eyes aimed in different directions. He dragged a corner of a cloth over himself and mumbled, "Go away."

"Not until I find out what's wrong with you."

"Nothing. Go 'way."

"No." I made myself comfortable. "Years ago you told me you wanted me to marry a warrior who would reign after Father and keep you on as procurator. Well, you've got what you wanted, haven't you?"

"Go away!"

"It's Epistrophos, isn't it? He's your problem."

Sphelos just groaned and covered his face with an arm, so I jabbed harder.

"I've heard an interesting story about certain goddesses whose measuring pots turned out to be larger than palace standard. I'm told that they've been cheating you for years and Epistrophos spotted it right away. Is that true?"

The arm was removed, the eyes converged on me, and

Sphelos heaved himself up to a sitting position, adjusting the blanket. "Yes. He laughed in my face when he showed me."

No man likes to be bested at his own lifelong skill by an amateur, so I could sympathize with his feelings. It was the way he had given in to them that disgusted me.

"I cannot see Epistrophos being content to be a procurator. I'm sure he'd rather heap skulls than pick grapes."

Sphelos did not wish to be comforted. He groaned and leaned his face on his hands. "He can *read*! He reads faster than I do. What sort of warrior bothers to learn to read?"

"The same sort as the procurator who learns to use a spear, I hope."

"What do you mean?"

"I mean you shame us, son of Briseus! You shame all of us. Is your life so much more precious than everyone else's that you would not risk it to defend your home?"

"I've told you! I'm not big enough to—"

"You're no dwarf. Every other man in the kingdom is busy practicing with shield and spear, and you lie here drinking yourself stupid!"

"You've got Enops and Bienor and now—"

I shouted louder, because I was afraid I would weep if I wasn't angry enough. "Why should they risk their lives protecting you? I came to tell you that you will always be welcome in Lyrnessos as long as I am queen, but if my future husband wants to throw you out with the slops, how can I argue with him now? This is what will happen to you!"

Whereupon I lifted the half-empty jar and heaved it over the railing. If there was anyone underneath at that moment, no one was ever unkind enough to tell me so. I stormed away, fighting back tears, wondering how my other brothers would react to the new order.

My flamboyant gesture with the wine jar had a gruesome echo the next day. The western end of the hill was so steep that a wall there seemed almost a formality, but it commanded the best view of the coast, so Mynes had posted lookouts there. He went around on inspection about noon, approached from the outside, climbed the hill, and clambered over the wall without being detected. The guards were under a tree, playing knucklebones. As they jumped to their feet, he ran the first man through with his sword. The second fled, but Mynes chased him, lifted him bodily, and threw him over the battlements. The fall broke his back; he died before dark. After that the sentries paid closer attention to their duties.

On hearing the story, I again sought consolation from Mother, and again did not receive it. She nodded vigorously, dewlaps flapping. "Just like his father! He is a warrior, that young man of yours."

"He frightens me!"

She sighed, patted my arm, and changed the subject.

Surprisingly, Sphelos took his harpy sister's chiding to heart. He proceeded to organize the older boys of Lyrnessos into a squadron of slingmen. Dozens of them jumped at the chance to play at being warriors. Many were already skilled, having served as shepherds, and even a stripling can pack death into a pebble. Mynes approved, of course, and soon the ominous rattle of flying rocks striking the palisade was a familiar sound near the palace.

Our fates are spun when we are born.

The sons of Euneus were everywhere, as if the palace had been invaded by a whole army of blond, clean-shaven Greeks. Usually clad only in shoes, greaves, and kilts, with swords slung on baldrics, they trotted from place to place, singly or together, barking orders and expecting them to be obeyed instantly.

Mynes wore a perpetual frown, although he sometimes remembered to grant me that grim, vulpine smile of his. Epistrophos rarely stopped smiling, yet he seemed more dangerous. When a delegation of priests and priestesses arrived with gifts for the new host leader, it was he who rejected them as inadequate and sent the whole holy army fleeing in terror. I was told he did not stop smiling the whole time he berated them.

A couple of days later I was nibbling a midday snack

under a tree in the courtyard when I saw him going by—
loping along as usual, flashing like bronze in the sunlight.
On impulse, I called out to him.

He spun around and ran straight to me. Gorgon thumped
her tail on the ground without rising; she approved of him
more than she did of his brother.

"Go!" he said to Ctimene and sank to his knees before
me, panting and shining all over with sweat. Ctimene fled.
He smiled expectantly.

"Oh, I must not interrupt you if you are busy." I was dis-
concerted by his stare.

"I am always busy—haven't you noticed? But I always
have time for a beautiful lady."

"Then, er . . ." I offered him my bowl of figs, no longer
sure why I had summoned him. "I just never seem to have
had a chance to talk with you. After all, you are to be my
brother-in-law."

He took a fig and ate it. "And Mynes is to be your husband. I don't suppose you have got much farther with him,
have you?"

"Er, no. He did enthuse for some time about that Dardanian horse we have in the stable."

Epistrophos laughed. "My brother is a very single-minded
person, Briseis. He never thinks of more than one thing at a
time. When he is sure that the palace is as safe as he can make
it and the war will not arrive until spring, then I promise you,
he will turn his attention to you and let nothing distract him."

"I look forward to it."

He cocked a golden eyebrow. "Do you? It may be too
much of a pleasure. Have you been wondering whether you
might contrive an exchange and marry me instead?"

"My lord! That is a shocking suggestion!"

"And a very intriguing one! Well? Have you?"

"Have you?" I countered.

"Oh, yes. I would marry you quite happily, Briseis, but he
would take it as a slight and feel honor bound to kill both of
us. So please don't suggest it to anyone." Epistrophos
reached out and scooped a handful of figs from my bowl.
His smile did not waver.

"You're joking!"

"No."

The worst thing was, I knew he wasn't joking. I stared fixedly at the golden fuzz on his chest. "I swear the thought never entered my head!"

"That's good. We're alike, he and I, aren't we?"

"To look at, yes."

"But there is one big difference between us."

"Tell me."

"You know why I like fighting, my lady?"

I risked a glance at his iron-gray eyes. "I can't understand why any man likes fighting."

"Most don't. A brawl, fine, but not real fighting. Run at a man with a spear in your hand and nine out of ten will turn and flee. I like it because it is so profitable. Kill a couple of men and take their armor and you have gained wealth. Kill a handful, as we did at Mysia, and you are rich. It is a vastly more enjoyable way to prosper than plowing or reaping. But Mynes doesn't see it that way. If you are to marry my brother, Briseis, you should know why he likes fighting."

"Then you had better tell me."

Epistrophos laughed. "Don't look so worried! It's perfectly simple. He enjoys fighting because he loves killing. He would rather slay a man than lay a woman, he says. I believe him. Keep that in mind."

The son of Euneus sprang to his feet and trotted away. He had never stopped smiling once, but he left me shaking.

7

Two Dardanian chariots came rattling down the Ida trail. I had foretold that our new knight would be arriving soon—an easy prophecy—and the lookouts had sent word of their coming, but they were still made to wait outside the gate until Mynes' permission arrived. By the time they reached the porch, the family had lined up in welcome, but there was a crackling tension in the air. Father was pale with fury, more visibly upset even than Mother.

Enops jumped down and marched up the steps to embrace them. He was eighteen then, big and bearded, and sporting his boar's tusk helmet—how could he have resisted that? Then he turned to Mynes, waiting with me beside him and Epistrophos one pace behind. Father began an introduction.

"I know who they are, my lord. Their deeds on the Caïcus are legend already." Enops came to them with both hands extended in greeting. "I am honored that my sister will have such a husband and Lyrnessos such defenders. If he will accept my humble aid, I shall be proud to follow the son of Euneus."

The crowd of onlookers broke into cheers. I was both relieved and proud. Mynes mumbled that he was happy to meet his future brother-in-law.

"What he means," said Epistrophos, "is that any knight trained by the fabulous son of Anchises is certain to be an outstanding colleague in battle. That's what you mean, isn't it, Brother?"

The following day, I squeezed into a chariot with Enops and Bienor. We drove down to the shore and eastward to our favorite swimming beach. The water was gloriously warm, calm, smooth as wine, but I could not keep up with my companions, who competed with each other ferociously in typical male fashion.

Gorgon and I had been sprawled on the sun-warmed grass to dry for some time before the others came puffing and dripping to join me. It is true that over the next hour or so we exchanged a few lewd quips as siblings will, but there was no thought of wrongdoing. None of us was unfamiliar with nudity.

"Mother seems reconciled to letting her babies grow up now," Enops remarked sleepily at one point.

"She had no choice," I agreed. "And she always accepts the inevitable as being exactly what she's wanted all along.

Father had no choice, either, but he doesn't have to divide up the kingdom—at least not yet—so he's happy."

"A pity Sphelos couldn't come with us. I saw him going off to practice throwing rocks."

"How can he concentrate beside all those lovely boys?"

"You're being unfair," I complained. "He is serving as best he can. Why aren't you hard at work gathering a war band?"

"Your pet Greeks have taken all the best men."

"Oh, come! There are plenty of husky woodsmen and sailors left."

"Briseis, dear child," Enops said in a fair imitation of Father's voice, "there is more to a war band than raw beef. Tell her, charioteer."

"The well-attended knight," Bienor said sleepily, but as if he were repeating a lesson, "will have trained his followers to handle sword, bow, sling, and javelin, cook meals, pitch camp, handle horses, repair chariots, strip armor from corpses, and function as porters. His troop is furnished with guides, healers, trumpeters, and heralds."

"You left out the augur and the bard," Enops said.

"Mustn't forget the bard."

"That's Aeneas!" I said. "What have Mynes and Epistrophos got?"

"Raw beef." Bienor yawned. "Brother, how's that bath attendant with the big boobs?"

"Not as tasty as she looks. The one with red hair is juicier. Sweetest little crotch you did ever see."

"You two are disgusting!" I said.

Bienor sighed happily. "That's not what they think."

"Does Aeneas approve of the sons of Euneus taking over Lyrnessos?"

Enops waved testily at flies. "He'd rather have them here than fighting for the Greeks."

"He will support the Trojans?"

"Oh, yes. He still dreams of replacing Hector, but he'll follow him if he has to."

"And you'll stay at Lyrnessos?"

"Don't know. I'm sure Mynes won't sit out the war here."

I came awake with a start. "What?"

"Dear baby sister!" Enops grabbed me and tickled. "You think that man will be satisfied to lie abed and toy with this fair soft flesh?"

I struggled free. "Stop that! And explain."

"Obvious. Mynes doesn't have his father holding his reins anymore. If the war comes to Lyrnessos, he can fight here. If it doesn't, he'll go to the war. And if the war fizzles out, he'll start one of his own."

"He'll fight Greeks? Agamemnon is his Overlord."

"His father's Overlord. Here he is his own man."

This time Bienor grabbed. "And you're his woman."

They both tickled me. I yelled and fought free again and scrambled out of reach. "Will he fight Greeks or fight Trojans?"

"I don't think he'll care which," Enops said. "Epistrophos will. He'll work out which side offers the most loot."

I reached for my dress. "You seem to have summed up those two very quickly."

"You disagree?"

"No," I said sadly. "No, I don't disagree."

My brothers took the horses to the stable. As I was removing my shoes in the porch, Mynes loomed up unexpectedly, wearing a scowl instead of his customary frown.

"Where have you been?"

"Swimming."

"Romping naked with naked men!"

I gaped at him. "You expect me to swim in my clothes?"

He grabbed my arm. He was faster than a hawk when he wanted to be. "I will not have you behaving like a wanton!" His fingers squeezed and I yelped.

"You're hurting me!"

He released his grip reluctantly. "You're my betrothed and must behave yourself."

"I was accompanied by my brothers."

"Pervert! Philaios saw you."

"You believe everything your pet sneak says? Well, until I am your wife, my brothers are responsible for my conduct, not you."

"You put them in danger, Briseis."

That threat was so outrageous that it left me speechless. He caught hold of me again and pulled me hard against him.

"You understand?"

I struggled, but he held me easily with one hand. He stank sourly of sweat and leather. I cringed before what I saw in his eyes.

"Let me go! How dare you bully me like this?"

"Behave yourself, or else I shall give orders that you are not to leave the palace. Is that clear?" Mynes pushed me away, turned on his heel, and stalked off.

The next time my brothers went swimming, I stayed home.

8

The grape festival was imminent, but when I offered to make Mynes a mask to match my own he turned sunset red and shouted that no future wife of his was going to shame herself at an orgy. End of discussion.

"You *are* as good as married to him, dear," Mother said, with some sympathy, "and married women *do* usually stay away until they have produced an heir."

True. Accidents did happen, although I had expected to dance with no one but him. I tried hinting that he should stay home and worship the god with me, but he went with the others. Everyone went, even Sphelos. I lay alone and sleepless on my balcony, hearing the singing and laughter in the distance and thinking of Polydorus.

The tales of isolated Greek raids still drifting in were old news, and it seemed the raiders had gone home for the winter. Mynes agreed to celebrate our wedding at the next full moon, when I turned sixteen.

Ctimene and I were passing the shuttle back and forth at
a loom in the queen's hall. We had been chattering about details of the marriage feast and had fallen into pensive silence, when in walked Bienor, an unexpected visitor. Even
more surprising, he was fresh from the bath, oiled and
scented, clad in sparkling white linen shorts—extremely
short shorts, as was his custom. Although he was still all
bone and sinew, even I could not deny that he was a striking
young man now—prince, charioteer, apprentice warrior.
Bracelets, necklace, the jewel-hilted sword all sparkled.

"By the smile of Apollo!" I said. "Have I forgotten a
feast?"

"I have been making sacrifice." He went to a window.

"I am sure the gods were surprised. If you're looking for
Mother, she is wallowing in the bath and will not appear
soon."

"No."

"Then to what do we owe the honor? Shouldn't you be
outside sweating and bruising? Which god?" I added suspiciously.

"Aphrodite." He spun around and came toward us with an
ominous glint in his eye, a gleam that had spelled trouble
ever since I could remember. He stopped when he reached
Ctimene and put an arm around her. "Sister, you own the
most beautiful slave in the palace. It would be good hus-
bandry to start taking children off her."

My twin had always been able to make me raise my voice,
if not always my fists. I raised it then. "Take your hands off
her!" I began. If I wanted his advice, I yelled, then I was
quite capable of asking for it. I had been defending Ctimene
from lechers since the day she arrived, I screeched, *and* he
was very high on the list of heartless wantons around Lyrnessos, *and* I had refused innumerable offers for her favors
and had always promised her that if she found a lover to
please her she had only to ask me *and* . . .

He had both arms around her now, and she seemed to
be both weeping and burrowing into his chest. He was
smirking.

"Oh, no!" I said quietly.

"Oh, yes."

Having much on my mind, I had noticed only vaguely that my slave was behaving oddly lately—chirruping one moment, mournful the next, withdrawn, then effusive, up and down all the time, very unlike her usual serene self. That this change had happened just after the grape festival had not occurred to me. She claimed that she had enjoyed herself there but did not know who had partnered her—not his name nor what he looked like under the mask. In my abstraction, I had not pressed her.

"It was you she met at the Dionysia?"

"It was I who cut her out of the pack. A dozen boys were after her, but Enops helped me—even if they did not know who we were, none of them wanted to argue with us. I carried off your little dove. We worshiped the god together all night long."

Intolerable Bienor and his tricks! Dionysia or not, how dare he seduce my personal body servant! And how dare she cuddle against him like that, as if he could defend her from me?

"Sister, I am asking you to keep your promise to her."

"Let her ask for herself! I can't believe she's so addlepated as to want anything to do with you."

"She loves me. I love her. I want her as my bedmate. I will be faithful and kind and make her happy." He attempted to look virtuous. "I have not touched another girl since I lay with her at the grape festival."

"You? Being chaste? I don't believe it!"

His grin grew even more lupine. "I didn't say that. Did you know you snore, Briseis?"

What? *No!* Intolerable! My anger roared like a smith's furnace. I clenched a fist, thought better of it very quickly, drew a deep breath, but before I could utter a single bellow, Bienor said, "Wait! It wasn't her idea. It was mine." Dark eyes gleamed up at me, overflowing with mockery. "Two nights after the festival, I climbed up to your balcony, stepped right over you, and went to where she was sleeping. She couldn't cry out, because it would have caused a scandal—that's what I told her, anyway! I kissed her a little

· and fondled until she admitted she didn't *want* to cry out, so that was that. . . . Since then, I've come in by the door. You do snore, but not much. Just once in a while. We find it reassuring."

Appalled, I said, "You've done this often?"

Smirk. "Every night."

I was aghast. Suppose Mynes heard a man had been seen entering or leaving my room? I shivered so hard I could barely speak. "She had only to ask me!"

"Had she?" A very rare expression came over my brother's face, but I knew my twin well enough to recognize it as sincerity. "She's frightened of you, Briseis. I know you're a good mistress, but you're still a mistress and she's still a slave. You've slapped her a few times. Don't deny it. You've always had a brute of a temper, and one day you may get really mad and order her beaten to raw bones—of course she's frightened of you!" He sighed. "You and I have always done more fighting than loving, haven't we? I was frightened of you when we were children. You used to rub my face in the dirt, remember?"

"I should never have stopped!"

"I'm still afraid of you! I'm afraid you'll refuse to keep the promise you gave Ctimene, just to spite me."

"That's ridiculous!"

"Then you consent? Darling, it's all right! She agrees! I told you she would!" He rearranged Ctimene in his embrace so he could kiss her, and then did so—hard and long, right in front of me. At first her fists were clenched against his back; I watched enviously as they relaxed and opened, and then her fingers began to dig into his flesh. If that was not passion, I did not know what passion was. Why could Mynes not kiss me like that a few times?

When the lovers paused for breath, I said, "Is this really want you want, girl?"

She was flushed and panting, eyes glittering like rock crystal. "Yes, my lady, oh yes!"

"Told you," Bienor said smugly, but he was pink too.

"You be kind to her!"

"Kind? I love her! I adore her. I swear it by Aphrodite!"

Well, at least he hadn't demanded that I give her to him, although that might follow. Ctimene thanked me with tears on her cheeks.

I hugged her and then Bienor, too. "Be happy. Brother, I'll hold you to your promise." I took another look at the two of them and sighed. "Why don't you go off and finish what you just started? I'm sure I'll get no useful work out of—"

They were gone, racing away hand in hand to find a bed.

How could I have objected? It was a very touching romance. I felt quite moved until I thought of my devious twin fornicating with my slave in my own bedroom while I slept—insolence! And sly! If I had tried to stand in his way, the young lout would have threatened to spread the story and make me a laughingstock. Bienor in love was a hard idea to swallow. How long would my rapscallion brother keep his promises? A month would be a surprise.

I set off in search of Father. Gorgon lurched to her feet and followed.

I found him slumped in his favorite chair on his balcony, amid a surprising litter of stools and tables and empty goblets, remains of some meeting that had not been cleared away. Automatically I checked the mirrored sea for signs of Greek raiders, but it bore only a couple of fishing boats. Lesbos was a blue haze across the mouth of the gulf.

"Father, I need to . . . Are you all right?"

He opened his eyes and peered at me uncertainly. "Mm? Yes. A headache, that's all. What's the matter, cygnet?"

"I need to talk to you!"

He sighed as if he had been afraid of that. "Pull over that stool, then. Here, by me. Closer. Now tell me."

I told him—my slave was at that moment rollicking in bed with my brother. He regarded me with puzzlement or disbelief, as if he had expected some very different complaint.

"But if Bienor has your permission . . . I don't understand your problem."

"I know he'll tire of her and that will hurt her horribly. With all the troubles Ctimene has known already, a broken heart seems an unnecessary addition. Can I make him marry her?"

"Marry? You want your brother to marry a slave?" Father rubbed his beard the way he did when he wanted to hide a smile. "Who is going to provide the dowry? Me? You?"

"You're telling me I'm being stupid?"

"A little unrealistic. Can you imagine what your mother would say? She'd shake Olympus!"

"Ctimene was wellborn."

He squeezed my hand, a gesture which I normally resented, but this time found oddly reassuring. "A noble can't marry a slave, Princess, no matter who her father was."

He meant, *What would people say?* which was Mother's constant lament. Even Enops had sneered at Sphelos for trying to turn Daos into a lover. Girl slave or boy slave, no matter. Pleasure, yes. Commitment, never.

"I think you're worrying unnecessarily, Briseis. Of course his infatuation will fade, and so will hers. None of us can go through life in a state of feverish passion, any more than we can eat beef at every meal. Affection and protection are the bread of life. A noble's concubine may fare much better than a freeborn wife. I've made my share of bastards, as I'm sure you know, but I look after them—see they eat well, even in lean years. If you can't trust Bienor to do as much for the girl, then do it yourself. It seems your slave has been given to a man genuinely fond of her. She is indeed blessed by Aphrodite."

"Meaning that most women are not?"

He glanced at me sharply. There was a nasty pause before he said wistfully, "I thought that was why you had come."

It wasn't. But since I was there . . . "He has shown no signs of loving me or wanting to make me love him."

Father sighed and reached out to pat Gorgon, who was sitting right by him with her tongue lolling out, staring at him and panting. "Love will grow in time. Remember telling me you wanted a protector? Mynes may well be the finest warrior I ever met, greater than his father. Perhaps Aeneas or Odysseus . . . but I suspect that even they would hesitate to meet the son of Euneus in battle. He will be strict, demanding, probably never very gentle, but you and the children you bear him will be as well guarded as anyone can be.

There is nothing more I can do, Briseis. I made him host leader. We swore oaths before the gods."

"But . . . Philaios was weeping last night—I heard him." I waited, but Father did not ask who Philaios was, which was a bad sign. "Mynes hurt some of the bath attendants, too, hasn't he? They complained to Mother and she said she would ask you to speak to him."

"I did. He promised to be more careful." Father spoke to far-off Lesbos, not to me. There was little a king could do to discipline his host leader. Altes of Pedasos was cuckolded by his son.

"Remember when Enops went off to seek his tassels?" I demanded. "You warned him that those who live by death are different from other men. They're natural killers, you said, like hawks or sharks. They don't see things the way we do. Are you going to marry me to a—"

"Stop!" Father snapped. "It's done. He's a hard man, but it's a hard world. Obey him, try to honor him in spite of his faults. Lyrnessos will be in good hands, strong hands."

"Yes, my lord." Who was I to pity Ctimene?

He offered a cheek. I stooped to kiss it.

I went away and left him to his own troubles.

9

That conversation blew away the mist. I could admit now that I really did not want to marry Mynes son of Euneus. But Father would do nothing, and Mother certainly could not. That left the gods. I strode out of the palace gates and down to the sacred grove.

There was no sign of Maera in her mossy, tumbledown hovel. The Lady would be home, of course. I went over to the rickety gate and was at once conscious of her presence, that warming sense of divinity in the air. The grove was very still, poised, anxious, full of the leafy, woodsy scents of morning. The last bells and flowering nettles still lingered among the yellow weeds, and the busy thrum of insects almost drowned out the distant singing.

I had not thought to bring an offering. I could go and fetch one, but the moment seemed too urgent to brook delay. When I lifted the gate on its leather hinges and stepped quietly into the precinct, the throb of holiness increased with a rush. My feet trod soundless on the soft litter. Sunlight filtering through the high canopy sparkled on the gnarled cypress xoanon, glistening with the fresh oil and honey of offerings. It was no more like a woman than usual, yet the restless shine of light on it added life, somehow, and the buzz of flies made a song for her, as if the old, old goddess hummed gently while she watched me approach. I knelt in the dampness before her, convinced I had been expected.

Unfamiliar birdsong twittered secrets whose meaning flitted always just out of reach. I searched the web of branches and could not see them, those mysterious birds. Then a faint breeze sighed through the grove, a warm breath. Leaves whispered. Speckles of sunlight danced everywhere like gnats.

"What is it?" I cried. "What are you trying to tell me?"

There were no words, only feelings. The goddess was there—behind me, before me, anywhere I wasn't looking. Laughing a little, teasing, taunting me that I could not understand something so obvious to her.

"You summoned me! What do you want of me? Speak!"

Never since I was a child had I felt the nearness so strongly. Feelings flowed and surged—joy and fear, sorrow and glory. Emotions gamboled in the riot of light and lurked in the deep shadow. Not in words, the meaning came. Anguish and terror. Foolish, transient mortals. Fate and duty.

A crow croaked and fluttered down onto the xoanon, barely arm's length from me where I knelt so still, barely daring to breathe. It peered at me with its fierce eye. A *solitary* crow is very rare, of course, but all I could recall from Helenus's lore was that it was a fearfully inauspicious sign at a wedding. A raven croaked somewhere on my left and the crow took wing.

"No!" I cried! "No, no, no! Not yet! I am not ready!"

I leaped to my feet and fled from the grove. I raced out of the gate without closing it, up the hill to the palace. Men were hurrying out the gate as I reached it. There were shouts of, "There she is!" and, "My lady?" and, "Quiet, fool! She knows already." They cleared out of my way, staring with frightened eyes as I rushed by them, through the maze of wattle huts that had invaded the outer courtyard. Women kneeling over their grindstones looked up in surprise, women with spindles paused in their urgent chatter, dogs barked, naked children stared. I ran up the steps to the porch, across the inner courtyard, through the portico, the vestibule. More servants were hurrying into the megaron carrying firewood, which was confirmation of my fears, for there were no feasts or sacrifices planned. Gasping for breath now, I stumbled up the staircase and started along the corridor. Mother appeared in front of me like a surfacing whale and threw out her arms. She was a huge, soft, immovable pillow. My headlong progress ended abruptly in her embrace.

"Calm yourself, dearest!"

"Where is he? What happened? *Let me go!*" My breathing rasped like a whetstone. I struggled in vain. She was shorter than me but much heavier, and a powerful woman still.

"Be calm! What will people think of you? There's no hurry. He isn't conscious. He won't know you."

"He's dead, isn't he? Dead!"

"No, dear. But the Archer has smitten him sorely."

I fought my way free of her smothering hug and tried to inspect her face in the gloom. She seemed pale, that was all I could tell from her expression. There were no scratches on her cheeks, but her hair was straggly and disheveled. She was lying to me, I was certain of it. There was a horrible taste in my throat.

"He's *dead!*"

"Shush! No, dear. You are not to disturb him. He's resting, being well cared for."

"He was all right when I left him. Just a headache, he said."

Her efforts to smile were a mockery. "Well, it is more than a headache now. No, I won't have it, Briseis! Stop! You listen to me. You have duties to perform now."

I ceased my efforts to get by her. "Duties?"

She hugged me again, but this time it was a different sort of hug, a sorrowful, motherly hug. "The land must have a king, dear. Mynes is getting ready."

"Oh, no! I won't, I won't!"

"Would you have me do it? Who do you suggest would be a suitable husband for me, dearest?"

I could say nothing but, "No, no!"

"Yes, yes. You see how it is. Come, now. You must be quick."

She clamped a thick hand on my wrist and led me along the passage. That grip—hand on wrist—was a grotesque parody of the marriage gesture, but I don't suppose she realized she was using it. Though her fingers were soft, they were powerful, and she dragged me past Father's door when I would have looked in. I could have broken loose had I exerted myself, I suppose, but one cannot treat a new widow so.

My father was dead. She knew it. I knew it. Probably everyone in the kingdom knew it, but the awful pretense would be kept up for as long as it took to secure the succession.

10

They bathed me, oiled me, scented me. The grand gown was not ready, so they robed me in the best I had. They tinted my face and nipples. They dressed my hair, draped a white cloth over it, and around my head wove a garland of pomegranate twigs.

Mother reappeared, restored to her normal impeccable grooming, although chinks in the layers of face paint showed pallor within. Her eyes were starkly dry.

"You look like a goddess, my dear," she said, her smile carved by a very bad sculptor.

I thanked her mechanically—if she could reap, then I could winnow.

She nodded approval and squeezed my hand. "If your eyes start to misbehave, look upward, dear. That staunches tears." She led me downstairs, and the others followed into the muddled assembly in the megaron, where more people were hurrying in all the time, all obviously newly washed and hurriedly dressed and frightened half to death. Only a small fire crackled in the center, but it smoked enough to make the hall acrid and stuffy on a hot morning in fall. Sphelos and Enops had been sacrificing a ewe, which should have been Father's honor. As they washed their hands two tortoiseshell lutes, one set of pipes, and a cymbalist began wandering at random over a musical landscape.

"You sit here by the hearth, dear," Mother said. "Mynes will be along very . . . Here he is."

My husband to be came striding in with his brother at his side, the two of them towering over the crowd that opened to make way for them. A garland like mine sat on his hair, which still hung wetly, and a couple of bloody scrapes on chin showed the effects of a too-hasty shave. On one shoulder hung a dolphin mantle, but he had not discarded those foolish Greek greaves of his—leather, though, not bronze. He took the chair at my side. Epistrophos sat next to him, studying the proceedings with an intent, darting gaze.

Mynes' iron-gray eyes searched me for signs of weakness. "Your father's sudden illness is a great shock to all of us. I offer my deepest sympathy."

"Thank you." That did not seem quite enough. "The gods mix good with evil, my lord. My fortune is to be sooner your wife."

"That fortune is mine, my lady."

"Briseis!" exclaimed Epistrophos. "He's improving!"

Was he testing me with his foolish humor? I would not be found wanting. "We may make a courtier out of him yet." We were about to make a king out of him.

"Oh, never! But if you aim at extracting one compliment a day, you may not fall too short."

"Only on my good days," Mynes said. "And this day is one of both sadness and great happiness. I confess, Briseis, that I have not been married very often. Your customs may not be those I know. Inform me what happens next."

"We have a feast, of course. There will be singing and dancing. Or there should be. I hope we get one song " My voice cracked. I took a few deep breaths.

"You will have songs, I promise."

But no chariot. I would not have my chariot procession, nor even a parade with torches, not in broad daylight. What sort of a feast would it be with Father stiffening on his bed upstairs while his family made merry in his palace? Brief, of course, just the minimum required for the people to know that we had been properly wed.

No one ate much. Some people drank too much, including me, but even unwatered wine could only make me feel nauseous, not soothe my ache or warm my heart. Dionysus had no power over me that day.

Our customs in the Troad were much like the Greeks'. After the feast, the bride uncovered her head to show her acceptance of the marriage, the guests sprinkled grain and nuts and fruits over the happy couple and sang hymns to them. The bride must eat an apple. Then the groom took her by the wrist and led her away to his home, with her mother going in front and all the guests rejoicing alongside, singing and bearing torches. The groom's best friend stood guard over the door of the bridal chamber until dawn, when the music and singing ended.

But in this case the groom led the bride upstairs to his room, and nobody followed.

The room was dim, because the drapes had been drawn against the sun, but it was breathlessly hot. No one had thought to bring flowers to perfume it. It smelled of men. All I could see was the bed platform waiting for me, with the cloths on it rumpled as if he had brought them in from the balcony himself and thrown them down there. He shut the door and stood with his back to it. Then he laughed.

I turned in surprise, for I had never heard him laugh before.

"I'm a king! You're the queen and I'm the king!" He laughed again, in sheer joy. "King Mynes, son of Euneus!"

"Not yet!" I meant that my father was not officially dead yet, but he misunderstood and frowned.

" 'Sright. I have to bed you first, so we're man and wife." He lurched forward and clasped me in his thick arms. He forced his tongue into my mouth. Dionysus had stolen his wits. I was a stone.

He released me crossly. "It must be done. Take off your clothes."

I turned from him and undressed with shaking fingers, telling my heart that I was always nervous at this stage and always enjoyed myself later. My heart did not believe a word of it.

He belched. "I know about women. I'm not like that runt brother of yours. Just because I enjoy boys does not mean I can't deal with women. I'm sure I will be able to make you all hot and sweaty when I have the time. At the moment the kingdom needs me more."

"Then this can wait," I whispered, standing there with my clothes heaped around my feet.

"I can't." He laughed again. "Look what you've done to me already! There! See the treat I have for you?" He came forward, naked and fully aroused. He took my hand and pressed it to his groin. "You have to give me the scepter, but first I'm going to give you mine." He nuzzled my neck.

I wanted to tell him to go and give it to Philaios, but I was sober now, unfortunately. My lack of response began to annoy him.

"Lie down!"

I crawled onto the bed and stretched out. He lay beside me. He did try, I admit—fondling my breasts, licking my nipples, stroking my thighs, but he might as well have been kneading dough for all I could feel. My hands lay at my sides as if nailed there. He gave up the pretense and glared at me, his eyes close above mine.

"Why are you so reluctant? Is there some other man?"

"No, no, no!"

"If you ever as much as touch another man, I'll cut out your womb and choke him with it."

"No, my lord. I just want a little love."

"Love?" He belched again. "Love? When you earn it. At the moment Philaios gets my love. Wives are for breeding sons and running households. Give me two or three big, strong sons, and I will love you for it. Do your duties and don't prattle about love. If you are an obedient, dutiful wife, then I will be a considerate and tolerant husband. I won't meddle in household things. Understand?"

I choked back a sob and nodded. Physically, he was everything I could have dreamed of, yet I, who had coupled eagerly with other men, was strangely reluctant to accept this one.

He rolled off the bed and went across to a fine chest of carved olive wood that Father had given him. In a moment he came back with a flask.

"Oil," he said. "You want to attend to this?"

I just shook my head, terrified I was about to disgrace myself by weeping.

He spread oil on his phallus, then told me to part my legs so he could apply some to me, working it into me with a finger. He tossed the flask away, parted my legs, and inserted his member with his hand as if he were putting a cork in a bottle. I closed my eyes, bit my lip, and tried not to cry out. Once he was in place he pushed himself all the way in by brute force. It hurt horribly. When he could go no farther and his full weight was on me, he tried to kiss me again and I turned my head away.

He growled furiously. "As you like. You just want to get it over with?" He raised his hips and thrust down again.

I did cry out then, and the next time. After that I restrained my sobs and lay there in silence as he hammered on me. It grew no easier—worse, in fact, as he became faster and frantic and more aroused. Finally he grunted and stopped. When he rolled off me, I turned my back and let the tears flow.

"Now you're my wife," he said, "and I'm king. I expect it will be easier next time."

I heard him shuffling around for a moment, dressing. The door closed as he went off to supervise the arrangements for his predecessor's funeral.

That was my wedding. Eventually I took a terrible revenge for it.

11

Mother must have had watchers posted, for in a very few minutes she slipped into the room, closing the door quietly behind her. I dragged a rumpled blanket over my nakedness and wiped my eyes.

Awkward in her finery, she came over to sit on the edge of the bed and frowned. "Not much fun?"

"None at all."

She held out her hands. I took them and she gripped mine tightly. "It will be. He has a lot on his mind just now. I am sure he will be a fine husband and a strong king. Don't expect the passion to start right away, my dear, but it will come. The first few times are not easy, but it gets much better."

My first time had been with Polydorus, and there had been passion aplenty then.

"Soon," she said, and sighed. "I had four years to learn to be a wife without having to be a queen. You must learn both at once, my dear. I am sorry."

I peered carefully at her face in the gloom, but I could see no scratches. Some of the paint had flaked off, though. "He's dead. You admit it now?"

"Hermes has come for him. It happened just after the wedding. *No!*" She clung to my hands. "No, Briseis! You will be Potnia, you cannot scar your cheeks."

I struggled briefly, then turned my head away.

"That is forbidden to us, dear," she said. "You promise?"

I nodded. She released me. I rolled over and sobbed. Not even allowed to mourn him properly!

She let me weep for a very few minutes, then she spoke in her practical, time-to-do-your-duty voice. "After the funeral, Mynes must receive the scepter. It should be done today, Panope."

I twisted around and rose on one elbow. *"Don't call me that!"*

"But you are a married woman now."

"If I can't even mourn him, then I will not forget his name. I am Briseis and always will be!"

She sighed and forced another smile. "As you wish. He would have been pleased. Do you wish me to go over the ceremony with you?"

"But why should . . . ? That is your duty!"

She shook her head. In sudden horror I lurched upright on the bedding and threw my arms around her, so that she almost overbalanced. "No! Oh, no! You mustn't, mustn't!"

She sat unmoving, tolerating me. "We've been married more than thirty years. I will not let him go on unaccompanied." She waited until my next outburst subsided. Her expression was as steadfast as Potnia's in the frescoes. "It is my privilege, Briseis. You cannot deprive me of it. The fates were kind, for few women survive so many births. The gods gave us great happiness. We came together like fire, as you and Mynes will, and after the fire faded, the love remained. Like molten bronze—when it cools, the mold and the cast have found a perfect fit. I learned to smile at his faults and weep at his virtues."

"You don't have to do this! When Hippodemia died, Anchises didn't—"

"Men don't. Women are different. I will not have people say I did not love him enough. We shall go on together. Besides, the world is changing. Lyrnessos is changing. I suppose I'm being cowardly, but I don't want to see what is going to happen. My mind is made up. Help me, please, by not making it harder?"

I sniffled and sobbed and reluctantly nodded.

"Now, your father always told me he would not want a

large retinue, and Mynes has agreed. Just one will do for me."

"Philona?"

"Mm . . . no, Megara, I think. She's been with me all my life and cannot have many more years. . . . Are you listening?"

I nodded dumbly.

"And you promise? No extravagant display, please?"

"Just Megara," I agreed, although it felt very wrong to send a queen on with only one attendant when she had lived surrounded by them all her life. She listed some bequests she wanted to make to her friends, a few personal treasures she would take with her. I nodded and nodded, struggling to concentrate and remember.

"Now, are you ready to be a woman, or do you want to stay a child for longer?" She smiled and squeezed my hand. "You can have ten minutes."

I shuddered and rubbed my eyes. "I am ready." But I did not think I should ever be ready. How much life and death must I pack into one day?

"Good." She patted my shoulder. "Now, about the ceremony. Anticleia will help you with the potions. You will not need very much the first time."

"What if the goddess doesn't come?" I whispered.

"Oh, I'm sure she will, because it is important that the people know she supports the new king. Have you ever known her to fail us?"

"No," I admitted. "But that was for you. Suppose she will not come at my asking?"

She took my hands again and held them. "She did not always come for me, either, Briseis," she said softly. "But she always came for the people."

"I don't understand."

"I just mean that sometimes I was not aware of the goddess as you all were. I usually was, but not always." Her eyes searched mine, seeking comprehension.

"You were *pretending*?"

"No. I'm trying to tell you that you may not always sense her with you, but that it won't matter. It just means that she

trusts you, as her priestess, to do what she would do or speak
the words of the ritual as she would. You are her representa-
tive, even if you are not her epiphany. And no one else will
notice any difference, I promise you."

I shivered. "I'll try. But I don't want you to go. Surely you
do not need to go with—"

The queen's voice rang out like Potnia's. *"Be silent!"*

I cringed back and she relented. "That is settled, Briseis!
There will be no argument. Now, about the giving of the
sword. Anticleia will help you with the potion. The goddess
usually begins with the blessing . . ."

By the time I had dressed, the wailing had begun. I was allowed in to see my father. He lay on fresh fleeces, clad in a
plain new robe. His face was a strange ivory color, oddly
shrunken, but otherwise he might have been sleeping. The
room was shadowed, unbearably hot, reeking of strong perfumes, and also full of women, wailing, shrieking, clawing
at their cheeks and breasts, tearing their hair. I pulled one
away from him—I could not even recall her name, but she
was the mother of two of his bastards—so I could take her
place, holding his head. I wailed and wept, for that was all I
was allowed to do. Who would want to be a queen if it meant
she could not even mourn her father properly?

Royal funerals should be foreseen so that they can be properly prepared, but the gods had sent no warning—neither to
me nor to anyone else. Give him his due, Mynes stinted
nothing that could have been provided in the time available.

Six black oxen with gilded horns pulled the catafalque
bearing my father, clad in his finest robe, anointed with rich
unguents, draped with his tasseled mantle. Immediately behind walked fifty women, barefoot and unkempt, wailing
and lamenting. Then came the sacrificial sheep and bullocks; Sphelos driving Mother; Enops and Bienor on foot
and wearing armor; King Mynes and Queen Briseis in a
chariot; the three hundred men of the army; the court; palace
servants, slaves, and mule carts with supplies for the feast;
the entire population of Lyrnessos.

I watched it all as if from a great distance, too numb to feel anything. When Mynes said, "Are you all right?" I stared up at him dumbly before I eventually said, "Of course."

He nodded approvingly. "In Greece, when a warrior dies, it is customary to hold funeral games in his honor—chariot racing, wrestling, and so on. His companions compete for his armor and trappings, so that only the best may inherit them. His leader may donate other prizes to honor his memory."

"My father was not much of a warrior when I knew him, but I expect he would have been flattered."

"Then I shall give rich prizes. It will be a good exercise for the army."

Chthonia take his army! She had taken my father.

The sun's heat was intense for so late in the year, but he could not feel that. He could not suffer now. He was bound for the realm of shades, of disembodied spirits. Then he must find his way over the river, with the help we should give him. And Mother at his side. Beyond that, they would go on together so they could live in the halls of the goddess for eternity. Would he meet Daos there?

The cortege wound its way through the town and along the shore to the pyre, where men were still at work, although they had already raised a pile of timber larger than a house. The body was transferred from the wagon to the bier, then the mourners advanced one by one to strew locks of their hair on the corpse. The court officials added gifts that Mynes had provided to accompany the king on his journey—robes, draperies, bowls, carvings. They were a generous provision, but many of the humble townsfolk brought treasures of their own, little things they had made themselves—figurines, weavings, wooden dishes—and those tributes had not been anticipated. His favorite dogs were laid at his feet.

The women's strident wailing was torture, but all my tears had been shed. I had none left, not even for Mother. She sat quietly on a chair, with her friends and cronies around her, reminiscing with them. I knelt and held her hand. Bienor stood behind her, struggling to keep his weeping silent.

Every now and again old Anticleia would offer her another sip of the poison, but eventually she stopped accepting it. Soon after that her words became slurred and her head drooped.

In the background, Megara and Perimedes were being dosed with poppy. The old woman had seemed more or less unconscious when she arrived, but the boy was still moaning and making a fuss.

The sacrificial fires blazed in the noon heat. Sphelos and Enops methodically slaughtered sheep and bullocks, drawing knives of curved bronze across their throats. Other men were butchering the carcasses, piling the fat upon the body to make sure it burned well. Wrapped in the hides, the bones were burned and sent up their smoky tribute to the appropriate gods.

Then I realized that Mother's eyes were closed. Her breathing stopped, started again, stopped, started . . . I shouted for someone to fetch Sphelos and Enops. They came at once, but she did not respond to their voices. Finally Mynes edged in through the crowd.

"Has she gone?" His voice seemed unnecessarily loud.

Anticleia took up a silver bowl filled with water, tipped it out and placed the cool metal to Mother's nostrils.

She bent to see, straightened up, and nodded. "She has gone, my lord."

"Are you sure!" I cried, jumping to my feet. "Quite sure!"

Mynes put an arm around me. "We are sure. Come, my queen." He led me away. I felt no need to weep on his shoulder.

Queen Nemertes' body was laid beside her lord's and swathed in more of the animal fat. I suppose someone made quite certain that she was truly dead, for that is customary, but I did not inquire. The two slaves were brought over and laid by their feet, and Enops, our warrior, cut their throats. Sphelos lit the pyre. At first the flames were invisible in the heat, but soon the smoke began to climb, and eventually the crackling of the burning pines drowned out even the wailing of the women. Now their souls were free and Hermes would lead them together to the shadow realms.

Later we feasted on the meat of the sacrificial animals. I gulped down one bite. I remember watching the children—the older ones gorging, the youngsters doubtful of the unfamiliar taste.

"You are weary, wife," my husband said. "We shall put off the rest of the ceremonies until tomorrow or the next day."

"No."

His eyes widened. "I am king now, Briseis."

"And I am the priestess of Potnia. In certain matters, I rule, my lord."

He did not like that, but he did not argue, not then. It was a thing that would have to be determined between us at a later date, for some men are unwilling to yield authority to their wives in anything. I think that is why the old ways have died out now everywhere.

When it was over, when the balefire had dwindled to embers and those had been doused with wine, the bones were gathered into the funerary vessel, which would later be buried beside my ancestors'. Then Mynes and I stood on a carpet to receive the acknowledgment of the townsfolk. In ones and twos they bent their knees to us and then moved on. I saw many eyes red with weeping, many bloodied cheeks. The common folk of Lyrnessos sincerely mourned their former king and queen, and that is a tribute few monarchs earn.

And still the day had not ended. As the court was assembling in the megaron, I joined Anticleia in the poky little herbarium next to the kitchen quarters. She seemed more gaunt and skeletal than ever, her hair a white cataract in the gloom as she stooped over a daunting display of clay bottles laid out on the table, but she tried to smile encouragingly.

"You will be a worthy Potnia, my lady!" Her voice was hoarse from wailing.

"I am big enough, certainly," I agreed, thinking of the frescoes.

She smiled in toothless approval and poured something into a goblet. Then she took up a larger bottle, shook it, and added some of its contents to the brew. She offered me the goblet.

"More."

She frowned and increased the dose a little.

"More!" I said. "Mother had it almost full."

"You are not accustomed to it! It can be dangerous, my lady. There are potent ingredients—poppy milk and henbane and aconite . . ."

I took up the bottle myself and poured.

Anticleia wrestled it away from me. "Fool! You do not know what you are risking."

"I am not going to risk being unworthy! Potnia must come!" I decided I had an ample dose there. It tasted even more vile than any of her other concoctions that I had tried in the past.

"You had better not wait too long, my lady. It will act very quickly on you, I think." The singing had begun in the distance. She took a joyful ribbon and tied the sacral knot in my hair.

"Come then. Let us go in." I took a couple of steps and felt the floor shift. "Mm. It is powerful, isn't it!"

To embody a major god is an experience of which I can say little, for mortal tongues lack the words required. Potnia did not come as a thunderclap, but filled me in a gentle flow of joy, as a pitcher is filled. As Briseis, I needed Anticleia's steadying hand until we reached the door of the megaron, but by then the goddess ruled and shook her off. Potnia floated into the dark expectant hall where the worshipers were assembled, kneeling in the shadows, waiting for her. We came to them along the narrow corridor that had been left for us, and even in the darkness the way was bright, so we could see every bowed head and the fingers we must not tread on. The throne waited, empty, unfamiliar, menacing; the floor obliging flexed and tilted, so that I moved downhill the rest of the way. We almost stumbled, turned, sat faster than I intended.

Sitting was better. My brothers and the shining locks of Mynes and Epistrophos were awash in singing that surged like sea waves all around. The music swayed with odors of apple and pistachio; we heard bright wraiths of perfume curling through the hall, quince and coriander. Potnia, goddess queen of Lyrnessos enthroned we were, and these were our people singing to us, seeking our blessing on their new king. How Mynes sweated in his tasseled mantle and boar's tusk helmet! I remembered how Briseis had seen him earlier, naked and aroused, the pale brown hair on his body, thin scars like white wires, bunched muscles quickly becoming a great weight pressing me down, flushed face close above mine, eyes closed, teeth bared as he thrust and thrust and I cried out in pain. A mighty man. The king. But to the goddess he was ephemeral, already dead, a rotting corpse.

The hall grew brighter, yet misty. I smiled at all their little ant faces peering adoringly at me, at Potnia. My ears rang with their paean. From far away, Mynes walked forward and knelt again to lay an ivory casket at my feet. Sphelos brought a golden vase, and Enops came, and others, while on the walls another procession took other offerings to another Potnia. Painted flowers swayed in the breeze, and dolphins curved through the sea.

My hand rose by itself and the singing died. I was on my feet, for I weighed nothing. Out of the glare, fat old Alcmene offered me the basket with the serpents. I took one in my right hand and watched with interest as it sank its fangs into my wrist. It was not venomous. I took the other in my left hand and raised them both to show them to my people and hear their cries of joy at the coming of Potnia Theron. I heard her speak, blessing the harvest and crops and herds. I suppose that when she was done with the serpents she threw them back in the basket as I had seen Mother do, but I do not recall.

Then others and, at last, Potnia Aphaea. She accepted the bronze sword and our arm raised it effortlessly overhead, although Briseis could not have done that by herself. She reversed it and held out the hilt to Mynes' strong hands. Again the goddess's voice boomed through the megaron, but what she said, I did not hear. I barely even registered his enraged face floating before us like a sun in clouds, and I do not recall him striking her, but he did.

Mother had often seemed dizzy and confused after the goddess left her, so it was no surprise that I fainted outright.

I do not remember. I was told later that there was little out-
cry, perhaps because everyone expected him to be struck
dead. He wasn't. He carried me upstairs in his arms. All I
know is that I awoke much later in his bed, in darkness, with
the worst headache I had ever experienced. I was streaming
sweat and yet my mouth was dry as ashes. I was a goddess
no longer.

I was Briseis, not quite sixteen, queen of Lyrnessus. A
married woman. That much I could be sure of, because I had
a naked husband snoring at my side and a very sore sticky
place between my legs.

BOOK SEVEN

PATROCLUS

1

In all the days of my mother and her mother before her, holy Potnia had never been known to prophesy. She was manifest at many ceremonies throughout the year and at some of them spoke a ritual blessing. Rarely she might comment on other matters, such as a shrine in need of restoration, and most recently she had assured us that the souls of Melite and Klymene were safely across the river. Judge, then, the consternation at the words she addressed to Mynes. "Take this scepter, although you will be least of those who have borne it, and the last. Your days will be short. You will father no children, and the son of a goddess will burn your corpse."

From his point of view, Mynes had much cause to be angry. He was a mighty man, designed by the gods to be a king; yet he was king only because he was married to me and it was my hand that gave him the scepter. Those were not easy concessions for him. Nor could he truly understand that I must sometimes be the goddess instead of his wife. He took the words he had heard coming from my lips on that first evening of his rule as deliberate challenge and public insult.

He could not believe that I did not remember those words. I was almost in tears before I persuaded him to repeat them, even in the privacy of his bed as we lay together in naked intimacy that first morning.

Then I did weep. "My lord, these are not my words, nor my wishes. I do not want you to die at any man's hand. I do not wish your reign to be short, and I will happily give you sons without number if Our Lady wills it! And I do not understand why the goddess should have said such things, because Potnia never prophesied through my mother."

"So I was told," he said grimly. "And that is why today you will stand up before the court and explain that you said those hateful things yourself and that it was not Potnia speaking."

I stared in dismay at those implacable gray eyes so close to mine on the pillow. "My lord, for me to disown the Mistress's words would be blasphemy. I cannot deny her. Ask me anything but that."

Thereupon he rose and took the baldric from his sword and gave me my first beating. I persisted in my refusal. He broke off to couple with me, but when he had done and saw that tenderness failed to move me, he went back to flogging, promising to continue until I consented to do what he wanted. My surrender did him no good, because my voice was not the voice of the goddess and convinced no one.

Thereafter Mynes beat me frequently, with his baldric when sober and his fists when drunk, for utterly trivial reasons—his bath water was not ready, or I had laughed too much at some other man's humor. When he had beaten me, he would mount me, for cruelty aroused him as nothing else. Ctimene saw all my welts and bruises, but I swore her to secrecy; and she never told anyone, even Bienor.

I will say no more of my marriage, except to tell how I ended it.

Kings come and go, but the land endures. The harvest had been bountiful that year, both in grain and fruit. When snow closed the hill trails and high winds barred the seas, we slept soundly, trying not to dream of spring.

The Kilikes, Leleges, and Dardanians were informed of the change of ruler in Lyrnessos and responded with royal gifts. Their heralds mouthed shapely phrases of welcome and posed delicate queries about the new king's policies. Mynes believed that diplomacy was men's business, so I did not hear his answers.

Although his sacrilege in striking the goddess while she was prophesying in the megaron had caused great distress, it was soon forgiven. In general the people approved of their vigorous young monarch—not that their opinion was asked or would have made any difference. He kept work gangs laboring on the defenses even while he continued to train his army and enlarge it. He appointed his brother host leader, although that honor meant little under a king who was himself a warrior.

While Epistrophos took his military duties seriously, he also found time to supervise the annual tallying of records. Poor Sphelos never knew when he would look up and see those cold gray eyes staring down at him. He did persevere with his slingshot squadron, and Mynes encouraged him in that.

I worried more for Enops than for Sphelos. Potnia's warning about a son of a goddess might mean Aeneas but could equally apply to any of my brothers. Although Mynes regarded them all with suspicion, if he were to select an enemy, Enops would be the obvious choice. Fortunately, Enops was aware of the danger and sensible enough to avoid giving offense.

Bienor remained astonishingly faithful to Ctimene. Given a trace of a chance, the two of them would be holding hands and purring like doves. She shared his bed every night, and I heard no gossip that he dallied with any others during the day. Enops still preferred variety, which could be very annoying for me when some maid or bath attendant was missing from her post. The women enjoyed the respite and apparently all enjoyed Enops, insisting they much preferred him to Epistrophos—he was just another sort of work, but Enops was fun. My brothers and my slave were enjoying life much more than I was.

Spring, usually so welcome, that year brought war. The Greeks assembled again at Aulis, their fleet larger and better organized than before. From Aulis they sailed around Euboea to the Sporades Islands and on to Skyros, which they sacked, although it was no ally of Troy's. When Poseidon sent a favorable wind, they struck out boldly north by way of Strati to Lemnos, where they were made welcome by King Thoas. Whether he truly supported Agamemnon's cause or knew better than to resist such a host mattered little, for at Lemnos they were able to muster and provision. Within days they landed on Tenedos, an island sacred to

Apollo. The shrines were spared, the inhabitants were not. Now the Greeks were within sight of Troy.

We Lyrnessians tried to ignore the dispute like children who pull the blankets over their heads while their parents fight, and with no more success. Aeneas had still not committed the Dardanian warriors to the Trojan cause, but Dardanian horsemen acted as Trojan couriers, carrying news north, east, and south to the allies. Day after day, these hardy men passed through Lyrnessos, sharing their grim reports with us.

The next blow fell on Lesbos, and we saw the smoke when Thermi and Methymna burned. Bands of refugees began arriving at our gates. Pinched as we were for space and supplies, Mynes refused them sanctuary, and after that our own land was no longer safe for us.

Soon we heard that the Greeks had sacked Larisa. They were on the mainland.

A solitary chariot came rattling down the Dardanian trail, driven by Ascanius son of Aeneas—a mere boy and very pleased with himself. The passenger was his grandfather Anchises, who was totally blind now but still erect and proud. Moreover, he was still family, so Mynes informed me grudgingly that I might attend the welcoming dinner. Probably Anchises had insisted on that.

War had ended the great feasts. Only five of us assembled in the echoing megaron. I was distressed that my brothers were excluded, although that merely showed how times were changing and a new king reigned. I did get to the throne ahead of Mynes, knowing that I would suffer later for my presumption. The others sat on chairs with their feet up on stools, little Ascanius smirking to himself at being included in a conference of monarchs. When we had eaten and drunk our fill, Mynes dismissed the servants and broke into the inconsequential talk with an abrupt, "What grave matter brings us the honor of your presence, my lord?"

Anchises took a leisurely sip of wine. Under his silver locks, his bony, weathered face still bore the dignity of kingship. It was from him that Aeneas had inherited his eagle looks.

"The Greeks have landed at Troy."

"So you said earlier. It is hardly unexpected news."

The old man lifted his snowy brows in mock surprise. "Unexpected to Hector, though! He swore they would die in the waves."

I said, "The son of Priam proclaimed as much in this very hall last summer. Do the gods favor Agamemnon more than Hector?"

The noble head turned to me with a smile. "No, but Agamemnon has found a man they do. His name is Achilles son of Peleus, prince of Thessaly, the youngest of the Greek leaders but by far their greatest warrior."

"He did well at Mysia," Mynes conceded.

"He has done even better since. Give him his due, though, Hector did not fall into the first trap Achilles set for him. Did you divine his purpose?"

Mynes exchanged glances with his brother. "It is fairly obvious now. He tried to lure the Trojans south?"

"He did. First Lesbos, then Larisa. Had Hector taken the bait, the Greeks might have been able to cut him off from his city. He was not distracted. But it ill befits the old to talk of deeds of valor. Ascanius, you tell the sons of Euneus what happened."

His grandson beamed and began to talk excitedly in his shrill treble. "My lords, the Greeks abandoned the ruins of Larisa and took sail again, heading north toward the Dardanelles, past Besik Bay. You know . . . Your lordships are doubtless aware there is no landing site on the cliffs north of Besik, only the Bay of Troy itself, and Prince Hector thought he saw his chance. He divided his army . . ." He paused, then said boldly, "My father says that was folly! He left half his forces at the city and led the rest around the bay and onto Cape Sigeum, so he had both sides of the bay guarded. He thought he had plenty of time, because the ships were rowing against wind and current, going slowly, but when he was into the trap, the Greeks also divided their forces. Half the fleet raised sail and reversed course, heading back to Besik with the north wind at their backs. The prince was now between the two halves of the Greek army! He had no choice but to withdraw and try to repel the landing at Besik. By the time he arrived, the Greeks were already ashore, and their van landed unopposed on Cape Sigeum and advanced upon his rear. By nightfall, the Trojans had withdrawn to the Scamander, and the Greeks had set up their camp."

"A tale well told!" his grandfather said fondly. "But now here is a harder test: Tell us what happens next!"

The boy raised his chin proudly, in a gesture worthy of his father. "Priam will send for Aeneas and make him Trojan host leader!"

"Perhaps. We can expect many days of hard fighting—farms and orchards destroyed, herds rounded up, the outlying parts of the city burned, until only the impregnable citadel remains. Troy may withstand a very long siege, but Hector has certainly missed his best chance of winning the war—probably his only chance."

"And you came to ask me whether I will march with your son," Mynes said.

Anchises chuckled. "I see you like blunt words, son of Euneus. Dardania has long counted Lyrnessos as kin and ally. Can we call on you now?"

"The greatest skill in warfare is to be on the winning side."

I saw a shocked expression cross Ascanius's young face, but his grandfather's gave away nothing while we waited for a real answer. Mynes remained silent also. I suspected that he had no answer, that he had never solved his ethical dilemma. The silence grew so weighty that I was certain a god must be present.

Epistrophos was first to speak. "The decision is not an easy one for him, son of Capys. We have ties of honor to both armies—on one hand to you by kinship and to Priam by our father's guest friendship, on the other to Agamemnon as our father's Overlord. We must also weigh our interests. Choosing the winning side may not be enough in this case. If my brother supports the Trojans, then Agamemnon—even if he goes home beaten—will certainly take revenge on our father Euneus. If we support the Greeks, then Troy may set the Leleges and Kilikes upon Lyrnessos, yes?"

"Did your brother expect kingship to be easy?"

Mynes roared with laughter and reached for the wine jug. "I like you, old man! If you were thirty years younger, I should dearly like to test you with a spear."

The old man smiled sadly. "I would gladly take that risk if the Thunderer would strip me of those years. But what answer do I take back to my son?"

"Your son?" Mynes refilled Anchises' goblet. "I have heard a prophecy that I shall die at the hands of a son of a goddess. Your son is reputed to be such a one. Did you lie with a goddess when you made him?"

Anchises frowned at so blasphemous a query. "Only in the sense that my late wife was priestess of Aphrodite in the old ways, as my daughter is now. It is a common enough way of speaking, meaning only that Aeneas is no ordinary man and the goddess has greatly blessed her servant." The withered lips curled in mockery. "Your own wife is priestess of Potnia, so you may yet find yourself with a son worthy to be hailed as semidivine."

Mynes scowled in my direction. "I find this equating of a mere cleric with a goddess offensive."

"But you Greeks do it too. Why, the son of Peleus . . ." Anchises fumbled to find his wine goblet. Ascanius reached over quickly to help him.

"What of him?"

"Achilles' Myrmidons hail him as the son of Thetis."

Mynes looked at his brother and then at me.

"You would seem to be between two of them," Epistrophos told him cheerily.

"Very amusing! Also blasphemous! Fortunately I put no faith in such suspect prophecies."

Helenus had warned me that augury made no difference.

"Fortunate indeed," Anchises said. "What answer do I take back to my son?"

"Tell him that whoever attacks my city dies on my spear. Otherwise, I shall make up my mind when he has made up his."

The old man chuckled. "That was exactly what I told him you would say! It would be my own answer, were I in your place, my lord."

2

Hector failed to bar the Greeks from coming ashore, but he held them penned on Cape Sigeum for several days and at times came near to driving them back into the sea. Priam never did replace him with Aeneas. Although the Trojans had great superiority in chariots, and their allies were flocking to join the battle, the Greek army was much larger. It secured its beachhead and began advancing doggedly toward the Scamander, which was still a formidable stream in late spring.

The mysterious incident of the duel occurred about the seventh or eighth day. No single mortal's eyes saw the whole event, for it was a dank, misty morning with clammy patches of fog drifting in from the salt marshes. I had the Trojan version from the Dardanians and later heard the Greek side of the matter, but only the gods know where the truth lies. A truce had been called at sundown so the bodies of the fallen could be decently cremated, and the pyres still smoldered, adding stench and smoke to the air. As the sun tried to throw off its hazy blankets, the Greek knights mustered their men for another day's battle.

The Trojans had an unquestioned leader in Hector. He was short on experience and imagination, but he could give orders and hope to have them obeyed. Agamemnon could do neither. He vacillated and temporized and lost his head; he frequently offended the men whose support he most needed, and he would not delegate. His only idea of strategy was to place himself front and center and tell everyone else to follow him, but he did not do that very often.

What mattered most was where a leader aimed his attack, because once battle was joined, he could do little except trust the gods and fight for his own life. Achilles had argued for days that the Greeks' best hope lay in the marshes, where

chariots were useless. An advance there would turn the Trojan flank and threaten the precious ford, throwing the defenders into panic. Let the main army feint at the center, he
said, while he led the best fighters along the edge of the
swamps. It was a difficult concept for Agamemnon to grasp,
but he had at last agreed.

That was why Patroclus and a war band of Myrmidons
were trudging through reeds and thick mud, amid a maze of
little islands and channels. To the Myrmidons' right, the
Salamisians were advancing on slightly drier ground behind the Greater Ajax. The Salamisians were unorthodox
fighters. Not for them the screaming charge and fast withdrawal. Encumbered by old-fashioned tower shields as high
as a man, reputedly each made of seven ox hides, they plodded through the fog like migrating trees, each spearman accompanied by an archer who could take cover behind his
shield and shower arrows on the enemy. Salamisians were
slow but irresistible. Any ground they gained they did not
readily give up.

The mist made every patch of reeds or rushes loom into
view like an enemy host, so that a man's battle cry leapt to
his throat and stuck there, to be swallowed unuttered when
the foes turned out to be only weeds. It was the worst moment in war, before the action begins, when the early morning blood is still sluggish, when a man cannot suppress his
heart's craven whispers that yesterday he was lucky but
today the gods may not be so kind—when his feet are ice in
the squelching ooze, his hasty breakfast lies like lead in his
belly, and his bronze armor feels heavier than a dead horse
on his shoulders. Or so I was told.

An island solidified out of the pearly haze ahead, with
two men standing there. Patroclus raised his spear to begin
a charge and opened his mouth . . .

"Greeks!" shouted one of the wraiths. "We are heralds,
come in the name of Hermes!"

The war cry died unuttered. "Patroclus son of Menoitios."

"Son of Menoitios, hear the words of Paris son of Priam."

"Speak and be quick about it."

"The noble Paris sends this challenge to Menelaus son of

Atreus: 'Let us two meet in personal combat. The winner shall be the husband of Helen, keeping her and her treasure. Thus let the war be decided and peace made.' ''

Patroclus's first thought was that the offer must be a trick. His second was to wonder how long he would have to keep his men standing in the icy mud. But the Salamisians roared approval, led by the great bellow of Ajax himself.

Achilles came running in along the front line, throwing up sheets of water. He was a giant to start with, but in bronze corselet and plumed helmet, bearing his round shield and great spear, he seemed more than human, and that day some trick of the mist magnified him even more, so that he loomed like a god over the battlefield. "What's holding up the war?"

"Heralds," Patroclus explained. "They bring a challenge from Paris to Menelaus. It's just a trick to gain time, so they can redeploy!"

Achilles swung around to scowl at the two misty shapes. "Or starve us out." Ever since they landed, the Greeks had been too busy fighting to forage, and now they were perilously short of food. Nevertheless, an appeal to the gods could not be denied. He marched the heralds off to make their plea to Agamemnon.

Patroclus led the Myrmidons to drier ground. The last man out of the marsh was Automedon, who frowned as he heard the delay explained. "Menelaus is a warrior. Will it work?"

Patroclus said, "Of course not." Two armies that had been slaughtering each other for days could not just watch a duel between champions and then walk away in cold blood. There were too many dead friends to avenge.

Menelaus, doughty fighter though he was, was not enthusiastic about the duel. "Paris is no true warrior," he roared. "He fights with a bow, which is the weapon of a coward. If he will meet me with manly spear, then I will gladly slay him. But no son of Priam can be trusted. Let them bring out the old man himself to swear to this accord, for it was he who began this war by refusing to return my wife to me."

So the preliminaries took a long time, while the two armies sat and shivered in companies, staring hatred at their opponents in the distance. Mist billowed and danced between them. Priam himself did come from Troy, driving his own chariot with Antenor at his side. Escorted by heralds and his senior vassals, Agamemnon drove forward to meet him in the trampled, shattered fields between the rival forces. The terms had to be hammered out in detail, because the Greeks insisted they must be richly recompensed for their trouble if Menelaus won. At last the two kings slaughtered lambs and poured out wine to Father Zeus, each swearing fearful oaths that he and all his men would abide by the result of the single combat, on pain of retribution by the gods. Then Agamemnon returned to the safety of his host, but Priam drove back to the city, strangely unwilling to watch his son fight.

Paris and Menelaus resumed their armor, the heavy bronze corselets they had discarded while they waited. They looped their sword straps over one shoulder and their shield straps on the other, then attendants set the helmets on their heads and handed them their spears. Menelaus displayed his two-star mantle dangling down his back and Paris a cape of leopard skin, which was typical of his flippant attitude. The sun had dimmed again, with mist floating in over the plain until the opposing armies grew smoky and faint. Nevertheless, the heralds gave the sign for the duel to commence.

The two men advanced slowly at first. Menelaus howled out his defiance and contempt, naming his opponent thief, pretty-boy seducer of women, defiler of hospitality, kithara player, and dancer. Paris, it was noted with disapproval, did not reply. Menelaus broke into a run with his spear held level before him. Paris continued his cautious approach until the last possible moment and then lunged, but the encounter took place much closer to the Trojan lines than to the Greeks'.

Spear tactics may not be subtle, but they require nerve and strength and skill, for no armor will withstand a direct blow from an ash-wood spear borne by a charging warrior. Each man tries to ram his own spear into his opponent, while at the same time warding off the oncoming shaft with a glancing blow of his shield, which is no easy task, as Paris showed by catching Menelaus's point at too steep an angle. His shield was ripped open, but it deflected the deadly bronze point far enough to save him. His own thrust missed completely. Weighted down with metal, neither man could come to a sudden halt. They rammed into each other, but in this case both men stayed upright.

Menelaus's spear had been torn from his grasp. Paris could not bring his to bear at close quarters. Menelaus seized it in his left hand while drawing his sword with his right. He would have done better with a dagger at that range; for the two men were still almost nose to nose, wrestling for the spear. Unable to stab, he swung a cutting blow at Paris's head. Swords are not meant to be used as axes, and the bronze shattered. Roaring, he grabbed Paris by the helmet and threw him.

Alas, the gods did not wish matters to end so simply. As the king of Sparta was methodically choking the Trojan prince to death with his own helmet strap, a flight of arrows came out of the mist. Menelaus was struck in the leg and slightly wounded, although not enough to stop him from bolting for safety. According to the Greeks, the attack was directed against them, pure treachery by Lykian bowmen. The Trojans claimed the culprits were Lokrians and could reasonably point out that Menelaus was much closer to their lines than to his own. Charitably, one might guess that some outlying patrol of one side or the other had not been informed of the truce and was confused by the fog. Screaming curses on the oath breakers, both armies snatched up their weapons and resumed the war.

Ever after, a rumor persisted in the Greek army that Paris had hovered near death until his supporters carried him back to Troy and tucked him into bed with Helen—whereupon, it was said, he made an instant, miraculous recovery.

Unable to stand the continuing heavy losses, the Trojans withdrew from the field that night under cover of darkness. At dawn the Greeks rampaged unhindered across the Sca-

mander, finding the land already devastated—farms, ham-
lets, fields, and orchards burning. Troy itself stood secure,
not merely the impregnable citadel with its high walls and
towers, but at that time the outer town also, behind ditch and
palisade. Most of the allies had withdrawn to the east, over
the hills or up the valley of the Simois, taking the herds with
them.

Military triumph did not solve the Greeks' supply problems. They needed provisions urgently, in large amounts.
Hector was no fool and had numerous devious brothers to
advise him. Whether from necessity or by cold-blooded cal-
culation, he had left only one source of food available to
invaders—the headwaters of the Scamander, land of the
Dardanians.

3

No swallows came to Lyrnessos that year. I rarely glanced
from a window without seeing rainbows or warriors battling
in the clouds. Out-of-doors I heard owls at midday. Mynes
disapproved of his wife being an augur. Even when a falcon
dropped from the sky and lay dead at his feet before a dozen
witnesses, he did not consult me. When I heard of it, I knew
that the end must be close. I could weep for Lyrnessos but
not for its king—nor for his wife, who would soon be freed
from a hateful marriage. I repeatedly urged my brothers to
flee the city, but they refused, even Sphelos.

"I am little enough here now," he said bitterly. "Beyond
the boundary stones I would be nothing at all."

Enops would not desert his people. Bienor would not
desert him, though I offered to let him take Ctimene. Together we stayed at our posts as our ship bore down upon the
rocks.

On the fateful morning, I was working on a weave more

ambitious than anything I had ever attempted before, Heracles slaying the Nemean lion. I knew I would never complete it, but concentration eased the strain of waiting. Anticleia and Phaedre were passing a shuttle back and forth at another loom; Alcmene was spinning while chatting with old Maera; Ctimene rocked Phaedre's baby and cooed at it. Clay weights tinkled in the breeze. Old Sime sat alone in a corner, smiling—she had been my wet nurse long years ago. I had freed her, and the best part of freedom for her was the novelty of absolute idleness.

Phaedre was the only companion I had enlisted since I became queen, because Mynes was so insanely suspicious that he bullied anyone I befriended, demanding to be told every word I spoke. She was a maker of cloaks, the highest rank of weaver, and I had summoned her once to advise me on a weaving problem and found her to be good company. She scorned the king's efforts to intimidate her. Thus I passed my days running the palace—which even Mynes admitted I did well—and waiting for the fall of Lyrnessos.

Gorgon came shuffling into the queen's hall. She was gray around the muzzle now but still capable of snapping at the youngsters in the pack to assert her authority as queen's dog. Wagging proudly, she laid a dead squirrel at my feet.

I heard the gods speak.

"Good girl!" I whispered. The Immortals had spoken to me through Gorgon before—and once with a squirrel, perhaps this very one. She wagged even harder and lay down to chew on the carcass.

Ctimene squealed in disgust. "My lady! Make her take it outside!"

"She has done well. Why don't you lead her down to the kitchen and exchange her prize for a juicy steak?"

Ctimene quickly returned Phaedre's baby and called the dog. The two of them went off together, one of them carrying the squirrel in her mouth.

Soon Enops stalked in with Bienor at his back; both sweaty and very much out of breath; both so visibly concerned about something that my heart rose to my throat and I looked away.

Enops said, "There is an eagle perched on the pine tree by the gate. It seems to have an injured wing. The other birds are mobbing it."

I did not look around. "Hardly unusual."

"The mobbing, no. But what does the eagle portend?"

Then I did turn to face my two handsome, doomed brothers and held out my arms to gather them to me. Bienor was the taller now—he would have been a big man if he had lived. "It means what I have already told you," I whispered. "Flee while you still can. I have not seen your names in the omens. Take a boat and sail away southward—now!"

They stared at me aghast.

"I am sorry," I said louder. "I cannot interpret this sign for you. My lord the king does not approve of augury."

"We will not desert Lyrnessos!" Enops protested.

Bienor said, "Hush!" He glanced around at the women, looking for Ctimene.

Epistrophos appeared in the doorway. "Ah! You have heard, my lady? What does it mean?" He seemed less harassed than the other two, but he had not paused in the porch to remove his shoes and his inevitable smile seemed forced.

Mine, I am sure, looked as genuine as it felt. After so many months of silent resentment, defiance was a true joy. "I cannot say. The king is displeased when I interpret omens, my lord."

"Speak! He wants to know now."

"The last time I ventured an opinion, he whipped me two nights in a row." There! After so many months of suffering, the secret was out.

"He did *what*?" Enops yelled. Bienor swore luridly and laid a hand on his sword.

Epistrophos frowned at them, then at me. "You should have told me about that, my lady," he said quietly. "I did not know."

"Complain to my brother-in-law?" I said. "You think I have no pride?" I wondered why I had never thought of it, though—it might well have worked. "You think you could have stopped him?"

"I usually can. I shall speak to him. There will be no more whippings."

"No," I said. "There won't be."

"That is true!" Bienor raged.

"Leave him to me, charioteer," Epistrophos said, not unkindly. "He won't tolerate meddling from you. Now, Sister, what do you foresee?"

"I am forbidden to say. I will not say, not if he comes himself and begs me on his knees."

"This is your last word?"

"It is."

Rebellion was sweet as honey, and he could see that. He shrugged and strode from the room without a glance at the women, who were all staring at the rest of us in dismay.

I walked out on the landward balcony. My brothers followed, so intent on me that they did not notice what I had already seen on the hills.

"What does the eagle mean?" Bienor demanded.

It was Enops I distrusted. "Will you be guided by me if I tell you?" I asked him, and he nodded. "It means Aeneas is coming, and the Greeks are at his heels like wolves. But you must not open the gate to him."

Enops uttered a groan of horror.

I hugged him sorrowfully. "If Lyrnessos lets Aeneas in, then it is doomed. If it does not . . . well, then we may have a chance, at least for a while. But we must stay within our walls."

"How do you know this?" His face was pale as barley meal.

If I told him the signs I had seen, he would not believe. "I just know. I am certain. Look up."

Bienor cried out. "She is right!"

There were men on the high pastures, and only a very large crowd would be visible at this distance.

"This is true?" Enops gripped my arms fiercely. "The son of Anchises?"

I leaned my head on his shoulder. "It is true. Oh, why did you not leave while there was time?"

"Many men," Bienor said. "It means fighting at last!" His pallor did not match his brave words.

"It means death if you leave the stockade!" I insisted.

"May we tell Mynes this?" Enops demanded.

I shrugged. "If you wish. Don't expect him to listen to you."

The army on the high pasture had been noticed. Out in the courtyard, someone began beating an alarm with heavy, metallic strokes. Conches blew, being gradually drowned out by shouting and general clamor. War had come to Lyrnessos.

4

Once the worst of the confusion had died down, Ctimene and I headed for the gate. The sun was already wickedly hot, the air still. Even the crows had fallen silent now. The walls were buttressed by a rampart of earth surmounted by a breastwork of timbers. Choosing a place where I would have a good view, I climbed up on the bank, greatly surprising a couple of sentries no older than myself. They were taut as strung bows.

"Where is this eagle?" I asked.

"It was on that tree over there, my lady," said the taller. "Its wing hung down like it was broken, we thought. But a little while ago it just flew off—that way." He pointed west.

Westward? That seemed prophetic somehow. I made a note to think about it later.

Dardanians were already limping up the trail from the orchards—a varied band of men, women, and children. The sons of Euneus came to the rampart to question them. Mynes must have noticed me standing not a dozen paces farther along, but he ignored me.

A white-haired man spoke for the fugitives. "We were tending the herds on the slopes of Ida, my lord. The Greeks came like a great wind up the Scamander valley, looting and burning—came so fast we had no time to organize. It must be Achilles himself. None else can move an army at such speed."

By then Achilles' reputation let him be in six places at once.

"And he is following you?"

The old man glanced nervously over his shoulder at the human ants still trickling across the high pasture. "He was, my lord. He sent men to drive the herds back to Troy, so he can't have many left with him now."

"How many is *many*?" Mynes roared.

"A few hundred only—two or three hundred."

"He's lying!" muttered the boy at my elbow.

If he was capable of working that out, then Mynes certainly was—the Dardanian wanted to be let in, so he would minimize the danger. At least fifty of the refugees had gathered below us by then, an exhausted, dispirited, and useless rabble. Would Mynes admit them and fight Achilles or keep the door barred and hope to be accepted as a Greek ally? Would he defy both sides? I sensed the presence of the gods. It was too soon to mourn the dead, but I saw the living as walking corpses, turning in a useless dance. All their hopes and pleas were as empty as the chirp of crickets.

No more were coming to the gate, though. The rest must be waiting under cover in the trees so we could not assess their strength. That meant they had a leader.

"Where is the son of Anchises?" Mynes demanded.

The silver-haired spokesman mumbled and stammered, trying to avoid admitting that Aeneas was involved at all without antagonizing the man whose word might yet open that vital gate. Then a small band of warriors emerged from the orchard.

Few had weapons or shields—and some were almost naked—but they held their beards up proudly, and Aeneas himself swaggered at their head. He had not changed in the three years since I had last seen him—he was still lank, arrogant, and aquiline, but now he was plastered with sweat and ochre dust. He wore a boar's tusk helmet on his head and boots on his feet. Between those he had only a sword and a rag like part of a tunic, as if the rest had been ripped from

him in the fighting or had gone for bandages. In spite of all
that, he still looked dangerous.

He saw me and waved, shouting, "Hail, Cousin!" Then he
put his hands on his hips and inspected the king above the
gate, although he could not have known which fair-haired
brother was which. "Mynes son of Euneus, I presume? Hail
to you also, Cousin."

Leaning his elbows on the breastwork, Mynes studied this
beggar who had arrived at his threshold with death at his
heel.

"What do you think of him?" I whispered to Ctimene.

"Oh, my lady! He is indeed the son of a goddess, perhaps
of a god also."

"He's impressive," I admitted, surprised to discover I
was proud of my cousin. There are times when arrogance
is admirable.

Mynes said, "How many able-bodied fighters do you
bring with you, and how many Greeks are after your blood?"

Acneas laughed. "Not enough and too many. You told my
father you would choose sides when I did. Well, my choice
has been made." He raised his voice to ring out for all the
world to hear—especially the defenders crowded along the
walls. "Will you be a tortoise cowering in its shell, son of
Euneus, or are you in a mood for a fight? If you are, I've
brought you a good one."

My husband's voice boomed back as clearly, "And if I
don't want your fight?"

"Then, by the beard of Zeus, I'll give you one of your
own! Let us in or we come in." The son of Anchises had
never in his life had to plead for anything and he was not
going to start now, even with his life at hazard.

"Is it Achilles?" Epistrophos asked.

"It is Achilles," Aeneas agreed. "The yellow-haired monster himself, and he's everything they say he is."

Ctimene touched my arm and pointed to the hills. A dark
shadow was spilling out of the forest like oil, and behind it
speckles of sunlight flashed like sequins on a hem. The
Greeks had arrived, driving herds before them. I nodded,
and a murmur of many voices along the parapet told me that

everyone had seen. The day changed ominously when the enemy was in sight.

Mynes smiled down at the suppliant who had dared to threaten him. "Too late! The dogs are closing. I can hold you off until they arrive."

Aeneas looked to the hills. When he turned back to face the gate, he was actually smiling.

"There is more to this than you know, son of Euneus! Must we talk strategy in public?"

"You must," Mynes jeered.

Aeneas looked in my direction. "Greetings to you also, sons of Briseus," he said ironically.

Enops and Bienor had joined me, although I had not noticed them come. They were both sickly pale. It was Bienor who answered.

"We cannot help! The gods have—"

Enops silenced him with a backhand slap across the belly.

Aeneas shrugged and turned to Mynes again. "Son of Euneus, I have drawn Achilles into a trap. We are the bait, yes, but I sent messengers ahead to Thebe and Pedasos. I sent others back to Alcathous and to the Lykians." He laughed as if his arms already embraced fickle Victory. "While the Greeks scramble around the ramparts of Lyrnessos like wolves at a sheepfold, our allies can close in. Three days will be enough."

"You expect me to take in a beggar? A man who sides with losers against winners is a fool."

"I beg for nothing! Except a spear. If you spurn my offer, at least give me a spear, for I must kill the son of Peleus."

Mynes laughed. "Spoken more like a true knight! What do you think, Brother?" He was a fighter, nothing but a fighter, and now he had the sweet scent of blood in his nostrils. He was trying to find a reason to side with the losers against the winners.

Epistrophos scowled at the hills, where the glinting river of bronze was still emerging from the trees with no end in sight. "I think there is no profit in this match. Don't commit yourself until you know the odds."

"Spoken like a poltroon!" the king sneered, but still he

hesitated. Kingship was not an easy craft, as Anchises had told him. He beckoned me impatiently.

I gathered up my hems and strode to his side, wondering what I should tell him. If he opened the gate, he would die, and good riddance. If he kept it closed he might live, at least for a while. My hatred of Mynes and my loyalty to Aeneas warred with my duty to the city, to my brothers, to everyone I knew.

Moreover, Helenus had warned me that I must never prophesy falsely, lest the gods withdraw their favor. The day was to come when I should discover the truth of that, but this was not to be that day.

"My lord?" I said cheerfully. "You were warned to beware sons of goddesses. Now you must choose between two of them, Aeneas and Achilles."

He glared. "I have spurned your gift in the past, Wife, but I see that I have need of it. Tell me what the gods have revealed to you."

"Only that I shall shortly be rid of a most unwelcome husband."

The great muscles of his arms bunched, and suddenly Enops was at my side with his hand on his sword.

"Stay out of this, cub!" Mynes barked. "Woman, as your king and your husband, I demand that you tell me: What is this omen you have seen that bars me from taking in this Dardanian rabble?"

I should have refused to answer. Then Mynes might have restrained his blood lust and Lyrnessos might even have survived. But the hatred and contempt that I had felt ever since my marriage flared up in me like madness, and I threw the truth at him. Yes, the gods' truth was the weapon I used to destroy my hated husband. Did any women ever take a more bitter revenge?

"My dog caught a squirrel. If it had stayed in its tree it would not—"

He yelled with laughter and his own disbelief destroyed him. "You call that an omen? Dardanian, I want to fight at your side. Open the gates to our kinsman!" He vaulted over the breastwork to drop at Aeneas's toes. Aeneas bellowed approval and the two of them embraced. The gate creaked open. Enops gasped with relief and drooped against the breastwork.

"Come," I said to Ctimene. "Let us leave the men to their play and go prepare the victory feast."

"My lady?" she gasped. "You foresee a victory?"

"I foresee victors," I said. "And they will want to celebrate."

5

The day had already taken on a strange tint of nightmare. Men and livestock trampled hither and yon without visible purpose, their bellowing empty of meaning. I could see everything and feel nothing, for there was no future to look forward to. The world ended at my toes, everything rushing toward nothing. I wondered if that could be a presentiment of death, but women did not die when a town was sacked. Men's troubles ended; women's began.

I went roaring through the palace, screaming orders until I had reduced the turmoil to sullen silence and herded every servant I could find into the already-hot kitchens. "Light the fires! Heat water. Bake bread. Prepare food! We have wounded arriving, who must be tended. Tonight we shall seat a thousand guests at a great victory feast." They obeyed me. They probably knew as well as I did that it would be Greeks who celebrated in the palace, but any sort of purpose was better than none. Slaughtering animals was men's work, and I found a few slaves and old men who could attend to it. I stormed back out to the courtyard and ran into a wailing mob of townswomen whirling like gnats. I gave them much the same orders—to prepare a celebration for their victorious husbands and sons—and delegated some of the forewomen like Lede to see I was obeyed. Priestesses I set to

praying, but I made no appeal of my own to Potnia. I knew
that the Immortals had made their decision.

When I was sure I had the women of Lyrnessos as busy as
their menfolk, I paused to wipe my forehead and ease my
hoarse throat. I found Ctimene still at my side, but weeping
like a spring, tears pouring down her fair cheeks in a horrible silent sobbing.

"Tush!" I said. "That does nobody good. Come with me."
I took her by the wrist and pulled her up the stairs behind
me. "You have nothing to fear! You are a slave now; you will
still be a slave tomorrow. And so will I. You must give me
lessons in how to behave as a slave, so that my new master
will not beat me." Whoever he might be, he could turn out
no worse than the one I was married to.

Her answer was a horrible wail, in which the only intelli-
gible sound was the name of Bienor. Unlike me, Ctimene
had a lover to mourn. I must honor her for that.

"Behave yourself!" I chided. "You are no longer my servant but my sister." We reached the top and I urged her along
the corridor. "Today I become a slave, but you become a
princess. You are the wife of my brother. As queen of Lyrnessos, I declare you married. He loves you, does he not? You
are of noble blood and certainly beautiful enough that men
will believe you are a princess if you are dressed like one."

The queen's hall was deserted, only the wind making the
looms tinkle their gentle song. I headed for the chests where
the spare weavings were stored, hoping to find a gown that
would fit my new sister-in-law, for certainly none of mine
would. The deception I planned would normally have been
impossible, but fortunately I had never kept Ctimene's
lovely hair as close-cropped as most slaves', and lately I had
yielded to Bienor's pleas and allowed her to grow it. Soon
fat Alcmene arrived, followed by Phaedre and her baby, then
Anticleia and others. I explained the game and they joined
in bravely, fetching jewelry and paints to adorn Ctimene. For
a little while we managed to forget our troubles and were actually laughing at the transformation we had achieved when
Aeneas came striding in with half a dozen armed Dardanians at his back.

He was still filthy and near naked, but he had looted a loaf of bread and a cold leg of lamb from the kitchens and was gnawing on them. Most of his followers were similarly engaged. Some of them were bandaged, many bore bloodstains, and all looked as villainous as any invading horde of bandits ever could. My companions squawked nervously. I frowned at the men's shoes, then realized that whatever damage they might do to our delicate plaster floors would be trivial compared to what would happen when the Greeks arrived.

Aeneas bowed to me with aplomb. If he felt shame at being a refugee, he hid it admirably behind royal arrogance. "Hail again, Cousin! I regret that we meet under such trying circumstances." He smiled as if challenging me to match his composure but spoiled the effect by continuing to chew vigorously.

I curtseyed. "My apologies, noble son of Anchises! I shall order your bath prepared."

"No time for that now," he said, waving the loaf airily. "We'll enjoy your hospitality later. I came to learn what the family seer can tell me of the Immortals' intentions."

I hesitated, and for a moment he changed before my eyes, or perhaps it was everyone else who changed. They faded and he stood more solid, as if he were real and the men behind him were only reflections on water. I blinked and the illusion was gone.

"You live."

Probably he had expected only some inspiring cliché, for his golden eyes widened in surprise, then narrowed. "I certainly intend to! Come here." He beckoned me with a wave of the bread in his hand and walked over to the window.

I followed him out onto the seaward balcony, leaving our companions behind. Astonishingly, the morning was still young. Lesbos lay sharp and clear beyond the shining sea, not yet dulled by haze. White seabirds soared serenely by as if the turbulent affairs of men were too trivial to notice. It was a day like all the others.

I was shaking, for I had prophesied without knowing I was going to. The wounded eagle was part of it, plus the sign

I had seen three years ago. "You must leave soon! You go
westward."

Aeneas tore off a chunk of meat; his golden eyes studied
me angrily while he chewed. "Not so loud! Are you suggesting I run away?"

"I am telling you what the gods have decided. You will
live. Most of the others die—Mynes, his brother . . ." I
thought of my own brothers and my throat tightened so I
could not finish. Why, oh why, had I baited Mynes into the
trap? All this blood would be on my hands.

"This is not welcome advice, Briseis. I am relieved to
hear that I shall not die just yet, but I cannot desert my
men—nor you and Lyrnessos, either, of course." But he was
not as certain as he wanted to be. For all his arrogance, and
unlike my foolish husband, Aeneas had enough faith in the
gods to believe their oracles.

"I can only tell you what has been shown to me, my lord.
Your destiny lies westward, and far away. I have known this
ever since the last time you came here. But you must go
soon!"

He grunted, still eating. "Do I kill the son of Peleus?"

"I have told you all I know. Now it is up to you to obey."

"I will not leave until I have tried, anyway. What of Lyrnessos? What of Briseis?"

"Of myself I know nothing directly, but the city must
fall."

He smiled skeptically. "We shall see. Your husband is an
impetuous young man and was a fool to open his gates to
me, because now he must do as I tell him. I have five knights
and he has two—only one, really, for Enops will follow me.
Cousin, I rule in Lyrnessos now, and I say we shall wait inside the walls and spit on Achilles and his Myrmidons. Unless he has sent word back to Troy for Agamemnon to bring
the fleet and rescue him, we shall crack the son of Peleus
like a flea."

I tried to take hope from his words, but I knew that he was
wrong. The gods had stolen his wits. "Does Mynes understand that?"

"I explained again. I used very short, simple words."

Chuckling, the son of Anchises tossed the lamb bone over the rail and wiped his beard. "I needed that! I was hungry. Now, I pray you will excuse me. It will take the Greeks at least another hour to come down from the hills and longer still to plan their assault, but I must make some arrangements to receive them."

I stared at the shore. The mud-brick hovels of the town itself were silent and deserted, but a fight had started on the beach. Four ships lay there, and nowadays anything of value was guarded day and night. Sunlight flashed on bronze. Armed men had seized the little fleet. One ship had been pushed into the water, but men were fighting on board, and more were wading out to it. There were a dozen bodies on the shingle. If the attackers were Lesbian refugees or Lyrnessian deserters, they would be preparing to sail, and that did not seem to be happening.

"An hour, Cousin? I was told that Achilles can move very quickly."

Aeneas swung around to look and roared, "Cesspits of Hades!" His followers came pouring out of the hall to see what angered him.

The fourth ship was now being dragged back up on the strand. I could make out about forty Greeks, enough to man all four in a pinch. The fact that they were not moving their prizes offshore showed that they felt capable of defending them against a counterattack. Did that mean they had reinforcements nearby?

Aeneas started barking orders. "We must not leave Achilles a way out! Sokos, go and find . . ." He ripped out another oath and ran with his men at his heels. I was suddenly alone on the balcony. The battle for Lyrnessos was about to begin.

6

The plans men bring to a battlefield are always the first casualties, and events unfold thereafter as the gods will. No mortal chose to make the beach at Lyrnessos a killing ground or declare those four smelly boats a trophy for which so many must die, but that is what happened. It was a small skirmish compared to the great butcheries on the Plain of Troy, but it was bloody enough. I, on my balcony, was granted the only clear view I would ever have of warfare, one glimpse enough for a lifetime.

Hours earlier—before dawn—Achilles had sent Patroclus ahead to outflank Aeneas and cut off any escape by sea. This task the son of Menoitios had accomplished brilliantly, for no one in Lyrnessos knew he was there until he stormed the ships and slaughtered their defenders. Having seen that the rest of the Greeks were already on their way down the hill, he chose to remain ashore and wait for them.

I doubt that even Mynes was stupid enough to contest the loss of four worthless fishing boats for their own sakes—not with the palace practically under siege already and any troops he sent out liable to be cut off—but Aeneas, with his mad dreams of encircling the Greek force and besieging the besiegers, saw those vessels as a strategic necessity, because even one of them would enable the hated Achilles to summon reinforcements from Troy.

The counterattack he demanded seemed impossible, because Patroclus and his men could be floating far out of range before any serious retaliation came near. Needing some way to pin the Greeks down until the infantry could arrive, Mynes sent Sphelos.

The first I knew of this was when a pack of adolescents poured out of the town onto the east end of the beach. They bore no armor or weapons visible at that distance, but I recognized Sphelos in the lead. They formed up in a line, arms whirling. Slings are deadly enough at close range, but the shooters themselves are vulnerable and need the support of armored spearmen. The youth of Lyrnessos had been sent to war without that protection. Not surprisingly, the Greeks raised their shields and charged. Most of the boys broke and ran, but Sphelos and a few others stood their ground to try for a second shot. They died. Although the Myrmidons chased the fugitives, spearing many, they were too well trained to become scattered. Patroclus called them back and attended to his wounded.

I stood on the balcony like a goddess on Olympus overseeing the follies of mankind. I kept staring at my brother's body, willing it to move, to show signs of life. All our lives we know that death is final and not open to argument, yet when we meet it we always have to learn that fact anew. Sphelos was dead. It was over. What had he achieved with his days in the sun?

Some of the boys danced around, peppering shots at the enemy, but staying too far back to be more than a nuisance. They were leaderless and had seen a third of their number slain. Who would expect them to hit a target now?

Mynes arrived in his chariot, with his war band jogging behind. On better days they were farmers, fishermen, woodcutters, masons, bakers, leather workers, hostlers. . . . I am sure they all wished it was one of those days. He dismounted at the edge of the beach and strode forward to meet the foe, fearsome as Ares in his armor and crested helmet. Against him stood a line of about thirty Greeks, all with bronze greaves and shields, spears and swords. Most wore helmets, but none was clad in full armor as he was, and some were clad in almost nothing. Enops had told me that many men spurned armor because they could move more nimbly without it, and some disdained clothes altogether, because fighting was warm work. The Myrmidons had been chasing Dardanians across the Troad for three days; not even a god could have done that in full panoply.

Mynes' field of view was badly restricted by his helmet, but he ought to have realized that he was chasing a swamp demon. Did he think his opponent was a lunatic? No sane commander would be accepting those odds when he could just embark and sail out of bowshot. Certainly Patroclus, ferocious fighter though he was, would have too much respect for his men's lives. In this case, though, he had seen what Mynes had not—Achilles and the Greek force abandoning the herds, leaving the main trail to the palace, and taking a shortcut across the fields. If the king of Lyrnessos wanted to stay and fight until it was too late for him to run home to the safety of his castle, then he would have to be humored, so it was Patroclus's duty to stand his ground. In warfare, small contingents are almost as expendable as peasants' vegetable patches.

The deluded Mynes stopped and brandished his spear. The Greek leader brandished his own right back at him.

"What are they doing?" Ctimene demanded at my ear. I realized that I had about a dozen companions beside me on the balcony, all watching this confrontation of ants as intently as I was.

"Shouting abuse, I expect." That, too, I had learned from Enops. "Knights like to know their opponents are worthy, so they proclaim their ancestry and titles."

Ctimene's "Oh?" said more about male behavior than a whole epic could have done.

Mynes son of Euneus son of Selepus, king of Lyrnessos.

Patroclus son of Menoitios son of Actor.

And so on. Then they would add insults, working themselves up into a suitable state of irritation for a duel that only one could hope to survive. Being virtually naked against an armored opponent, Patroclus could honorably have called on his men to join him in a charge, but they were outnumbered and he wanted to keep the preliminaries going as long as possible. Mynes' war band was more than willing to leave the contest to the two knights, so when their king tired of the wordplay and began lumbering forward, the Lyrnessians stood their ground.

He stabbed at Patroclus, who deflected the blow with his shield and jumped sideways, striking past the edge of Mynes' shield. It was a glancing blow that failed to penetrate the cuirass. That was where bronze had it over skin. But shingle is not the easiest terrain for a man in armor, and Patroclus could dance around his clumsy opponent. The contest between agility and invulnerability continued as the two men repeatedly struck at each other. Their supporters jeered and cheered.

Meanwhile the spectators on the parapets had observed Achilles' approach and realized that Mynes and a sizable portion of the Lyrnessian forces were going to be overwhelmed very shortly. Aeneas sent off runners to warn him and tried to keep Epistrophos from going to his brother's aid by throwing a cordon across the gates. Epistrophos abandoned his chariot and led his war band out over the wall, thus leaving Aeneas so bereft of defenders that he had no choice but to accept the battle. He led out his Dardanians, going around to the west in the hope of taking Achilles from the rear. Of course Enops went with him. Everyone now converged on the beach, where the duel continued.

Patroclus later told me that Mynes was the better man, but Patroclus was an unusually modest warrior. He was badly handicapped by his lack of armor and physically exhausted before the fight even began. He did incredibly well to keep it going as long as he did—which was long enough—and he managed to move the contest closer to his own followers. Eventually the odds caught up with him. He deflected Mynes' spear downwards and tripped over it, gashing his calf. Mynes raised the spear to kill him.

The war bands charged, but the Lyrnessians had farther to come than the Myrmidons. Mynes was driven off before he could slay Patroclus, and the fighting became a free-for-all. Man for man, the Greeks were better trained and vastly more experienced, but weight of numbers prevailed, pushing them back. Patroclus had struggled to his feet, unable to put weight on his wounded, bleeding leg. He deflected a spear with his shield and fell headlong. Again Mynes prepared to kill him, but he took a few moments to jeer and that was Patroclus's salvation.

Achilles came roaring onto the west end of the beach, with a straggle of the fleetest Boeotians and Myrmidons at

his heels and hundreds more following them. All the women
around me on the balcony screamed in unison. The Lyrnessian spearmen turned and fled, abandoning their knight.

Flat on his back, Patroclus managed to parry Mynes'
stroke, and then Achilles arrived. He had the same problem
Patroclus had, in that he was not wearing armor, but even so
he was more than a match for the son of Euneus—bigger,
stronger, more nimble, and wielding a longer spear. I yelled
in joy as I watched my husband's frantic parrying and futile
attempts to strike his opponent. He backed away, and his
destiny followed him relentlessly. I was told later that very
few men lasted as long when pitted against the terrible son
of Peleus, but his ordeal ended all too soon for me. Achilles'
great spear skewered him right through his shield and corselet, meat on a spit. I cried out with joy as my husband went
down. I watched his limbs thrash when the victor put a foot
on him to haul out the spear. They were still twitching as
Achilles ordered two men to collect the dead man's armor
while he himself went in search of another opponent. I am
fairly sure that Mynes was still alive while he was being
stripped, but after that he lay still, and I knew I was a widow.
Despise me if you will, but I sang my thanks to the gods.

The fleeing Lyrnessians did not go far before they ran into
Epistrophos, who rallied them and brought the combined
war bands into battle, roaring challenge to the man who had
slain his brother. That developed into a good duel, but it was
soon swallowed up in the general melee. I did not see much
of it, because Aeneas and the other Dardanian knights had
arrived at the Greeks' rear with their war bands. Enops was
with them, and my attention was completely taken up with
trying to keep track of my brother in that raging tumult of
men.

He did very well. He slew two Boeotian knights and numerous rank and file who failed to get out of his way quickly
enough. I screamed and wailed with my companions at his
very success, because I could see that he was being stalked
by the murderous giant leader, who could only be the
dreaded Achilles himself. Being singled out by Achilles as a

worthy opponent was a shining compliment, of course, but a very deadly one. As it happened, before Achilles could reach him, Enops challenged Peisander son of Maemalus, who was almost as lethal as the son of Peleus. Thus my second brother died.

Time soon washed the blood from the beach of Lyrnessos. Uncounted years have rolled over a battle that only I remember at all. I have often wondered if Enops enjoyed it. Was the adventure he had gone to seek worth all the effort, three years for a handful of minutes? Was glory sweet enough to mask the bitter taste of death? Epistrophos, who had fought for gain, took no profit in the end, and Mynes . . . Oh, Mynes! How did the man who enjoyed slaying feel when Achilles slew him? I do hope he had time to appreciate the experience.

By the time Enops fell, the fight was almost over. Lyrnessians and Dardanians were fleeing into the trees or the town and even into the sea. Bienor had been waiting on the sidelines with Enops's chariot and made an effort to retrieve his body—I suppose in the hope that he might be still alive. He whipped up the horses and drove straight into the slaughter. A Greek spear took him in the chest, pitching him backward out of the car.

Ctimene screamed at my ear. I whirled around and grabbed her wrists before she could tear her cheeks.

"No!" I yelled. "You must not!"

"Bienor!"

"Bienor is dead and you are alive! You have to live!"

She stared at me in uncomprehending horror. She would be worth far less to the victors if her face and breasts were scarred. The same was true of me, so I could not mourn my brothers fittingly, any more than I had been able to mourn my parents.

I had no inclination to mourn my husband.

There is little demand for adult male slaves, so the men are slaughtered when a city falls. Women and children belong to the victors. Nobles of either sex may hope to be ransomed, although that is never guaranteed, and I knew of no one who would ransom me. I had wakened that morning a queen, but henceforth the best I could hope for was assignment as concubine to some important warrior. At worst . . . I could not even imagine the worst.

The Lyrnessian losers fled off to the woods, of course, homeless outlaws. Some of their womenfolk tried to follow, but the Myrmidons were experienced sackers of cities and quickly sealed the gates and manned the walls. I had expected tumult and panic, but an eerie, ominous silence settled over the palace. All the usual bustle was absent: the whir of potters' wheels, the thump of hammers, the cheerful singing of artisans. Once or twice dogs barked—but only briefly. There was a fearful clamor of screaming when the invaders located the Dardanian wounded. That did not last long, either.

Clad in my finest gown plus all the gold and jewels I could find, I went down to the megaron. A multitude of girls and women flocked in behind me, wailing and weeping. Almost all of them had scored their faces; many displayed bleeding breasts also. The sight infuriated me as if they were proclaiming aloud that they had loved their menfolk more than I loved my brothers.

"Silence!" I commanded. "Be silent, all of you! If you wish to remain with me, you must be silent. I will tolerate not a single snivel." Bearing the scepter of Lyrnessos, I settled myself on the throne and directed Ctimene to the inlaid chair that Epistrophos had used, where she sat in white-faced immobility, staring fixedly at nothing as if she had been shaped by a potter's hand. The womenfolk of the palace stood back in the anonymous gloom and struggled to hush their frightened children. Old Maera tottered in, looking as if even she had been shaken from her normal serenity by the disaster of the last hour. I sent a maid to fetch a stool for her.

Then there was nothing to do but wait. I spoke a silent prayer to my brothers' shades, explaining why I could not mourn them properly. I rehearsed, over and over, the words of submission I would say to Achilles when I surrendered the scepter. Gorgon lay at my feet, tongue lolling. The tension grew unbearable, until I was praying for the Greeks to come. Whatever they did would be better than the suspense.

"Here they are!" proclaimed a tenor voice outside the door. "Knew they must be somewhere."

Women and children were packed eight or ten deep along the walls by then, and the sound made them all squeeze back harder, as if they could disappear into the frescoes. I clutched the scepter more tightly and waited.

"A fair haul!" replied a bass. "Let's see what sport we've found."

Five men strolled in, peering uncertainly around them in the gloom, laughing and exchanging predictable obscenities. They all held spears and carried shields on their backs; they all wore tasseled mantles. Four of them wore nothing else except greaves and shoes, but the fifth had a tattered, bloodstained tunic as well. That one was very large and very blond.

Gorgon growled. Her ruff bristled. In all her years, she had never threatened anyone, but she knew these intruders were dangerous. Before I could speak, she leaped up and charged, barking stridently. The big yellow-haired man impaled her on his spear. I should not have been surprised, but I gasped in horror, choking back a scream as I stared at the pathetic heap of fur, suddenly so tiny and so useless. For the first and only time that day, my eyes filled with tears. I had not wept for Bienor or Enops or Sphelos, but I almost wept for Gorgon.

"Well, well, well!" said the tenor voice. "Behold the goddess!" The big man stood before me, one fist clutching the blood-wet spear, the other raised to his forehead in mocking salute.

Achilles! I could forgive the dread son of Peleus for slaying my husband—thank him, even—but never for killing Gorgon. All the pretty speeches I had prepared fled from my mind, so I could only stare in horror at the monster. Not that he looked like a monster. In spite of his size, his face was boyishly pretty, framed by golden curls, flushed with victory and thoughts of the orgy that was now his due.

He laughed. "She's a big one, isn't she? By Hera, there's a shapely udder!"

"You can have the nymph if I can have her decorations," said the tenor.

"That will do!" a third snapped. "Greetings, Queen Briseis."

I ignored him. Licking my lips, I began to stammer: "Noble s-son of . . . In the name of Potnia, our . . . My lord, I yield my city to . . ." I lurched to my feet and held out the gold-studded scepter of Lyrnessos, trembling so hard I almost dropped it.

The blond giant grinned, displaying a wide gap in his front teeth. He stepped forward, fingers reaching.

"I'll take that." The man who had addressed me halted him with a hand on his shoulder. Leaning on the butt end of his spear, he took the staff from me and raised it in salute, smiling gently—amused at my absurd queenly pretensions, naturally, but not openly mocking me for them. "My lady, I am Patroclus son of Menoitios."

I had never heard that name before and was puzzled to know how he could overrule the great Achilles. He was strikingly handsome, with curly brown hair and a marked pallor. His right leg was bandaged, which was why he had been limping. . . . I peered in confusion from one man to the other.

"And this is Menesthius son of Borus, nephew of Achilles. In stature and in valor, he is not unlike his famous uncle. Peisander son of Maemalus . . . Automedon son of Diores . . . Arkesilaos son of Promachos."

Four Myrmidons and a Boeotian, those five young thugs were absolute masters there. If they chose to cut me in pieces or throw me on the floor and rape me in sequence, no one in the whole world could deny them their pleasure, but Patroclus was supporting the fiction I had staged, that they were noble visitors calling on a queen. Remembering the hundreds of witnesses in the background relying on me to show them how to behave in this calamity, I found my voice.

"It is you who honor me, son of Menoitios." I sank to my knees. "I cede the city to you."

The Boeotian Arkesilaos guffawed. "Isn't that nice of the wench?"

"I'd rather wrestle her for it." Menesthius reached for my breasts.

"Stop that!" Patroclus barked, bringing them to heel again. "The men of Lyrnessos died bravely—cannot you honor their women's courage also?"

"I'd rather test their endurance."

"By Ares, even their dogs were brave!" Patroclus roared. "Since you slew the last defender of Lyrnessos to your fame, you can take the body out and give it an honorable place on its masters' pyre."

The giant's fair face flushed dark in the gloom. His hand swept to his sword. Patroclus watched, expressionless.

Menesthius paused, then growled, "You shouldn't be walking on that leg." He sheathed the sword and stalked away to survey the assembled women.

Patroclus tucked the scepter under his spear arm and held out his other hand to raise me, although he was obviously unsteady on his feet. His fingers were icy cold, his smile curiously diffident. "Are there any others here of noble birth?"

I indicated Ctimene, who was still frozen on her chair, seemingly unaware of what was happening. "My sister-in-law."

He frowned and shrugged. He must have seen women in shock before. "Will either of you fetch ransom?"

"Not a single ox," I said bitterly.

He chuckled. "You are worth a lot more than any ox, Queen Briseis."

Menesthius headed for the door, driving a girl who could not have been more than twelve who was struggling under Gorgon's weight. The next morning I saw the body lying behind a bush in the courtyard, but by then I understood that the death of a dog was only one raindrop in a cloudburst.

Patroclus said, "Tell them to submit, my lady. There will be less unpleasantness."

I swallowed the millstone in my throat and nodded, "What orders must I give them?"

"Call out the makers of cloaks and the bath attendants, any others you think may be of special value."

They were all of special value to themselves. I looked around the multitude of frightened faces in the shadows and found my voice hiding somewhere. "Makers of cloaks and bath attendants go to the hearth. Er . . . with their children?" I asked Patroclus, and passed on that command when he nodded. "Scribes?" I asked hopefully, "herbalists?" but he shook his head.

About thirty women and as many children had crept out of the throng and assembled between the pillars. The Greek knights looked them over and rejected most of them, sending them back to the mob.

"Tell the rest to go out now," Patroclus said softly. "Explain that men are all much the same in what they want."

Shuddering and hating myself, I passed on the command. "Women of Lyrnessos! You will go now to your new masters. They are not monsters, but strong warriors all. Do as they tell you and they will treat you well." I did not believe that, but I had no comfort to give them. They and their children were booty—women can sink no lower than that and still live. Their menfolk had failed them.

The Greeks began herding them out of the megaron, cutting out a few of the prettiest and sending them back to join the group at the hearth. Loud male cheering erupted in the courtyard, a sound like feeding time for the palace dogs.

With an angry mutter, Patroclus sank down on the throne. It was a sign of weakness, not of power. I registered his appalling pallor and the blood running from his bandage. "My lord! You must let us tend your wound."

He peered at me as if his vision was blurred. "In a moment. When the mob's gone." He smiled, somehow registering apology, tolerance, and distaste all at the same time. "It's all they fight for, you know."

"My lord?"

"Farmhands, herdsmen . . . What do those boys care about the fair Helen? How much loot do you think trickles down to them? They were dragged from their homes and families to come here. They risk their lives, see their friends die around them. Their reward is to take pleasure from women who cannot refuse them. That's all."

I said, "Oh!"

He sighed. "There's something about battle that rouses lust in men. Ares and Aphrodite. Stags fighting for the right to cover a herd of does."

I stared in bewilderment at this so-astonishing Greek. He was not the boor I had expected. His cynical musing reminded me of my father. He, too, had been a Greek.

Ctimene remained in her stony trance. Maera crouched on her stool, watching and listening like a spider. The score or so girls and younger women by the fireplace were huddled so close together that I could not be sure of their number. The last of the others disappeared through the door to meet the howling mob outside.

"They'll survive," Patroclus said. "Which is more than the men did. Your husband died well, my lady. He was a great fighter, as I discovered to my cost, greater than I. I offer my condolences. And your brother Enops, a mighty warrior."

"I had other brothers also."

"I heard of no other sons of Briseus."

"They were not knights, but they were just as brave. And they are just as dead."

He sighed. "Forgive me. Sometimes we forget. Be assured that all the dead are being given proper rites. We Greeks do not make war on corpses. Achilles is very particular about that. He ordered sacrifices for all, even the Lyrnessian lowborn."

I thanked him, and truly the news was a great comfort to me—at least as far as my brothers were concerned, and

Epistrophos too, for he had not been a bad man. Mynes, for all I cared, could have lain in the dirt for the dogs to eat, with his soul doomed to roam the gloom forever.

"Is not the son of Anchises a relative of yours also?"

"Aeneas? A third cousin or thereabouts. He survived."

Patroclus cocked an eyebrow. "How are you so sure?"

"Omens, my lord. I have some skill in augury."

"Praise to the Immortals!" He regarded me with a new intentness. "So Achilles could have saved himself a chase? And what else do you prophesy?"

"Troy is doomed, but I am sure you know that. I cannot tell you when it will fall, but fall it will. That you are about to bleed to death unless you let us help you. The old priestess is skilled, and I have some knowledge of herbs and healing."

The racket outside was not as loud as before, but now it sounded more human and less animal, and somehow that made it worse—animals are stupid; men are cruel.

"You are a remarkable woman, Briseis. Achilles will be interested to meet you." He made an effort to rise and sat back quickly, wincing at his weakness.

I was embarrassed for him and waited until his eyes opened, but then I dared to ask, "Like a stag fresh from battle?"

Many men would have struck me for insolence; dozens of women in the palace were being punched and pummeled at that very moment for less reason. Patroclus just let a smile draw up the corner of his mouth, which made him seem younger and very beautiful. "You certainly have nothing to fear from this stag tonight. I need help in walking. My charioteer should be out there, Alcimus son of Polyctor. He has white hair. Fetch him, please."

"At once, my lord." I hurried to the door, wondering if I would be dragged away and raped before I could explain my mission. Raped or robbed, because I was still loaded with treasure.

8

I came out to the vestibule, carpeted now with discarded clothing and copulating couples. I could hear worse things happening outside in the portico, but fortunately I did not have to venture that far. The tall youngster standing by himself, watching the sport with an envious smirk, was obviously a noble, for his greaves were of bronze and silver flashed on his sword hilt; his long tresses were white as flax.

I said, "My lord?" my voice sounding shrill and birdlike. "The son of Menoitios needs help! He sent me to fetch—"

Alcimus had gone. I turned and ran after him. Before I even reached the throne, he had received his orders and was on his way back out to find another helper. Patroclus smiled bravely at me, although he must have been feeling ghastly from lack of blood.

I grabbed Ctimene by the shoulders and shook her, bringing a sudden reawakening of terror. I scolded her to behave herself. She whimpered vaguely, as if she were half asleep. The charioteer returned with a man whom he addressed as Ctesios, and who was obviously disgruntled at being dragged away from the festivities. They lifted Patroclus between them and followed us out of the megaron—me bearing a shield, Ctimene a spear, and Maera the scepter.

Fortunately we did not need to go out to the portico or the courtyard, but I could not shut out the screaming and laughter, and I had to listen to many terrible stories in the days that followed. To be fair, most of the Greeks were ordinary young men who merely took the reward they had fought for. Apart from their long hair and shaven faces, they could have been sailors or woodcutters from Lyrnessos, and they used no violence on women who submitted. What happened in the courtyard was the work of a few: pure brutality—rape, sodomy, savage beatings, every perversion possible. It was the final act of the battle, the victors' triumph, for men who can degrade their enemies' women and children like that know beyond question they have won. Some of it was vengeance for dead friends. And no sooner was it over than the other half of the Greek force, those who had gone chasing Aeneas, came back and began it all again. Such is war and always will be.

We navigated the corridor, stepping over, between, and around occupants, until we reached the herbarium, a small and pungent room. Its walls were lined with shelves above, boxes and baskets below, and at the best of times there was little room around the massive central table. Then there was even less space than usual, for two girls and four men were present, all naked and all yelling in ferocious argument, close to blows. Forgetting that I was queen no longer, I screamed at them to get out. And they did, like sheep! Barely pausing in their contention, the men gathered up their clothes and weapons and departed, taking their victims with them, still arguing.

The table, which was normally cluttered with jars, bowls, packets, and mortars, had been cleared to expose a surface ominously stained with ancient blood. I told the men to lay Patroclus on it, facedown. He was barely conscious.

"Water!" I told Ctimene. "Hot if you can find it." She wailed in horror, so I turned to Alcimus and snapped, "You go with her. And you," I told Ctesios, "guard the door so we are not disturbed." They jumped to obey me as if I were the Great King of Mycenae.

I tied a tourniquet around Patroclus's leg to stop any further loss of blood, then cut away his bandage. The wound in his calf was deep and ragged, much worse than I had expected and certainly much more serious than anything I had ever treated. Maera inspected it with her nose practically on his leg; we exchanged shocked looks.

"Bah!" she said. "Terrible job! You'll have to take these stitches out and start over."

I was not competent! I had sewn up a leg only once, a slave's, and he had died. Our male healers were slain or fled. I knew many herb wives far more qualified than I, but even if I could find one and rescue her, she would be in no state now to perform a delicate piece of surgery. Maera's age-crippled hands were not deft enough. I must do the job myself.

"My lord, have you no men of your own who can deal with this?"

"Not here," Patroclus said resignedly, "and one of them did what you see. The matter is urgent. Go ahead."

Shaking, I turned to the shelves. "We have poppy."

"No! Just something to bite on."

I was relieved by his refusal, for I had no idea what dosage he could tolerate in his weakened state. We had lesser painkillers—wine, willow, safflower—but any of them might be dangerous to him, and none of them can match poppy milk anyway.

We must be quick, before he weakened any further. Alcimus and Ctimene returned with four pitchers of steaming-hot water, and Maera found needles and good linen thread. I gave Patroclus a bone spatula to bite on and told the men to hold him still, although that proved unnecessary, for he bore the pain without a groan, barely twitching. First I cut away the old stitches and rinsed the wound. The great tendon in his ankle had not been severed, so he would walk again if he lived. Repeatedly we loosed the tourniquet to discover the source of the bleeding, and then I would try to sew it up, speaking the appropriate prayers, while Alcimus promised offerings. It was only on the fifth or sixth try that my stitching stanched the flow and we dared close the muscle. I applied a healing ointment made from flax, lentils, and caper leaves, then sewed the skin together. Maera removed the tourniquet, nodding approval as the leg regained its color and no blood spurted. When I replaced the bandage and stepped away, she whispered, "Now it depends on the gods."

Patroclus was completely limp. The spatula had fallen from his teeth and the pulse in his neck was very faint. If Hermes was coming for his soul, he could not be far away now.

My fingers, which had been steady enough until then, began to shake violently. I had the men turn him over on his

back and propped his head on a pillow improvised from
some bags of dried herbs. He was still alive, but he would
not remain so for long unless we could waken him. I dispatched Ctimene and Ctesios to fetch fleeces, more hot
water, a fresh tunic.

"Alcimus," I said, "would you go and . . ."

No, he wouldn't. The charioteer folded his arms and
glared at me. "I do not leave this room until the son of
Menoitios tells me. Nor do you." I doubt he was any older
than I was. He was the blondest person I had ever seen, all
white and pink, so he looked like a child, but I had no doubt
he meant what he said. Remembering the screaming I had
heard earlier, I wondered what atrocities this baby-faced
Greek could dream up for me if his leader died.

"He'll come around shortly," I said without a blush. "I
was only going to ask you to get a room ready for him."

But our patient was in deep sleep. We spoke to him and
shook him without response. He was about to die on us, I
was certain.

"Hand me down that bottle," Maera said, pointing.

I gave it to her, noting that it was scaled with wax and so
dusty that it must have been standing on the shelf for years,
obviously a desperate recourse, not to be used lightly.

She broke the seal, removed the stopper, and held the
opening under Patroclus's nose. For a moment nothing happened, then he choked, coughed, and pulled a face. His eyes
opened blankly and steadied. I had never seen lips so white
manage to smile.

"All done?"

"All done," I agreed with relief. As Maera stoppered up
her miracle cure, I asked, "What's in that flask?"

She chuckled. "This and that. Mostly goat urine."

"Things to do," Patroclus muttered, making a feeble effort
to rise.

"You stay right there!" I said sternly.

He sank back, yielding to his weakness. "Yes, mistress.
Whatever you say. I'm thirsty."

I gave him wine, well watered. When Ctimene returned
with the fleeces, the men helped me make him more com-

fortable. Now Alcimus did not argue when I sent Ctimene and Ctesios to prepare a room, although he did not exactly smile, either. Patroclus submitted without protest as I removed his tattered mantle and washed him from top to toe. He was no stranger to wounds, for I counted eight white scars on his body. I was reaching for a tunic for him when the door flew open behind me.

"Patroclus!" An earthquake shouldered me aside and hurled himself on top of my patient. "Friend!" he roared. "Dearest friend! Your wound opened? Are you all right?"

Patroclus spluttered feebly through the mop of red-gold hair that had fallen over his face. "I was all right until you arrived. I am being treated most royally."

There are some moments in one's life one never forgets. I told you that Mynes could fill a doorway. Achilles could fill a megaron—not just with size, although I never met a larger man, but with the sheer blaze of his soul. Suddenly there was no room to move in that cramped herbarium and all the fears I had briefly forgotten rushed in around me so I could not breathe. I was a widow, a slave; my brothers were dead. This titan was master of Lyrnessos. Clasping the tunic to me, I cringed back against the wall, choking.

"Praise to Athena! You certainly smell royal enough. Ravishing!"

"Well, you stink like a goat pen. Get off me!"

"You *are* all right," Achilles said, his voice husky with relief.

"Thanks to Queen Briseis."

Achilles straightened up, dominating the little room. He raked back the tawny drapery of his hair and inspected the other two occupants—Alcimus was Patroclus's charioteer, attending him as was his duty, and I was . . .

I was a mess! I was soaked with blood and water and oil, the paint on my lips and nipples smeared, my hair bedraggled. I had been playing surgeon and then bath attendant while wearing my finest court gown and half the treasure of the kingdom. My efforts to make a good first impression on my captors had come to nought.

Admittedly, Achilles was in no better shape—filthy,

bloodstained, and stinking from a three-day battle, a hairy, muscular giant, in a ragged mantle thrown over one shoulder and pinned under the other arm so that it hung down to give a very scanty minimum of cover. Shoes, bronze greaves, a baldric, and nothing else. He was younger than I had expected, yet there was nothing boyish about him. His nose was high and straight, his square jaw gleaming with bronze stubble, the glow of his great eyes as blue and dazzling as summer seas. Red-gold waves trailed down to shoulders thick as meal sacks. Think how you expect Hermes to look when he comes for you, and you may have some slight idea of the man before me.

Blood rushed to my face and I lowered my gaze.

He took the tunic from my hands. Understanding, I lowered my arms to uncover my breasts and then endured his stare. At last he hooked a finger under my chin to raise my head again. I had forgotten how other women had to look up to men. I was accustomed to being an Amazon, a female colossus. Alongside Achilles, I felt *dainty*. The wonder in his eyes said he must be thinking much the same as I was—he had found a woman he could kiss, if he wished, without having to bend over.

"Briseis? I did not know such beauty still walked the earth."

My heart crashed against my ribs. I could have said the same to him. I could have said that we had been made for each other. But a slave must not presume so.

I whispered hoarsely, "I am yours to command, my lord."

"If you don't need surgery," Patroclus said, "I recommend her as a splendid bath attendant. You need a rest, and Zeus knows you need a wash. Troy won't disappear if you take an hour off. Aeneas escaped, of course."

Achilles spun around. "And how do you know that?"

"The Lady Briseis is also skilled in augury."

Remembering Mynes' attitude to seers, I wished he had not said that, but Achilles raised a massive fist to his brow in salute and there was no mockery in his dazzling blue eyes. "Are you a goddess?"

"No, my lord. I am mortal."

Patroclus laughed weakly. "So you have nothing to fear. Are you going to stand there gaping at her all day or do something?"

Achilles reacted to that with a strangely uncertain expression. No, he did not blush, but I wondered if this notorious son of Peleus, prince of Thessaly, leader of the Myrmidon host, sacker of cities, conqueror of Lyrnessos, and so on, could possibly be shy with women. It seemed absurd. The rutting stag fresh from battle was not behaving as he should.

"My augury depends on the whims of the gods, my lord." My voice sounded gratifyingly steady. "My beauty I cannot judge, but I do know how princes should be made welcome, and none greater than the son of Peleus has ever graced these halls." Surely he would not refuse me!

The notorious sacker of cities raised golden eyebrows and produced an incongruous dimple to the left of his mouth. Then the smile spread and another appeared on the right. "An honor I shall be happy to accept."

"I beg you to give me a few moments to prepare the bathroom." I remembered that I was still encrusted with jewelry and there were hundreds of rapists rampaging outside. "May I have an escort, my lord? In case of trouble?"

The son of Peleus looked puzzled, for danger was not something he ever considered. "Trouble? Oh, the men, you mean? Just tell them you are under my protection and they won't bother you."

"Go with her, Alcimus," Patroclus said quietly.

9

The kitchens were a swarming, sweating chaos of ravenous men, women, and even some terrified children, all battling for food and access to the hearths. Men intent on washing were guarding cauldrons of water on the fires, but Alcimus both commandeered the water and conscripted the rightful owners to carry it. His arrogant scowl and the silver studs on his sword hilt were all the authority he needed.

I led the procession to the bathroom, dreading what disarray I might find, but what I discovered was a bolted door. I hammered and shouted, and in a moment it creaked open on its pivots. Kopi's frightened, childlike face peered out.

I pushed my way past, demanding, "Who else is here?" but to my joy there was no one else present and the room was still in the immaculate state of readiness I insisted on. Towels and clean garments lay folded on the shelves and the bench was spread with clean fleeces. Truly, this was Potnia's doing! "How long have you been hiding in here?"

"A long time, my lady." Kopi backed away, staring fearfully at Alcimus and the men behind him.

"I realize you were protecting yourself, not the room," I told her warmly, "but it was well done. You will be rewarded."

"Rewards are not up to you," said Alcimus. "But she's scenic, so I'll put her with the prizes. Lay those over there," he told the men with the cauldrons. "You need anything more, widow of Mynes?"

"No, except Achilles must be shown where to come."

"It shall be done." He watched the men depart and then followed with his arm tight around Kopi. "What's your name, girl?"

I did not hear her reply, but he was comely enough to have brought a smile to her face. If it was to be one man at a time and lust was what was on his mind, Kopi could certainly cope. So could I. I knelt before the image of Potnia and thanked her for keeping me from harm that day.

My beads and bangles and other adornments went into an empty jar. I folded my gown and laid it under the bench, sponged myself, slung a tasseled belt around my hips, all as Mother had instructed. How glad I was that she had not lived to see this day of horror! I sat to comb my hair, prepared to endure a nerve-racking wait and wondering if I could satisfy a man anymore. My marriage had taught me that male nudity foretold suffering and humiliation. I barely remembered what rapture was, for in Mynes' bed I had found only pain and humiliation.

But Achilles did not keep me waiting. I jumped to my feet and bent my knee to him as he entered. He looked me over briefly, then averted his eyes.

"Are you sure you want to do this? I can bathe myself, you know."

What sort of a conquering hero was that?

Astonished, I said, "Quite certain, my lord," but my heart drooped. Was he another Sphelos? He had embraced Patroclus very warmly. I had watched him carry his friend off in his arms like a child, with Patroclus's head nestling on his shoulder. To cover my disappointment, I took up the jar in which I had placed my jewelry. "This belongs to you, son of Peleus."

He scowled in at the contents. "Perhaps a trinket or two."

I did not understand his displeasure, because I had not yet been told about Agamemnon's greed, but I knew that things were starting badly. I went to tip water into the tub.

"Your husband beat you, I see."

Dismay! It was four or five days since Mynes had last taken his belt to me, and so accustomed was I to being sore all the time that I had forgotten the purple and yellow trellis on my back. I hung my head.

"Yes, my lord."

Achilles frowned. "Why? How did you displease him?"

What could I say that he would believe? Mynes had rarely bothered to think up reasons by the end. He whipped me because he enjoyed it. If I thought up some more credible explanation, I would have to confess to being wanton or willful or lazy, and then Achilles would despise me.

"He punished me for speaking of an augury I had seen, my lord. It foretold that Lyrnessos would fall." That was true, although it had been three beatings earlier.

The brilliant blue eyes widened incredulously. "He beat you for passing on the gods' words?"

I nodded.

"You spoke to him alone or to others also?"

"To others," I admitted, my face burning.

"That was wrong of you," Achilles said reluctantly. "Such messages are sent to kings, not to the common herd. But his response still verged on impiety, unless you were disobeying his express orders on the matter. When next the Immortals speak to you, confide their words first to me or to Patroclus."

He saw me in his future!

"Gladly, my lord!"

"Auguries are matters of grave importance." He laid his greaves on the stool and lifted his baldric over his head. I went to remove his mantle. He pointed at the pot containing my discarded treasure. "Put that by the door in case we forget it."

Puzzled, I did as I was told. I also slid the bolt so we should not be disturbed. When I returned, he was already in the tub, busily rubbing his feet. I went to kneel beside him and sponge that astonishing expanse of back.

"The son of Euneus was a great spearman," he said, "a worthy foe. Epistrophos, too. Your own brother Prince Enops was equally valiant. I was sorry to hear that you lost other brothers also. No, don't stop, I'm enjoying it. Aeneas must be in Pedasos by now. What else can you tell me about him?"

"He hoped to trap you here, my lord. He sent messengers to summon the tribes." I owed Aeneas no loyalty; he had fled the field.

"Good. Let them come. Tell me about the town of Thebe."

To Hades with Thebe! Why was this godlike man spurning me? Was I not desirable? I was very nearly as naked as he was and could not be more obviously available. When I had begun to think I must soon rub his back raw, he held an arm out sideways for me to wipe, and then I began to suspect. When he bent his head and said, "Do my hair now," I knew that he was hiding his nudity.

Bashful? A sacker of cities? As I ladled water over the heavy gold mane, he rubbed fingers through it busily, bent forward so it trailed on his knees.

"A towel, now."

I went for a towel, although this had certainly been the fastest bathing I had ever attended. As I handed it to him, the absurdity of his modesty suddenly exasperated me. I felt insulted, which a slave can never be. I lost my temper, which a slave must never do.

"Do you wish me to turn my back, my lord? Or go away? I assure you that I am not a frightened virgin."

He looked up at me sharply.

I glared right back at him. "I have seen men before!"

"Have you ever seen one like this?" He sat back and lowered his knees.

No, I had not. There was more to Achilles than normally met the eye, considerably more, more than I had ever seen on any man, or would ever see on another. Elatos had been wrong—men do not all stand equal. Achilles' manhood was already fully tumescent, erect and proud as the Great Tower of Ilium. It was impossible! He would rip me open and I would bleed to death. But then I remembered that bath girls with far more experience than I had always assured me that what mattered in a man was always *how* and never *how much*. I began to quiver with a strange sort of trepidation—fear, yes, but also excitement.

"My lord! I am flattered that I have aroused you so quickly."

"It doesn't frighten you?"

Poor man! That was what had been bothering him. How many women had run screaming from his bed?

"If any woman can accept that, then I can, my lord." Aphrodite was daring me to try and promising unknown joys if I succeeded. I knelt down and clasped the wonder in both hands. It was as rigid as the trunk of an oak, gnarled with dark veins. I touched the huge head with the purplish eye peering angrily out of its covering, stroked my fingers down to the coppery undergrowth at the base, gently cupped the great sack hanging beneath. The tingle had spread to my nipples. "I am eager to try, at least, my lord, if you will just be gentle at first?"

The dimples reappeared, first left, then right. He took my face in his hands and the fire of his kiss withered all my remaining doubts. A moment later, he was out of the bath, splashing water everywhere, and we embraced, body against body. He bent his head a little, I raised my face, and we were mouth to mouth, a perfect fit. His fingers dug into the bruises on my back, but I did not care, feeling only his great manhood hot and hard between us, his arms like oak beams around me, the sweetness of his tongue on mine. Before I knew it, we were on the bench together, kissing and fondling like maniacs, exploring each other. Soon I realized he was waiting for my word.

"Now!" I said. "Yes! Now!" I spread my legs and guided him to the hot moistness opening to receive him. There was no pain, only irresistible pressure, a slow stretching gradually turning to joy. Deeper and deeper. Wonderful! More pressure, deeper yet.

He paused. "All right?" he whispered.

"More!"

I had thought he was all the way in, but there was more. Deeper still, until red fur pressed against black. He rested a moment, then pulled back—which was another miracle—pushed in again, moving with steady strokes that sent surges of pleasure through my entire body. The long-forgotten rapture of the goddess crept over me. I gasped at the rising thrill.

He stopped—shocked, disappointed. "I'm hurting you?"

"No!" I screamed, pounding my heels and fists on his back. "Go on! More! Harder!"

He resumed thrusting, faster and faster. We rose to glorious struggle, red pounding on black and black rising to meet red. I raked his flanks and buttocks to spur him on. Soon, soon, the holy fire began to burn in my loins again and blazed into climax, belly and toes and breasts and tongue, flame after flame until I was all gone, ash upon the wind. Achilles started to moan, so I reached down and gently stroked his scrotum. He gasped with joy and came to fulfilment also, his titanic body out of control, muscles heaving in fearful spasms, hammering up and down on me again and again with no end or mercy until I was sure he would kill me. But the passion dwindled and faded until he collapsed, spent and sated, a dead weight like a whole ox crushing me.

Only streaming sweat remained, frantic breathing, the

heavy beat of hearts, all fading to the intense peace that comes from nothing else.

He said, "Mm?"

I turned my face and slid my tongue into his mouth. He took it joyfully. If this was death, he could slaughter me as often as he liked.

"The one thing he cannot abide," Patroclus told me the next day, "is women weeping. After all, if a man cannot defend what he claims to own, then by what right does he own it? The rules are very clear. When a strong man slays a weaker, he is entitled to take the loser's possessions, and those certainly include his women—sisters, daughters, bedmates." The gentle brown eyes twinkled. "They especially should be happy at the improvement, surely? So Achilles will tell you. He understands mourning, within reason, but women who cannot accept the facts of life infuriate him. When I saw you on your throne yesterday, conquered but proud, I knew at once that he would approve of you. You have great courage, Briseis, and without courage even a woman is nothing."

But that was the next day.

I bathed Achilles a second time and dried him. When I had finished oiling that superb body, I was more than ready to be raped and pillaged again. He smiled ruefully at my enthusiasm, fending off my groping hands.

"I have orders to issue, Briseis. I have hardly eaten or slept in three days."

"Forgive me! I am thoughtless!"

He kissed my fingers. "I must eat, but sleep can wait a night or two. Give me an hour and a meal and you will be astonished."

I thought he was bragging. I was to learn that the son of Peleus bragged by telling the truth.

The family quarters had been taken over by the Greek leaders for themselves and the women selected as prizes, many of whom had never even seen those rooms before. The queen's chamber was set aside for Achilles, and there I spread a meal that would have fed a dozen normal men. There, in due course, he came to me.

I expected to serve him, but he was starving, and before I had poured out the wine, he was already seated at the tables, stuffing himself with both hands. Even as he gorged, his eyes were on me, and the welcome greed in them had nothing to do with food. Here was the rutting stag Patroclus had prophesied! Very soon he drained his goblet, wiped his mouth with a hairy forearm, and rose to his great height.

"That bed is too small!"

I laughed ruefully and went to his embrace. "It is the largest in the kingdom." I moved experimentally against his tunic and found the lump I expected. "As are you, my lord."

I led him out to the balcony, where I had spread a thick pile of Dardanian fleeces. The night was warm, the stars glorious. I could hear wailing in the distance and some cruel, drunken laughter also, but I could ignore them, because the man at my side required all my attention.

Our hands trembled with haste as we stripped away each other's clothing. We sank down together on the bedding and coupled eagerly, rolling and tussling, for there was now no edge we might fall off. It was over all too quickly. Briefly I saw my feet against the sky and felt his weight crushing me in glorious subjugation. I cried out first, then he did, and we came to fulfilment together.

"Oh, Briseis, Briseis!" he murmured in the sated, breathless calm that followed. "Oh, what I have won today!"

Tears prickled under my eyelids. I had won much more than he had—a mighty lover, but also a peerless protector. Then he astonished me as he had promised he would, for instead of withdrawing, he began moving inside me again, at first gently, then with more confidence as his member stiffened, and soon he was back in the full frenzy of lovemaking all over again, this time for longer. In later days I was to witness even greater feats of stamina from him, but then he had reached the limits of even his strength. When he found peace, I pulled a blanket over us and in moments heard the slow and even breathing of sleep.

Such escape was not for me. Under the uncaring stars, I

cuddled against his warmth, seeking comfort while the torments of the day yammered through my mind like stampeding cattle. Bienor, Enops, Sphelos—all gone. Lyrnessos fallen. Men slain, women abused. I was a queen no longer, only a chattel. If, I told myself, I could remain the chattel of Achilles, then I need fear nothing more. Was this, somehow, the true meaning of that oracle I had seen so long ago? Had Mynes been one eagle and Achilles the second?

I was not aware of sleep until Enops came to stand over me in a dream—his hair matted with blood, his bone-pale face staring down at me reproachfully. He repeated what he had once said of Sphelos.

"A prince should not try to make a slave into a lover!"

"Why not?" I cried. "Can it not be so, just this once?"

He shook his head and faded away. Bienor took his place, holding his hands over the bloody hole where the spear had struck him. *"A prince cannot marry a slave, no matter who her father was,"* he told me sadly.

"Of course not!" Sphelos said. *"What would people say?"*

"But he can love her!"

I must have spoken aloud, because Achilles wrapped his arms around me. I thought he was Mynes and screamed in terror.

"Briseis! What's wrong?"

The mists of sleep rolled back. I clasped him tightly, buried my face on his hairy chest, and wept until I choked.

He let me sob for a while, then kissed away my tears. "Now tell me. Not all dreams are portents."

"My brothers came to me!"

"They can have no reproaches for you," Achilles said sternly. "Or for me. All the fallen were given proper rites. Did they bring you some warning from the gods?"

I thought perhaps they had, but I gasped and said, "No, my lord. They ordered me to serve you well."

He chuckled, already much wider awake than I was. "They had no need to return from the Fortunate Lands to tell you that! Are you ready to obey them?" We could not have slept for long, but the passion of his kiss slid naturally into more lovemaking.

Bed with Achilles was not all brute copulation, although there was plenty of that. He joked, tickled, teased, and flattered. He was full of surprises, being boisterous, gentle, and passionate by turns, but also considerate, never letting the play grow serious again without making sure I was still willing. Most welcome of all was his tenderness, for often in the calms between the storms, he was content to hold me in his powerful arms and talk—not disappearing off to sleep, not jumping up and rushing away to attend to other business, but just being attentive and affectionate. Few men can manage that. I never knew a lover to match him.

By the time he left, just before dawn, I had summed up Achilles as a simple man; and in many ways he was, always walking in straight lines, pursuing one quarry at a time. Fighting, debating, carousing, loving—whatever he happened to be doing consumed his complete attention, and he knew no half measures. Watch him fighting and you would call him a monster, implacable as Ares. See him wrestling and romping with his Myrmidons and you would take him for a vastly overgrown boy. At planning battles and moving armies in the field, he outshone any of the Greeks, even the wily Odysseus, and he hoodwinked both Aeneas and Hector more than once. He was a man's man, if that means that his followers worshiped him without reservation. But he also had an insatiable need for sex, and especially so after a battle, as I learned that first night.

Yet his experience of women before me must have been limited. When I experimented to see if the technique Polydorus had taught me for peeling parsnips would work on a cucumber, he squealed in alarm and demanded to know what I thought I was doing. I paused only long enough to say, "Being greedy," and continued until I achieved the result I wanted.

Just a simple warrior, I thought, but there were depths to Achilles that I did not even suspect until it was too late.

10

Achilles led his little army out at dawn, although the Troad was infested with enemies and he had no idea where they were or how they might combine against him. According to Patroclus, he reasoned that the Dardanians would need time to regroup, the Leleges and Kilikes would remain on the defensive, guarding their own walls, and the others—those who had been lured from afar by Trojan gold to oppose the Greek landing—would see no merit in picking a fight with him now. He was going to seize Thebe, just as he had seized Lyrnessos.

The king of Mycenae, who had probably never even heard of Lyrnessos, had ordered a minor foray up the Scamander valley to forage. Achilles rounded up the nearest herds, sent them back to camp, and took off after Aeneas on his own initiative. Now, having seen that the whole south coast of the Troad was his for the taking, he wanted to finish the campaign and keep all the glory for himself. Agamemnon never forgave him.

Achilles' rear guard was barely out of sight before Patroclus explained some things Achilles had not mentioned, things that had me cursing the name of Agamemnon, praying to all the gods to strike him dead. His shadow lay across my future like a pestilence.

In theory Patroclus had been left to hold Lyrnessos, but he was as weak as a new-hatched sparrow and in great pain. I found him lying on a pallet on a balcony, giving orders to Alcimus. When I appeared, he terminated the lecture with, "Do whatever you think needs to be done. Succeed and be honored, or fail and be scorned."

"But—" The boy turned and saw me and scowled.

"That's how Achilles delegates."

"Yes, son of Menoitios." The son of Polyctor thrust out his downy chin and stalked off without another word.

Patroclus sent a weak grin after him.

I offered greetings and knelt to unwrap his bandage. "Achilles didn't leave you enough men, did he? All the women will run away!"

"They won't. Are you planning to?"

"No," I admitted. Why flee into the hills to starve or be captured by someone else? "I suppose not."

"See?" said the experienced sacker of cities. "And you don't even have children to worry about. Their menfolk are all dead or fled. Half of them were slaves in the first place, so they're no worse off than they were before. They'll do as they're told and go where they're sent. They will find Greek fields no harder to till and Greek babies no harder to bear."

All around, our spring-green fields lay empty of sowers and hoers. Sheep and lambs strayed untended, for not one boy over thirteen still lived. No crops would grow in Lyrnessos this summer, no trees be cut, and the olives would rot unpicked next winter. Forest would sprout in the ruins.

With a shiver, I turned my attention to Patroclus's wound. It was puffy and red, but the pus did not smell of rot.

"I've seen better," he said. "Do you have bitter yarrow root?"

When he described the plant he wanted in detail, I had to confess that I had no knowledge of it. He was unfamiliar with the names we used and I with his, but he knew far more herb lore than I did and infinitely more about wounds. There was nothing to be done then, he said, except offer sacrifices and wait for the gods' decision. If the fever dropped by the fourth day, then he would probably live. Otherwise not.

I settled myself on a cushion to keep him company. No man could stand comparison with my stupendous Achilles, but I could admit that Patroclus was very handsome, superbly proportioned and not in the least feminine, despite his long lashes and mop of curls. The little hairs on his chest grew in spirals like artwork on pottery.

We discussed the sacrifices he would have Alcimus make for him and to which gods they should be burned. He wanted to hear about the local divinities, and I told him of many wonderful cures that Potnia had granted. We talked of war, omens, fertile Thessaly. My tactful queries about King Peleus and the royal family failed to reveal whether Achilles had a wife, children, or a favorite bedmate.

Patroclus yawned. "I'll try to sleep awhile now. I had a disturbed night." A brilliant smile gleamed briefly through the pain. "But more restful than yours, I expect."

With my bruised lips and half-smothered yawns, I could not deny the charge. "But I suffered most willingly. I hope to endure many more such ordeals."

"Oh, Briseis!" He was shiny with sweat, breathing faster than a resting man should, but he held out a hand to me and pulled me down to sit by him again. He spaced his words as if he were breaking bad news to a child. "Listen. I am sure that the son of Peleus feels about you as you do about him, but what you are suggesting will not be possible."

"Oh, I do not ask that he marry me. Just to be his bedmate will give me happiness enough. I will gladly serve him, please him, bear him children, if only he will protect me and keep me safe in his house."

"But that decision is not his to make. He is the mightiest warrior the Greeks have, but he is only a follower. As Overlord, Agamemnon is awarded the finest prize when a city falls. Unless she is a fearful hag, that means the queen in all her finery. You are no hag, so you—"

"No! The gods cannot be so cruel! Where is he, this Agamemnon? It was Achilles who sacked Lyrnessos, not he!"

"That does not matter. The army awards the prizes, and the Great King gets the best. You will be allotted to Agamemnon."

"I don't want . . ."

Who cared what a slave wanted?

"Then Achilles could buy me from him?"

Patroclus closed his eyes as if I were being excessively stupid. "I am not talking of ordinary booty, Briseis, although the Great King gets the best of that, too. You will be more, a prize of honor, and that could never be traded. Besides, can you imagine the son of Peleus ever trading for anything? Bargaining? Haggling? He would sooner die in chains."

"This is terrible!" I whispered. "What can we do?"

"Nothing. Take what moments of happiness you can and accept the will of Zeus."

The will of Zeus is very obvious in hindsight, but only Zeus knows it beforehand. When I had made my patient as comfortable as possible, I hurried off to question the other prizes. I wanted to hear what they had learned from their partners in the night, especially if they had learned how we were going to be allocated.

So began the strange last days of Lyrnessos. I who had been queen was now a slave among slaves, but habits linger and the others acknowledged my authority. The Greeks respected me as Achilles' bedmate. Even corpse-pale Alcimus never took pleasure of me as he did many of the other women.

A score of women and almost as many children inhabited the royal quarters. Some of the prizes seemed crushed, others displayed heartrending courage. Kopi and Polydamma had always been slaves and could revel in unaccustomed idleness and luxury. Phacdre, who had lost her freedom, husband, father, and two brothers, consoled herself with her baby. Ctimene spent hours just staring at walls and whispering Bienor's name, although she had been through a similar experience only two years before and should have been better able to bear such troubles than the rest of us. As for me, my thoughts were occupied by the looming prospect of Agamemnon stealing me away from Achilles. I was not ready to admit that it was inevitable.

My adviser and guide must be Patroclus. By evening he was clearly weaker than before, but he bore the pain without complaint. When he was alert, he welcomed my company. As twilight fell, I brought up the topic again, and this time I said aloud what I had barely dared even to think: "I love Achilles!"

What sort of fool must he think me? A man kills another

and rapes his widow, so she thinks she is in love with him. Better to be Achilles' chattel than the wife of Mynes.

Patroclus sighed. "So do I. So does everyone who knows him. You impressed him greatly, Briseis." He frowned at me as if puzzled and then laughed faintly. "You need not look at me like that!"

"Like what, my lord?"

"I am no rival, child! Achilles and I are as close as men can be. I would die a thousand agonizing deaths for him. No one will ever come between us, but our love has nothing to do with the sort of love you can share with him. Nothing would please me more than to see the two of you united. Normally he is wary of women. He is afraid they will break, and his strength will hurt them. But you are different. He wakened me this morning to rave about you. I have never known him take to a woman the way he has taken to you."

Praise to the Lady! I wanted to scream with joy. He returned my love! "Then tell me how I can elude Agamemnon! There must be a way."

The shadows flowed back into Patroclus's face. "There may be a way to deceive Agamemnon, but how will you deceive Achilles? You expect me to betray him?"

"Betray? No—"

"Listen. My father was a landgrave in Locris. When I was thirteen I killed a man. A boy, really, for he was my own age, a dear friend. A group of us were playing knucklebones, but we had raided his father's wine store. Being drunk, we began to quarrel. Words led to blows, and we forgot we were no longer squabbling puppies who can do each other little harm. He punched me on the jaw. That hurt, so I knocked him down. He died."

I said, "No! That's terrible!"

"Yes it was. His father and uncles would take my life in retribution. They were rich in land and herds, so even if they would accept a blood price, they would set it so high that my family would be beggared. I ran to my father and told him what I had done. He ordered up his chariot and we drove away before I could even bid farewell to my brothers—and I have never been home to Locris. We traveled north for many days to the court of my cousin Peleus, and my father begged him to give me sanctuary.

"The son of Aeacus was still a strong warrior in those days, almost as great a spearman as his son is now. I was scared of him. He looked me over sternly, questioned me straitly, but seemed to approve of what he learned. 'My son needs a companion of his own rank,' he told me. 'He is younger than you, and you can be his guide. Go and serve him.' "

Hermes might be coming for his soul soon—we both knew that—yet Patroclus smiled to himself as he relived the memory.

"You may imagine that I was not pleased to be appointed nurse to an eight-year-old royal brat. I had some fuzz under my loincloth and thought myself a man. I was even a killer and not quite as ashamed of that as I should have been. Having no choice, though, I went to seek out Achilles and found him in the pasture, breaking a horse. When he was pointed out to me, I was sure there had been a mistake, for he was taller than I, even then. That was an unpleasant surprise. When I told him of the new arrangement, he seemed no happier about it than I was. He studied me with those great big blue eyes.

" 'Can you throw a javelin?' He shouted to one of the men to bring two javelins. As it happened, I rather fancied myself with a javelin. I tried a throw and was pleased with the result.

"Achilles' cast fell short of mine. He shrugged and said, 'Then let us see who can run fastest.' We raced; I won again. He called for a bow. Lifting rocks, driving chariots—the same. Spears, staves, jumping . . . I won every time, but he seemed determined to find something he could beat me at, if we had to stay out there all summer. Finally there was only wrestling left to try."

Patroclus broke off, panting in his fever.

I dabbed his forehead with a linen cloth. "You should rest now and finish the tale later." It did not seem to have much point or relevance. He must be slipping into delirium.

"Almost done. He didn't want to wrestle, but I insisted.

He was big and fast and amazingly strong. We grappled and strained, trying to throw each other, and then I deliberately shifted my weight so he could throw me. He didn't. He started to laugh. That made me furious, but he clung to me so I couldn't break free—and I certainly couldn't throw him—and all the time he was howling with laughter, until finally I had to laugh too. We fell down and rolled on the grass, shrieking with laughter, as boys will."

"I don't understand!"

"Oh, he'd been losing deliberately, all the time. He'd been satisfying himself that he could beat me at all those things. When I tried to let him win at wrestling, he knew I knew. . . ."

"And you have been friends ever since!"

"I have hardly ever been out of his sight since, but that is not the point! That is the only time I have ever known Achilles to cheat, and he cheated to lose, not to win. Why? Because his father had chosen me to be his tutor, but he was already better than me at anything a boy thinks important. He could have made me seem quite useless, but that would have been a criticism of his father's choice. He was thinking of his father's honor."

"I think his father was a better judge of men than he was."

"I should hope so! He was only a child. Don't you understand, Briseis? Honor is the world to Achilles. Honor matters more than life, more than anything. He is the best in everything, so he cannot be less in honor. No matter how much he loves you, he will not win you by deceit. If the army awards the premier prize of Lyrnessos to Agamemnon, then Achilles will not contest the choice."

The son of Menoitios closed his eyes wearily. "I don't cheat either."

The next day he was running a high fever, crying out for Achilles in his delirium. Alcimus sacrificed another twelve bullocks to Apollo.

That was not the only blood the son of Polyctor shed that day. He had his men crop the prisoners' ears. In Lyrnessos we had not marked slaves because everyone knew who they were. Although it was a trivial wound, the children did not understand and their screaming went on all day. Fortunately, we prizes were exempt.

Next morning, Patroclus was weaker and quite insensible. That evening we saw pillars of smoke in the east—not enough to be a town burning, Alcimus said, probably large funeral pyres. We thanked him for sharing his knowledge with us.

On the fourth day, Patroclus's fever broke. His wound still festered, but he said he was going to live, and I pretended to believe him.

Near sunset, a ship brought Achilles. He rushed straight to Patroclus and stayed with him for a long time. Then he sent for me to attend him. He was so haggard with exhaustion that I wondered if he had slept at all. I had to shake him awake in the bathtub. He went straight from there to the bedding on the balcony.

"I have meat and bread here," I said firmly. "You must eat before you sleep." I sat down beside him on the fleeces and practically forced the food into his mouth. He was amused, bleary blue eyes trying to twinkle through his fatigue.

"You are mothering me!" he mumbled, mouth full. "I like it."

"I am happy to please you in any way, son of Peleus." I stroked the golden hairs on his chest. "I may lie with you?"

He smiled blearily. "You can dance on me and I won't notice."

"I'll be here if you want me, my lord—I'm a light sleeper."

He was unconscious before he had finished smiling his consent. I stretched out at his side, and already I felt as safe there as a babe in its mother's arms.

Before dawn, I was awakened by the presence of a naked man pressing against my back. For a moment I felt sheer terror, thinking it was Mynes. Then I remembered with joy that Mynes was dead and this was a greater man, one I could love. I reached behind me and confirmed that the tree that had grown between us was what I thought it was. A hand cupped my breast. Fully aroused though he was, he spun out the lovemaking in long, lazy indulgence until, when at last he rolled me on my back and entered me, we were both aching with the need of it. The vigorous ending was brief but ecstatic. There is something especially satisfying about early-morning loving under the covers: the scratchy blankets, bed-warmed skin, the cozy, intimate scents.

I guessed there would be more, and there was. Lots.

After we came drifting back from the dreamworld for the second or third time, I said, "What happened at Thebe?"

Blue eyes studied me in silence for a while. "We won."

"I am glad." That pleased him, perhaps surprised him, although it was true. "And it went well?" I really did not know what I meant by that—how could a massacre go well?

"I underestimated King Eëtion! I thought a man with grown sons would be a pushover. He wasn't."

"You . . . He's dead?" I had liked grumpy old Eëtion. His daughter was Hector's wife. His youngest son, Pollis, had been the second man to make love to me.

"He died magnificently. He will be long remembered." Achilles released me and sat up. He rose in the chill morning air and looked around him, glorious as a god. Then he stalked indoors to find clothes. I had displeased him, a bedmate talking business.

I later learned that Achilles himself had slain Eëtion and all seven of his sons also, one after the other. The bards still sing of it.

Around noon, the rest of the army returned on foot from Thebe. Having left it as thinly garrisoned as Lyrnessos, Achilles now planned a strike at Pedasos.

That night the whole palace echoed with the clamor of feasting, of drunken roistering, songs of triumph, women laughing or weeping. I remained on the balcony with Patroclus. Despite his pain, he kept refusing my offers of poppy milk. It was after one such offer that he uttered the nearest I ever heard to a complaint from him.

"Wounds and sickness are the worst part of war. I always

pray to Athena that my death be quick, if it must come in battle."

"Is that not true of any death, my lord?"

He smiled faintly in the starlight. "Of course. Who would want to shrivel into hateful dotage and be mocked by the young? Better by far to die on a spear in one's pride and strength."

"Why do you fight?"

My query puzzled him. "Your realm has been torn from you, you have seen your menfolk slain, and yet you wonder why men fight?"

"No, I ask why *you* fight, my lord. How had Lyrnessos offended you that you bore its people so terrible a grudge?"

"Ah! Mm!" He ran a hand through his curls. "Well, I fight because I am in a war. I am in a war because I choose to be. I choose to be because I am a knight bred and trained. Ask the sailor why he goes to sea or the farmer why he tills. Could I let Achilles come and fight without me to look after him?"

"I see." I held a cup for him to drink.

"Do you? I don't think you do." His hand fumbled for mine. "I'm not sure a woman will understand this. I fight because my friend fights. I could not be his friend otherwise." Starlight glittered in the gentle eyes. "It is a dangerous question, Briscis. Don't ask it rashly."

When the feasting was over, Achilles came to check on his friend. Then he laughingly said he had work for me and carried me off to bed in his arms. I confess I was apprehensive, not knowing what sort of man he was when he was drunk, but I was soon reassured. Wine had very little effect on him. He did not need it for courage, and it could not loosen his tongue because he always said the first thing that came into his head anyway. It certainly could not make him any lustier than he was normally, and the world did not contain enough of it to make him pass out. Compared to other men he was always drunk—permanently intoxicated with the sheer joy of being Achilles.

Next morning he led the army off to the west and Pedasos fell two days later, with the usual bloody slaughter.

Aeneas escaped—again—and so did Elatos son of Altes, the Lelegian host leader, but Mestor son of Priam was among the dozens of knights slain. His former charioteer, Polydorus, was absent, confined to Troy by his father's command.

In less than half a month, with a mere thousand men, Achilles had shattered the fighting strength of the Leleges and Kilikes, grievously maimed the Dardanians, and taken three cities. Now he must let Agamemnon into the secret and tell him of the booty waiting to be collected.

I was part of that booty.

11

Achilles dallied in Lyrnessos two full days before he picked out a crew of strong oarsmen and sent them off to Cape Sigeum. Certainly his men had earned a rest, and if I suspected he was delaying matters just so he could keep me for himself a little longer, why should I complain?

We were both very young, burning with first love, insane with it. We almost murdered each other in glorious struggles all night long—and not rarely during the day as well. It seemed impossible that the gods would deprive us of such happiness.

But the word did go to Agamemnon and next morning the Greek fleet came in sight. Achilles sailed out to accompany it to Thebe, where the ceremonies would begin. Already women were trooping up and down to the beach, transporting anything that could be moved: food and wine, textiles and armor, cook pots and chests of treasure, furniture, perfumes, and livestock. The palace reeked of oil as men prepared it for destruction.

Patroclus was on the mend, but his sickness had left him drawn and strangely intense. I found him perched on a stool, being shaved by Amphidora. I could have counted his ribs from the far side of the balcony.

"You are not going to walk on that leg, I hope?"

"It is hard to walk on one."

Amphidora snarled at him, threatening to cut off his chin if he spoke again. "Or smile!" she added angrily.

He managed to smile using only his eyelashes. How many knights would have taken such impudence from a bath attendant?

I fretted impatiently until she finished, consoling myself with the promises Achilles had showered upon me not an hour before. He had told me I was precious to him, more wonderful than any woman he had ever met. He had sworn he would never part with me. I could still see his flushed face close above mine, feel his weight and the slickness of sweat and soft hair trailing in my eyes, hear that urgent whisper in the breathless aftermath of love, "I have earned the paramount prize! Even Agamemnon cannot deny me that. You shall be my prize of honor, if I have to choose between you and all the treasures of Holy Troy."

At last Amphidora was dispatched to prepare a bath. I repeated what Achilles had said. Patroclus shook his head gloomily. "I can't believe Agamemnon will grant him precedence, no matter how great his triumph. He's only the son of a backwoods chieftain to Agamemnon. The man can't admit there's more to Achilles than size and muscle. Agamemnon has so little tactical skill himself, he doesn't even recognize it in others. He's probably convinced himself by now that this whole foray was his idea right from the first."

His response chilled me, although I had expected it. "Then will you let me try my plan?"

"It won't work, Briseis. Achilles will never descend to trickery, not even for you."

I marched across and waved a fist in his face. "He doesn't have to!" I was near choking with anger and frustration. "It is up to you, son of Menoitios. Don't you value your friend's happiness?"

"I'm supposed to teach Alcimus honor, not trickery."

"So you'll let Achilles be cheated of his rightful prize?"

Patroclus groaned. "I suppose not."

I said, "Thank you!" and dared to stoop and hug him.

Weak and pale though he was, he smiled even more beautifully than usual. "Don't do that! You'll bring back my fever. Tell Alcimus I want him."

I went off to outwit the son of Atreus.

I had nothing to lose.

I had everything to lose.

At noon smoke darkened the eastern sky, and soon thereafter the fleet returned. Some of the ships carried on, heavy laden with booty and captives, bound for the Bay of Troy or the slave markets of Lemnos. The rest pulled into shore at Lyrnessos.

Alcimus led the prizes downstairs. Every woman was primped and painted, except me; every one clad in the finest gown she had ever worn, except me. I was bundled in a nondescript robe of shabby brown, with my hair hacked short, no longer than Ctimene's.

In the megaron, he proceeded to decorate us with gold and silver and jewels—beads, brooches, bracelets, diadems. Most of the women had never even seen such treasures before. Some reacted with fright, while others laughed and flaunted their glory before their children. Ctimene and I were especially favored, but as soon as he had finished loading us with precious things, I set to work rearranging matters. Rings, brooches, gold diadem—all went in trade for strings of beads until I had converted my finery to seven necklaces. Patroclus had forbidden Alcimus to interfere with me, so all he could do was sulk. The rest of the women were happy enough to oblige me in my whims, although only Phaedre and Ctimene were in on the plot.

We waited for what felt like a lifetime. Oh, how we waited! The megaron was bare, even the throne gone. We spoke in whispers, trying to comfort frightened children. I said prayers to Potnia, asking her to repent and guard us, the last of her flock. There were moments when I was convinced she was there with us, and others when I was sure she was not.

Meanwhile the Greek leaders had disembarked. They admired the towering piles of booty displayed on the shore and the cowering ranks of women and children beside them. Agamemnon made what he called a lavish distribution of these riches to the knights who had collected them and to some of the senior kings, although he again demonstrated how skimpy his ideas of lavish were. The loading began, with women wading out to deliver the goods to the ships. There was a huge surfeit of livestock, which could not be safely driven back to Troy and for which the Greeks lacked pasturage anyway, so hundreds of sheep and goats and cattle were sacrificed in great hecatombs—better to let the gods have them than leave them there at Lyrnessos for the defeated survivors skulking in the woods. After all that, at long last, the kings trooped up to the palace for the victory rite.

We prizes had been led out to the vestibule, but still we could see very little of what was going on. Perhaps you can imagine how we were feeling. Or perhaps you can't. Some of the older children were vomiting with fear. But eventually the courtyard was filled with armed Greeks, and Agamemnon called for the prizes to be brought forth.

Alcimus's boyish voice began calling the roll. "Amphidora, a skilled bath attendant, with a female infant and wearing a necklace of two strands of crystal, a sealstone of agate carved in the likeness of a gryphon fighting a bull, and a diadem of gold embossed in rosettes and spirals."

His choice of Amphidora to be first was a good one, for she had nerves of bronze. Holding her daughter's hand, she sauntered out with her head high, onyx hair gleaming in the sun, flounced dress of green and red and white displaying magnificent breasts. The troops cheered thunderously, knowing that there would be even better to follow—skilled weavers, beauteous bath attendants, comely freeborn women with young daughters. One by one, the fine-clad prizes emerged into the dazzling sunlight and formed up in a line at the top of the steps, like mares at a Dardanian horse fair. Phaedre and her baby went next to last, leaving only Ctimene and me, holding hands, trembling in unison.

Then Alcimus spoke exactly the words he had been given:

"And finally, my lords, two ladies of noble birth: Queen Briseis, widow of Mynes son of Euneus, and Princess Ctimene,
widow of Bienor son of Briseus."

We walked forward.

She went first—that, too, had been arranged—and she
was very lovely, a worthy prize for any warrior. She did not
care who chose her, but she had tasted love and was willing
to aid me in finding mine. Her gown was a magnificent
thing, her finery flamed around her.

I, in contrast, apparently wore none, for my seven necklaces were hidden under my dress. I had padded my belly
to suggest I was in the early stages of pregnancy—a cal-
culated risk, but I had to assume that a man as rich as the
king of Mycenae would have more interest in his own car-
nal pleasure than in gaining an extra slave brat—and my
rough-chopped hair was dulled with dust. I hoped that I
had not overdone the deception. Would Agamemnon question why the second-ranked prize had been so poorly gar-
nished?

The first face I saw was that of Odysseus son of Laertes.
My heart, which had been flapping like an eagle carrying off
a sheep, suddenly became a whole flock of geese in turmoil.
That glowering man had already noticed that something was
awry. He knew me, and no one deceived the king of Ithaca
for long.

Then my darting eyes found Achilles—great arms folded
defiantly and jaw clenched. My heart fell clear to the halls
of Hades. He never deigned to conceal his feelings, and the
matching scowls and glares of the Myrmidons at his back
confirmed that things had not gone well at Thebe.

As the wistful, lustful jeers of the rank and file died away,
I identified Agamemnon. He was a domineering, dominating figure—not built like Achilles, of course, but huge and
burly. Sunlight flamed on embossed greaves and silver-
studded sword, long black tresses trailed from under his
boar's tusk helmet, his tasseled mantle flaunted the lions of
Mycenae in gold on flaming red.

I forced my fists to unclench. As soon as the Great King
turned his back on us to address the army, I grabbed Phae-

dre's baby and she gave it to me. After the long hours of waiting, it stank worse than the pits behind the slave barns.

"Behold these fair prizes, my lords, the fruits of victory from Lyrnessos! Who were the heroes? Who is worthy to take first choice?"

The captains began the response Agamemnon wanted. "Son of Atreus! Son of Atreus!" The war bands took it up with no great enthusiasm. To make a safe bet certain, he had arranged for his Mycenaeans to be heavily represented. It had worked for him at Thebe, but ironically the prize he had won there was the despicable Chryseis, who was to cause so much grief later. Only the Myrmidons dissented, calling another name and being shouted down.

Agamemnon preened for several minutes before he raised a hand for silence. "You honor me, noble Greeks! I accept your award with true humility." The first statement was more than the truth, the second an outright falsehood, but he strode eagerly to the far end of the line and began working his way along it, frowning as he saw all the wealth that would be allotted to others.

I was shaking so hard I feared I might drop my sleeping, stinking bundle. Was the baby a clever deterrent or an added attraction? Would Agamemnon question why I was not richly embellished like the others? Would he value a baby and a future baby more than a pretty body like Ctimene's? And even if he did choose her as I hoped, would he lead her off by the hand or—and this was my greatest dread— proclaim aloud that he chose Queen Briseis? Then all my deception would be in vain, because Achilles would not condone fraud. If the Great King demanded Queen Briseis by name, Briseis he would get.

How could the brat sleep when it reeked so? I pinched it. It cried out. I nipped with my nails: *Be louder!* It howled satisfactorily. At my side, Phaedre did not notice my ploy, but she fretted anyway. She was right to be concerned, because neither of us knew what would happen if Agamemnon chose me while I was holding the baby. An appeal to what Alcimus had said would not likely carry much weight with the Great King of Mycenae.

He arrived in front of me. I kept my attention on the child, although I sensed that I was as tall as he was. *Ignore me!* I thought. *I am shabby and unadorned. I wear a plain gown. I am obviously pregnant, and I have this stinking, howling baby.* I shook it and screeched at it to shut up as if my wits were slightly addled. But I was well aware that I was strong and voluptuous. I wished I had dared stain my teeth and paint sores on my face.

Agamemnon barely glanced at me before taking another step. Ctimene—may the Immortals cherish her soul!—blushed all the way to her big rosy aureoles. Her golden adornments flamed in the sun.

"Truly you are lovely, Queen," said the Overlord, but he spoke to her and not the assembly. No one else heard the man's unfortunate error. "Come and honor my bed."

Taking her in a marriage hold, hand on wrist, he led his prize all around the court to taunt the lusts of lesser men. The army dutifully yelled its envy. I relaxed with a rush of breath—done it!—and passed the stinking infant back to its mother with a quick word of thanks. Only then did I dare glance again across at Achilles, who was staring open-mouthed, unable to believe his good fortune. He was too far off to see exactly what I was doing as I fumbled at my throat to pull the necklaces into view.

Agamemnon handed over his trophy to the care of a willowy charioteer and addressed the company again. "Greeks! Who comes next in honor, second in your regard?" He might have phrased the question more tactfully. He had no need to be paltry. The Spartans and Mycenaeans began chanting the name of Menelaus, but the other knights felt they had done their duty and could now vote as they wished. The war bands took up the roar: "Son of Peleus! Son of Peleus!"

Looking better pleased, Achilles came forward, following the same track Agamemnon had, starting at the far end of the line. He gave every woman a smile of approval. When he arrived in front of me, blue eyes frowned at my hair, my shapeless smock, the hodgepodge collection of beads. If he asked about the baby—if he asked anything at all—my plan would unravel in a heap.

"Oh, be gentle, my lord," I whispered. "I am a virgin!"

"*Briseis!*" He managed not to laugh, but the effort turned his face tile red. Only that morning he had complained about some gashes my claws had opened on his buttocks. "Oh, you hussy!" He swept me up in his arms as if I weighed nothing and strode back to his cheering Myrmidons. I nibbled his ear all the way across the courtyard.

12

Less than an hour later, I was at sea, a new and alarming experience. The waves were bigger and more boisterous than I had expected, and the hull that had seemed so large on the beach had become very small. Patroclus and I were crammed in together in the little shelter at the stern, looking out at Alcimus framed in the doorway. He was helmsman, beating time with one hand and clutching the steering oar with the other. Our cargo was mostly bedding—blankets and pillows and goose-down quilts. Patroclus and I sat enthroned atop a frothy mass of this, and more of it was packed in under the crew's benches and along the central walkway, and yet we still rode high in the water. The rowers strained at their oars, a double line of them, twenty to a side.

"My lady, you worked a wonder at the choosing."

"Not I, son of Menoitios. It was Lady Potnia's doing."

"Was it? She had an able assistant, in truth." A smile brightened his deep-shadowed eyes. "Who won the prize—Achilles or Briseis?"

"I am very grateful for your help."

"Don't ever mention it to Achilles. Today he is too happy to question how his happiness came to him. Keep him that way."

"He really does love me, doesn't he?"

"Hasn't he said so?"

"He promises he will never part with me. Could there be more?"

"More? There is everything, Briseis. I have never seen the lad so besotted. Aphrodite has driven him completely out of his wits."

"Oh, what a terrible thing to say!" I protested in delight. "Go on!"

"True it is! He raves. He swears he will take you home to Thessaly and marry you."

"*Marry* me? A prince cannot marry a slave!"

"And who will tell Achilles so? He will have you as his wife, to bear him sons and rule his household and reign as queen by his side when—far off may that day be—his noble father must cross the river. He rambles in delirium. I'm sure he will come to his senses when the fever goes down."

The last remark was nonsense, of course. Whatever Achilles said Achilles meant, and we both knew that. Too overcome to speak another word, I threw myself across Patroclus and wept on his chest. He wrapped an arm around me and chuckled.

"You are laughing at me," I mumbled.

"No. I am laughing because my friends are happy."

Neither of us mentioned the black smoke coiling up into the sky behind us. When we drew closer to Lesbos, Patroclus risked calling for the sail to be raised. Then the willing ship bared white teeth at the waves and raced forward like a stallion over a meadow. We rounded the cape, caught the heavier swell of the open sea, and headed north. I saw Ida from afar, as I never had, and watched it dwindle from my life. Patroclus pointed out Tenedos, the ruins of Larisa, Imbros, and faraway, towering Samothrace. We turned Cape Sigeum as the sun was setting, with the rowers heaving and sweating against the current. We entered into the Bay of Troy at dusk, when a full moon was rising over the shining citadel.

"There it stands, Briseis," Patroclus said. "At least you get a chance to see it before it burns. Another month and Troy will be no more."

He was wrong, of course. A month later the Greeks had
razed the outer town, but the citadel on the hill endured unharmed. A year later, that had not changed.

That magic evening, while the moon turned from gold to silver, nothing seemed real at all, as if I had been transported
into one of the bards' tales of ancient times. The size of the
Greek camp surprised me, as did the number of ships basking on the strand like black cattle. My family was dead, my
home torched, and I was adrift in a world of dream. I wanted
Achilles, and yet I was perversely glad he was not there, so
I could adjust to this strange new life without his rampant
sexuality looming over me. The person I really wanted—and
the realization jarred—was my mother.

As soon as the keel grated on the shingle, Alcimus de-
tailed four husky rowers to carry Patroclus's litter. No one
took any notice of me at all, which was a novel experience.
I waded ashore and followed the procession through a tangle of ropes and smelly leather tents until we arrived at the
fine timbered lodge. It was not a palace, but it was Olympus
compared to the commoners' quarters.

I did not get a proper look at the interior until the fire
blazed up to illuminate the megaron—and fill it with smoke,
of course. I gaped around at the agglomeration of furniture,
the weapons that scaled the walls like the sides of some
giant bronze fish, and finally at the ashen-faced Patroclus,
reclining on a heap of fleeces with his eyes closed, exhausted by the journey. The girl kneeling beside him, clutching his hand and sobbing, had lit the fire and set a cauldron
of water to warm, but that seemed to be the limit of her abilities. Not too helpful.

I was weary, too, jangled by a tumultuous day, and also
ravenous. All my life my reaction to hunger had been to yell
for a servant, but I had enough wit to understand that the future would be different. I knelt at his other side, feeling his
brow for fever. He opened his eyes, smiled faintly.

"Briseis, this is Iphis. Iphis, Briseis."

"The gods be with you, Iphis."

She stared at me, then repeated my name carefully.

"Briseis is Achilles' prize of honor from Lyrnessos."

She twitched a smile that did not imply understanding.

"Lord Achilles will be back tomorrow," he added.

At first glance she was a beauty, all curves and downy soft, and her face was truly lovely, framed by hair that sparkled with highlights of gold and copper and bronze in the firelight.

I said, "What do you need, my lord? Wine, water, food?"

"I couldn't eat. A little wine would be welcome."

I looked inquiringly at Iphis. She stared back at me and bit a voluptuous lip. The potter was skilled; the jar was empty.

"Fetch some wine, Iphis," I said.

"Oh!" She smiled and jumped up and headed for the porch at a pigeon-toed run, apparently quite willing to be helpful if properly directed. She was a child in a woman's body, and a curious choice for Patroclus. I would have expected him to want more from a partner than simple animal copulation.

She returned in moments with a wine flask and a silver cup, which she filled and gave to him. Patroclus sacrificed, drank, then handed the cup to me.

"Perhaps I am hungry." He was mumbling as he fought off sleep. "Iphis, find some cheese and bread. If you can't find any, ask Alcimus. Enough for three people, please, cow-eyes?"

She simpered at the compliment and hurried off to obey. She did have very beautiful eyes, but she had other bovine attributes to go with them. I would have no problem managing Iphis.

"Be gentle," Patroclus murmured, without opening his eyes.

"My lord?"

"The world is a difficult place for her, but she tries her best."

"You love her?"

After a moment, he muttered, "I like her. She's willing and she smells nice." He added, "And she never gossips." Soon he was asleep.

                    *   *   *

Achilles arrived at noon like a cheerful thunderstorm and
swept me into bed at once, but that was just his greeting.
When night came, he settled down to serious lovemaking.

Soon that rough-timbered lodge was my home and sleepy
postcoital contentment my most familiar condition. Nothing
dispels care like frequent bouts of lechery, and whether he
chose to be obstreperous, languorous, or demonic, no man
was better at it than the son of Peleus.

Time passed, and I adjusted to my new life. I made friends
with other well-bred captives, especially Hecamede and
Melantho. I ran Achilles' household, shared his bed, and
waited like everyone else for Troy to fall. Patroclus healed
and returned to both the fight and the joys of Iphis, much to
her relief.

The camp was crowded, noisy, intolerably windy, and
dusty, but I had rather be there with Achilles than in a
palace without him. A palace *with* him would be better still,
but it was the constant fighting that made me long for the
end of the war. Time and again he went off raiding with his
Myrmidons—joyfully, as if war were a wonderful game. I
tossed sleeplessly through the nights until he returned and
coupled with him insanely from dusk until dawn when he
did. Winter, when it arrived, was drear and unpleasant, but at
least I had him at my side every night.

He never called for another woman and I never refused
him. He never raised his voice to me . . . except once, and
then I had stupidly provoked him.

It was the night he returned from sacking Abydos, and we
were alone, which happened rarely. He was stretched on the
floor, and I was kneading his back to work the stiffness from
his muscles. The raid had gone badly. He had lost men. The
palace had been torched before it could be looted, so he had
brought back little plunder, and Agamemnon had kept almost all of it. Any man might be grumpy under the circumstances, but I had never known his good humor fail before.

"Why do you fight, son of Peleus?"

He grunted, then said sharply to the ox hides under him,
"What in the world do you mean, woman?"

I knew at once I had erred, but it was too late to withdraw the words. I pushed down on his shoulders, pressing hard. "You were born to wealth, heir to a kingdom. You have lands and slaves and a people to rule. Why do you risk your life and your men's lives here in Ilium fighting battles that have nothing to do with Thessaly?"

He rolled over on his back, taking me by surprise. The oil jar went flying as his great hands hauled me down on top of him. His teeth were bared in a snarl.

"Are you implying that there is something wrong with fighting?"

"No, no!"

"That it is folly, perhaps?" His fingers dug into my arms.

"No, no! I—"

"What else should I do? Herd goats? Because the gods have made me so much greater than all other men, you expect me to stand before a mirror all my life, admiring myself? Lie abed fathering children? Be content to be the son of Peleus and bask in my father's reputation? Is that what you suggest?"

He crushed me to him until I could hardly breathe. I stared in dismay into those blazing eyes. Too late I recalled tales of the fabulous battle rage of Achilles.

"I m-mean no offense, my lord!" I stammered. "Is it Helen's honor, or the shame of Paris . . . ?" My voice dried up in despair.

"No, none of that. I won you in battle! Do you regret that?"

"Oh, no! No! Never!"

He studied me for a moment longer, and then the grinding grip eased, the anger faded into annoyance. "Women! You don't understand, do you? Well, I expect you understand babies, which I don't. I fight for glory, so that Peleus will be remembered evermore as the father of Achilles. Is not that an ambition?" It was also a surprising admission, for he worshiped his father. "We are all mortal, Briseis. Nothing of a man survives except his bones and perhaps children to revere his memory. Any fool can sire children, but I will be remembered forever as the greatest of the Greeks." The dimples popped into view simultaneously. "And Briseis will be remembered as the woman Achilles loved."

He kissed me then to block any chance of my asking more stupid questions. From there he went right into demonstrating the love part.

Whenever he captured knights worth ransoming we had houseguests—mostly Trojans, but some from distant lands, Paeones or Lycians. Achilles accepted their paroles and treated them generously.

The one I remember best, and the last, as winter was closing down the fighting, was Lykaon son of Priam. He charmed Achilles and Patroclus with his good humor and courtly ways, and he was kind to the dull-witted Iphis. He spent almost a month with us, sharing our meals, sleeping on a cot in the porch. Neither he nor I ever mentioned his visit to Lyrnessos, but I frequently caught him staring wistfully at me, and I think his memories of our wild night together were as pleasant as my own. In the end, Achilles lost patience with the unending negotiations and packed him off to the slave market on Lemnos with a shipload of other prisoners. They were to meet again, briefly.

It was about then that I said farewell to Ctimene. Agamemnon had summoned her to his bed a few times, but the first time he chose her he did not remember her name or where she had come from—he had enough women in his stable to glut a war band. Late in the summer he gave her away to a hairy-limbed knight from Arkady, Oros son of Ormenos. Her old sparkle began to return, so he must have been an improvement on the Great King, but Oros lost an eye in battle. Deciding that he had fulfilled his obligations to the Overlord, he sailed for home, taking his booty with him. Very few Lyrnessos women remained in the camp by then.

I saw Agamemnon only at a distance until that fateful spring day when we met as he was returning from a funeral. Next morning the festering resentment between him and Achilles erupted in council, and Achilles gave me to him.

BOOK EIGHT

AGAMEMNON

1

The heralds, Talthybius and Eurybates, were aging warriors who had followed their lord to Troy because they had no sons to send. Often in happier days I had plied them with wine and honey cakes when they brought messages to Achilles. Now I followed them along the beach in sullen silence.

Plotting murder. That dog-faced son of Atreus! By stealing me from Achilles, Agamemnon was defying the Immortals. As Athena, the Mistress had always favored Achilles above all others, and as Potnia she had accepted my service in Lyrnessos, manifested herself in my flesh. Had she not just sent a sign, coming in the guise of a swallow to bless Achilles' house? She would aid us!

She would have to do it quickly. Achilles had said he was going home, so he would embark at dawn to gain a full day's sailing. I had often watched the Myrmidons run the ships out, and they needed only minutes after the sacrifices had been made. In this case the need to load their loot and personal gear would delay them a little, but I must be back there by first light, ready to go with them.

How could I, if I was in Agamemnon's bed? I had advised Chryseis to stick a knife between his ribs when in that situation, and this advice now seemed warmly profound but hardly realistic. Even if I could catch him unaware and could then somehow evade the guards and reach the Myrmidon fleet before it sailed, I would have created a blood feud beyond nightmare. It would destroy me and Achilles and all Thessaly as well. Murder was not practical.

My gruesome brooding ended when we reached the smoking remnants of the feast. Satiated with meat and wine, men lay in the shade of the ships, some sleeping, some vigorously copulating, others waiting their turn with the overworked women. I felt many eyes examining me, the woman who had torn the Greek army asunder. Helen's beauty had begun the war—was mine to end it? The curious rose to their feet and followed us, so that we trailed a crowd of onlookers when we approached the flapping, gay-striped canopy where Agamemnon sprawled godlike on his throne with the senior kings on stools around him, frogs around a swan.

There Eurybates stopped me, while Talthybius went on alone. It took him a few moments to gain the Overlord's attention, but then Agamemnon lifted his big head to stare at me. Spectators fell silent. He beckoned impatiently. Eurybates gave me a shove. The Great King's brutish features were flushed, his black locks straggling and windswept. For all his purple and gold, his rings, necklaces, and bracelets, he was more boor than king—and this was Zeus's deputy on earth! The sweaty rabble drifted in behind me, closing around the royal canopy and bringing shadows with them. Knights and lowborn stared.

"Here she is at last!" he bellowed. "Come, child, and greet your new master. Closer!"

I did go close, close enough to stand over him. He probably expected me to hurl myself at his feet—I was a slave, and a single spunky glance can bring disaster on a slave— but I knew I had Athena at my side, so I curled my lip and sneered down into his piggy, bloodshot eyes with all the contempt I could muster. My insides curdled with fear, but I must have managed to hide it, for he scowled and lurched to his feet, a big man but no taller than I.

"She's a sizable heifer, isn't she, my lords? Too good for that upstart brat of Peleus's! See the fine set of milk jars here? Yesterday she flaunted them for us—like this." He ripped my dress open to the waist.

Why should *exposing* be different from *being exposed*? I felt myself blush scarlet and needed all my willpower to keep my arms at my side.

The Great King chuckled and turned to survey his audience. "Are they not worthy to comfort a king?"

There was no response at all. Some men drank, others scratched, and the rest looked nowhere. Their Overlord had

thrown away the best fighter in his army just to possess a
woman, and their contempt was a stench in the air.

Angrily Agamemnon pulled me to him, bent me backward, and pushed his wine-sodden mouth on mine. His
baldric and necklaces dug painfully into my breasts. Astonished and outraged, I kept my eyes open. So did he. For a
long moment we stared at each other. Then he straightened
me up and released me.

He turned away. "Take her! Put her in a kennel where she
belongs."

As I gathered the remains of my gown around me, I heard
old Nestor raise his creaky voice. "Call for the bards, my
lord, and let us hear some inspiring songs of noble deeds by
the heroes of yore, Dryas or Exadius or some such, for truly
there are no men their equals in these lesser times. . . ."

"Not a promising beginning, darling," Alcandre purred as
she escorted me through the Mycenaean encampment. "Men
need to be flattered—you know that!"

"He's a boor!"

"Oh, an absolute lout, but it is not your job to demonstrate
it, certainly not in front of the entire army. I fear Achilles has
been spoiling you, dear." Her smile was perfectly genuine,
in that she obviously enjoyed sharpening her claws on me.

Darling Alcandre! *Dear* Alcandre, looking lovely as ever.
The Fates were weaving a complex web. Queen Alcandre of
Pedasos, Queen Briseis of Lyrnessos, and Princess Chryseis
of Thebe had been the paramount prizes of their respective
cities all on the same day, and now Chryseis's departure had
thrown me into Alcandre's clutches.

I must rethink my plans. Agamemnon had been faking
that kiss, so whatever had inspired him to steal me away
from Achilles was not lust. If he did not summon me to his
sleeping chamber that night, then I had Alcandre to deal
with instead. Escape might be possible after all.

"We must find a needle so you can sew up your dress," my
companion said sweetly. "I'm sure we have no others of
your size."

"Mother always told me that stature is a sure indication of

noble blood." My retort was rewarded with a nasty glance, for Alcandre's father had been a common sailor, although an uncommonly rich one after his daughter caught the eye of old King Altes.

We had passed the largest building the Greeks had raised on the cape: the Great King's high-peaked palace, which towered over its entourage of barns, tents, and sheds. Ahead of us lay another landmark, the compound where Agamemnon kept his women. It had been a single hut when I first came to the cape, and I had seen it grow to a hamlet of a dozen buildings surrounded by a stockade. More than two score women captured in the previous year's fighting still dwelt there. Many others had been sent back to Mycenae or distributed to senior followers, but in general Agamemnon was as stingy with women as he was with inanimate loot. He hoarded them.

Every hoard needs a dragon. Even the Overlord was not fool enough to overlook the difficulties of confining scores of female beauties within a camp of thousands of bored young men, so he had appointed a warder—Alcandre. Achilles would leave at dawn. It was her job to make sure I did not go with him.

I was annoyed when the guards at the paddock gate saluted her and even more annoyed when I saw her private cabin. It impressed me more than I would have admitted—a roomy bed, a couple of chests, chairs, lamps, jars of oil and wine, artistic weavings hung on the walls to keep out the relentless Trojan winds, while the hearth would have been a great luxury in the winter. The former queen of Pedasos was doing very well in her petty tyranny.

A couple of the other huts in the paddock looked substantial enough, but most were despicable kennels of branches and hides. At least two score women were sitting around in idle boredom or tending children or chatting through the stockade to men loitering outside.

"Thallata!" Alcandre shouted. "Come here! Take off your dress," she told me. "Do sit down, darling. Care for some wine?"

Very slick! Thallata was a former bath attendant from

Lyrnessos, so once one of mine and now under Alcandre's orders. She nervously returned my smile as she was handed my torn dress and told to go and sew it up.

The wine was excellent. When I complained that I had not eaten all day, another girl was sent to fetch food. I was being shown the advantages of cooperation.

"He really put his mark on you, didn't he!" Alcandre said, sipping wine and eying the scratches on my breasts with undisguised amusement.

"Does he play rough in bed?"

Shrug. "So I'm told." Not her problem.

"What happens tonight? Do we parade in rows for his approval?" I was not as ignorant as I pretended. From gossip at the washing place I knew that Agamemnon would sometimes come in person to select a bedmate for the evening and sometimes just send orders for one to be sent over. Then Alcandre would choose.

"Tonight? Tonight Eurymedon will tuck him in and kiss him good night. His charioteer, I mean." She smiled at my surprise. "He was very *up* at the council this morning. By the time you arrived, he was definitely *down*. Very down. He will drink himself to sleep. No company needed."

That explained the clammy kiss. "How long will he stay down?"

"No way of telling. Sometimes for days."

"And he has no use for women? Boys?"

"Never boys. No use for anyone. When he is very up, he may call for three girls a night."

I digested this information in silence for a moment. Already the day was growing old, the shadows long. I could see no way to enlist Alcandre's willing help. It would have to be direct challenge, Achilles style. The only question was whether to bully her into submission now or wait until dark and crack her on the head with a water jug.

"He won't stay down forever, so I can be certain of finding myself in his bed sooner or later?"

"Oh, I don't think he wants you just to weave blankets, dear."

A basket of bread and cold meat arrived for me and I set

to work eagerly. Thallata brought back my mended dress. I thanked her.

Alcandre poured herself more wine, forgetting to offer me any. "We must find you a corner of your own. I do wish I'd realized sooner that you would be joining us, Briseis dear! I reassigned Chryseis's quarters. Newcomers usually have to settle for a patch of straw in that hovel over there, next to the latrines, but I'll try to find something a little more suitable in your case."

"Would it help if I groveled in the dirt and kissed your feet?"

Alcandre chuckled and showed her lower teeth, making the water jug gambit feel even more tempting. Granted, she had some cause for bitterness. Like me, she was a widow. When the Myrmidon horde came over the walls of Pedasos, old Altes had dragged himself from his sickbed and tottered out with a spear in his hand so he could die as a warrior. Achilles had extolled his courage and done him the honor of slaying him personally. She should by rights have been ransomed long ago, because her stepson, Elatos, had escaped the sack and still led the surviving Leleges. Even more important, one of Priam's wives, the mother of Lykaon and Polydorus, was her stepdaughter. But we captives had heard nothing of any offer being made.

"Let us understand each other," I said with my mouth full. "You can play slave master as much as you want with the others, lady, but not with me. When I have eaten, you will show me the rest of the accommodation, so I may choose the building I prefer and the women who will share it with me."

This defiance made her purr with delight. "You will not be the first queen who has learned to do as she's told here, darling."

"I intend to be the first who doesn't," I said calmly. "I know how you run this place, you and your special cronies. I know you can order women whipped or caged, that you decide who goes to the washing place or shares the wine and any treats that came along. I know about the fortunate lovers visiting by night and of women meeting friends outside, too. All it takes is your favor, isn't it? Well, you're not going to order me around."

"And what makes you so special, cow-eyes?" Her smile was imagining me tied to the whipping post already.

I gestured expansively with a rib I was enjoying. "First, you admit I will find myself nose to nose with Agamemnon sooner or later and you have no way of preventing that. When I do, I can tell him all sorts of fascinating stories. In detail! That tall Spartan of yours, Thibron? Would he swear an oath before Zeus that he and a few chosen friends never spent a night here in the compound? Or that fat Argive, Telandros? A truly lusty knave, from what I hear. He—"

"You would not dare!" Medusa must have eyes like that.

I laughed. "No? You can't frighten me, Alcandre, because I know secrets you dare not let loose. I can tell the Great King why he never received any offer to ransom you. If that doesn't puzzle him already, I can point out that it should. Did he really promise you a rich husband? That's what the rumors say—that if you guard his little doves here, he will see you wedded to a wealthy landgrave back in Greece. But if I explain that the reason the Trojans will have nothing to do with you is that you had an incestuous affair with your son, Elatos, then I think any prospect of marriage is going to fade like dew in the—"

She leaped to her feet. "He will not believe your vile gossip!"

"I think I can convince him. If I have to. Shall we discuss terms?"

We discussed terms.

Intending to be gone before dawn, I had no real interest in sleeping quarters, but the fuss I made about them distracted her from my real purpose. I eventually settled on a shed that seemed relatively windproof. It would hold four, and I was fortunate to find three Lyrnessos women I could trust to share it with me.

After that, it was easy. If you know anything at all about slaves I need not tell you that there was a secret way out of the compound. My new roommates sniggered as they explained how the sentries were bribed. They promised to attend to that for me, happy to oblige. The hardest part was staying awake until the camp had fallen silent and all the rest of the paddock was asleep. Then my accomplices went first, scrambling quietly through the hole behind the water jugs. They were not merely unobserved in this, they actually had to go in search of the guards they were supposed to be distracting. I followed them out and vanished into the dark like a fish that slips from a hook.

2

The moon rolled through cloud like a silver plate. At first I went westward, tearing my legs on scrub and startling cattle, but no men saw me. When I felt safe from notice, I headed north until I reached the end of the camp. To my surprise, the Myrmidon sector was as dark and silent as all the rest. The hour was too late for the customary singing and reveling, but if the ships were to sail at dawn, there should be some preliminary activity in evidence and there wasn't. I paused to catch my breath and consider this new problem. Obviously I could not go with Achilles if he was not leaving. Some omen must have forced him to postpone his departure.

Myrmidon sentries would be more alert than the Mycenaeans had been. If they caught me they would not harm me, but they would be amused that the prince's prize had come sneaking back to him under cover of darkness. In the morning someone would share the joke with a Boeotian or a Cretan and soon it would be all over the army like a rain shower.

But I could not possibly go crawling back to Agamemnon without learning what Achilles was planning. No smoke blew from the chimney, and I would not dare disturb him if he were asleep, but how could he possibly be asleep? I stood paralyzed until I remembered the swallow. Then I raised my arms and cried: "Potnia Athena, hear my plea! As a slave I have nothing to offer you, but let me become the wife of Achilles, whom you favor, and all my life I will heap your altars and burn sacrifices to you! Every month I shall bring a splendid new gown to adorn your image. Let me speak with my love."

I set off over the moon-silvered grass. By fortunate chance I came in downwind, so the dogs caught my scent and gathered to greet me without barking. No guard challenged, and I was congratulating myself on having arrived unseen when a hand grabbed my shoulder and spun me around. Sheer terror muffled my scream.

"Briseis!"

"Patroclus!" In my relief I tried to embrace him, but he caught hold of my wrists and held me away from him.

He was swathed in a dark mantle, a dim shape in the gloom, and his voice sounded unnaturally cold and harsh. "If the Great King thinks he can make amends this way, he is more of a fool than I took him for."

"What?"

"He stole you in full view of the army. He must return you the same way and give many shining gifts in compensation, too. Nothing less will—"

"He did not send . . . I escaped!"

"Oh, you chaff head!" Patroclus released me and ran fingers through his hair. "You know what they do to runaway slaves! Agamemnon will scour the camp to find you. He will have you flogged or give you to the rabble. He will claim that Achilles put you up to—"

"I can be halfway to Thessaly by then."

"Briseis, Briseis! That can never be. Never!"

Shocked and hurt, I began gabbling protests, but Patroclus put a powerful arm around my shoulders and urged me away from the lodge. In my distress, I edged close to him, taking comfort from his strength although he was moving me in the wrong direction.

"Dear Briseis," he said, his voice so soft that the wind almost stole it. "Yes, Achilles loves you. He loves you as he has never loved any woman and probably always will. But it is not because of you his heart is breaking. It was not just you that Agamemnon stole from him, it was honor, and that you cannot return to him. He grieves over losing you, yes.

Were you dead, he would sorrow deeply and give you lavish rites. But death would be an act of the gods, which no man can do more than endure, submitting to their will. This is worse, far worse, because it was a mortal who shamed him before the army."

"But Thessaly—"

"No, Briseis! He may decide to go home, because he came to fight for glory and he can earn no glory fighting for that brute. But to slink off with you hidden in his ships . . . can't you see? That would make things worse by a hundredfold! Then men would say that he had been unmanned by love of a woman, that he cared more for his concubine than he did for the war. You expect the son of Peleus to steal you from Agamemnon and flee in the night like a thief? Like that wastrel Paris?"

"He stole me from Mynes!"

"He won you by valor and the strength of his arm. He cannot fight Agamemnon for you—he would, and joyfully, were it just between the two of them. He is not Paris, who destroys his people for the sake of his lust. I am disgusted that you could think such things of Achilles." Patroclus released me with a sigh. "Forgive my hard words. It has not been an easy day, has it? Go back to the Overlord. Submit to your fate, woman."

The moon rushed behind a silver-tipped cloud, pitching the world into shadow. Was there nothing I could do?

"At least let me go to him and say a word of—"

Patroclus's hand caught me when I would have gone past him. "No. Must I drag you back to the Mycenaeans myself? If you truly love Achilles, then you will forget him and cause him no more suffering. Begone, Briseis! And hurry, before you are missed. Do not provoke the Great King's anger, for that will solve nothing."

He kissed me. It was a brief, brotherly kiss and more precious than all the gold of Troy to me that terrible evening. Before I could say more, he strode away into the dark.

Fool that I was, I did not believe what he had told me.

"Goddess!" I cried. "Help me! Help Achilles!"

Silent and ominous, a great white owl soared out of the

darkness, flashed over my head, and was gone to the west.
My heart leaped with joy, for the owl is the preeminent symbol of Athena. Never since my childhood vision of the two
eagles had I seen a clearer sign. She was telling me that
Achilles was not in the lodge at all! He had never returned
from the shore, where he had gone earlier. I started to run.

Three times Athena's owl soared silently overhead, leading
me always westward, even to the edge of the land, high
above the low-grumbling surf, and there the wind made
boisterous efforts to tip me over. I could see nothing down
there in the darkness except the white teeth of the breakers.
Men had gathered eggs on these cliffs earlier in the spring,
but they had worked in teams, in daylight, using ropes. Yet
the goddess led me to a place where a descent might be possible, where a section of the face had fallen away, leaving a
notch above and a steep ramp below. Muttering prayers, I
dropped to my knees and made the attempt.

I had moonlight to help me, but the wind tried to pluck
me from every perch. The slope was worse even than I had
expected—a loose-packed jumble of rocks and gravel, slith-
ery grassy inclines, boulders big as chariots, a few bushes,
banks of loose dirt. Soon my knees were scraped, my dress
ripped, my fingers bleeding. About halfway down I passed a
spring that dribbled on me spitefully for the rest of my descent
and made the terrain even more treacherous, slick with mud.

Achilles had spent the day and half the night lamenting
alone on the shore, beseeching the gods to redress the wrong
he had suffered, reminding them of the offerings he had
given them in the past and seeking a sign that his pleas were
being heard. Knowing how the Olympians may manifest in
mortal form, he might well have jumped to strange conclusions had I suddenly emerged from the darkness to accost
him.

That did not happen. Working my way down a slippery
face, I failed to realize how close to the booming sea I had
come. It snatched me from my perch, sucked me down into
blackness and a stunning shock of cold. Waves swung me up
again like a boy pitching rocks and tried to smash me against

the wall, but Achilles leaped across the weed-slick boulders and caught my arm. For a moment he wrestled Poseidon for me, chest-deep in a madness of roaring white foam. When the water dropped back to try again, he was able to scoop me up and spring to higher ground. I was scraped and bleeding and soaked. He knew I was no Immortal.

He carried me to a patch of sand little larger than a bed and there set me on my feet. I clung to his great bulk, shivering violently. He began ripping off my wet clothing, and then I tore at his. Normal speech was impossible. We shouted at each other over the thunder of the waves that crashed in white tumult nearby, hurling spray at the stars.

"Briseis! How could you . . ." *Boom!* roared the surf. ". . . sent you?"

"Athena!" I yelled. "It was Athena, Athena herself."

He caught that name at least, for he bared his teeth in triumph. He dragged me down to the cold sand and gathered me in his arms. His skin was clammy, his weight crushing, and his hair flopped on my face in salty rags. The noise was a little less there, and he could shout in my ear. "I have prayed for a sign . . . Athena . . . She brought you!"

"She led me!"

"Bright-eyed Athena! This is the sign! . . . will be returned to me!" He roared his joy. *Thunder!* echoed the waves, hurling stars upward to the sky.

What followed was a strange passion indeed. We had much to say to each other, but we were lovers reunited, naked and desperate, and Aphrodite inflamed us—his mouth on mine, his hands everywhere, his manhood already huge and hard, rubbing in my groin, seeking entrance. He, who had given me away to another, struggled to possess and subdue me, while I, who wanted him so much, resisted frantically, clawing and biting his salt-wet skin. Love is not always tenderness. Too much can be a torment, and that night we held back nothing. He plunged into me in one shattering thrust, all the way. I had not expected so much so soon, agony and yet joy. I screamed. I screamed again as he withdrew and thrust again. And again. I kicked and clawed at his back, wild with love and rage, pain and pleasure, all at the same time.

"Mine!" he roared, and I felt the refrain repeating with every impact: *Mine! Mine! Mine!*

A slave cannot resist, but I was a past and future queen. I would not submit like a mere brood animal, so I fought as if he were Agamemnon himself raping me. He hammered his body on mine. I bit, scratched, and pummeled until suddenly my lust for him triumphed, my body melted and surrendered in howls of ecstasy. With a great cry, he threw his head back and spilled himself into me in convulsions that went on and on beyond belief.

At last he fell quiet, gasping for breath, but sprawled like a dead man on top of me. I held him while our hearts thundered and the waves roared. I wanted to lie there forever, one flesh with Achilles. He had not withdrawn, and I knew what that meant.

"We must hurry. We must be gone before they miss me."

After a moment he grunted and raised his head to stare into my eyes. "What?"

"Go home!" I said, "home to Thessaly—now, tonight! This is the message the goddess sends!"

"No."

"Yes!" I cried. I was helpless in his embrace, but I could plead. "You must go home! Beloved, you are mortal. You have proved your courage beyond all doubts; you have won great booty and honor; you need fight no more." The surf boomed, rushing and dragging on the rocks. "You cannot keep winning for ever! Home in your father's hall, live out a long and happy life. Don't you see? *Stay here and you will surely die under the walls of Troy!*"

"Go home in shame?" he roared, for his rage was still on him. "Nay, all day I have prayed to mighty Zeus for justice, and he has sent you as a sign that he will grant my plea. Bright-eyed Athena will see to it! He will give victory to the Trojans and drive back the Greeks until they come and clasp my knees and beg me to fight. Agamemnon will send you back with rich gifts! That *pig*!" he snarled, and I felt his manhood move within me. "That dog!" The next thrust was firmer, harder. I gasped in protest, but he paid no heed. "That dog-eyed *pig* son of a *whore*! Just *watch* his triumph over *me* shrivel before the *wrath* of the *gods,* see his *pride* crumble." The words grew louder, the strokes fiercer. "When the Trojans rage around the ships, then he will crawl to me. Then he will give you back!" My protests were swallowed in a suffocating kiss that seemed designed to suck the heart right out of me.

There was more, much more. He took his fill of me that night and I showed no mercy either—love knows many forms and ownership is one of them. When it was over, he helped me up the cliff and escorted me to the border of the Mycenaean camp, although Agamemnon would surely have soared to new heights of folly had we been seen together. I reached the paddock and its secret door undetected.

By then I had completely accepted Achilles' reading of the omen. I forgot that my voice had prophesied his death, just as it once had prophesied Mynes'.

3

Alcandre must have learned of my midnight escapade, but we both knew that one word of it to Agamemnon would bring disaster to both of us. For the rest of my stay in the paddock we treated each other with cool civility.

Day after day the Myrmidon ships remained on the beach, the army waited for orders, and Agamemnon did nothing. A brief delay to regroup after the pestilence ended would have been reasonable, but the pause dragged on. And on. Trojan allies were seen in the hills, the Scamander was falling, the marshes dried out. The lesser kings were reported frantic at the Overlord's inaction, yet still he procrastinated. He never sent for a woman. A man who has no use for a bedmate cannot be much use for anything.

Achilles had banned all contact between the Myrmidons and the rest of the Greeks, even ordering the women to use a spring farther up the cape instead of going to the washing place, but old Maera made her own laws and brought me news.

"Never saw a man who could stay furious for so long as that big lad of yours. He just sulks in his house all day or takes long, healthy walks by himself. Anyone speaks to him, he bites their heads off."

"He must be missing me?" I dared not ask outright who shared his bed, for although I hated to think of him pining for me, I feared even more that he might not. I was certainly missing him.

She cackled. "He hasn't told me if he is. He thinks it's all an Athena problem. If you want Aphrodite to intervene, you'll have to ask her yourself."

I prayed to Aphrodite, certainly. I prayed to Potnia and every other goddess I could think of, but why should they listen to me? I was a slave and had nothing to offer them.

One morning when the moon had shrunk to a thin curl above the dawn, heralds went by proclaiming a muster. We heard the gongs and trumpets and later a great deal of shouting in the distance, but that was all. Exactly what happened was never very clear, although all news came to us eventually, if only by way of illicit lovers whispering through the chinks of the fence.

Agamemnon had addressed the whole army. That was folly, because he had little insight even for the captains and nobles, and absolutely no feel for the lowborn. Whether he was trying to be humorous or thought he was in some way testing the war bands' mettle, he began by stressing all the difficulties of the Greek position—the invincibility of the walls of Troy, the strength of the Trojan allies, and so on. He may have been working up to a rousing call for effort, but his listeners concluded that he was calling off the siege. In enthusiastic tumult, the troops stampeded to the ships.

Odysseus son of Laertes saved the day. He snatched the scepter from Agamemnon's paralyzed hand and rallied the knights. Then he waded into mobs of malcontents and laid about him. An oaf named Thersites had gathered a following by accusing Agamemnon of greed and cowardice. Even Achilles had not gotten away with that. Odysseus clubbed Thersites down with the Overlord's own scepter and dispersed the mutineers.

Obviously the Greek army was a useless rabble without Achilles to lead it. Would Agamemnon swallow his pride and try to win him back?

As the dreary day was drawing to a close, the herald Talthybius came to the paddock and informed Alcandre that I was to attend the Overlord that evening.

"It will be a welcome break in the monotony," I said after my gooseflesh subsided. "He can't be much worse than an attack of diarrhea." This raised the best laugh of the day and a good deal of agreement.

"You have nothing to fear," one of the Dardanians said. "This morning won't have helped much. When his spirits are down, so is his prodder. You'll have a good night's sleep in a comfortable bed."

As Alcandre and I inspected the available gowns, I said, "I wonder if he's thinking of sending me back? Perhaps he just wants my advice on how to propitiate Achilles' anger."

She made a skeptical noise. "Don't count on it, dear. He does not take advice from slaves. He rarely takes advice from anyone, more's the pity. I can't advise you what to expect. Sometimes he's royally gracious. Sometimes it's just, 'Strip and lie down!' Or crouch. I understand he likes to play horses."

"That's good. Then I won't have to look at him." I could pretend it was some other man on my back.

Preparing the night's victim was a communal effort, and in my case there was the added complication of finding garments my size. Eventually I was draped in a seven-layered flounced skirt of red, white, and green and an open-fronted bodice cut from a simpler gown. A Kilike freewoman fashioned a hat for me, and we found some red leather sandals that did not pinch my feet too severely. Even Ctimene had never done a finer job on my tresses than those many skilled hands did. Bathed, oiled, painted, and scented, I was ready long before the heralds came for me.

The experts in the paddock were insisting that the Overlord must soon be *up* again. When that happened, he would lead out the army and meet disaster—so Achilles had predicted. From my point of view, the sooner the war resumed the better, so I should do as much as possible to encourage Agamemnon. If I could inspire him to raise his spear to me, he might feel up to waving it at the Trojans. It was that thought that led me blunder into the second of my three great mistakes.

I was taken to a small lodge, not the main hall. As the door creaked shut behind me, I removed my shoes and sank to my knees, alone with the king of men. Even keeping my eyes respectfully lowered, I could tell that the furnishings were lavish, with fleeces covering the floor and bright weavings the walls. Tables and chests were exquisitely ornate and inlaid, lamps twinkled through the smoke, and a fire crackled on the central hearth. A bed in the corner was piled high with many-colored quilts.

"The lovely Briseis!" Two hairy legs strode forward and a hairy hand was offered to raise me. Inspecting me with wet-lipped approval, he led me by the hand to a couch near the hearth and settled in close against me. He was trying to be gracious, not just strip-and-open-up, but he still oozed power and arrogant virility. He was robed to the thighs in a rich mantle, the twin lions of Mycenae on a red background, draped over his left shoulder and clipped under his right arm with a gold pin . . . a gold diadem, and three or four gold bracelets, nothing else. He was certainly not dressed as if he intended to discuss sending me back to Achilles with gifts and apologies, nor as if he planned to consult me as a seer. His interests were strictly physical.

"Magnificent!" He ran fingertips over my right nipple. His eyes were bright with lust, but no telltale bulge showed in his mantle yet.

I tried to hide a shiver. "You are kind, my lord."

"I hope you will be. I anticipate an exciting evening for both of us." He turned to the table at his side, and ladled wine from a silver bowl with a silver rhyton shaped like a bull's head. I was more interested in the other table, whose meats and breads and cheeses would be a welcome relief from the slaves' monotonous bland mash, but I accepted the goblet he offered with a flaunt of eyelashes.

"So do I, my lord." The wine was pleasantly flavored with honey and a trace of linseed. "Delicious!" I heaved a sigh that made his eyes widen.

As I had no choice in the matter, no one could criticize me for submitting to him or even encouraging him to be as speedy as possible, but I would feel untrue to Achilles if I enjoyed myself in the process. Now I realized that this resolution might not be easy to keep. The man oozed power. He was a Great King, equal of Egypt's pharaoh or the Hittite emperor. I was very aware of the muscled thigh pressing against mine, the rugged warrior's body at my side, covered with black fur like a bear's, and the many empty nights since Achilles and I raped each other on the sand.

"Drink up! We have a bowl to finish." He drained his cup.

I obeyed; he poured me more. Fool that I was, I was thinking only of the intimate nuzzling that might be required of me and how much more bearable it would be with a bellyful of wine. I overlooked the other indiscretions I might be tempted to. "This room is beautiful, my lord! You have an eye for beauty."

He preened. "Ah, wait till you see Mycenae! But even with all its treasures and all the riches I shall take home with me from the sack of Troy, the lovely Briseis will shine brightest of all!"

That was close to one of Achilles' favorite lines, and I resented it. I had no intention of ever going near Mycenae. The goddess had promised.

"I am no expert on great palaces, my lord. I am a judge of fine textiles, though." I fingered his mantle approvingly, letting a fingernail scratch his nipple.

He shrugged. "One of Clytemnestra's. My wife weaves much better than she humps."

Oaf!

"Then we complement each other!" I touched the gold pin. "And this is very fine work." I fluttered my eyelash banners again.

Subtlety was wasted on him. He thought I liked the pin. "It came from the sack of Thebes." He launched into a long explanation.

"The booty from Troy will be even greater!" I leaned across him to place my cup on the table.

A sweaty arm slid around my shoulders. "But at what cost? So many fine warriors have gone down to Hades already, and so many more must follow. I do not lack valor in battle, as you must know, but I confess that I mourn the dear friends I order out to die." He dipped the silver rhyton to refill my goblet. "To be a king is a heavy burden. I toss sleepless on my bed at night, tortured by responsibilities."

"If you are to lose valuable sleeping time, my lord, you should do it to better purpose."

"A Great King is a lonely man!"

He had lost his earlier cheerfulness. I began to worry.

"You are not alone now, my lord." I stroked his thigh.

He grunted. "Ah! And how long, oh gods, how long? When will Zeus fulfill his promise that the towers of Troy will fall?" The cup he was clutching on his knee was empty, so I raised mine to his lips. He turned his face away. "The Lord of Storms promised us that we would loot Priam's treasury and ravish his women. Or so Calchas said. Ah, that despicable son of Thestor! Was he wrong? He will never give me a straight answer. Fool that I ever was to trust our hopes to a seer so useless!"

I took a drink while I appraised this new topic. I also eased my hand around to the inside of his thigh. Agamemnon responded with a sudden lurch, tightening his grip on my neck, pushing his hand down to fondle my breast. He leered his wet lips at me. "But enough of troubles! I must appoint a senior—what was the word you used? Consort? I have so many bedmates that one must be paramount. You are the obvious choice, my dear, for none of them looks so much like a goddess as you do."

"You flatter me, my lord." I drained my cup. His abrupt changes of mood were making my head spin.

"Not at all! You quite outdo Chryseis in beauty, although I confess that the little patch of red fur on her pudendum used to excite me extensively. I look forward to seeing yours. We must find splendid gowns for you to strut around in, and jewels and gold. Chains of gold! Bracelets and bangles! Jewels! I will load you with royal treasures! Onyx! Agate! Alabaster white as your fine breasts! Hematite! Chalcedony! Sardonyx! Jasper! I will make you a marvel for men to behold!" He sprayed me with enthusiasm. "And you must not remain in that paddock with the rest of the stock—no, no! You will stay here from now on in my private quarters. There is room enough in that bed for three when I choose to entertain others. You shall be a credit to the Great King, my beauty!"

Horrors! To submit to him was unavoidable, but to let him load honors on me would be a betrayal of Achilles.

"My lord! You are presuming too much!"

He scowled, his already flushed face darkening. "Presuming?"

"You do not know if I am worthy, my lord! Would you judge a horse only by its looks? Would you set a value on it before you had tried it out?" To avoid his favors, I would have to be very disappointing, even if he ordered me whipped for it.

He chuckled throatily. "Sly heifer! I hear you are an augur of great skill."

"Oh! Er . . . Yes! I have seen omens."

He clasped a hand around my throat and pushed my head back against the crook of his elbow, peering into my face with dark, suspicious eyes. "What omens?"

I was drunk, yes. Suddenly I was also frightened, for I had never met a man so mercurial. I did not know whether he wanted to seduce me or choke me. "Good omens, my lord! Great omens!"

"Tell me!" His fingers tightened, digging into my neck.

"The fall of Troy!" I squealed.

He licked his lips. "Yes? Yes! Go on! Who sacks Troy? Achilles?"

"No! You do! Zeus has decided! The time will come when you will fill its streets with Greeks, ravish its—"

He crowed with triumph and dragged me on top of him. His kiss was slobbery yet violent. By the time it had finished he had torn away my bodice. "More! Tell me more!"

"What else is there to tell?" I cried. "You will crush the Trojans and slay them. You will take everything they possess."

"When?" His fumbling hands slid down to my waist

"Now! Soon!"

"Up!" he snarled, having trouble with my heavy skirts. He heaved me upright. "This is a true message from the Thunderer? How do you know?"

He hauled my dress down as I rose, so I swayed naked before him, clutching his shoulders for balance. The room spun around me, and I did not know what I was saying. I think I spoke of dreams, for those are safest. Whatever my words, he believed them. He reeled to his feet with a howl of triumph. With one hand gripping my arm and another thrust between my legs, he lifted me bodily and staggered across the room to throw me on the bed—whatever his faults, Agamemnon was a man of enormous physical strength. Ripping off his mantle, he fell on top of me.

I knew what I was doing in that situation. We wrestled erotically for a few moments, but then he stopped slobbering in my mouth so he could bark more questions, demanding details of the supreme victory I was prophesying for him. When I hesitated, he punched and pinched me and yet still did not stop pawing and squirming. Did he want a seer or a bed slave? Realizing what terrible things I was saying, I reached for his groin, but found nothing there or very little—no parsnip, just a pea pod. The next time he rolled us over, I wrenched myself around to take it in my lips. He grunted with surprise and pleasure. I sucked and kneaded, confident that he would not force me to answer more questions while I was doing so. He pulled my legs closer to him and began fondling me clumsily. That hurt, so I mouthed him even faster, and soon I had a manly hunk of meat to work with, hot and firm, although no match for Achilles' great shaft. Deciding this could be no worse inside me than the finger he had inserted, I tried to change position.

"Don't stop!" He pushed my head down.

I went back to work on him again and, now that he was forcing a second finger into me, redoubled my efforts. His free hand gripped my hair and pumped my head up and down, almost choking me. I had always used mouth work as an appetizer, never the main meal, and I found the results revolting. Agamemnon evidently did not, for he squealed at the first spasm, thrashed like a landed fish several times, and eventually went limp, sweating and gasping as if he had done all the usual work.

I rolled free of him, spat out his slime, wiped my mouth on a quilt, and lay still at his side, shivering with revulsion. I was almost sober by then, although the bed seemed to be spinning still. I strove to remember exactly what I had told him. What he wanted to hear, certainly, which is always the safest thing to say to kings, but I had been reporting it as the will of Zeus. Although Agamemnon might have forgotten by morning, the Immortals would certainly remember my presumption. True, I had been in a very difficult situation, but Maera had taught me that the deed counted, not the intention. I had done what Helenus, years before, had warned me never to do—I had foresworn the gods.

My brooding was interrupted by an enormous snore from the Great King. I rose and spread a covering over him, while doubting that anyone so furry needed one. I went back to the hearth for a long drink of sweet wine, then sat there naked, sensuously toasting my skin and enjoying a delicious solitary supper, with only the porcine grunts from the bed spoiling my pleasure. When I could eat no more, I piled fleeces and quilts beside the hearth and lay down to enjoy whatever sleep I would be allowed, expecting to be summoned in an hour or two.

Several times I heard him thrashing and mumbling in some sort of nightmare, but he did not awaken until dawn. When he did, he did not notice me at all. He crashed around, cursing and knocking over furniture, then went charging out, leaving the door open and already bellowing orders.

I dressed and strolled back to the paddock. The camp was
in an uproar. Whatever I had said or done in the night, the
Overlord was aroused at last.

4

Achilles had not been totally fair when he accused Agamemnon of shirking battle. On occasion I had heard him praise the
Great King's valor highly, describing him as a bull who spent
twenty-nine days a month chewing cud or servicing cows and
the thirtieth in full charge against everything in sight. That day
the bull charged. He stirred up the army like a mule kicking
over a beehive, bellowing at the knights to lead out their war
bands, exhorting, berating, barely patient enough to wait until
the men had been fed. I heard later that he had babbled something about dreams and messages from Zeus, but whatever he
said was good enough to convince the other kings.

So began a four-day battle that saw the bitterest fighting
of the war. Forgotten were the courtesies that had marked
the previous year—staged duels, truces to bury the dead,
ransoming of prisoners. Savagery reigned supreme.

Before the onset of winter, Achilles had driven off the
Trojan allies, destroyed their towns, razed Troy back to the
citadel walls, and penned the defenders inside them. Spring
floods and then pestilence had extended the stalemate, but
now the action could resume. So confident were the Greeks
that they took along a mule train loaded with scaling ladders. When the racket of their departure died away, only the
captives remained in camp, plus some sick and wounded. A
few women set off southward toward Larisa in hopes of es-
caping, but I doubt if any eluded the men and dogs guarding
the palisade. Most of us walked over to the western ridge,
from which we could view the day's action like spectators at
a chariot race.

Alcandre and I found a sun-warmed slope overlooking the camp. It was a halcyon day, blustery and yet warm—the silver-blue bay salted with white seabirds, fresh grass peppered with iris and anemones, bright green landscape streaked by stretches of yellow-flowered broom. The sky was alive with birds. A perfect day for battle.

On the far side of the bay, the white-towered citadel on its eminence seemed very insignificant to be the cause of so much suffering and slaughter. Only a black stain below it marked where the town had stood, for whatever would burn had burned, and winter rains had disposed of the ashes. Another couple of years' neglect and the ruins would vanish altogether, although the citadel itself will surely remain forever, the towers built by gods.

By the time we had taken our seats the Greek van had reached the end of the bay, but to us it was merely a dark smudge on the plain, moving very slowly. Nothing was going to happen for some time, and we should see very little at that distance. The land beyond remained eerily empty. I was confident of a Trojan victory that would force Agamemnon to admit his folly and send me back to Achilles. Where Alcandre's loyalties lay I could not even guess.

Eventually I tired of futile small talk. "What makes men so savage?" I demanded. "Why must they fight all the time?"

She looked at me oddly. "Would you rather still be married to Mynes?"

"I suppose not. It seems like a long time ago."

"They say Achilles is infatuated with you."

"And I with him."

"The goddess grants that sort of passion to few mortals."

Did she refer to Elatos? For a moment we teetered on the brink of intimacy. She was the first to turn away from the precipice. "But we cannot condemn men for fighting today. They have done nothing so far. I shall complain to someone."

I laughed politely. "They're not heading up to the ford. The lower reaches must be passable now. And look! The Trojans are coming out to fight."

"Do you suppose Agamemnon knows that yet?"

"He would have sent chariots ahead to scout. He'll be able to see them soon." I wondered if he would be surprised by this show of defiance. Achilles would not have been.

The Trojan host emerged and headed south along the shore toward the Greeks, whose advance had been slowed by the need to cross the river. I found it hard to believe that those distant blurs were not just shadows of clouds, but were thousands of breathing, sweating men marching out to slay or be slain. Then another tongue of darkness began flowing out of the hills. Soon another came into view down the valley of the Scamander. Agamemnon would have no need for ladders that day.

A battle must be the most devastating experience imaginable for those involved, but it is boring to watch from a distance. When those four shadows merged into one, Alcandre and I could make out no details. We heard no screams and saw no blood, only a haze of dust on the wind. In the struggle for Lyrnessos I had seen men die. In the previous year's fighting, I had been worried ragged knowing that Achilles would be always in the thick of it. This was only shadows on the land.

We heard great stories later, of course. Noble deeds of valor were hailed by the bards, fine knights perished in glory, innumerable lowborn bled in the dust, forgotten by all but the families they had left behind. The Trojans were supported by Lykians, Dardanians, and Lycians, who brought a considerable superiority in chariots and archers; and Hector was a more effective leader than Agamemnon. Without Achilles to direct them the Greek knights were a swarm of gnats lacking aim and cohesion. The hero that day was Diomedes of Argos, who seemed to be everywhere at once, steering, inspiring, and personally slaughtering, but second best was not good enough.

For a while in mid-afternoon, the Greeks made progress and the battle rolled slowly toward Troy, but when the best contingents were forced out by sheer exhaustion, the winds of war turned. Hector threw in good troops he had been holding in reserve, a tactic Agamemnon could never arrange.

By the end of the day, the Greek front was struggling back across the river, sore beset. The dogged Salamisians with their tower shields fought a stubborn rearguard battle to cover the retreat, and for a while the action became almost a personal duel between Hector and the Greater Ajax. The onset of darkness forced both sides to retire from the blood-clotted field.

Long before that, though, the injured began slinking back into camp—in chariots, on mule carts, or hobbling on makeshift crutches. With the healers at the front over-whelmed by the numbers, the women came to the aid of their captors. Those who had no training fetched water and bandages and bedding. Others, like Alcandre and me, were bandaging, stitching, soothing, and cutting out arrowheads. I noticed old Maera lending a hand, although I got no chance to speak to her and none of the other Myrmidon women seemed to be present.

Tents and sleeping sheds became makeshift hospitals, places of nightmare reeking of blood, loud with screams of pain and the weeping of dying boys. They lay all over the floors with corpses being carried out as fast as fresh wounded were brought in. Have you any idea how fast blowflies can cluster on a wound? Did you know that a dead man stinks like a latrine? I had not seen the horrors of the battlefield, but I saw horrors enough. At one point a woman began laughing maniacally in a corner of the shed where I was working, a sound so horrible that a lot of the onlookers cried out in fear, thinking a demon had entered. I rushed over to silence her, as much as anyone could rush when the floor was carpeted with bodies. She was kneel-ing beside a lanky youth, and I can still see the horror in his eyes and the pallor that made his face shine like a moon in the dimness. She was laughing because she rec-ognized him as one who had raped her, but he had been wounded in the groin and was never going to rape anyone again. I dragged her away and threw her out into the sun-shine. By the time I got back to the boy, he was dead and stinking like a latrine.

*   *   *

It was long after sunset when I staggered back to the paddock and flopped down on my straw. I was reasonably well satisfied with the results of the day. True, the Trojans had not rolled up the Greeks like a blanket as I hoped they would. The honors had been about even, but the Greek morale was utterly shattered. They had set out in the morning expecting to sleep in Priam's megaron with beautiful Trojan women, and now they were back where they had started in the first days after their landing, penned behind the Scamander.

Much of the army hardly slept at all that night. They were kept busy at the palisade, strengthening it from a fence to keep livestock in to a barricade to keep Hector out. For the first time in the war, the dead were left lying where they had fallen.

5

Fighting resumed the next morning as soon as there was enough light to tell friend from foe, which was not always easy even by day. Most contingents had some sort of distinguishing mark, like the horns on the Mycenaeans' helmets, but mistakes could happen in the heat of battle. A leader might easily find himself and his men surrounded by the enemy, or run his men to exhaustion following his chariot. Some, like Odysseus and the Greater Ajax, did not use chariots at all, but most would drive out ahead until they saw a profitable opening, then summon up their war band by waving their mantles and dismount to lead it on foot. A charioteer had the trickiest job of all. He must watch out for trouble approaching while his leader was engrossed in combat, blinkered by his helmet. When the engagement went well, he was expected to drive in and collect the armor looted from the enemy dead. If things went wrong he must be ready at all times to dash back into the fray and rescue his knight; and yet he had to keep his team out of danger as much as possible, because it was an easy and profitable target for archers. Chariots were the fastest and most vulnerable pieces on the board and the armored knights the strongest and slowest.

I saw none of the morning's fighting, for Alcandre and I were again tending the wounded. Toward noon we went back to the hill to see what was happening, and it was about then that the gods tipped the scales against the Greeks. More and more Trojan allies were arriving, not especially decisive in numbers but bad for morale. Furthermore, storm clouds swept in from the north, bringing ominous peals of warning from Zeus. Everyone knew what it meant when thunderbolts fell on the Trojans' right, the Greeks' left.

The climax came when the large force from Pylos ran into serious trouble. Normally it was most ably directed by old Nestor in his chariot, but that time he overreached himself. Diomedes brought the Argives to his rescue, but they were all driven back by a Trojan assault, and the sight of Diomedes withdrawing sapped the Greek will as nothing else could have done. Soon the front was falling back on the palisade, the camp was filling up ominously with fighters who had fled the field, and our peaceful hillside was being invaded by sullen-faced but apparently able-bodied men.

"I think, my dear," Alcandre said with a frown, "that we should retire to our quarters. That is, unless you are of a mind to be gang raped?"

"It is a little early in the day for that," I retorted. "By all means let us make a tactical withdrawal, as everyone else seems to be of the same mind." Of course, I was secretly exulting. Achilles' predictions were proving as perceptive as always. Agamemnon would soon be crawling to him like the worm he was.

We found the camp teeming with men, for many knights felt that they had done a fair day's work and earned some rest for themselves and their war bands. Agamemnon himself had returned to rally the missing parts of his army; and now he was riding his chariot up and down the beach, in and out among the ships and tents and buildings, waving his

mantle and bellowing his head off. When he was good he
was very good, and just then he was at his best. He rounded
up several hundred men, raised their chins, and led them
back to the battle, which by then had almost reached the palisade. There, in the last hour of daylight, the Trojan assault
was brought to a halt by a coalition of Cretans, Spartans,
Mycenaeans, and Diomedes' Argives.

I heard only scraps of that news, though, for I again became
involved in tending the wounded. I spent a long time sewing
up dying men while their comrades held them down for me.
It was disgusting, hopeless, soul-wrenching work. Three out
of four would die. It would have been kinder to have speared
them on the battlefield, although at least those who died in
camp would be given decent rites. The thought of all those
abandoned bodies on the plain was frightful, the worst abomination the war had yet produced. Whatever had happened to
the bright oaths the knights had sworn to Athena?

As the sun set, rain began spattering, to add to the general
misery. I managed to escape, dragging myself off in the direction of the paddock. I had almost reached it when a deep
voice called from the shadows.

"Briseis!"

I jumped and spun around. Two men came forward, with
a dozen or so followers trailing at a respectful distance.

"Son of Laertes!" I swept a courtesy as well as I could in
a filthy, blood-spattered slave's wrap. My hair was a thicket
of swamp grass.

"And the son of Neleus. This is the former queen of Lyrnessos, my lord. You understand now how wars can be
fought over beauty?"

"My eyes are not as sharp as they used to be," Nestor said
with a rasping chuckle, "especially in this sort of semi-
twilight, but I cannot recall ever regretting the fact as much
as I do at the moment. I never met the fair Helen. How
would you rank the two of them?"

"That would depend entirely on who was listening. The
daughter of Briseus is certainly endowed with greater acu-
men. My lady, you have been putting your enforced leisure
to good use."

"It is fortunate, my lord, that the gods gave at least half the human race some sense."

Nestor chortled. Odysseus glanced around to see how near his followers were and then moved closer to me, bringing his companion with him. He spoke softly.

"Am I correct in believing that you would rather be reunited with the son of Peleus than remain where you are, my lady?"

My lady? I distrusted the king of Ithaca when he used flattery. "Slaves have no preferences, my lord."

"Yes, they do. But they are rarely invited to express them."

He won a smile from me with that. "Then, in confidence, I admit that there is some truth in your supposition, noble son of Laertes."

"You may be able to promote that state of affairs. You must know Achilles better than anyone else does except Patroclus. Supposing—and we are speaking hypothetically, you understand—supposing some person wished to send an emissary to treat with him. Who would be the wisest choice? Whom does he trust most among the captains?"

My surge of joy was swiftly tempered by alarm. Flattering as it was to have my judgment sought, this was dangerous ground for a slave. "Why, either of you noble lords yourselves would—"

"Leave us two out of consideration. I am aware that some men credit me with what they perceive as an unseemly subtlety of speech."

The king of Pylos chuckled. "And the young resent old men lecturing them at wearisome length."

"My lords! I swear to you that I have never heard Achilles speak thus of either of you. In fact I cannot recall him ever censure any man of quality. It is not in him to find fault with others."

"We believe you," Odysseus replied, "and we love him for it. But pray answer my question." He hesitated and then put the problem squarely. "If you were Agamemnon seeking reconciliation, whom would you choose to send to plead with him?"

To be consulted on such a matter was a heady sensation, although I could not believe they needed my advice. I took a moment to consider, mostly wondering what these shrewd kings really wanted of me. The rain was gathering confidence.

"I believe that no one ranks higher in his estimation than his kinsman Ajax, my lords."

They exchanged glances as if I had merely confirmed their own conclusions. Nestor nodded. "Still just supposing. It is often thought prudent when petitioning a king to present one's case through some courtier who has his ear and trust. We all know that Patroclus son of Menoitios is like a second shadow to Achilles, but he may be reluctant to importune his dear friend. If a proposal such as we have hypothesized were to be directed to Achilles, who among his followers would be most inclined to favor it?"

Ah! Now we had come to the sharp edge. Here they probably did need my knowledge of the Myrmidon contingent. Fortunately I could answer without hesitation. "Phoenix son of Amyntor is a doughty warrior, yet a prudent man whose counsel Achilles values above all others'."

"So?" Odysseus favored me with one of his rare smiles. "We are grateful for your help. Tonight the Overlord will be holding a feast for the Greek leaders. That is a reasonable assumption, is it not, son of Neleus?"

"He ought to," Nestor agreed. "I can recall many precedents. . . . We shall see what we can do to incline him in the appropriate direction."

"I think it would help the cause if his many prizes of honor were present to grace the hall with their beauty. Briseis, will you see that they are prepared and ready when he calls for them?"

These two men were the shrewdest of the Greek leaders, and I was fairly certain that I approved of whatever they were up to. "I shall do whatever I can, my lords."

Odysseus smiled grimly. "And so shall we. May Athena Our Lady smile upon our efforts."

Their efforts were effective. Agamemnon was persuaded to hold a feast for the knights and summon his women to adorn

it. When old Talthybius came puffing and flustered to the
paddock, he was astonished and gratified to discover that we
were already dressed in our finery. He led us through the
drizzle to the Great King's hall and bade us wait for a few
minutes in the porch. Through the wide doors we could see
firelight and the flicker of lamps, while the smoke drifting
out brought scents of roasting meat that made my mouth
water. A deafening roar of voices revealed that the wine was
flowing already. Men kept hurrying past us, bringing more
food, more stools, more dishes.

Talthybius returned with Eurymedon son of Ptolemy,
Agamemnon's charioteer, the two of them struggling with a
wooden chest, which turned out to be loaded to the brim
with gold and silver and jewels. They pulled out this treasure in handfuls, thrusting it at us as if they were ladling stew
into bowls, a queen's adornment for each of us. I received
four mismatched necklaces, rings of hematite, jasper, carnelian, ivory, and amethyst, half a dozen bracelets, and a hat
covered with gold sequins that was far too small for my
head. I exchanged it for a filigree coronet from the woman
next to me and no one objected. All that mattered was the
overall impression, I suppose. The Greeks were in need of
reassurance after the drubbing they had received that day.
We were to be symbols of what they had achieved already, a
display of Agamemnon's glory.

Then we were ordered into the hall.

"To do what?" I whispered to Alcandre.

"Scintillate," she said with one of her catlike smiles. "Os-
cillate your bosom at them, dear, and make them drool."

I looked over the throng of virile warriors. "What happens
if they make me drool, though?"

"Ah! Well, I suspect you'll be disappointed. Come to
think of it, try not to stir up the Overlord too much."

We separated. I proceeded resolutely into the mob, staying well clear of the Great King's throne. The hall was loud,
eye-nippingly smoky, and jammed to the walls with knights
and their charioteers—eating, drinking, shouting, laughing,
and arguing ferociously over the events of the day. Most
were on stools or chairs; but others were standing, and not a

few lay stretched out on the floor in a sleep of exhaustion. The jollity was forced, with some long faces glowering through the chinks in it. The Trojans were at the barricade, waiting for dawn. Their campfires twinkled like all the stars of heaven on the plain.

I noted fierce fiery-haired Diomedes holding court amid a buzz of admirers. "Fight on, of course!" he shouted in answer to some question. "If anyone wants to go, let him go. I stay until Troy falls or I do, as my father would have done. I recall . . ." He launched into one of his interminable stories about his father.

Odysseus stood alone at the far side of the room, nursing a gold cup and thoughtfully assessing the assembly. He was another who would not consider quitting. But Menelaus, now—one glance at his face was enough to make anyone think of launching a ship and getting out while the getting was good. The red-haired king of Sparta looked as bewildered as a puppy whose bone has been stolen. His brother sat humped on his throne, scowling morosely at the floor and speaking to no one, as if he hated parties and wanted to go home to bed. Down again, obviously.

That was the strangest feast I ever attended. Forty beautiful women had just paraded in and hardly an eye looked at them. When men had that much on their minds, anything could happen. It had better happen soon, because the Trojans were at the gates.

A large hand gripped my arm. I looked around into the big blue eyes and carefree smile of the Greater Ajax. He was perched on a stool too low for him, clutching a bowl heaped with meat and bread.

"Hungry? Won't you share this with me?"

"I'd be honored, my lord!"

"The pleasure is mine." He pulled me onto a thigh as massive as a pony's back and tilted me back to lean against him. "Eat up."

I selected a juicy bone to nibble, grateful to the gods for leading me to so enjoyable a companion. I never heard anyone speak an unkind word about the son of Telamon, as either fighter or person. He was Achilles' cousin, built on the same titanic scale, with golden hair and a face to dream of. A little innocent flirtation with him would pass the time most agreeably.

As I ate, I said, "I have heard great tales already of the last two days, my lord. Men sing your praises to the heavens."

Ajax shrugged, which was for me a sensation akin to a small earthquake. "Who cares what men say? Far too many good men will never speak again. What women say may matter more."

I sucked juicy fat off the rib I was holding. "I'm not sure what you mean, my lord."

"You have been bandying my name about, Briseis."

I peered at those apparently guileless baby-blue eyes so close to mine. "Me? Bandy? I don't even know how to bandy."

He boomed laughter, another earthquake. "If Achilles ever tires of you, head for my tent, won't you?"

"I do not belong to the son of Peleus any longer."

"That injustice is about to be put to rights." His smirk said he was in on the plot, whatever it was.

"I mentioned you only to report that Achilles honors you above all other men."

He raised flaxen eyebrows. "Oh, no! You implied that I would be a suitable ambassador. No one has ever attributed such skills to me before. My strong arm has been praised often enough but never my tongue." He chuckled at my embarrassment. "But that is the whole point, isn't it?"

He lifted a silver goblet from between his feet and held it to my lips. As I drank, a horny hand gently closed around my breast. When I had done, I peered in the general direction of Agamemnon, but he was hidden behind a noisy group of Cretans.

"Flattered as I am by your interest, my lord, I wonder if you should demonstrate it so publicly? Some men are overly suspicious and see conspiracy where none is intended."

Ajax frowned. He had not even thought of that. "I enjoy fondling a beautiful woman! Too many of my friends will never know such joy again, and by another sunset I may be with them. That's what you're here for, isn't it? What harm can there be?"

If he didn't know that, where had he been this last half month? Pretty though he was, and a mountain of strength in battle also, Ajax was not Achilles.

"I equally enjoy being cuddled by a beautiful man. I did not say there was harm, only that others might think so." I popped a tasty morsel in his mouth and let him lick my fingers.

Even bone weary, as he must have been, the king of Salamis was amusing company, cheerful and attentive. All around us men were refighting the day's battles, but he would not speak of them. He had dismissed the war from his mind until the time came to fret about it again, just as Achilles would have done. He told some amusing stories of life in Salamis and laughed uproariously at tales of mine, as long as I did not make them too subtle.

When heralds began shouting for silence, I reluctantly made my excuses and slipped away to the porch, but there I lingered to watch and listen. Old Nestor was on his feet, haranguing Agamemnon in a way no one else would have dared. Dispensing with his usual loquacity, the old warrior was as brutal as a battle-ax: the Greeks needed Achilles and it was Agamemnon's fault that Achilles was absent. He even said, "I told you so," but that was his privilege. The Great King would have to send back the woman Briseis.

Praise to the goddess!

He returned to his stool in a silence so profound that I could hear ripples lapping on the shore and even a distant owl, which was probably Athena laughing. Agamemnon glared around to see if anyone would argue, and no one did. His face, already flushed from the wine, grew darker yet. He heaved himself to his feet.

"Very well, my lords, I admit that an error was made. My words may have been tactless. How much must I pay the boy to bring his men back into the war? What gifts will appease his pride, do you think? Ten bars of gold, mm? Seven brand-new pots of bronze? Yes, and I'll throw in twenty precious, shining bowls as well."

No one spoke.

He walked forward to the fire. "And seven gorgeous women from Lesbos, well skilled in household crafts!"

I bristled. What about me? Did he really think he could keep me?

No, he tossed me onto the heap. "And the Briseis girl." He peered around at the deathly hush.

Someone coughed inquiringly.

"And . . . and, if he wishes, I will swear a solemn oath before the gods that I have never coupled with her as man and woman naturally do."

This outrageous blasphemy was met with a sigh of relief that seemed to come from every set of lungs in the hall. He had phrased it very carefully, though. I wondered if the gods would accept such hairsplitting.

Now he turned and strode back to the throne. Perhaps he was relieved not to have been struck down by a thunderbolt already, because he raised his voice and roared out the praises of some fancy horses he would contribute. Those won murmurs of admiration, although everyone knew that Achilles already owned the best horses on the cape. Encouraged, Agamemnon stopped emptying his treasury and began heaping promises instead.

"And, if the Immortals favor our cause, then Achilles may choose any twenty of the fairest Trojan women—other than Helen, of course—and fill his ships with Priam's wealth!" He was growing more and more excited now. "When we return to Greece, I will adopt him as my own son and give him one of my three lovely daughters to marry, whichever one he chooses!"

I bristled again.

"I'll ask no bride gifts for her. Nay, I will grant him lands—seven fair cities I will give him as my son-in-law!" He rattled off their names. Six were unfamiliar to me, but I caught the name of Hire, where Euneus ruled.

Fool! I thought. *Idiot!* He still did not understand. Achilles had already chosen the wife he wanted. Could this foolish king not understand that this was the whole problem? Or part of the problem, at least. Why did he not just offer to recognize Achilles as host leader, which is what he had been in fact? Give him command of the Greeks and tell him to go and take Troy—that and me and a public apology would probably be enough. A few gold bars as well wouldn't hurt.

As if to emphasize his blindness, Agamemnon concluded in a roar. "But he must acknowledge that I am Overlord!" He flopped back onto his throne, panting and glaring.

After a moment, Nestor rose. "Truly, my lord, these are wondrous gifts! I cannot recall their equals in any comparable situation, whether in the noble tales the bards sing or in my own experience, extensive though that has been. We must dispatch emissaries to the son of Peleus to plead our cause and tell him of your munificent offer. Let me suggest . . ."

As he was working his way around to naming names, I hurried off into the night.

6

The envoys took the easy path along the shore, guided by the myriad fires of the camp, while I had to travel by the inland way, stumbling through scrub and brush in a drizzle that hid the stars. Nor were living men all I had to fear, although they might rape me, drag me ignominiously back to my captivity, or cut my throat for the treasure I wore. Much worse was the thought of all the unburied dead on the battlefield. Fortunately for my resolution, the petty difficulties of finding a way overland in the dark kept me too busy to worry about the ghosts that must be haunting the encampment, wailing for proper rites to free them. I tripped and fell many times, ripping my dress and shedding jewels in the process, but I arrived at the Myrmidon camp unmolested by man or beast or wraith.

The emissaries had traveled faster, but on reaching the

Myrmidon camp they had to treat with Automedon, who was officer of the watch that night, then send for Phoenix and ask him to plead their case. By the time they had done all that, I had crept up to the back of Achilles' lodge and pressed my ear to a chink in the logs. He was playing the kithara and singing, and the familiar sound brought an ache to my throat and added tears to the rain on my cheeks—I was home! I would not be able to stay, of course, but the urgency of the Greek plight was so great that the settlement could not wait until morning. As soon as Achilles accepted Agamemnon's terms, he would go back with the envoys to be reconciled and receive his gifts, including me. How I would get there in time to be handed over and how I would explain my bedraggled condition when I did so were problems I was prepared to leave until later.

The dogs in the porch erupted in barking. Automedon shouted at them, and I slipped around to the front corner in time to watch them sniffing and growling at the visitors, dark against the brighter sea behind them. The music had stopped. Achilles' voice boomed out almost at my side:

"Friends! Good friends, welcome! Come! Enter!" I risked another peek as he strode out from the porch, the kithara still under his arm. He reached for Ajax's hand, which was a tricky decision, because neither age nor rank nor reputation distinguished the two kings, but Patroclus hurried out to lead in Odysseus. Behind them came old Eurybates and another herald, even older, followed by the two Myrmidons; and they all disappeared inside without noticing that the dogs had found another visitor.

When I had rubbed enough ears and been thoroughly licked and wagged at, I slid like a ghost into the porch to see what was going on. Old Phoenix was beaming, while Automedon, hovering behind him, was grinning like a young shark at the prospect of being able to harness up Achilles' chariot again. Iphis and . . . *Diomede*? Oh, no! I could understand Achilles taking another bedmate, but surely he could have chosen one with more brains than that buttery cow from Lesbos? I should perhaps feel flattered that he had sought out the only woman in the Myrmidon camp who approached me for size, but how could he bear her stupidity, her lumbering walk, her raucous jackdaw laugh? I stamped my foot angrily. Even Iphis was directing worried looks at her darling Patroclus, guessing that he was about to return to the battle, but that witless Lesbos she-bear was still smiling. She had not realized she was going to be sent back to the troops.

Well, if Diomede was the best substitute Achilles had been able to find, he should be all the more grateful to get me back.

Now I realized that I need not have hurried, because nothing important was going to happen for a long time yet. When kings come a-calling on business, all the formalities of welcome must be observed, and Achilles was ever a scrupulous host. Fine weavings were being spread on chairs and stools, wine brought, libations poured. Automedon stoked up the fire; Patroclus laid out meat on the cutting block. Shivering, I fumbled around that porch I knew so well until I found a towel to dry my face. I kept my eyes on the proceedings, though, so I could disappear if anyone came out to fetch anything.

Achilles' bronze tresses were not as well oiled and combed as they should be, and his tunic was a sickly yellow one I disliked; but apparently the repulsive Diomede had been doing a reasonable job of looking after him. Too good! I could not be certain in the poor light, but I suspected that was a love bite I could see on his neck. Shameless slut! I had never marked him anywhere that could not be hidden by a tunic. Or almost never.

It seemed to take years for the meat to be roasted on the many-pronged forks, while the men drank and spoke of inconsequential matters. They did not talk about the war or the Trojans or the men who had died, or any of the thousand things that must be burdening their minds. Horses they discussed, and the sailing off to Euboea. I could have crawled there on hands and knees and still arrived in time.

Odysseus and Ajax were peerless knights both, yet very different men, which was why Nestor had chosen them. The wily king of Ithaca was a negotiator supreme, exactly the

ambassador to talk Achilles out of his anger, and yet his very
subtlety might undermine him; for Achilles, being notoriously blunt spoken himself, might distrust that cunning
tongue. Hence Ajax, a man even more forthright, had been
sent along as a token of good faith. If his life depended on
it—and it very well might—the king of Salamis would not
let his colleague skirt an issue or shade a truth.

At long last the visitors completed their second feast of
the evening. Conversation faded into an expectant hush. Automedon poured out another round of wine and then sat
down, glancing excitedly at the other faces. The two old heralds moved their stools back, while Iphis and the Lesbos
whale retreated to a shadowy corner. Achilles was facing the
door, with Odysseus on his right and Patroclus on his left.
Ajax and Phoenix had their backs to me.

Achilles looked inquiringly at Phoenix and began the proceedings. "What can I do for you, old friend?"

The son of Amyntor cleared his throat. "My lord, I beg
you to hear the words these noble kings have brought for
you."

"I am always glad to listen to them, for I esteem them
above all men."

Odysseus raised his cup in salute. "You are ever gracious,
son of Peleus, ever the peerless host. We have dined well
tonight, both here and with the Overlord, but good cheer and
fellowship must yield now to a serious matter. Sad are the
tidings I bear. These last two days have seen great slaughter
and sent many fine men down to the dark halls of Hades.
Having driven us back to our palisade, the Trojan host
camps on the plain beyond, waiting only for daylight to
renew its assault. The Thunderer encourages them with
omens; Hector rages in his pride. All the Greeks are agreed
that tomorrow he will overrun our defenses and fire our
ships"—he paused to appraise his audience—"unless you
return to the battle."

Achilles sat stony faced in his great chair, Patroclus
frowning and chewing a fingernail, Phoenix nodding
somberly, Automedon failing to hide his glee.

Odysseus continued. "So the Great King has sent us to list

the many splendid gifts he will give if you will set aside your rage and return to the fight. Ten bars of gold, he offers . . ."

As he ran through the list, word for word like a herald, I watched Achilles, but his expression was politely attentive, revealing nothing of the triumph he must be feeling. It was only as Odysseus finished recounting the merits of the fabulous horses and began listing the promises of future benefits, that even I, who knew him so well, had my first inkling of the appalling truth   he was not preening over his victory No, his knuckles whitened when he heard of the seven maidens from Lesbos. When the tally came to the beautiful daughter in marriage, ropes moved in his forearms. I wanted to scream. He was going to refuse!

He was going to *refuse*!

Odysseus came to the point where Agamemnon had demanded that Achilles acknowledge his suzerainty—and left that out. He did not need to mention it. The daughter in marriage had said it all.

"All these great gifts he offers, if you will only forgo your anger and return to the battle."

Silence. I watched the truth dawn on their faces, as if Iris herself walked around the hearth touching each of them in turn with her wand—Patroclus's and Automedon's and finally Odysseus's smile fading to horror. Ajax's face was hidden from me.

"So?" Achilles said quietly. "So it is I who must yield to Agamemnon, is it? Well, I will not gild my words. I despise men who say one thing and mean another." His voice grew louder. "So the truth. He wants me to fight for him! Why should I? What for? It doesn't matter how hard a man fights or doesn't fight, everyone gets the same reward. What fairness is that? I risked death, day in and day out, and what have I to show for it? A pittance! Crumbs and crusts!" Angry words flew out like sparks from a fire. "Fighting, pillaging . . . a bird foraging for its young . . . I brought it all back for that cur while he cowered in the camp. Twelve cities by sea, eleven by land. That's what I've taken for him. What I gave him. And what do I get of it? Precious little!" He was roaring, gripping the arms of his chair as if about to crush them. "And the dearest of all, my bride, taken from me! All those other stay-at-homes and he takes *my* prize! Mine! My prize of honor! And now he tries to buy me with her?"

He surged to his feet and pointed an accusing finger. "What are we doing here? *Why are you fighting the Trojans, son of Laertes?*"

Odysseus gaped at him, speechless. He had told me once why he fought. Achilles himself fought for honor and glory, measuring them in booty and beautiful women.

"Helen, wasn't it?" Achilles roared. "Wasn't Helen why we came here to fight the Trojans? So, are the sons of Atreus the only men who love their bedmates? I loved Briseis just as much as Menelaus loved Helen, even if I did win her with my spear. And that foul wretch took her from me in full view of the whole army!" He thumped a fist against the pillar. The house shook and showers of dust fell down, sparking in the fire.

"Tricked me! Shamed me! You think I can ever trust him again? The army gave her to me. You think I want her back as a sop from that pig-faced thief, like a bone tossed to a dog? Never lay with her? You believe that? Well, he can keep her now and hump her as much as he wants. Let him fight Hector himself. You and the others can help him if you want. You've been doing well without me, haven't you? Built a big, strong stockade, haven't you? Keep right on. Hector never came so close when I was around. And that's Agamemnon's offer? Daughter in marriage! Son-in-law? He can keep her. Keep it all, all of it." He struck the pillar again and again. His fury lashed the megaron like whips of fire. "If that's his offer, then I sail for home at dawn! I have riches enough there for one lifetime, and I'll take home enough for many more. Gold and bronze and silver, fair women—yes, shiploads of wealth I take to Thessaly to make men wonder! What need have I for—"

Odysseus found his voice. "You are not being consistent. A moment ago you complained—"

"Consistent? *Consistent?* It is the son of Atreus who is consistent. Consistent coward, consistent cheat!"

Cowering in the outer darkness, petrified with horror, I

watched his great chest heave as he fought for control. Achilles, Achilles! Whatever had gone wrong? His prayers had been answered, the prophecy fulfilled. Agamemnon had admitted error, promised to return me, offered incredible gifts as well. What was wrong?

He took two giant strides to tower over Odysseus, who craned his neck to stare up at him. "I spit on his gifts and promises. I would not accept ten times what he offers, no, nor twenty! He cheated me once—now I should trust him, should I? Not if he gave me the world would I trust him. Nor take his wretched daughter, be she lovely as Aphrodite. My father back in Thessaly will find a bride for me."

I moaned aloud, but no one heard. They had eyes only for that furious, raging giant.

"Fight for Agamemnon? No, I'll fight no more. What use is wealth to a dead man, son of Laertes?"

Amazingly, Odysseus answered him. Few men would have been so brave. "That is cowards' talk!"

Achilles balled a fist, then he spun on his heel and stalked back to his chair. He threw himself down in it and reached for his wine cup. His eyes blazed deadly blue and his voice choked with passion. "It is wisdom, a truth told me by the gods. If I stay and fight, then I shall win glory, but I will die here, under the walls of Troy. Die young. *Die soon!* If I go home, my life must be dull, but it will be a great deal longer."

It is a wonder I did not cry out then, because *those were my words*! My voice had warned him that he was mortal, that night on the beach. At the time he had paid no heed. Now he was treating my plea as a divine prophecy, foretelling his death. Had I spoken on my own authority or as the goddess? I did not know!

"Ha!" roared Odysseus. "A long, dull life? Obscurity? Anonymity? A goatherd, forgotten as soon as the ashes cool? Is this the son of Peleus I hear?"

Achilles bared teeth at him. "I asked you first: What use is wealth to a corpse? What joy can a dead man have of a woman, however fair? Tell me; I've been wondering about that. The gods have given me a choice, so I choose life.

Tonight we load our ships. Tomorrow at dawn the Myrmidons sail for Thessaly. Go back to Agamemnon, both of you. Tell him his tricks didn't work. Find another way to stop Hector." He drained the cup and held it out. Automedon scrambled up to fill it.

Going home to Thessaly! And I would go with them if I had to hide under a bench. . . . Had Achilles seen me lurking out there in the shadows? Was he secretly speaking to me? My heart flailed like a bird in a snare.

Patroclus chewed his lip, watching Achilles but knowing better than to speak. Odysseus opened his mouth and closed it again. He shot a bleak look at Ajax and shrugged. Their mission was over. The offer had been refused. The embassy had failed. He laid his feet on the floor and gripped the arms of the chair. . . .

"Oh, my dear Achilles!" said Phoenix. "I have been silent too long. If I have not spoken out these last days, it is not because I approve of your actions. Bear with me now if I speak my mind at last?"

Achilles glanced at the two strangers and grimaced. "Must it be now, old friend?"

"I think it must, much as I love you."

"Then speak, as I love you."

"Your father appointed me your tutor and your guide. I dandled you on my knee when you were a babe and rejoiced to see you grow to glorious manhood. I taught you the ways of a warrior. I tried to teach you how to comport yourself in council. You have been the son I could never have—you know that tale—so I speak to you as a father and as I truly believe your father would speak to you now, were he here. Dear boy, quell your anger! The gods themselves can be placated with offerings and prayers! Is your rage so much greater than a god's?"

Achilles glared.

The older man shook his head in sorrow. "I would not say this before, but I can say it now, because Agamemnon has offered fine gifts, a great fortune. He will return the woman Briseis, whom you love so dearly. He has publicly made many noble promises. He has sent the noblest of his captains

to treat with you. Yet you spurn these men, your friends?
Humiliate them? Humiliate the Great King? Achilles, my
son, what more can you want?"

Achilles did not reply, just stared, dark as thunder, veins
standing out in his forehead. I had never wanted to mother
him before, but I did then. I wanted to run to him and clutch
his head to my breast, to baby and comfort him. He gave no
answer because there was no answer—not if he believed my
prophecy. What honor was worth certain death? If Agamemnon were to kneel and clasp his knees before the whole
army . . . but how could the Great King of the Greeks do that?

"Take the gifts, Achilles! If you spurn them now and repent later, when the ships are burning, then you will have to
fight as hard and there will be no gifts."

Achilles found his voice. "No, I won't. We sail with tomorrow's dawn. Three days homeward if Lord Poseidon
sends a good wind."

Phoenix sighed. "You are leader, you decide, but think
what will follow. Yes, you will be hailed as a hero in Thessaly. Yes, your father will weep tears of joy when he comes
running from his gates to embrace you. The people will marvel at the wealth of booty and the fabled beauties you have
won. But then? But then Peleus will say, 'So Troy is fallen
and the war is over?' What do you tell him, Achilles?" The
soft voice was sand in a wound. " 'No,' you will say. 'Troy's
walls still stand. Helen's captivity endures. The Greeks were
sore beset when I left, likely to be overrun and slain, their
ships burned. But Agamemnon insulted me, so I did not
want to fight for him anymore. I was angry and came home.'
Is that what you will tell him?"

Achilles' eyes flicked in the direction of Ajax, then to
Odysseus, then back to Phoenix. He swallowed hard,
squirming like a child at this reproof.

"Have you done?"

"No, I have not done. I trained you. I taught you weapons
and horses and tactics and courage. No, not courage. You
never lacked that until now. But I trained you as a knight,
and I presented you at the altar of Athena in Phthia to take
your oath. You remember that oath?"

"I remember that oath." The sweat on Achilles' face made it shine like polished bronze in the firelight. "To be first in battle? I have been true to that oath. No man in the army had been truer to those words than I. To honor the bodies of my enemies with proper rites—always! To respect the honor of my followers? Have I ever stinted any of you anything? Have I ever given you anything and then taken it back? A pretty cup? A cloak I regretted parting with? No, not a spoon! Do I speak the truth, son of Diores?"

Automedon nodded his head vigorously.

"Son of Menoitios?"

Patroclus nodded also.

"And the rest?" Phoenix sounded close to tears. "The part you missed out?"

"To respect the honor of my leader? You think I have forgotten?" Achilles bared his teeth. "But answer me this, son of Amyntor—is not Agamemnon a knight also? Did he not swear that same oath? How often do you see him in the forefront of the battle? And what of respecting the honor of his followers? Ha! What of that? Do not ask me to esteem that man! Much as I love you, I will not take it, not even from you!"

I waited for Ajax or Odysseus to tell of Agamemnon's feats in the last two days, but neither spoke.

"Accept the gifts and swallow your anger," Phoenix whispered, so quietly I could barely hear him. "You cannot slink away like a kicked cur before the war is over!"

Achilles thumped his fist on the chair a couple of times as if he were in pain. Then he straightened up and glanced at the visitors. "You have my answer, my lords: *I will not fight!*" He turned to Phoenix and made a visible effort to control his fury. "It is late. Hear that rain! Stay here with us tonight. We'll make up a bed for you." The hint to the others was typical Achillean subtlety, a bronze blade through the belly. Then he added, "I am sorry I cannot accept your counsel in this, old friend, but that will not come between us. You know I never bear grudges! Let us talk again in the morning and decide then whether to stay or go."

Odysseus glanced at Ajax, but the son of Telamon did not

seem to have noted that subtle shift in Achilles' stance. Did Achilles mean it or was he just softening his refusal, deferring to old Phoenix's feelings? I could not judge.

Odysseus raised his cup. "A libation, then, to Zeus, who will decide between the Greeks and the Trojans tomorrow, and to the Lady Athena, who gives honor and valor to her warriors."

He tipped a few drops into the fire and then drank. The others copied him, although clearly Achilles had not liked the wording of the prayer.

"Son of Peleus!" Ajax rose to his feet like a great bear and lumbered around the fire to lay a massive hand on Achilles' shoulder. "I am not skilled with words as others are, but I must say this, and I am your guest, so you will hear me. When a man is slain—a son or a brother—his family will take a blood price so that the village will not be rent by feud. Even the immortal gods set aside their anger when rich offerings are made to them. But not you! No, your heart is stone. You will not yield, although we bring the entreaties of all the Greeks, your friends and comrades, those who have so honored you in the past and seek to honor you in the future. Your friends, Achilles? Think of your friends! They are dying!"

And Achilles, who had reddened like fire when the others spoke, now went pale as ice. He stared up at his accuser much as Odysseus had earlier had to crane his neck to him, and with the same horror and disbelief.

"Helenus son of Oenops," growled the son of Telamon, "Oenomanus, Menesthius son of Areïthous, Trechus . . . and I must not forget Tlepolemus! Yes, the mighty son of Heracles was slain by Sarpedon! I could go on until dawn listing the noble fallen. Anchialus and Oresbius, Iphinoös son of Dexius—remember how he fought at your side at Larisa?"

Achilles groaned and closed his eyes, but still the grisly catalogue continued.

"Teuthras. Aeneas felled both Orsilochos and Crethon, the sons of Diokles. Oh, so many have died in the last two days! How many more must die tomorrow, when Hector storms our camp?"

No! No! I thrust knuckles in my mouth to stifle a scream. Ajax had found the answer. Simple, unsubtle Ajax had gone right to Achilles' heart when the others had all missed it— he would fight for his friends.

But the big man blundered by this opening like a wolf jumping into a sheepfold and then jumping right back out again without noticing all the juicy lambs cowering in the corner. "While you sulk here! You're making a terrible fuss over one miserable girl. The king's offering you seven girls and his own daughter as well! Come on out and fight."

Achilles' head jerked as if he had been slapped in the face. He sprang to his feet, and from there he could look down even on the son of Telamon. "Need me to save your ships, do you?" he roared. "Well, it was your idea to camp at that end of the line. Live with that. If Hector attacks this end, I'll defend it."

For a moment the titans glared at each other. Then Ajax sighed and turned away, shaking his head in disbelief. Odysseus and the two heralds rose and headed for the door. It was the end, and the worst possible end—Achilles would neither take me back and frght for Agamemnon, nor would he sail home to Thessaly and safety.

I fled into the dark.

BOOK NINE

ACHILLES

1

The lamb had turned on the wolf. Two days earlier, Troy had been besieged, but now the Trojans invested the Greek camp. At dawn Agamemnon led out his host in a strategy both simple and absolutely typical—he put his head down and charged the enemy like a goat. There was an alternative, as Achilles was to show him before that day of sorrows ended, but the Great King did not think of it nor listen if anyone else did.

Hector, advised by some god, fell back before the assault, biding his time. The fighting was brutal and bloody, but eventually the ferocity of the Greek attack was blunted by exhaustion. Agamemnon himself was wounded, as were many others among the Greek leaders. Then the winds of war shifted and Hector brought up the reserves he had been saving, advancing in five columns against the whole width of the palisade.

I knew very little of this at the time, because I was again busy aiding the wounded. Those who had survived the night were writhing with wound fever, and we barely had time to feed and tend them before more casualties were brought in. The rain had stopped, so we were able to minister to them in the open air, where the stench and the flies were less bothersome. Offsetting that, we had run out of bandages, poppy milk, sinews to stitch up wounds, firewood to heat water. At times patients were arriving so quickly that we barely had time to whet our knives.

The Pylosian dressing station, the next one to the north of us, was being skillfully run by Nestor's consort Hecamede, whom I had not seen since the dismal day when I quarreled with Chryseis, but she was hard-pressed to keep up with the butchery. When she appealed to us for help, I took three other women and went to join her. Motherly as ever, she greeted me with a hug and a warm smile.

"Start with this doughty warrior," she said, leading me to a stocky youth sitting on the grass. "He has a broken leg to splint. He can ogle your charms while you work. Lucky lad—now he'll sail home a hero and be running after girls again in a month."

Her words brought a grin to his ivory-pale face. He was soon telling me of his narrow escape and how a Trojan chariot wheel had gone over his shin. I did what I could with it, trying to be gentle, although I suspected his running days were over.

Perhaps it amused the gods to reunite me with Hecamede. She had been present when Chryseis provoked me, and that had been the first stroke of the ax. Now she was to be present when Nestor himself swung the final blow that toppled the tree. From then on, no matter how many others it might drag down with it, even the Immortals could only watch it fall.

Our work site was a long strip of grass between two ships, sheltered from the wind. About noon we were relieved to notice a lull in the flow of new patients, not realizing that this meant the Greeks were retreating and abandoning their wounded. Hecamede assigned me to aid a tow-haired boy who had been run through by a Trojan spear. I pricked him a few times to pretend I was sewing up the gaping hole in his belly, then bandaged him with his own loincloth. He was in fearful pain and told me over and over about his home near Kyparisseeis, of the farm he would inherit, of the wife his parents had promised him when he returned, while all the time his life's blood trickled into the grass. I knelt beside him, holding his hand, wiping his forehead sometimes, giving him sips of wine, but mostly just listening.

Nestor arrived at the stern of the ship in a jingle of harness and squeak of wheels. Both he and his charioteer were dusty and sweat streaked, their horses foaming, and they had brought in a casualty. Women clustered around to help, Hecamede among them.

"Quickly, now!" the old king said. "For here is Machaon son of Asclepius, lord of Trikke, who has been struck in the shoulder by an arrow. We have cut off the ash-wood shaft, but the barbed head remains in the wound, so you will have to dig it out with a sharp bronze blade and treat the wound with soothing herbs before wrapping it soundly to staunch the blood. Listen well if he gives you direction, because he is as skilled at healing as his great father." And so on. Nobody could state the obvious more clearly than Nestor. It was when he was being subtle that he was dangerous.

Machaon was laid under the curve of the hull only a few paces from me, and women knelt around him. I kept my head down, attentive to my patient, reluctant to attract the old king's attention in case he had noticed my extended absence the previous evening.

"She's not as beautiful as you," the boy said, "but she's still the prettiest girl in Pylos."

"I'm sure she is."

A new shadow fell over me, and my heart jumped as Patroclus spoke almost at my shoulder. "Son of Neleus, tell me of the battle! Achilles has sent me to learn who has fallen, who is injured, and whether the Trojans can be stopped." He did not notice me at his feet.

Nestor turned around with deliberation and peered at him. His beard seemed to bristle.

"So the son of Peleus cares enough to ask, does he? I am surprised to hear this. You may tell him that the news is bad. Agamemnon himself is wounded, and many others also. The Trojans are over the ditch and palisade and press hard upon us. Come to my hut and share a goblet of wine with me, so I may tell you more."

"Nay, my lord, your offer is welcome, but I must return at once. Achilles is not the most patient of men. I shall tell him about Lord Agamemnon and the son of Asclepius here."

". . . brown eyes soft as a doe's," the boy whispered, "and when she laughs, it is springtime."

I smiled and nodded, not daring to look up at Patroclus, standing there almost close enough to touch.

"Tell him also," Nestor said sternly, "of Odysseus and Diomedes, wounded both! Tell him that the Greeks are dying and the ships are about to burn. Ah, if I only had the strength of my youth, son of Menoitios!"

He launched into a very long story about cattle rustling long ago, before any of the rest of us were born. Patroclus's feet twitched, but he stayed and endured the shower of words. My mouth smiled vacantly at my patient as my hands dabbed the sweat from his brow, but my ears did not hear his ramblings. Machaon whimpered under the knife. Hecamede brought cups of wine from the lodge. And still Nestor droned on.

"Do you not recall, Patroclus, that day when Odysseus and I came to Phthia to seek the help of Achilles in this war? Your father was there, and Peleus also. Do you not remember what your father told you that day? 'Achilles is mightier than you,' he said, 'but you are older. Give him always your wise counsel, for he will listen to you.' Is this not the situation he foresaw in his wisdom, Patroclus?"

"I have tried, my lord! He is adamant. He will not fight!"

And at last the old man came to the point. He swung the deadly ax of words. "Aha! So he said, my boy, so he said! But did he forbid *you* to fight? Do not all the Myrmidons fret as you do, eager to join the battle? Return to Achilles and tell him how hard-pressed we are. Beseech him to give you command, to let you lead out the host. Flaunt his mantle so the Trojans will think that you are he. They will turn and flee before you, but he will not have broken the oath he swore."

"Yes!" Patroclus cried. "That may work! I shall go and tell Achilles what you propose!"

His feet vanished from my field of view as he ran down to the beach. Nestor chuckled softly. Realizing that I was smiling at a corpse, I set the cold hand down upon the grass, closed the boy's eyes, and stood up. Nestor had gone over to peer at Machaon and had his back to me. I took off after Patroclus. As I rounded the bow of the ship, I saw him not far off but with another man, and I stumbled to a halt.

"Briseis?" Hecamede's voice at my back was full of marble-hard authority. "I do not think that would be seemly." She sounded just like my mother.

I turned in dismay. "The boy is dead."

"He lasted longer than I expected. Let us find a living man for you to care for. Come."

♀

When Patroclus emerged from the shadow of the ship onto the sun-bright shingle, he almost ran into Eurypylos son of Euiamon limping along in full armor, leaning on his spear. His right leg and greave were scarlet, his features white as cloud and drenched in sweat.

The message to Achilles was urgent, but Patroclus could not refuse a friend in need. He took Eurypylos's arm over his shoulder and supported him, although he was a big man and faint from lack of blood. As they staggered along together, Patroclus barked questions. The mumbled answers were all bad. The Trojans had pushed archers and spearmen through the palisade and their chariots were following. Ajax was the only major Greek knight left in the field, fighting a desperate rearguard action, being steadily pushed back upon the ships. Between the splash of the ripples and the harsh breathing of the wounded, the din of battle was now audible. Ajax against Hector? Man to man, yes, but not army against army. Ajax knew no more strategy than a badger.

They passed Odysseus's camp and came at last to Eurypylos's. Men ran down to help, many of them wounded and bandaged, but between them they carried their leader up to the tents. Patroclus made sure he was in competent hands, then took off as fast as he could run.

Achilles was using the closest of his ships as a watch-tower, balancing precariously on the gunwale near the stern post and staring grimly southward toward the battle. He must know that he would soon have to choose between fight and flight. His followers were huddled on the deck nearer the bow: Phoenix, Eudoros, Peisander, Menesthius, Automedon, Alkimedon; all were haggard with worry, all leery of provoking their leader with any ill-considered word. The rest of the ships were loaded with spearmen, practically climbing on one another's shoulders in their eagerness to see, many of them already armed.

Patroclus leaped up and swung himself aboard. The men at the bow hurried aft to hear his news, but for a moment he could only gasp for breath.

Achilles jumped down to the deck. "You look ready to weep. Tell me."

Patroclus blurted out all the bleak tidings of the dead and wounded and the Trojans triumphant. He followed them with howls of reproach, speaking as he had never spoken to Achilles before. "How can you stand here and do nothing? Have you a rock for a heart? Your friends are dead or dying."

Achilles' blue eyes turned cold as the winter sea. "So they need me? Where were they when I needed them?"

"Do you expect them to ask you again? You think the Trojans will stand back and let them come?" Patroclus fell to his knees. "I know you said you would not fight, but you did not say the rest of us could not. You never said that! Let me go, Achilles, please! Let me lead out the Myrmidons. Give me your mantle so the Trojans will think I am you. They will flee before us and the camp will be saved."

Achilles scowled at the twitching, shuffling leaders, at the anxious rank and file on the other ships, and then back toward the distant battle that was not now distant enough.

"It won't work. There's such a butchery going on down there that your arrival won't even be noticed."

"We must do something!"

Achilles considered the matter. "I swore I wouldn't fight . . . true. I did not swear I would stay angry, did I?"

"We can go?"

"All right, you can go. Launch the ships."

Patroclus howled, *"What!?"* The knights at his back moaned in dismay.

Achilles pointed across the bay. "Sail that way."

Accustomed though they all were to his brilliance, they did not comprehend. He grinned at their bewilderment.

"The Trojans are about to take the camp, you say? They must have committed every man they've got, yes? Then they see the son of Peleus about to take Troy. What will Prince Hector do then, poor thing?"

Automedon bellowed his war cry and vaulted over the side. A moment later the others followed him—Alkimedon, Phoenix, Eudoros, Peisandor, Menesthius—yelling to their men, heading for their own contingents, shouting orders.

As Patroclus rose, Achilles grabbed his shoulder in a bruising grip. His blue eyes flamed. "This is a feint, you understand? Nothing more! As soon as the Trojans cross the Scamander, you will embark and come back! You cannot take the city, son of Menoitios. The whole Trojan host will close in on you. You must not let them cut you off from the ships!"

"I understand," Patroclus said.

For a moment longer, Achilles held on, staring doubtfully at him, but then he let him go.

Patroclus went.

3

Within minutes, the men had fetched their weapons and thrown them aboard. Eager hands rushed the hulls down the beach in a frantic race to be first. Without waiting to raise masts, they ran out the oars and began beating the rippled silver, driving across to Troy. Achilles watched them go and then strode back to his lodge to sacrifice to Zeus and pray for their safe return.

Fearing him and his Myrmidons beyond all others as they did, the Trojans must have been wondering how far they could push before they roused the lion. They knew who camped at the north end, and when those ships set out across the bay, the whole grisly three-day battle for the Greek camp must suddenly have seemed like a mere diversion to draw them away from the walls. Abandoning the assault, they raced off to rescue the city—chariots and mounted Dardanians in the lead, infantry straggling far behind.

The Greeks' first reaction was despair and cries that Achilles was abandoning them. We flew to the sea's edge or scrambled up on the ships to watch. Then came understanding and screams of triumph. He was not going home—he was going to Troy!

The feint against the city was an impromptu solution to a desperate situation, a brilliant tactical stroke, but there had been no time to plan it properly. If Achilles had led the sortie in person, he might well have relieved the pressure on the Greeks without having to fight at all. The Myrmidons could have sailed back, laughing at a bloodless victory. Or they might have gone on to take Troy—who but the gods know? Alas, he stayed in the camp, and only Patroclus had heard his explicit orders.

The plan began to unravel even before the expedition was halfway across, because into the leadership gap blundered Menelaus son of Atreus. Being as deceived by the feint as the Trojans were, he ordered more ships launched and led a second flotilla off after the Myrmidons, determined that no man would get to Helen before he did.

Patroclus's vessel beached unopposed, and he was the first to leap ashore. Crew became war band, exchanging oars for spears just in time to meet a charge by some of the Trojan allies, mostly Paeones from the far west and Lycians from the far south, who had borne the brunt of the Greek assault in the morning and then withdrawn to regroup. They put up a creditable fight, considering that they were facing fresh troops in a battle they had not expected. The Lycian leader was the great Sarpedon son of Zeus, who had been wounded in his struggle with the Rhodians when he had personally slain Tlepolemus. He had distinguished himself again that morning at the palisade; now he rallied his men once more to slaughter Greeks. Undeterred by—or perhaps

not deceived by—the mantle of Achilles, he faced off
against Patroclus. Sarpedon would have won fairly easily
had he not been exhausted and weakened by his wound, but
there is no fairness in war. His death was both a supreme
personal triumph for the son of Menoitios and a major blow
to the Trojan cause. A bloody struggle developed around the
corpse.

By the time it was over, the Trojan vanguard was crossing
the Scamander. That was the moment when Patroclus should
have sounded the retreat, but the Myrmidon war bands had
gone swarming across the plain like ants, heading for the
citadel. Achilles might have been able to whistle them back.
Patroclus did not even try. Either he saw the second flotilla
coming and assumed that the diversion had been converted
into a full assault, or else blood lust jangled his wits. Whatever the reason, he and his men went on to the walls of Troy,
where no Greek had come since the previous fall.

Their attack was hopeless, for they lacked ropes and ladders. Three times Patroclus himself tried to climb up, only to
fall back. At the fourth attempt, he realized that the gods were
not going to give him the city and ordered withdrawal, but by
that time it was too late—the Trojan chariots were arriving. So
was the second wave of Greeks. What had been launched as a
diversion developed into a major battle, a major disaster.
When the Greek force fought back to the ships, it took with it
the body of Patroclus. Wounded, cut off, and surrounded, he
had been hacked down by Hector himself.

So perished the noble son of Menoitios.

4

I knew nothing of this, not even whether Achilles had gone
himself or sent Patroclus in his stead. The battle was too distant for us to make out any of it, although the dark-tasseled

thunderclouds that Zeus sent to cloak the city warned us that the fighting must be serious. We certainly had no time to worry about it, for the Trojan departure brought a new tide of wounded flooding in. Some of them had lain on the field for hours, playing dead. Neither side had been taking prisoners.

About the time the storm cleared the far shore and the Greeks began embarking, I was seized by a demon, something that had never happened to me before and never would again. I was steadying a man's head while a Greek doctor amputated his smashed leg and cauterized the stump. The patient stopped screaming and rolled his eyes up to stare at me accusingly. Exactly the same thing had happened to the last one, only minutes before.

"Dead," the doctor said sadly. "Next?"

The four soldiers who had been holding the man down now rose and hoisted his corpse between them to remove it, but I rolled away, moaning and gasping for breath. I choked; my whole body shook uncontrollably. Hecamede knelt and gathered me into her arms like a child, holding me tight and muttering comfort until the fit began to pass, yet my teeth still rattled so hard that I could barely speak.

"It is his ghost! Punishing me!"

"No," she insisted. "You are just overtired. You have done wonders here and it is time you had a rest. I need one too."

"There are so many still needing help."

"But you have done your share. You couldn't bandage a pricked thumb at the moment, far less wield a knife or a needle. Come."

She led me over to the king's lodge. Even on that short journey I could see that the camp was in strange disorder with wounded men wandering aimlessly, laughing inexplicably; apparently whole men striding by with empty, staring faces; and far too many fly-infested corpses not yet claimed by their comrades. Above all that ran a bustle of seemingly aimless business, like a buzzing of wasps, with heralds and runners trotting back and forth; but that may have been the first sign of returning order as Nestor, Idomeneus, and Odysseus took control of events.

When Hecamede and I had washed, she found a garment

to fit me, a white linen chiton. Although I was breathing normally again and my hands were steady enough to comb out my hair, I remained strangely distracted, a twig caught in a mountain torrent, swirled and whirled around and carried onward with no will or purpose of its own. Even on the day Lyrnessos fell I had known the gods' will and understood that all I need do was submit to whichever one of the victors claimed me. Now I did not know who owned me, what the gods expected of me, or if they still spoke to me as they had in the past.

Nestor's lodge was larger than Achilles' and furnished in much better taste, which I am sure was Hecamede's doing. The megaron was hung with bright weavings instead of weapons and lacked the appalling clutter of furniture Achilles favored. Apart from a couple of women attending the children, there was no one else there at all, so we sat on fine chairs in the porch and drank honeyed wine from silver cups. I gulped it down in complete silence while Hecamede talked, but I kept thinking of the way the dead man had looked up at me so reproachfully, and I heard nothing of what she was saying. At length I noticed the ships straggling back across the bay, waving their banks of oars.

"They're returning," I said. The Myrmidons had gone into battle. That was important, was it not?

"So they are," she said, calmly refilling my goblet. "Well, let us send someone to gather news." She dispatched a girl and ordered another to bring us cheese and barley flour to sift into our wine.

I wanted to run to the Myrmidon encampment myself, but I recalled that she thought that this would be improper behavior, so I contained myself as well as I could and tried to listen as she made small talk about anything except the war. But there *was* nothing except the war, nothing else under heaven. It overshadowed our lives totally.

"There has been a lot of rain, hasn't there?" she remarked. "Most unseasonable. See, Ida is still shrouded in cloud."

"I expect the Scamander will be rising. The armies will have to use the ford."

She pursed her lips and tried again. "White looks good on you."

"My brother-in-law always said so. Achilles likes me in red."

"Ah. This is a beautiful table, isn't it? All these inlaid ivory plaques! Griffons and eagles. Such splendid work!"

"It came from Lyrnessos. It was one of Mother's favorites."

Hecamede winced and stopped evading the subject. "Now that Achilles is back in the war, I am sure you will be returned to him, child."

"I don't know if Achilles is back in the war. He may have sent Patroclus to lead the Myrmidons."

"Whoever was leading," Hecamede said, "they saved the day." Certainly the emergency seemed to be over; the ships were returning, and it was too late for the Trojans to resume their assault on the camp. Tomorrow would bring a fresh start.

I was floating somewhere over my own head. Her words seemed to come from a long way away, and to answer them required enormous effort. "Agamemnon may withdraw his promises."

"Not after the fright he got today. He would rather give the treasures to Achilles than have them fall to Hector."

"Achilles will die under the walls of Troy."

Hecamede wailed in horror. "An augury? Who says so?"

"Not me. My mouth said it, not me." That seemed humorous, so I laughed uproariously and drained my goblet. This time she did not refill it.

The first ship to beach was one of the Spartan craft, but it contained men of many contingents, for they had piled aboard any vessel they could reach in the confusion. Antilokos son of Nestor was sent to break the terrible news to Achilles. I knew nothing of that.

"What is all that shouting?" Hecamede said.

"I don't know." It seemed very far away. It could not concern me. Nothing concerned me.

Then the woman who had been sent to learn the news came hastening back with two armed men at her heels.

"My lady!" she gasped. "The heralds are shouting for Briseis. The Great King wants her."

"You! Come!" said one of the spearmen.

I decided he was speaking to me. I rose and turned to make my farewells to my hostess. I got as far as, "Thank you for all—" before my arm was seized in a lion's grip and almost hauled out of its socket.

I made no protest and was released as soon as my feet were moving, but if I was not thereafter rushed through the camp at spear point, the difference was almost too slight to notice. It did not matter. I did not care. How much of the strange floating feeling came from the demon and how much from Hecamede's wine, I do not know.

But I was not taken to the Great King's sleeping hut. We went instead to the council hollow, which was already filled with men. I stood where I was told, beside the empty throne, trembling under all the thousands of angry eyes glaring at me, fiery young warriors remembering fallen comrades. More were arriving all the time as knights led in their war bands. Many were still in armor, sweaty and spattered with blood, fresh from battle; but how many would not arrive who had been there the last time? How many had died when the army tried to fight without Achilles? It was my fault! Everywhere I saw wounded, even among the nobles— Diomedes, Odysseus. I recognized spearmen I had treated in these last three days, but I saw no liking anywhere for me, the Lyrnessos slut who had bewitched their leaders into folly. Why had I been brought here to face their anger?

A group of young women entered and was set where Odysseus pointed, on the far side of the throne from me; but still my mind floated from surmise to conjecture, making no sense of this, even when men arrived bearing bars of gold, shining silver bowls, big bronze cauldrons with legs, and all of these were spread before my feet, which was where the son of Laertes wanted them. I stared down at them, uncomprehending. The demon had not yet released me.

The hollow hushed. I heard horses and voices. Agamemnon trudged in, leaning on his royal scepter and scowling at me in passing, before lowering himself onto the throne. His ugly face was pale and he had his right arm in a sling. Odysseus, after a glance around to make sure nothing was missing, limped across to the place Nestor and Idomeneus had saved for him among the knights.

Achilles came running down the slope.

It was a long time since I had seen him in armor, in sunlight, and I had forgotten how he blazed, huge and terrifying. His shield hung on his back, his sword at his side. Only his spear and helmet were missing, probably left with his chariot, but a fury of battle flamed already in his eyes. He glared around the assembly without seeming to notice me at all. The roar he directed at the Overlord must have been audible over half the Troad.

"Why are you wasting time here when there are Trojans to kill? Come! Make war!"

The army exploded in wild cheers but did not move. I wondered why his red-gold hair was so tangled and filthy, his face smeared with dirt. Even then I did not understand.

Agamemnon struggled to his feet but had to bellow for silence, while Achilles fidgeted impatiently. "Be still! How can any speaker address an assembly if it will not listen? This is welcome news we hear. Some of you have thought ill of me because of that quarrel, and I admit I spoke rashly. The gods sent a great folly into my heart and stole my wits, and much harm has come of it. Any of us, the lowest or the greatest, can be so deluded at times. Now I will make amends." He paused and glanced at Nestor and Odysseus, who both nodded sternly. Agamemnon sighed. "Here, before you, behold the rich gifts I promised the son of Peleus if he would return to the battle. He rejected them yesterday and now has come back to us anyway, but I shall still deliver what I promised."

"The gifts do not matter!" Achilles shouted. "We can attend to that another day! Our business now is to go forth and teach the Trojans what war is. They are out there on the plain. Will we let them camp there? Come, let us drive them back to their city!"

The army cheered again and stayed right where it was. I smiled proudly at him, although I knew even in my bemused

state that I did not really want him to go and fight. Fighting
was dangerous.

Odysseus frowned and rose. Agamemnon sank down on
his throne as if grateful to be relieved of the need to argue.
The assembly hushed.

"Son of Peleus, we all welcome you back, and we all
share your desire to go and do battle. But the hour grows
late. The men have put in a hard day already and cannot fight
more without rest and food."

"Food?" Achilles bellowed. "How can you think of *food*
when there are Trojans out there alive? If the hour grows
late, then all the more reason to make haste!"

"Nay, save your anger for the morrow. At dawn you may
lead us out and we shall gladly let you show us how to slay.
But now accept the Great King's gifts. And attend while he
swears a solemn oath before Zeus that he never lay with that
girl of yours."

At his sign, a group of charioteers rose to gather up the
treasures spread out on the grass. I watched with puzzled curiosity until a hand touched my arm and I looked around into
the crinkled smile of old Eurybates the herald.

"My lady?"

"Me?"

"I am to have the honor of escorting you again, my lady."

"Oh? Where to?"

Now it was his turn to be puzzled, but he motioned me
forward, and I obeyed. I would rather have gone to Achilles,
although even in my peculiar daze I could sense that he had
other things on his mind and did not want me just then. As
we left the assembly, another herald dragged in a squealing
pig, which Agamemnon subsequently sacrificed to Zeus
while swearing a solemn oath that he had not bedded me. I
did not witness the ritual, but I assume his denial was
phrased as carefully as it had been the previous evening.

Guided by Eurybates, I led the procession that wound its
way along the shore to the Myrmidon encampment. Behind
us came the seven women, young men burdened with precious metal, others leading horses. By then I had realized
that I was being returned to Achilles, and yet the joy and tri-

umph I should have been feeling was strangely muted by the fog the demon had cast over my mind. As we neared our destination, I saw the last of the ships being dragged up on the shore and men giving up the blood and sweat of battle to the cleansing sea, but I also heard the cries of wounded being treated. I started to shake again.

The herald took my arm to direct me between the ships and then the tents. Another, even more discordant wailing broke through my daze. The fog lifted and the gods told me what had provoked Achilles' new fury. With a shriek of dismay I broke into a run.

Men lay sprawled on the ground before the lodge, throwing dirt over their heads in convulsions of unbearable grief. Patroclus's body rested in the porch, surrounded by the Myrmidon women, all howling and weeping. Hurling them aside, I thrust my way through and fell across his pitiful, blood-streaked corpse. Oh, Patroclus, Patroclus! My parents, my brothers—not for them had I been allowed to mourn as I had wanted, but for him I could tear out my heart. Too late I realized how vital he had been and how great the abyss his departure must leave in all our lives. Alone among all the great warriors I had known, he had been a truly compassionate man. I remembered his kindness to me when Lyrnessos fell, his calm courage as death flirted around him in the days that followed, his unfailing gentleness. Screaming, I raked my face and throat and breasts, crying out his name and my desolation.

5

Of course Odysseus was right—it was far too late to take revenge on the Trojans that day—but Achilles' anguish would not let him rest. He left the assembly as soon as Agamemnon had sworn his oath and drove off alone in his chariot. It

is said that out beyond the palisade he came on a Trojan war
band. Lacking a charioteer to handle his team, he could do
them no harm, but he drove straight at them, roaring his hatred. And the Trojans, seeing this fiery fury thundering at
them out of the sunset, turned tail and fled, panicked by the
mere sight and sound of Achilles. I cannot swear to the truth
of this tale, which was one the bards were to sing in later
times, but I am inclined to believe it. He was certainly a long
time returning to the lodge to resume his lamenting, and his
mood was bitter beyond reckoning.

When he appeared, I was still holding Patroclus's head,
but I had wept my eyes dry. The great crowd of mourners
had mostly wandered sadly away. All Greeks are demon-
strative in their grief, but Achilles did nothing by half
measures. He hurled himself down on the body and
lamented again, alternating between howling his misery
and swearing the awful revenge he would take on Hector
and the Trojans. His sorrow reawakened my own, and I
shed more tears. Darkness had fallen before his sobs
faded.

"My lord?" I whispered.

After a moment he raised his head.

"May we begin the rites, my lord? Wash him?"

He groaned, but then he nodded and heaved himself up.

Aided by the other women, Iphis and I washed the body,
anointed it with the finest oils we possessed, and wrapped it
in a lordly shroud. Then Achilles and the other Myrmidon
knights bore the bier along the shore to a flat space north of
the camp. Almost the whole army paraded behind—not only
knights but war bands also, the lowborn of valleys and islands who had followed their lords to Troy, for no man had
been more respected than the son of Menoitios.

When Achilles returned and went into the megaron to remove his armor, I followed, expecting to attend him.

"May I help, my lord?"

He went on with what he was doing. No one could help.
Nothing would help, except vengeance. I left him to his
sorrow.

All night we mourned. I did not sleep, although once my

weakness forced me to go in search of food. Achilles did not eat anything, as far as I know. He had gone alone into the night, and if he slept at all, it was out there on the cold ground.

He returned as the first hints of dawn began to soften the darkness. I never enjoyed watching him go off to war, but I never shirked my obligation to prepare him as best I could, for that is as much the duty of a warrior's woman as welcoming him back. I had cleaned his armor, banked up the fire, set cauldrons of water to warm, put the stool ready on ox hides by the hearth. He halted in the doorway, and I suddenly feared he would order me out.

"You must be chilled, my lord. A wash will warm your limbs, so they will not betray you in battle."

Sighing, he came forward. He shed his tunic, sat down. I knelt to remove his greaves and then began to wash him by the dancing flicker of the fire. There was nothing sensual about that washing; I might as well have been grooming a warhorse, for I was readying this giant to go out and kill. My thoughts were of how I had washed Patroclus—when he had been wounded in Lyrnessos and now as a corpse. Remembering the prophecy, I wondered if I should soon be performing the same office for Achilles.

Much the same must have occurred to him, because as I was wiping his shoulders, he suddenly said, "You prophesied my death."

I dipped the sponge in the steaming water and wrung it out with a savage twist. Strange thoughts leaped through my mind, doubts and wild hopes and slinking terror. "I warned you that you are mortal. It is merely common sense that you cannot forever be first in battle without—"

He clasped my chin in his horny fingers. "You said that if I remain to fight at Troy, I will win everlasting glory but die here, never returning to Thessaly. You said that these words came from Athena!"

Perhaps even then I might have repented. I could have claimed a misunderstanding and denied I had spoken for the goddess, but in my folly I quailed before the flash of fire-light in his eyes and mumbled, "I do not remember."

So do we follow our fates. I failed to deny the false prophesy and thus foreswore the gods again. Helenus had warned me that the Immortals are not mocked.

"You! My prize of honor!" Achilles' voice was bitter as untimely death itself. "I could not bear to go without my honor, so I stayed. Because I stayed, Patroclus died. Mighty I sat here on the shore—useless! Terrible is anger, sweet as honey, but now my anger is for Hector. *Him I must slay!* Then I shall not complain of whatever destiny the gods send. Though I never return to kneel at my father's feet and strew his hall with treasure, though I will not comfort him in his old age or give him the honorable burial that is his right and my duty, I must fight now. No prophecy will keep me from this battle. Today I will make many new widows weep in Troy. They will learn that war has been easy until now."

"Do it!" I said. "Destroy them who slew Patroclus and may Athena aid you." The words came from my heart, but they left a bitter taste on my tongue.

The sky beyond the doorway was brightening fast. Clamoring pots in the camp summoned men to eat; horses bugled their eagerness to run. I rubbed Achilles with sweet oil, combed out his hair, clad him in a scented tunic of fine linen. I had set a table of food nearby, but he was little interested, grabbing scraps from time to time as if unaware what his hands were doing. He strapped on his bronze greaves and his heavy cuirass. I hung his starry mantle on his back, clipping it at his throat with a gold pin. He slung his sword over his right shoulder, his shield on his left, and by that time Automedon was at the door with his chariot. Always before he had gone joyously to battle, but that grim morning he said not a word. He donned his helmet, took up his great spear, and strode out.

Thus I sent forth Achilles son of Peleus to smite the Trojans.

One man among thousands should make no difference, but Achilles had the gods on his side. He led out the army as Dawn scattered rose petals on the peaks of Ida, and Posei-

don sent a roiling sea mist to mask his movements from
the foe.

Having learned the danger of leaving his city undefended,
Hector made the best choice available to him by electing to
defend the ford. He was certainly justified in expecting Scamander's lower reaches to be impassable for the Greeks, because the river had always been a Trojan supporter and that
day it was glutted with rain from the mountains, dangerous
and swift. His allies were weakening like timbers rotting
under his feet, but he put them with the Dardanians in the
forefront and kept the Trojans themselves on the east bank.
Thus he held his best troops in reserve, as he had the previous day.

As he had the previous day, Achilles outflanked him. At
first he headed for the ford, racing ahead of the army in his
chariot, sweeping aside enemy scouts and skirmishers like
spiderwebs. Other chariots followed, but the war bands
skirted the marshes, obscured by mist. Only when they
reached the river did the chariots turn back to join them.
Hector had to reverse his deployment and rush his motley
host downstream along both banks to block a possible Greek
crossing, and that left his army divided by the river.

The Dardanians were the first to make contact, charging
out of the mist. They fought well, but many of the allies who
should have been with them had gone in the opposite direction rather than stay and fight Achilles. Aeneas and Achilles
met in battle again, and again my cousin escaped into the
fog and confusion.

There were allies present, though: Lydians, Thracians,
and others. Some had come a long way to die on the Plain
of Troy. And there were Trojans also, for among those who
died in that battle on Achilles' spear were two sons of Priam.
One of them was Polydorus. His father had forbidden his
youngest and favorite son to fight, but he had wanted to be
with his brothers.

When the massacre was over and the defenders had fled
back upstream, Achilles led the Greeks into the river. No one
else would have dared to challenge Scamander in his spring
pride, but the men would have followed Achilles into the

Styx itself; and somehow he got most of them across, despite ferocious resistance from both the river and the Trojans holding the far bank. At times the stream was choked with bodies; when the sun burned off the mists, the waters ran fiery red.

As more and more Greeks came ashore, the allies broke and fled upstream. The four-day slaughter had left them little stomach for further struggle, and Priam had run out of gold to pay them. Achilles followed, harrying and hounding without mercy until they had dispersed in the hills. With them went the Trojans' last hopes. The war was as good as won.

The Trojans themselves fell back toward Troy in good order with their rear guard putting up a valorous resistance until only Hector and his personal war band remained outside the walls, close by the Scaian Gate. Having closed off all possible escape routes, the rest of the Greek army sat down to wait for Achilles, who had given very specific orders that only he was to harm Hector. When he at last arrived, burning across the plain like a deadly star, Hector's men fled within, leaving him alone. The defenders shouted down repeatedly for him to follow, but he stood by his chariot, refusing to budge even when his parents came to add their appeals. Eventually the massive gate was banged shut at his back, barred, bolted, and barricaded.

Only the gods know for certain what moved him to make that fatal decision. Even if he dreamed of defeating Achilles in single combat he could not have hoped to withstand the entire army. The time was long past for thoughts of parley, of giving back Helen and paying recompense. That stern, dutiful man I met so briefly had spoken with affection of his wife and infant son, proclaiming his obligation to protect them with his life, and yet he must have seen that now he was throwing his life away, leaving them defenseless. Perhaps he knew that he had lost the war and could not face the reproaches of his family and peers. Pride was the strength that let the knights face death for a living, and pride was their weakness. Agamemnon could not bear to lose Chryseis, Achilles, me, or Hector Troy.

Stranger yet, at the last minute he leaped aboard his car,

lashed his team to a gallop, and fled the field. (I wept when I heard that.) Did the son of Peleus seem so superhumanly terrible that even the great Hector's nerve failed him? Achilles pursued, of course, and the two chariots went racing around the citadel while the Trojans wailed and the Greeks shrieked in derision.

Close to the walls, the terrain was cluttered with the ruins of burned hovels. If Hector's purpose was to draw Achilles within bowshot of the defenders, he was defeated by this debris and the inspired driving of Automedon, who repeatedly cut him off. Around and around they went, the gap steadily closing. At last Hector reined in his lathered team and jumped down to make a fight of it. Achilles dismounted likewise, and the two men ran at each other with shield and spear. They met in a peal of bronze. Each managed to deflect the other's blow and stay upright, but Achilles was the first to recover and line up a second stroke. He rammed the point into Hector's throat and stood over him until he was dead.

Thus died Priam's greatest son—a failure, and apparently, at the last, a coward. So Achilles proclaimed him and so the bards deride him still. But the bards are Greeks and I later heard another version of events from Laothoë. No matter— he was dead; Achilles had avenged Patroclus and doomed Troy. He left a cordon of troops around the city to maintain the siege and led the rest of the army back to the camp in triumph. He stripped Hector's corpse himself, strung thongs through its ankles, roped it behind his chariot, and dragged it home as a trophy of war.

6

I spent most of that day brooding in the megaron, which seemed more than usually gloomy without Patroclus's brightness. I prepared for the funeral feast, assembling wine and livestock, sending parties to the end of the cape to collect driftwood for fuel. The wounded men left in camp did my bidding without argument, and of course the other Myrmidon women obeyed me. The strapping Diomede I sent back to the troops, assuring her that her services were no longer required, and I set Maera to look after the inconsolable Iphis.

Casualties returning from the battle by the river told us of the Trojan rout. When dust clouds informed us that the main army was on its way back to camp, I began preparing to receive Achilles, assuming that he would, as usual, return ablaze with triumph. I dressed in a chiton of fine linen, set cauldrons by the fire, and laid out bedding. Many times I had welcomed him back from forays, and lovemaking had always been his first priority—usually second and third priorities also. After being deprived of his embrace for so long, I was hungry for it. Patroclus would not have grudged us this consolation.

Alas! He clambered down from the chariot as if every bone ached and plodded by my waiting smile without a glance. I followed him into the lodge. He hurled off his armor, turning away when I reached out to assist him. His face and hair and limbs were caked with dirt and dried blood, but he ignored the steaming cauldrons, snatching up the tunic I had set out.

"May I not bathe you, my lord?"

"I will not touch water until my friend has received his rites." He stalked toward the door, pulling on the tunic.

"That is obscene! You would not offer sacrifice to the gods without washing your hands. Will you honor your friend in that revolting state? You degrade his memory!"

Horrified at what I said, I clapped a hand over my mouth. Achilles stopped. Slowly he pulled off the tunic again and dropped it on the floor. Then he stalked back to the hearth and sat on the stool without looking at me. I dipped the sponge and began to wash him, not daring another word.

As I cleaned his face, I realized that he was weeping, staring fixedly ahead and streaming tears that had washed little runnels through the filth and dried blood on his cheeks. He had had his revenge, but Patroclus was still as dead. There was so much blood on him that I was frightened of finding some horrible wound, but it all seemed to be Trojan blood, until I reached his right forearm, and there I discovered an ugly gash. It had stopped bleeding, but it gaped. I dabbed at it cautiously. He winced.

"I should sew this up."

"Leave it."

"It will make a scar."

"Leave it!"

I submitted, but we both knew it was an omen. His body bore no other scars. He had never been wounded before.

"You won a great victory, my lord?"

He grunted.

"You have avenged the son of Menoitios?"

He sighed. "Many times. And Hector is dead."

"I am glad." I moved a kettle of clean water closer and knelt to clean my master's legs. Unlike every other time I had welcomed him home from battle, my attentions provoked no salute.

"And Priam lost other sons also. He will recall this day when he rues his folly in sheltering the despicable Paris." Achilles spoke as if to the shade of Patroclus, not me at all, but then he added, "Lykaon! Remember him? One of your bedmates?"

Shocked, I almost dropped the sponge, for I had never mentioned my earlier escapades to him. He had never asked. Lykaon himself must have told him, when he was a prisoner.

"Before I met you." I washed Achilles' feet vigorously, not looking up.

"Young fool! I thought I'd seen the last of him when I sent him off to Lemnos, but he came back. I met him in the river and he had the gall to beg for his life. Because he'd been my guest! Imagine! I told him there could be no mercy now, not since Patroclus died. I told him I was a far better man than any son of Priam, and since I must die at Troy, then he certainly must."

I did not speak.

"He told me his brother died earlier, Polydorus."

At that I must have made some sound, because Achilles snarled.

"Him too?"

"I knew him. He was young to die."

"Well, he's dead. They're both dead. Hector is dead. And Patroclus is dead."

I had not finished, but he rose and strode over to the discarded tunic. I scrambled to my feet, shaking.

"May I not even dry you, my lord? Oil?"

He paused for a moment at the door. "Daughter of Briseus!" His voice grated harsh and unfamiliar, a stranger's voice. "It would have been far better that you had died in the battle for your city. Then Agamemnon and I would not have contested over you in bitterness and many brave men would not have died." He slammed the door behind him, shaking the whole lodge.

To bring Patroclus back, he would have given up me or his own life or all Thessaly, and possibly even his father, Peleus. I could not disagree with his words, but that did not stop them hurting. Shocked and dismayed, I crumpled down on the heaped fleeces of the bed and wept.

Soon old Maera crept in like a sly black woodlouse. She must have seen Achilles depart and appraised the situation exactly.

I sat up, wiped my eyes, and barked, "What do you want?" My throat hurt.

"Very little." She perched on a stool of carved olive wood. "But you want Achilles back and that is a great deal to ask of the gods."

"Why? Why should it be? They gave me back to him, as he knew they would. I don't understand! He has always said he loved me."

"He loved Patroclus more."

"It was not my fault!"

"Maybe it was." She held up a tiny, twisted hand to block my protest. "Why did he not go home to Thessaly when he said he would? Had he left you, Patroclus would still be alive. Men like to find others to blame for their own mistakes. Take Hector, now."

"What about Hector?"

She screwed up her wrinkles in a grimace. "Achilles dragged his corpse back to camp and left it beside the bier. He plans to do it further mischief."

"No! Not Achilles! He wouldn't. That is against the oath of knighthood."

"It is worse." She wrung her twisted hands, more upset than I could ever recall seeing her. "It is an offense against the gods and all that is fitting. He is sore in his heart, that mighty man of yours, sore indeed. Be careful, Briseis! However much he loves you, he may take it into his head to put you away now. He does not want the other men to think he lost his head over a slave. Who else is left to be angry at? Every time he looks at you, he will remember Patroclus."

As I did then, for I had always taken problems to him. "What can I do?"

Maera shrugged her tiny shoulders. "Wait and pray. He does not want to be happy yet. When the funeral is over and he can go back to fighting, he may improve." She rose and headed for the door. "Watch what he does with the body. I fear the fury of the gods if he does not return it."

I rinsed my face and went outside. On the grass in front of the lodge, a mountain of bronze glittered in the evening light—swords, cuirasses, helmets, and all the other accouterments of warriors—a tumulus of armor that his followers had stripped from men he had slain that day. I wondered what Sphelos would have thought. It was worth a kingdom and the dogs had been pissing on it.

The porch was still littered with Agamemnon's gold bars and silver bowls. As I was pondering where they should go, Automedon came striding up from the tents, lithe and fresh scrubbed, looking as if he still had mother's milk on his chin but enormously pleased with himself. He tapped his forehead to me.

"Lady Briseis! Is the son of Peleus ready?"

"He has already gone."

"Oh!" He frowned, nonplussed.

"You have done well today, son of Diores?" I could see the glow of victory running like fire under his skin.

He grinned. "Achilles' charioteer at the Battle of the Scamander? All my life I shall be honored for that." He began to turn, paused. "Er, my lady?"

I must be the only slave in the Troad who was so addressed. Patroclus had begun the custom, and the others had copied him. "Charioteer?"

"Does he want . . . Has he mentioned . . ." He shuffled his feet. "Am I to sleep here?"

I did not know. I had thought I understood Achilles and now he was a stranger. Normally a knight was attended at all times by his charioteer or another highborn companion, but no one would ever replace Patroclus. Poor Automedon was so eager to please and his task so impossible.

"He hasn't said. I . . . Were it my choice, I would rather be here to be sent away than absent and have to be summoned."

He replied with a worried nod and half a grin, but I had just noticed the seven skilled maidens from Lesbos beside the corral fence, preening under the attentive banter of a group of spearmen. Achilles had given no instructions concerning them, either. If any of them had ambitions to replace me in his bed, they had the sense not to let me know it. Anything would seem good to them after their long captivity in Agamemnon's slave barn.

Dare I? "How is Alexandra?"

Automedon smirked. "Big enough for triplets."

Almost every woman in the camp was with child or nursing. I was an exception. I took a deep breath and gambled. "Achilles wants those girls distributed among the knights. Will you attend to it now?"

His eyes went very wide. "I am to decide?"

"And take first choice. Shall I present them to you?"

I was running a great risk, but if Achilles planned to keep one of them as a replacement for me, my cause was already hopeless. I escorted my eager young companion across and introduced the gaggle of beauties, then left him there to make his decision. He did not seem to find this task an imposition.

Pillars of sparks soaring into the dusk led me toward the feast, but that was a male ritual, involving clashing of weapons and loud declamations of the departed's great deeds; and later the knights would circle the bier in their chariots. I stood in the background to watch the lambs and bullocks being slaughtered and butchered, their blood caught in silver cups and tipped out as offerings around that still, white-shrouded figure. None of this seemed to me to have any relation to the Patroclus I had known, but I tended to forget the mighty fighter I had watched duel with Mynes. I preferred to remember the gracious companion, the man who had told me he fought because his friend did—and who had died because his friend had not.

I went back to the lodge and there found Eriphyle, one of the seven. She was a sweet-natured girl, something of a wit, and a striking beauty in a lean sort of way, daughter of a prosperous ship captain in Thermi.

"I see the son of Diores has excellent taste," I said.

She laughed, tossing back her long hair. "Obviously the Fates have been kind to him! I think they could have done worse by me, too." The lightness of her tone was hiding a serious question.

"Much worse," I assured her. "I understand he has no brothers and will inherit rich estates in Thessaly. Alexandra has never complained of his treatment of her."

Relieved, she sighed. "My mother used to say that happiness was a warm bed and a full cook pot. I have had those for the last year and am starting to think that there must be more."

"Whatever else there is, I suspect Automedon can supply it."

"I should keep him, you mean?"

"Definitely. Spare no pains."

She chuckled, her color rising. "Or pleasures?"

"None at all!" Later, as we prepared a meal together, I heard myself say, "Smiles."

"What?"

I had not meant to speak aloud. "Happiness," I explained. "That's what else is needed—warm bed, full pot, and people whose faces light up at the sight of you." I suppose I was won-

dering what Achilles would say to me. He must have learned
by now how I had disposed of the seven maidens of Lesbos.

Eventually we heard horses being returned to the paddock, which meant the chariot parade was over. We spread
out the bedding on either side of the hearth, undressed, and
slid under our respective covers. Then we lay in silence.

The door creaked open and squeaked closed. Automedon
hesitated in the darkness, peering from one sleeping place to
the other. Eriphyle helpfully sat up and held out her arms,
letting the blanket drop so the firelight could gleam on a figure somewhat on the slender side, but very shapely—
shapely enough, evidently, for he flashed across the room in
a shower of cloak, tunic, greaves, and shoes and plunged
naked under the cover she raised to admit him. Locked together, they disappeared behind the stone circle of the
hearth, out of my sight. Soon I heard whimpers of girlish
pleasure that I found overdone, unbelievable, and intensely
annoying. They served their purpose, though, for they were
soon joined by deeper, masculine moans. The skills
Agamemnon had praised in the seven maidens of Lesbos
were not confined to spinning and weaving. Then Eriphyle's
feet were over her ears, Automedon's pale buttocks were rising and falling in the firelight, and I could hear the gasps as
each thrust went home. They cried out their joy quite shamelessly. I rolled on my side, almost awash myself and trying
not to grind my teeth.

I waited in vain for Achilles. He spent the night wandering the cape, beset by ghosts and unable to find peace.

7

The day dawned cold and gloomy, with spattering rain and
heavy clouds threatening worse to come—fitting weather
for funerals. Work parties and mule teams cut timber in

lands south of Besik Bay and gathered together the scores of Greek corpses on the plains. Trojan bodies, identified by their shorter hair, were left to the birds and foxes. The jailers cordoning the citadel made sure that the defenders knew this, jeering at their impotence to aid their dead.

Patroclus was not the first Greek knight to die at Troy; but the Myrmidons strove to make his funeral exceptional, heaping a pyre larger than four houses on the northern cape. Achilles himself carried the corpse up and laid it at the top. He cut locks of his hair to strew over it, and all the other nobles followed him. More animals were slaughtered for blood sacrifice and hot-burning lard to cover the body. Patroclus's armor was sent with him and many rich gifts, including four horses, his two favorite dogs, and twelve young Trojans whom Achilles had captured the previous day for just this purpose and whose throats he now cut with complete disregard of their screams for mercy. A couple of human attendants would have been generous, a dozen seemed excessive, but who would tell him so? With a few choked words of farewell to his lost friend, he set the fire a-burning.

It did little but dribble smoke in the dull air until Achilles offered sacrifice and prayer to Boreas, which can be a rash act. Then the clouds darkened even more, the leaden waters of the bay began to fleck with white, and the god came raging. Flames leapt higher than the towers of Troy.

It was a fitting tribute to a noble man, and I was deeply moved—up to that point. I disapproved strongly when Achilles lashed Hector's corpse behind his chariot and dragged it around the blaze. I saw many angry frowns and knew that only Achilles could have done such a thing without provoking protests. No one dared object, least of all a slave like me. I was already unhappy about the Trojan dead lying unburied on the plain, for they had fought bravely and deserved decent rites. Many of the women in the camp were quite distraught, especially those who knew they might have relatives out there. Neglect was bad enough; actively dishonoring a body was despicable. Where was the happy, great-hearted Achilles I loved?

I thought I saw him that afternoon, presiding at the funeral games, when the knights competed for the dead man's gear. Such sweaty man nonsense had little interest for me, but I was happy that Diomedes of Argos won the main event, the chariot race, because his prizes included Iphis. She could have done much worse and the follower he later gave her to was a kindly man, who treated her well.

Achilles had donated many other lavish trophies. He presided with perfect courtesy, being gracious even to Agamemnon. When tempers rose, he adjudicated fairly, quenching the heat with calm good humor. I am sure he deceived everyone except me, but although I was watching from a distance, well wrapped in a heavy cloak against the wintery gale, I eventually realized that what I was seeing was a massive effort of will, Achilles playing Achilles, although until then I would not have believed him capable of such deception. His rage and pain still burned inside, unappeased even by the death of Hector. When he came to the lodge that evening, he spoke barely a word to me. I would rather have had him berate me for my insubordination in disposing of the women than just sit there, staring into space. He spent the night in the open, and when I went looking for him, I saw him standing alone, staring into the dying embers of the funeral pyre in a whirl of snowflakes.

Next day he dowsed the embers with wine and collected Patroclus's bones. He ordered the other remains gathered together and a mound heaped above them, but a modest one, not the great tumulus everyone expected. The funerary urn, sealed with fat, he interred at the crest, just below the surface, where it could readily be found again. He was certain his own bones would join his friend's very shortly.

The storm he had summoned continued for days, tormenting the shivering troops around Troy. He rarely ate, hardly spoke. Worse, at night he lay uncaring at my side while young Automedon copulated like a goat on the far side of the hearth. That was so unlike Achilles' old self that I found it more terrifying than anything else. When he did sleep, wraiths and evil dreams came to him; he muttered and mumbled to them or wakened crying out. Clearly the gods had cursed him.

Even old Maera was at a loss to advise me. What could we do to placate the Immortals? I kept hoping some senior captain would intervene—Nestor or Odysseus—but even they did not dare. When I tried to enlist the help of Phoenix, he walked away before I had uttered a dozen words. No one would risk Achilles' smoldering fury.

No one was happy. The Greeks needed someone to fight, but the Trojan allies had fled the field and the Trojans themselves were sealed up within their circle of walls, unreachable. There they would remain until they had eaten their horses, their mules, their stores, and ultimately the sparrows and the rats. That would take months.

One morning—I had lost count of the days—I awoke suddenly as Achilles sat up at my side and began tying on his greaves. The hall was dark and cold, with only the first gray traces of dawn showing in the clerestory. Under the blustering of the wind I heard quiet sounds from the other side of the hearth and guessed what had disturbed him. He pulled on his tunic and rose, preparing to go out and face another day of misery.

I decided I could not. I must speak if he killed me for it. As he strode toward the door I rose on my elbow.

"Going in search of glory?"

Automedon's moist nuzzling noises stopped instantly.

Achilles spun around. "What did you say?"

I sat up, throwing aside the blankets. "I say you are a fool, son of Peleus! The gods promised you everlasting glory if you stayed and fought at Troy, so you did and *they have given it to you*! You destroyed the Trojan army and your name will be sung forever for it. The city will fall in time. What more can you want? What more can you find? What sort of knight makes war on corpses?"

Automedon choked.

Achilles was too astounded to say more than, "Be silent!"

I leapt to my feet, stark naked. "I will not be silent! My love for you demands that I speak out. The gods insist on it. Do you not see that your contempt for Hector has brought their wrath upon you? Was he not a worthy foe? Did not the

Immortals love him in his time? And now you desecrate his corpse! That is unworthy of knighthood, an insult to the memory of Patroclus, a shame on your father's name. Relent, Achilles! Accept a proper ransom, a great ransom if you will, but return the son of Priam to his family so that his soul may find peace. I tell you that if you do not, then you will find no peace, not here nor in the underworld to come!"

All through my rant, he stood rigid in the shadows. When he spoke, his voice was quiet. "Show me this ransom." He spun on his heel and walked out, closing the door without a sound.

I sagged with relief. Sweat streamed off me in rivers, but the lightning had not struck me down. Or at least not yet.

Automedon was sitting up, staring at me openmouthed.

"You heard him!" I said. "Get me a chariot." A plain white robe, I decided. A head cloth, no jewelry.

"Chariot?" he squeaked. "He didn't—"

"You will make me walk to Troy?" I rummaged in a chest to find what I needed. "Or do you expect me to beg for help from Agamemnon or Ajax? Someone must take the word to Priam." The Myrmidon heralds had both died in the pestilence. Achilles had never appointed replacements, so far as I knew, and Automedon was not arguing otherwise.

He groaned. Desperately wanting to do what was right, he must have been wondering what Patroclus would have done in this situation. Patroclus would not have let Achilles get himself into such a fix.

"My lady, he swore he would never accept ransom for the body!"

Fortunately, I had not known that. "Then he has obviously changed his mind or is considering changing it. You heard him tell me to arrange it, and I must do my master's bidding. *Now*, son of Diores!"

"But a woman . . . ?"

Heedless of my nudity, I turned to glare at him. "I may not rule, but I am still queen of Lyrnessos. I can drive a chariot as well as you can. Must I tell the son of Peleus that you refuse to assist me?"

Staring down at Eriphyle as if he feared he was seeing her

for the last time, he said, "No, my lady. Will you let me go
with you?"

"No. You would only get shot. Just bring me a chariot."

8

I dressed in haste. As I was making sacrifice to Hermes, I realized that my mission could have more than one purpose. In
Troy I would speak with the Trojans, yes, but I could also
appeal to the mighty Trojan gods. From its hiding place
under a hearth stone, I retrieved a gold bracelet Achilles had
given me.

I went out just as Automedon drove up in the uncertain
predawn light. My posturing had not cowed him; he was
merely perplexed by Achilles' decidedly ambiguous orders
and still frantic to do what was expected of him. I protested
when he reached down a hand, but he said gruffly, "You
won't get out of the camp without me."

He was right. I accepted his help to clamber up beside
him, grabbing for the rail as he flicked the horses into mo-
tion. "I am grateful. I am only trying to help Achilles." The
unrelenting wind tugged and buffeted at my cloak. The air
felt cold enough for snow.

As we descended the slope to the shingle, he said, "Just
promise me I'll get a proper funeral."

I looked at him sharply and saw hints of a wry grin under
his coppery stubble. The son of Diores would never have become Achilles' charioteer had he lacked courage.

"Achilles has realized he is in the wrong. If I fail, he can
disavow me. I only hope that you will not suffer also."

"You are worthy of him, my lady."

"I try to be. We all do."

Automedon had certainly done his best for me, choosing
two sprightly ponies and a lightweight wicker chariot that

had once been some Trojan noble's racing car. No one paid heed to a charioteer exercising his team along the beach, and there was no reason why he should not take his woman along if he wished—or another man's if he thought he could get away with it—but a woman driving alone would have attracted notice. The only women there were captives.

He drove me to the palisade, then jumped down and opened a gate. I was relieved he did not try to accompany me all the way to Troy, for although he was nowhere near the size of Achilles, I could not imagine myself throwing him out of the car. He stood there, staring after me until I was out of sight.

At that time of year I should have met a beautiful spring morning with larks singing and dew sparkling on crocuses and hyacinths. Instead the gods' displeasure had turned the world a looming gray—gray sky, gray sea, even grayish hills. There was nothing much to see anywhere. Ares' feet had stamped down the original settlements into charred timbers and tree stumps, and fields had become groves of thistles. Droves of blackbirds fluttered up from time to time, disturbed by my passage, and mostly they flew away to my right, which was encouraging. I could guess what they had been eating. The lower river would be passable, but that had been the site of the greatest slaughter, so I carried on upstream to the ford, and there I did see bodies. *I am doing this for you, too,* I told them, averting my eyes.

Until then, I had been enjoying my ride, for it was my first excursion out of the camp since the day I squelched Chryseis. I had not been so alone in years. I had forgotten how pleasurable a chariot was—wind in my face, the sprightly bouncing, the challenge of guiding the team to the smoothest way. My first glimpse of the unburied dead changed my mood abruptly. As I drove north, I began to feel very naked and small and presumptuous. Even if I could evade the Greek beleaguerers and enter the citadel, the Trojans might deny me a hearing or hold me for ransom or do any one of innumerable bad things.

Some Trojan might plant an arrow in my chest before I

reached the gates, but when I was seen to be a woman, sheer curiosity ought to win me a hearing. I would be in greater danger from the Greek besiegers, although they might assume that a solitary charioteer was just some hothead braggart wanting to jeer at the defenders.

Troy stood on the edge of the plateau, but the approach from the south was gentle enough that I kept the horses at a trot. The citadel loomed over me much larger than I had expected, and perhaps the war had made it more impressive by wiping away the humble buildings that had once huddled around it. Arrogant the Trojans undoubtedly were in their day, but their hauteur was understandable when their towers touched the sky and their walls of smooth, tight-fitted blocks seemed so impregnable. Within the citadel, the flat-roofed houses rose in terraces to Pergamon, the shining palace.

Fortunately Achilles had concentrated his forces on the inland side, and there were no Greek tents to seaward, no chariots in sight. I was halfway up the hill before a foot patrol saw me. The leader shouted, and they all began to run.

The trail to the Scaian Gate crossed a level wasteland littered with charred timbers, pockmarked by foundations of vanished houses. To the left of the gate the Great Tower jutted forward foursquare from the wall, soaring ten times the height of a man. The gods of Holy Troy had stood at its base for untold centuries, but now they had been taken into the citadel for safekeeping and only the plinths remained. To the right of the road stood the house of sacrifice, overtopped by the wall behind it. Farther to the east was the Dardanian Gate and another tower.

I almost choked on an unexpected surge of fear as the city loomed up over me like a stone monster. Suppose they kept me, made me stay? Troy was a trap; it was going to burn. I could not turn back now, for the Greeks were almost within range.

"Who comes?"

I reined in and looked up at a line of very startled faces and an ominous glitter of bronze. Humility would get me nowhere.

"Queen Briseis of Lyrnessos. I must speak with the son of

Laomedon." I glanced around again. "Be quick, or I'll start growing feathers."

The Greeks were advancing with drawn bows. They probably thought I was an escaped slave stealing a chariot, so any minute they would start lobbing long shots. Personally, I could not imagine why anyone would try to escape *into* Troy now, but men don't always think so clearly.

"Last time we met, lady, you said I was not welcome in your house."

I scanned the battlements to find the source of that familiar mockery—Paris himself, the cause of all the trouble. He was bareheaded, dark tresses rippling in the wind, younger than I remembered. His smirk was as detestable as ever.

"That day I gave you a message from the Cloud Gatherer, my lord."

"Do you bring another this time?"

"My words now are to your noble father, for his ears alone."

Fortunately Paris had ordered the gate opened while he baited me. Bars fell with somber thuds, and one of the great flaps creaked wide. Ignoring the Greeks' shouts, I urged the team forward under the huge stone lintel into a narrow paved street shaded by high walls on either side and filled with armored men, all glaring at me suspiciously under the brows of their helmets. Hands caught the horses' neckbands and halted them. The gate thundered shut at my back.

Trapped.

"This is a sad reunion, my lady."

With sharp relief I looked down at the white hair and sad dark eyes of Helenus, whom I would trust more than any other Trojan. He wore a simple, drab brown tunic, not princes' wear. His hair and beard were matted, and his face seemed more lined than I remembered it, smeared with the ashes of mourning.

"You expected me?"

"I expected someone, but not the pleasure of seeing you again." He swung up to stand beside me. "It was Cassandra who foresaw you, but she did not divine your name." He waved the men away from the horses. "Drive on, widow of Mynes. I will take you to my father."

Easier said than done. The street's upward slope was gentle, curving to the left, but the horses were skittish in the cramped, crowded place. It was only when we drew away from the gate and the guards that I was able to spare another glance for my companion.

"We grieve for both the dead and the living," he said quietly, not looking at me.

"I hope I can do a little to ease your burden, but it will not be much."

"Ease? I do not know your purpose in coming here, Queen Briseis, but Cassandra foresees that you bring doom to the city."

Startled, I cried out, "No!"

He shrugged with numbed indifference. "A quick end may be a mercy now." He refused to say more.

I wish I had seen Troy in its glorious past. I almost regret my glimpse of it in that grim present, when hordes of refugees crammed it far past its normal capacity. Noble houses were packed like fish jars, with faces peering down from every roof and balcony. The streets were cluttered with makeshift lean-tos and livestock, whose filth had splattered the formerly snow-white walls, the bright-painted beams and columns. Time and again I had to wait for a way to be cleared for the horses. Mingled stenches of ordure and bad food and unwashed people made my eyes sting, and the very air seemed dark with despair. The future must be worse.

We wound our way up the hill—it was not far—until we came to the yard in front of the palace gates, and even that was packed with refugees, mostly women and children, huddled in patient misery around their few remaining possessions, living out the last days of the city, hour by lingering hour. Leaving the chariot with a slave, we climbed wide marble steps to a high and spacious portico, the first empty space I had seen. The airy courtyard beyond it was full of refugees of another sort, between marble benches, under four silvery olive trees—the tall, stiff figures of the gods who had so long guarded the Scaian and Dardanian gates. Age had split the wood and faded the painted pottery, yet they were an awesome assembly still, somehow more pathetic than the human debris in the streets.

"Briseis, child!" Two women advanced toward me from opposite directions, each trailing attendants. The one who spoke was tall and lovely, for even trappings of mourning could not conceal the wondrous beauty of Helen. Trials and sorrows had not withered her. Her youth surprised me, but I had been only a child when she came to Lyrnessos.

"How wonderful to see you again, and how tragic that our reunion must be thus!" She took my hands and looked me over with a wistful smile. "Yes! I foretold your beauty and I was not mistaken."

I regarded the soft curves of her cheeks, discretely scored by nails and delicately smeared with ash, the luster of the auburn locks so tastefully unkempt, the black gown judiciously rent to display one perfect breast. I tasted gall. "And I was not mistaken when I foretold the anguish that followed you, my lady."

She shook her lovely head in agreement. "Truly I am cursed beyond all women to have caused such a terrible war. Women's beauty should bring joy to men. How sad if it be a cause for their contention!"

Not by voice nor look did she condemn me, but my claws sprang from their sheaths. "It was not over me that my husband and my lover fought."

"You love the terrible Achilles?" Her fingertip traced a line on my cheek. "You have been mourning. Not for the son of Peleus, not yet. For Hector? He praised your beauty highly. All Troy mourns for Hector, and none more than I. Among all my brothers-in-law, only he was kind to me."

Helenus was staring at her with undisguised loathing. "You will excuse us, Princess? My father—"

I turned toward the other woman, and she screamed at the sight of me. *"No! Take her away! Kill her!"* She waved her hands in a frenzy, as if terrified of me, as if trying to ward me off. Cassandra was reputed to be the fairest of Priam's twelve daughters, and yet she did not seem so then. Her face and neck were deeply scored, the scabs inflamed, and she had torn out some of her hair, leaving dark blood among the golden roots. Where Helen was peach-smooth and curved, Cassandra was hard, angular, burning with strange light, like a carving of rock crystal. She fended off invisible horrors as she railed. "Slay her now! Cannot you see she comes seeking revenge? She will lose the dread Argives upon us!"

My skin crawled. I tried to back away. Helenus put a protective arm around me and edged me past his ranting twin.

"Hush, Sister! She comes as a guest."

"She comes as a destroyer! She brings the horse that will throw down our walls!"

"Don't let her upset you, child," Helen remarked. "It is a pleasant change to hear someone else being the object of her ravings. She does not understand the sorrows she causes." She drifted in our wake as Helenus hurried me along. Helen knew her sorrows. And no one else's. I shook myself like a wet dog.

In the background, Cassandra still howled. "Cut off her head, but you won't. Ah, mercy! We sail in the same ship! Slay her!"

I hated Troy. It deserved to die. I hated Helen and Paris and Cassandra and their whole family. I was trapped in a tomb full of corpses and maggots.

9

Helenus led me into the very heart of Pergamon, to the megaron where Priam had ruled for two generations. Alas, it was no larger or grander than Lyrnessos' had been. The four great pillars were more massive, but smoke stains had blurred the wall frescoes to ghosts and the designs on the floor were scuffed to bare plaster. Only dead ashes lay on the central hearth under the drab daylight filtering down from the ceiling. The throne of Tros itself, back in the shadows of the eastern wall, was a simple alabaster chair less imposing than the wooden one set beside it for the queen. For the first time I realized how much my father had achieved in his tiny realm. And all this was fated to perish as that had.

I had assumed that the two of us would be alone together when I met with the king, or almost so. To my dismay, the hall was crowded with men and women, about a score of them standing in morose silence, apparently waiting to hear what dread message I brought. There was little else to do in Troy by then. I saw Helen and Paris standing together, although not especially close, then faces I had seen long ago in Pedasos. These were the surviving members of the royal family: sons and wives, daughters and husbands.

Eyes demurely downcast, I followed Helenus forward to the hearth, then turned to approach the throne. I knelt before the king but did not clasp his knees, for I had not come as a supplicant. Nor was I a herald. I was very close to a fraud, a traitor, a spy. I forced myself to look up, and my first clear sight of Priam snatched my breath away.

He was terrible—huge as Achilles but very old, a great tree towering on some wind-racked cliff for uncounted years, twisted and mutilated, yet still defiant although the soil had washed away from its roots and most of its branches had fallen. He was ragged and filthy in his mourning, his silver hair and beard straggling around a ruin of a face that must once have been beautiful and now was only leather and bone, ravaged but imperious, a rock long lashed by the pitiless sea. But a rock cannot suffer. Still he waited for me to speak, staring down at me with tortured eyes until I found my wits.

"My lord, I am Panope, daughter of Briseus and erstwhile queen of Lyrnessos."

"Taken there as prize by the accursed son of Peleus." His voice was a rumble of millstones.

I nodded my assent, struggling against tears or perhaps shame that I could love the man who had slain so many of this old man's sons.

"What has he done with my son's body?"

"My lord . . . it lies on the ground, spurned and untended." The woman at his side howled like a wounded dog, but I saw

only the agony that convulsed Priam's face, the clenching of
his massive hands. I cowered down so I need not watch. I did
not describe how Achilles liked to drag the body around Patroclus's grave behind his chariot.

"He sent you to tell us this?"

"No, my lord. Not exactly."

"Then why are you here?"

"Because this abomination is an offense against the ways
of men and gods, and against Achilles himself. He injures
himself and his noble father. This morning I told him so."

"Why should he need to be told?" Priam thundered.

I shuddered, huddled on the floor at his feet as small as I
could make myself. "I don't think he needed to be told, not
now his anger has . . . No one else would tell him! But he
did not rage at me as I thought he would, my lord! I told him
it was wrong and he should accept a fitting ransom and release the body. He just said, 'Show me this ransom!'—my
lord."

The megaron was very still.

"We have offered ransom. It was scorned."

"I think it would be accepted now," I whispered.

"You think? You do not know?"

"I hope. I pray."

"But he has given no orders? He sent a slave, not a
herald?"

"He did not send me. I just came. To tell you."

"The dogs prowling 'round our walls know naught of
this?"

"No, my lord."

More silence.

Queen Hecuba's bitter croak spattered scorn at me. "You
love this monster? You let him fondle and caress you with
his killer hands? You melt in his embrace and open yourself
to him?"

I raised my head to stare at her. Despite the ravages of age
and childbearing, despite the sagging breasts and sunken
cheeks or the gray locks matted with mourning ashes, some
of the legendary beauty lingered still, like a sunset glow.
And the eyes. Her eyes burned like Medusa's.

"Yes, I love him. He is not always thus."

She opened her shark jaws to rail at me again, and her husband said, "Be silent. Rise, widow of Mynes. You are welcome to our halls, for you have no part in Achilles' shame and do the gods' bidding in coming here. Saw you omens or auguries? Or what moved you?"

I clambered unsteadily to my feet. My eyes swam with tears. "None, my lord. It was my love for Achilles that brought me. Yet he may turn his anger against me for doing so. Send a herald back with me and—"

"No!" Priam, too, rose up. Even seated he had dominated the megaron and on his feet his great height and age made him more frightful than Cronos. "Heralds have failed. I will go myself and treat with the son of Peleus."

The hall erupted in yells and protests, none louder than the screams of Hecuba. The terrible old man shouted them down, brandishing his staff until they all shrank from him.

Then it was my turn. "My lord," I cried, "I bring no promise, no safe conduct! I came only to—"

He turned his mad glare on me. "You came upon the gods' errand. The Storm Lord himself sent you."

Several sons and daughters yelped again in protest.

"Disgrace!" he bellowed. "Shame! Oh, widow of Mynes, I cringe with shame when you look upon these vermin. Trash, they are! Dregs! Once I had many fine sons, fair sons, strong warriors, and now you see the parasites left to me in my old age." He lurched at them, and they fled before him. Weeping and raging at the same time, he drove them from the megaron with his whirling staff. Still he shouted back to me: "Yes, woman of Achilles, I will go with you to the frightful son of Peleus and if he slays me for it, I will not care—not if he will just once let me weep over the body of Hector. Go, all of you! Out of my sight! Begone!"

He paused by the door, leaning on the jamb to catch his breath, then went out. I was alone with the queen of Troy.

"Old fool!" said Hecuba. "Madman!" She rose with a grimace of pain, still stately although bowed by age. When I tried to aid her, she recoiled. "Do not touch me! Your hands are foul; they have caressed Achilles. Oh, how I detest that man! I suppose we must offer you food, child. We are not down to rats yet."

Even had I not been plaything of the hated son of Peleus, to Hecuba I would still have been only a juvenile camp slave, widow of a very minor chieftain and a serious nuisance who had put mad ideas in her husband's head. She turned me over to a quiet-spoken, much younger woman, while she herself went off—so I assumed—to track down Priam and try to badger some sense into him.

Laothoë, my new hostess, surprised me with a warm embrace. "My son was greatly smitten by you, widow of Mynes."

I realized then that this dumpy Laothoë must be Priam's most junior wife, daughter of Altes of Pedasos. She had tasted as much tragedy as anyone, having lost both her sons to Achilles' spear at the Battle of the Scamander, but she put me at ease, or as much as I could ever be at ease in the house of fears and sorrows, and led me off to her own quarters, where she had her maids attend to my toilet. With only one well inside the walls, water was precious, but they sponged and oiled me and clad me in a simple robe.

The two of us ate on a high balcony of Pergamon, over-looking the whole world: the Bay of Troy, the Greek camp, Imbros and Tenedos and far-off Samothrace, the blue ribbon of the Dardanelles with the shore of Thrace beyond it. Nothing stood above us except golden Apollo. We wept together, speaking at length of sunshine days before the war came, she shedding tears for her sons and I for my lost youth. I told her how Polydorus had taught me love—not understating his technique, of course—and spoke of Lykaon's outrageous seduction.

She laughed and said that it sounded just like him. "I must tell those tales to Priam. My sons were his favorites—"

"Except for Hector?"

"Of course Hector. Hector had no equal." She sighed.

"Why did he stay outside the walls to challenge Achilles?" I demanded. "Even if he had won, what could he have hoped . . ." I studied her sorrow for a moment. "Is there something I don't know?"

Hesitantly she said, "It may be." Then she shrugged and began to speak of Polydorus again.

"Please!" I persisted. "I knew Hector and would not think wrong of him. What was his purpose?"

She was very reluctant to say more, insisting that she did not know—it was only suspicion, just guesswork—but at last, when I had sworn never to tell anyone, especially Achilles, she put her fears into words.

"He must have known Achilles would pursue him when he fled, yes?"

"Yes, but . . . an ambush!" I cried, and shuddered, imagining my lover struck down. "Archers hidden in the ruins?"

Laothoë bit her lip and whispered, "That is what I suspect."

"So what went wrong?"

"The gods decreed otherwise, I presume."

I shuddered again, this time thinking of Hector finding himself alone and betrayed, his plan in ruins. "Who? Who was supposed to be there? When Priam railed against his sons today—" Which of them had failed Hector? But obviously my companion did not know and my prying was causing needless pain. I veered away. "Will Priam really dare go back with me?"

She smiled fondly, wiping away tears. "I expect so. He is like Zeus. Once he has made up his mind, none of us can do anything."

Mention of the Storm Lord reminded me I had other business to consider. "I must go and worship Our Lady."

"The streets are very crowded," Laothoë said quickly.

Was that alarm in her eyes? Was she my hostess or my jailer? Perhaps Priam had given orders to isolate me—Priam or one of those surviving sons he reviled. The Trojans certainly had no cause to trust me, Achilles' toy, but what harm could one lone woman do? What could they fear, other than Cassandra's cryptic croaking?

"I brought an offering." I displayed my bracelet. "My lady, I have been Potnia. I cannot visit Troy and not go to her shrine."

Laothoë winced at this truth and even argued a little more,

but eventually she ordered cloaks and head cloths brought for us. She took no servant when we set off for the shrine of Athena, nor did she venture outside the palace, leading me instead through furtive passageways as if trying to keep my presence a secret.

At the shrine, her hand had not even touched the latch before the big gold-studded door creaked open. The priestess standing there was past middle years, but as tall as I and vastly imposing in her rich many-colored gown and the sacral bow tied in her hair. She knew or guessed who I was, for when I moved to kneel, she reached out to stop me.

"We are sisters in the sight of Our Lady, widow of Mynes." She embraced me and urged me inside, slamming the door on Priam's junior wife with some curt excuse about private devotions. "You are welcome to the shrine. I am Theano daughter of Kisseus." Her name meant nothing to me, yet her manner seemed to imply that it should.

The cramped chamber was dank and dark, droning with flies attracted by the sacrifices. I turned to kneel before the goddess, the Palladium, most holy of all representations of Pallas, who is Athena and Potnia and others. She was vastly ancient, somewhat less than life-sized, holding a spear. Although her features were clumsily painted, the faint light coming from somewhere overhead clothed her in awe and mystery, while the richness of her vestments and adornments shamed the simple bracelet I laid it at her feet.

"Potnia Athena, Pallas, Our Lady, mother and virgin, accept this poor token. If by your favor I ever have more to give, then I will honor you greatly. I pray you to guide Achilles, whom you have always favored, to forgo his anger and return the body of Hector. I pray you to keep him safe in battle so he will not die under the walls of Troy."

"You ask a lot for one little bangle," said a man's voice.

With a cry of fury, I leapt to my feet and glared at the figure standing back in the shadows.

His eyes shone golden as he stepped forward to embrace me. "And will you pray for your family also?" The mockery in his voice would have curdled vinegar. A year had worked no improvement in Aeneas. If the eagle was molting a little,

I could not detect it, and the arrogance—well, he would still be arrogant when he was two months dead.

"I did not expect to find you here. Did you run the wrong way this time?" I spun around to complain to the priestess. "I came here to worship, not to endure this man's insults."

"You came upon her business," Theano responded. "She heard my prayers and sent you."

That I had not expected. "Me?"

"Our Lady sent you."

"She and others," said Aeneas. "I saw you in a dream. You brought Lord Poseidon to aid me. He snatched me up in a golden cloud."

Only now did I see the implications and turn away, trembling. Cassandra had known. If any son of Priam learned of this, I would die before nightfall. "Madness! I am nothing but a slave."

"The slave of Achilles. You can take word to him."

"Stop!" I moaned, wondering who might be listening. "I came here to worship the daughter of Zeus. If you have something to say to the son of Peleus, send a herald."

"Fool!" Theano snapped. "You think we could get a herald over the wall alive?"

She would not attend the goddess with ashes in her hair, but her cheeks and breasts bore scars of sorrow—some old, some still raw. No one in all Troy was not mourning someone. I noted again her assumption of familiarity, but I hated the feeling that I had been trapped by these two, and my fear made me lash out with angry words.

"Is this a fitting place to plot treason, my lady? Pray rather that silver-eyed Athena stiffen this downcast cousin of mine with true warrior courage. You degrade your office by aiding him in his betrayals."

Aeneas gripped my shoulder and spun me around to face him. "She is not aiding me. I am aiding her."

"What help are you?" I yelled. "Are you still sulking because Priam will not appoint you host leader? Is it wounded pride that makes you sink so low?"

He flinched, his arrogance pierced at last. "I do it for my son, my father, and . . . Remember young Akamas? He's dead. Iphidamas dead. Archelochus dead. Laodamas dead. Demoleon dead. Coön—"

"Stop!" I screamed, clapping my hands over my ears.

Theano sank to the floor and clasped my knees. "My sons, but not all my sons. I must save the few I have left. And my dear husband."

My first suitor—the boy who had been Aeneas's charioteer—had been Akamas son of . . . son of . . . Antenor, a senior Trojan counselor, related by marriage to the House of Priam. "Oh, lady, does your husband know that you plan to betray the city?"

Aeneas said, "Of course he does. But no one is trusted now. When there are Dardanians on the watch, there are Trojans. When there are Thracians or sons of Priam. *Will you take word to Achilles?*"

"Not Achilles," Theano said, rising. "Odysseus. When he and Menelaus came on embassy, they stayed at our house. He has a subtle mind."

So did she. The son of Laertes was far more likely to accept this abomination than Achilles was. I turned in dismay to the goddess. She was answering my prayers also, for if the city fell, Achilles need not fight under its walls. He might yet live! How could I refuse? "I make no promises," I whispered, "except that I will take your message to the Greeks. Not for you, Cousin, but for the mother of Akamas, I will do it. Tell me what you propose."

10

Toward evening, orders came that I was to be taken to Priam. When I was brought to the door of the megaron, he led me in by the hand and sat me on the queen's chair.

Like me, he was draped in black. He had been bathed and groomed, so now he seemed much closer to the godlike ruler

I had always imagined, with dangling silver locks and snowy beard but bare of jewelry or adornments, as befitted a bereaved father and suppliant. Although his arrogant, bony face was still haggard with suffering, he had shed the wildness of his grief and gained a grim dignity. If he thought he was going to his death, he intended to go proudly. Servants set out small tables bearing food and wine. Left alone then, the two of us nibbled but more from custom than appetite.

He treated me with wondrous courtesy, although he was still a mighty king and I was only the captive playmate of his worst enemy. My heart ached for him, for it seemed my efforts to resolve his sorrows would bring him to his death. He questioned me at length about Achilles, what sort of man he was, and I answered fully, although I had to confess that he held mysteries for me that I had not even suspected until recently.

"Anger?" He did not smile, but I sensed a little of the amusement that the very young inspire in the old and wise. "Great warriors are always men of great anger, child, because anger is the only thing that can overcome the dread of death that lurks within all of us. But anger must be reserved for battle and the foe." He pondered for a moment, as if recalling examples he had known—after all, he had been a very great warrior in his day and king in Troy since long before I was born. Priam of the Ash Spear, the bards called him. "They are often capable of very great love, also, men of mighty passions. Drab souls or dreamers do not make strong fighters. When such a man makes a mistake, then he can be most terribly wrong."

"You have described him exactly, my lord."

But was he thinking of Achilles or of a father who had loved a wayward son too much? If he had sent Helen back to Menelaus and thrashed Paris to the doorstep of death as he deserved, his city would not be cracking around him now.

He moved on to question me about Peleus, so I reported what I knew, which was only the little I had learned from Achilles and Patroclus. After Peleus he began to ask of Agamemnon, displaying a surprising familiarity with the quarrel between the Overlord and Achilles—information wrung from prisoners, I assumed.

"And is his wound as serious as he pretends?"

"*Pretends,* my lord? Why should the Great King? . . . . I don't know."

The wily old man almost smiled then, amused at my confusion. "While he is afflicted and unable to fight, is not Achilles effectively in charge—leader of the Greeks?"

"I suppose so." He did not have the title, but his orders were being obeyed as if he did, and that was certainly a convenient arrangement for all concerned, especially Agamemnon. I had not seen that, but Priam had.

As the sky darkened above the clerestory, he clapped his hands to summon bearers with torches, then led me down to his treasury, a great pillared chamber stacked to the timbered ceiling with chests and hampers, hoarded riches of a city old as the gods.

"Choose!" he growled. "You know the man. What will move him?"

Nonplussed, I said, "Gold, I suppose, my lord."

"There is little of that left." He nodded to a servant, who led the way to a corner containing a dozen or so bright ingots that must be last survivors of a great pile, for the floor all around was clear of dust. The porters began carrying the bars away.

"What else?" Priam said. "Pick out what will please him and do not stop until I say so."

It was a dream beyond avarice. Tended by torchbearers, I explored the maze, pointing out anything that caught my fancy—artifacts of silver and bronze and fine woodwork inlaid with ivory or crystal or faience. But Achilles already owned many such treasures, so I mainly chose heaps of the famous textiles of Troy, dozens of mantles and robes and blankets and splendid weavings. The boys ran with their burdens and came back for more, until at last Priam called halt, saying that one cart could carry no more.

I followed him back up the narrow stairs, feeling dazed. "Son of Laomedon, you are offering a richer bounty than Agamemnon gave to lure Achilles back into the war." To ransom a dead body!

"What better use can I find now for my riches?" he growled.

The chariot I had appropriated stood waiting, but the horses in the harness were larger and better than the two I had driven. The little man hunched on the bench of the mule cart looked to be almost as old as Priam himself. I could see nothing but grim determination in his unmoving posture, so either he had not been told where he was bound or, like his master, he no longer valued his life very highly.

As torches flamed in the dimming courtyard, there was one last ceremony to perform. Supported by her women, Hecuba shuffled out bearing wine in a cup of gold, so that Priam could pour out a libation to Zeus. Servants offered a silver basin and pitcher of water.

The queen was not reconciled to his mission. "I have known you do many foolish things in your time, son of Laomedon," she rasped, "but never one to match this. Pray to the Lord of Storms that he will protect you in your folly. If he truly expects you to undertake this madness, he will send you a sign."

"We shall look for it." The old man washed his hands, made his prayer, returned the cup to her without another word, and headed over to the chariot. That was all. His wife stood staring after him. I hoped they had made their farewells earlier, in private, else that was a bitter parting from the woman who had borne him nineteen children.

I climbed up beside him. He took the reins, and one of his sons threw in the heels. We began to move, out into the narrow streets made even narrower by livestock and the refugees who had chosen the shaky security of Troy. The road we followed was not the one by which I had come on my arrival, but steeper and more twisted, and we should have made little progress had we not been preceded by a squad of princes armed with staves. They clubbed a passage through the mobs for us and brought us at least to the western gate. When the sentries on the walls confirmed that there were no Greek patrols nearby, the gate was opened to let us out into the night and the wind.

Boreas's icy hands tugged at my robe and hair and nipped my flesh. I clung to the rail with freezing fingers. The air smelled of snow. Down the steep hillside we plunged, and

Priam kicked out the wheels to slow our descent. The mule cart rattled behind. Under stony clouds, a last red stain of sunset lay along the western rim of the bay—Cape Sigeum, where the Greeks were, where we were headed. I did not expect us to progress much farther than one bowshot from the walls before the Greek army fell on us like a net. What would happen then, I preferred not to try to imagine.

"Look, widow of Mynes!" The old man pointed a long arm to the north. His old eyes were incredibly sharp. I could barely make out a speck riding the high winds.

"An eagle?"

"The bird of Zeus." That wasn't quite a smile that disturbed the grimness of his jaw, but it was close to one.

"And on the right! Your prayer has been heard, my lord."

"May my other prayers be heard also."

We descended the slope without mishap and turned to the south. We had no choice of route, except in detail. Wheels squeaking on their axles, clumping hooves of horses and mules, all seemed to make a racket that should be audible on Lemnos. More than the freezing cold under the stars made me shake; I kept seeing vague flickers of movement in the darkness, not knowing whether they were ghosts or living watchers. I sensed eyes in the night. Yet still no one challenged. An owl soared by, silent as the wispy clouds. I knew her and rejoiced, for she is less fickle than her father. As we neared the river, the wind brought the sickly-sweet reek of death. I shuddered.

"Will you ransom them also, my lord?"

"I have sons here too," Priam growled.

Shamed, I gulped an apology.

He reined in at the river's edge to let the horses drink, and the mule cart came to a halt behind us. In the sudden silence I could hear the horses' splashing and waves slapping in the distance. Then my companion uttered a half cry, half gasp of alarm. I looked around and saw a vague pale shape approaching, a figure of white fire in the darkness. I felt my hair stir.

When singing of Priam's journey that night, the bards claim he was guided unseen into the Greek camp by the

Pathfinder himself, sent by Father Zeus. It's a fine tale, but I cannot vouch for the truth of it. I did not see Hermes, although I do not deny the possibility. I thought at the time that it was Alcimus, clad in a white chiton, his ash-blond air streaming in the wind. I jumped down and ran to him.

I neither liked the son of Polyctor nor trusted him. He had probably seen Priam at the oath taking on the day that Menelaus and Paris fought their duel and would recognize him now. To slay Priam would be to gain everlasting renown. When he tried to go past me, I stepped in front of him.

He scowled mightily. "Haven't you caused enough trouble, girl?"

"Trouble? I have brought a herald from Troy to offer ransom for Hector's body. That was what Achilles told me to do."

"Not according to Achilles, it wasn't! You think he sends slaves to negotiate with kings?" Darkness hid his sneer, but it sounded like Alcimus's voice, not the way a god would speak. "If this gets out, there will be uproar and scandal."

"Automedon told him where I went?"

"He didn't have much choice. Achilles picked him up by the throat and shook him. One-handed. If you thought he was angry at Agamemnon, wait until you meet him now. Out of my way, woman."

"But it's only an old herald!"

"Old herald?" Alcimus peered past me. "And what's in the cart—firewood?"

"Of course not."

"And suppose Agamemnon gets his hands on it?" He pushed past me and strode over to Priam. "You travel at a strange hour and on a strange road, old sir."

Priam responded calmly. I stumbled over the coarse grass to the mule cart and clambered up beside the driver. Moments later we started across the river. My driver, Idiaos, hardly spoke at all on the journey and whatever Priam and his guide said to each other I did not hear. There were no bards there to eavesdrop, either.

Of course Alcimus's words had left me apprehensive,

wondering what sort of welcome I would receive from Achilles, but I was fairly confident that the glorious ransom Priam had brought would turn aside his anger. It was a relief to know that we were expected. Having learned what I was doing and probably confirmed it from the watchers on the shore, Achilles must have given orders that any embassy emerging from Troy that night be allowed to pass unquestioned. I had not been mistaken when I detected eyes in the night.

So I was no longer frightened of being molested by cutthroats or Greek patrols, but I was cold and bone weary and very worried about Achilles' reaction to Priam. He would certainly not be expecting the old tyrant himself, the man whose arrogance had caused the war, father of Patroclus's killer.

By starlight we drew near to the palisade, where Alcimus jumped down and ran off into the dark. No sentries were in sight when chariot and mule cart drove through the gate, but he did not bother to close it behind us, so I expect the guards had just withdrawn out of view. Keeping well away from tents and ships, we clattered northward along the seaward spine of the cape until we were level with the last of the campfires, and then turned east. When we came to the back of the lodge, not a single dog barked. That may have been the gods' doing or more of Achilles' efforts to keep this midnight encounter a secret.

11

I followed close on Priam's heels as the old giant strode through the porch. After the darkness of the night, the hall blazed bright, with a huge fire spitting on the hearth and white smoke roiling and billowing. Beyond it, Achilles sprawled back in his great chair, Eriphyle was just clearing

dishes from a table beside him, and Automedon chewed
lustily on a goose leg.

The wind had masked the noise of our arrival. Achilles,
wearing only a white cloth around his loins and a tasseled
mantle draped over his shoulders, was not ready to greet visitors. Yet I thought I had never seen him look more like a
god, for the mist of hair covering his limbs and chest
gleamed in gold and bronze so that he was clad in fire. Perhaps I was just viewing him afresh through Priam's eyes,
and the illusion was momentary, for his face drained of color
as the massive old man advanced.

Automedon sprang up to honor the visitor, obviously not
comprehending who he was. Moving stiffly but with royal
dignity, Priam knelt before Achilles and clasped his knees.
Achilles stared down at his white head, dumbfounded, not
reacting even when the old man took each of his hands in
turn and brought it to his lips. Then Priam looked up with
grief-filled eyes and spoke in a rumbling, broken voice that
roused warlike echoes from the weapons on the walls.

"Son of Peleus, I have brought great ransom to offer for
the body of my boy. Many fine sons I had, and all the best
of them are dead now, most of them slain by these hands of
yours. I have kissed those hands—what father has ever done
as much? Hector was the finest of my sons. If you cannot
pity me in my sorrow, then I beg you to think of your own
father, who is of an age with me. Think of his grieving as he
sits uneasy in far-off Thessaly, worrying night and day what
fate may overtake you here at Troy."

Achilles licked his lips, still shocked. "For a moment,
there . . . As you came in, I thought you *were* my father!"

"He is more fortunate than I, for he can still hope for your
safe return, while I have watched my flowers cut down
under my walls. Oh, son of Peleus, give me back Hector, I
beg of you! Give him back that we may award him rites befitting the great warrior he was and send his shade in peace
across the river."

"You came yourself! I did not expect . . . That needed no
small courage, my lord!"

Then Achilles seemed to shake himself awake. He took

the king's hands and, rising, lifted him to his feet. Priam straightened and they gazed into each other's eyes: the ancient, eroded warrior of former days—fearfully vulnerable and yet unbowed—and the virile young killer who had slain so many of his sons; the king who had ruled so great a realm and the juvenile warrior who had come blazing across the seas to smash it. There was not a finger's width between them in height. In breathless silence they studied each other, and then Achilles' face crumpled in pain. With a muffled sob, he clasped his arms around Priam and embraced him. Whether he was thinking of Peleus or Patroclus or even perhaps of Hector, I did not know, but I suddenly began to shake with the release of tension. There would be no bloodshed now. This embassy was not destined for miserable failure like the last one to plead in the lodge. Priam had come in person; Agamemnon had not.

Only Priam's face was visible to me. His eyes were tightly closed, but his cheeks glistened wetly in the firelight. When the two men stepped apart, I saw that Achilles had been weeping also, and I remembered the old king saying that great warriors must be passionate men.

Abashed, Achilles wiped his eyes with a knuckle. "Truly, the gods are fickle, my lord. To you and to my father both, they gave many great gifts: wide realms to rule, uncounted warriors to lead, untold wealth. But to him they allowed only one son, who will never return to console and defend him in his frail old age. You were blessed with many sons and have lived to see them die. Which fate is more cruel? I do not know, my lord. I see only that we must accept the portion the gods send down to us and bear it with all the courage we can find, for courage is our only recourse. Our ends are spun when we are born. I cannot return your living son to you, but I will give up his body for fitting burial. Automedon, bring a chair for our guest."

"First let me see my son!"

Priam's demand almost broke the spell. Achilles' face flamed. "Sit, old man! You will see him when he is ready to be seen. Until then, you stay here and do not provoke me."

Flinching, Priam took the chair Automedon placed for

him. Achilles gave him a final glare and then strode out of
the megaron, beckoning the rest of us to follow.

"Where is it?" he demanded.

" 'Round the back, my lord," said Alcimus.

Around to the back we trooped, where we found old
Idiaos still hunched on the cart, shivering piteously. Achilles
told Alcimus to take him inside and let him warm up, then
he began struggling with the ropes that held the cover. Eriphyle and Automedon and I gathered around to help.

"There's plenty of it, certainly!" he muttered. But when
he hauled the leather off, he growled deep in his throat.
"What folly is this? Blankets? Old clothes? Am I a village
bride that he seeks to delight me with such trash?"

"No, no, my lord!" I cried. "Take them into the light and
see! I chose them myself. They are fabulous weavings, rich
cloaks, fine mantles—soft rugs emblazoned with heroic
scenes, my lord! All men will marvel when they adorn your
father's hall. I have never seen their like. There are gold bars
underneath."

Achilles groaned and leaned on the heap, embracing it
with outspread arms and resting his face on it. Automedon
and I exchanged worried glances. We waited, shivering in
the north's cold breath.

"Briseis," Achilles said without raising his head, "you
bring me these gifts to tempt me from my sworn path. I gave
Patroclus's shade my oath that I would never surrender the
body of his killer. How can I do this now? Tell me!"

"Fabrics will burn. Give Patroclus his share and he will
not mind."

After a moment he sighed. "Aye, I can do that. Come
then." He straightened and with a grunt lifted a huge pile in
his arms. "Let us take them in. Briseis, make the corpse presentable."

Washing corpses is women's work and I was his woman,
so who else would he turn to? He strode off with his load.
Automedon followed, equally laden.

Teeth chattering in the wind, I looked to Eriphyle. "The
more help the better."

She said, "Yes," with little enthusiasm.

"Go and round them up, then. None too near their term or suckling."

"They will all be in bed!"

I laughed, and the sound was shriller than I expected. "Bring them anyway. If a man is busy, let him finish what he's doing of course. I'll get torches, water . . ."

"Perfumes?"

"Definitely perfumes," I agreed.

Perhaps the gods had sent that bitter weather to preserve Hector's body, for it was not as rotted and bloated as I had feared it might be. It also bore a pungent fragrance of pine like the extract we used to purify latrines. While that could not completely mask the odor of decay, it had deterred the camp dogs from scavenging the flesh, and I surmised that some of the Trojan women had been tending the corpse in secret. Eriphyle returned with six or seven helpers, and we took turns at the work, grateful for the darkness that concealed what we were doing. I had washed Hector son of Priam once before, in Lyrnessos, but I could not relate my memories of the pompous young prince to that inanimate lump of bad meat. We doused it thoroughly in scented oils, wrapped it in rich weavings, and then bore it over to the mule cart for its journey home. We had done the best we could, and I dismissed the women with my thanks.

By the time Eriphyle and I had cleaned up and returned to the lodge, Achilles and Priam were eating a ceremonial meal together, being served roast lamb by Automedon while Alcimus stood guard outside to stave off any unexpected visitors. In a dark corner, old Idiaos doggedly chomped his few remaining teeth on what might be his last good meal.

Host and guest were trying to conduct a seemly conversation and having great trouble finding safe topics. Time and again the talk would die away, leaving them staring at each other with wonder and disbelief—and perhaps some mutual admiration. Gold bars had been stacked beside the hearth; every chair and table in the hall was draped with choice textiles. Studying Achilles carefully, I began to hope that the flames of his anger had at last burned out. I could tell that he was well pleased with the riches the night had brought and the joyful knowledge that Agamemnon would lay no hands on them. If the removal of Hector's body would not stem his grief, then nothing would.

The fire collapsed gradually into embers and ash, and he did not order it stoked. My eyelids kept sagging.

"Briseis!"

I jumped. "My lord?"

"Prepare beds in the porch for our guest and his servant. They are weary and will want to make an early start."

Eriphyle and I gathered up blankets and fleeces and trooped out.

"There isn't room for a pair of cats, let alone those two!" she whispered, looking around at all the pots and boxes and cauldrons.

Alcimus stepped in from his watch, his flaxen hair glowing under the stars. "I don't think you need do much," he said, sounding quite pleasant for once. He was well satisfied with his night's work.

"If you would be so gracious as to move those chests, my lord," I wheedled, "then we could spread these cloths on them. I imagine that will do?"

"They can't sleep on those!" Eriphyle protested, as Alcimus began demonstrating his brawn.

"They aren't going to. My father once told me that the reason guests sleep in porches is so they can make a fast getaway. Isn't that right, son of Polyctor?"

He chuckled. "They know they must be gone before dawn. That's my job."

So it was done, and we put down only token bedding. Achilles brought out the two men, discussing with Priam the terms of a truce for the Trojans to collect and burn their dead.

Eriphyle and I withdrew to the interior to help Automedon clean up after the meal and restore some sort of order. More than ever, the hall now resembled a treasure chamber and the problem of finding enough room to sleep was as bad there as it had been in the porch. We cleared places on either side of the hearth and heaped them with gaudy Trojan rugs and fleecy blankets.

I was kneeling to arrange them when the door thumped shut. Achilles stood there for a moment and then advanced into the fading glow of the fire. I rose to my feet, conscious of my heartbeat. He looked around, surveying the litter of loot the night had added to his wealth, then put his hands on his hips and stared at me. I could not tell whether he was about to strike me or throw himself at my feet and weep, or anything in between.

"Did I do wrong?" I demanded bravely.

"You are a madwoman, Briseis!"

My pulse quickened at his smile—not quite his old smile, but close!

"My lord was angry with me, I heard."

"I was *furious*! I thought the Trojans would keep you. I was afraid I had lost you."

"Oh." Encouraging! "A slave wouldn't fetch much ransom."

Eriphyle, bless her, pulled Automedon down on their bedding and began distracting him, which she never found difficult.

Achilles shook his head. "A live slave is worth more than a dead prince, much more. Or is to me." While not as inarticulate as Mynes, he had never been a man overflowing with tender words—action was his specialty—but even he knew that this was a time for words. He was doing his best.

I wanted better. I felt I had earned it. He had given me away, refused to accept me back, and then when he did get me back, he had spurned me.

I folded my arms. "I am relieved to hear you prefer me to a corpse, my lord. On the other hand, if slave and corpse are both left to lie around doing nothing, there cannot be much to choose between them."

He took a step closer. "I have been neglecting you."

"You have."

"I am sorry. I let my grief blind me." He unpinned his chiton, but I made no move to help him. "Alas, Briseis, had I been given a choice between you and Patroclus, I would have chosen him, so perhaps it is as well that the gods do not offer us such choices. It was only today, when I feared I might have lost both of you, that I—" he drew a long breath "—that I realized . . . that I saw that if the gods are to cut my life so short, then I should seek to enjoy what is left to me. I realized how much you mean to me." He looked at me wistfully, like a small boy seeking his mother's forgiveness.

"Tell me about that."

"I'd do better at showing you. See?"

"Showing lust and showing love are hard to tell apart."

His lip crooked in a smile, producing those absurd dimples. "Oh, that's mostly a matter of timing, isn't it? If I promise to go very, very slowly?"

Automedon and Eriphyle were going very, very fast to show that they weren't listening. My nipples had begun to tingle.

"You can't even give me a hint?"

"If the Trojans had demanded Agamemnon as your ransom, I would have delivered him in chains."

"I suppose that's flattering, although I never suspected you of loving the son of Atreus. So you got me back for nothing. Tell me exactly what you are going to do about it."

"This." For so huge a man, he could move very fast. He had not kissed me since the night on the beach, but he tried to make up for that in one overwhelming embrace. In no time his crushing strength around my ribs, the intoxicating taste of his mouth, the sheer heat of his passion, melted my anger and made my head spin. Memory plays tricks. It seems in retrospect that the one devastating kiss continued without interruption while he tore off my clothes and eased me down to the bedding, entered me, urged me to agonies of rapture, and eventually followed me into release. Only when he lay sprawled upon me in limp exhaustion did our lips part, and by then I was already clawing at him, eager for more. Priam must have been back in Troy before we let each other sleep.

12

Now summer came dancing back to the Troad. Achilles was up at dawn, spreading word of the truce he had granted the Trojans—news that raised some eyebrows and much speculation but was universally welcome. Now the dead would be buried and the war soon resume, so the army rejoiced. Greek ships beached under the city walls. Greek guards watched and jeered as Trojan work parties cut firewood and gathered corpses, while any man who tried to escape was run down, brutally beaten, and returned to the city to eat up his share of the supplies. Troy was doomed and everyone knew it.

So was Achilles. Everyone knew that, too. I alone would not accept the prophecy my tongue had spoken. As I bathed him that evening, I made a determined effort to persuade him to leave. Automedon was off herding Trojans, so we had the lodge to ourselves.

"The gods promised you glory. And they have given it. You have won the war. Troy must fall. You can go home now."

He regarded me with eyes as blue and dangerous as the sea. He was not quite the old Achilles, for his ribs were more visible than they had been, and spiky tufts stuck up from his scalp where he had cut off locks to lay on Patroclus's bier. But the wound on his forearm was healing cleanly and his manhood was already demonstrating that the curse had been lifted. "Cheat? Try to escape my side of the bargain?"

I wrung out the sponge, trying to meet that spear-like stare. "They may have relented."

"Then they will let me go home in good time. But I don't believe that. Do you?" His hand closed around my arm.

"Athena favors you above all men."

"I could not have slain Hector without her aid."

"Then why should she withdraw her favor now?"

"Because I run away, perhaps?" His smile grew wistful, as if death were an embarrassing weakness. "Hector's death doomed Troy. Other gods will want vengeance for it—Apollo certainly, who stands on the crest of Pergamon. Zeus must decide, and he has told us how he will choose." He went on before I could argue. "Besides, if there is still a way to save the mash, Agamemnon would find it. No, my love, I stay here, fighting while I can and dying when I must. I won't run like Hector."

"You asked Odysseus what use a dead man had for a woman. What use does a woman have for a dead man? What happens to me if you die?"

He dragged me onto his lap and hugged me until I could hardly breathe. "I don't know, dearest," he said sadly, his chin resting on my head. "You and Peleus son of Aeacus—you both need me. I have thought about this long and hard, and all I know is that there is no second best to glory. I must strive and the gods will judge. They set the price and I must pay, even if that price be early death. I sent Patroclus to fight and did not go with him, so he died, and that weighs strangely on my heart. I will not shirk again. I am Achilles and will not be less."

I braced myself to tell him how Antenor and Aeneas would make his task so much easier, but he was through with serious talk.

"Short life makes pleasure precious, yes?" He slid the wet sponge inside my chiton to make me squeal. In moments he had me as naked as he was, wrestling on the floor.

Trojans cut firewood and the Greeks built ladders. When they weren't making ladders, they were sharpening their weapons. In a way those were happy days for me, restored to my lover and my lover restored to me. The nights were even happier, because Achilles, having decided that life should be enjoyed, pursued this end with all his customary single-mindedness and the endurance of a bronze goat.

Yet Patroclus's death was an unhealed wound. When he was restless, I would do what I could to soothe him. Even in the middle of the night, if he awoke to stare at the darkness and brood upon his coming fate, his very stillness would waken me. Then I would reach out to him, and he would respond desperately. When Aphrodite departed, she would send Sleep, the greatest comforter of all.

Wary of unleashing his terrible rage, I procrastinated until the very last day of the truce to mention Antenor's offer, and then I told it to Achilles, because to go first to Odysseus seemed disloyal. Even that blunder might not have mattered had I not topped it with another.

All the leaders had been tearily busy since dawn preparing for the morrow's assault, and when at evening Achilles stalked up to the lodge in search of comfort, he was in a testy humor, hungry, dust caked, and hoarse. I watched him come, for I loved to see his scowl break into a lover's smile at the sight of me. I returned his hug, then restrained him when he would have gone inside, for Automedon and Eriphyle were in there.

"Look!" I said, and pointed to the grim citadel across the bay, glimmering like a wraith against an indigo sky.

"What of it? I hate it."

"So do I. Let it burn! Can you topple its towers and throw down its gates, son of Peleus? Because I can."

He folded his great arms. "What visions are you seeing now, Briseis?"

I drew a deep breath and spilled it all out as fast as I could. "The priestess of Athena in Troy is the wife of Antenor. When I went to honor the goddess, she begged my help and made me promise to bring you this message. Tell Achilles, she said, that if he will swear to give us safe conduct, we will open a gate for him by night. Fifty to go free—some men, some women, many children. None of the House of Priam except one daughter."

Achilles' face had darkened like the evening sky. "War is men's work!"

"Athena's work, and I was given this message in her shrine. The sign will be to build an altar to Poseidon outside the city, but where it can be clearly seen from the walls. You must build a great horse, symbol of the Earthshaker, and that

will be your pledge that you agree and will let them pass.
Two nights after you consecrate it, Antenor will open the
postern by the eastern tower. Let them out, then you go in,
and Troy is yours."

"Treachery?" he muttered, but he was tempted—I could
see it, although indecision was unfamiliar territory to him.
"Where is the glory in winning a city by treason?"

"How many more Greeks must die if you do not?" And he
among them. "How many months must you wait? How soon
will Agamemnon return to the field to steal your triumph?
Take it, son of Peleus, take it!"

He snarled at the distant citadel. "Why didn't you tell me
this sooner? Why two nights? Why Poseidon?"

"It will take them two nights to pack the watch with loyal
followers. And Aeneas said that Poseidon—"

There was my second mistake.

"Oh?" Achilles said. "The son of Anchises? Your cousin
is part of this, is he? He escaped me at Lyrnessos. He escaped at Pedasos and on Scamander's banks too. And now
he hopes to escape from me again? Three times but never
four. It is undoubtedly a trap, a foul plot to deceive you and
kill our best warriors."

"They swore before Athena—"

"No!" roared the son of Peleus. "Where is the glory in it?
After so many brave men have died in honor, I will not be
known as the trickster who took Troy by cheating!" His eyes
flamed with fury, his great hands grabbed my shoulders as if
ready to shake me. "I will not shame the brave men who are
prepared to die defending their city by killing them in their
beds. Speak no more of perfidy—not to me nor anyone else,
Briseis!"

Oh, folly! Cringing, I promised.

"Tomorrow we will batter down the gates." He released
me and walked into the lodge.

He was never malicious. Having rejected my interference, he dismissed it from his mind, and that night his
lovemaking was a huge and shameless romp, full of
laughter and tickling and absurd gymnastics. He hardly

slept at all, and before first light he was off to war, eager
for battle.

I moped all morning, staring across the bay at the citadel
just too far off for me to make out what was happening.
Once in a while a ship would go or come, but the only news
that reached us was that the fighting was fierce. About noon
the herald Eurybates came to the lodge to tell me that
Agamemnon wanted me, although he could not say why.

"Perhaps his wound has sickened again," I suggested, "or
he wishes to consult a seer? To interpret a dream?"

I dared not refuse the summons, however uneasy it made
me. I felt even more perturbed when Eurybates led me directly to the Great King's sleeping quarters. It must be a
medical problem. His wound had opened. But, as I paused
on the threshold to remove my shoes, the sights and smells
of the hut brought back memories of that one degrading
night I had spent there, and suddenly I remembered how I
had prophesied then. I had *pretended* to prophesy. My words
to Achilles on the beach had been a misunderstanding, but I
had told Agamemnon that the gods would give him Troy
without Achilles' aid, and I had known I was lying when I
said it.

He slammed the door on the sunshine, gripped my head in
both hands, and pressed a slobbering kiss on my mouth.
Right away I knew what had happened. He was obviously
up, more *up* than I had ever seen him. Drooling with excitement, he gripped my arm and hastened me over to the bed.
He would not dare this outrage if Achilles lived.

I should have been flattered that his first act on hearing
the news had been to steal me back, but the truth is that I
was too shocked to care. I offered no resistance when he
ripped my clothes from me and threw me down. I endured
in silence as he nibbled and pinched and prodded, trying
to win some reaction, even a cry of pain. I said nothing
when he climbed on top and impaled me. Mute I endured
his battering.

I knew that gods were present. There on that bed I had
forsworn them and there they began my torment. Three
times I had mocked them—on the beach with Achilles, on

that bed to Agamemnon, and a third time when Achilles had questioned me. I had not denied my false prophecy. Three times but never four . . .

They punished my false prophecies by making them come true. Achilles had won glory and died young for it, as I had predicted, and now Agamemnon would take Troy without his help.

When the Great King had obtained satisfaction and rolled off me, sweating and gasping, I began to laugh.

He roared. "You find this humorous? You are mine now, woman. The son of Peleus is dead!"

I sat up and spat at him. "And so are you! Know you not a curse when you see one? Every man who has ever lusted after me is dead now, except you, son of Atreus. You will not long survive."

EPILOGUE

The fire had burned out and the crone fallen silent. The storm was only a memory. Somewhere a bird sang, and the first smoky tendrils of dawn peered through chinks in the ruin. Cold and stiff, I eased my aching back. If a youth had suffered so much in the long listening, I wondered how her ancient voice had endured the telling.

"Was he wounded in the heel?"

"Who?"

"Achilles. That was supposed to be the only mortal part of him."

She coughed hoarsely. "Arr! You have been listening to the bards. Have I not been telling you he was all mortal? He was fighting before the Scaian Gate with his back to the Great Tower of Ilium. An arrow took him in the leg, behind his greave. Paris claimed credit. Why would any man boast of such a deed? Aye, it was vengeful Apollo guided the shaft. Achilles was not badly hurt, but he fell and the Trojans rained down missiles and arrows on him. They sent men over the walls, and a major battle developed above him. By the time Ajax carried him out of the fray, his life had drained away from many wounds."

"What of the fall of Troy?"

"What of it?" she croaked. "Odysseus knew of Antenor's offer. Whether he learned it from Achilles or some other source, I never asked. The Greeks worried it around and around in council and then decided to accept. They built a fine wooden horse, dedicating it to Poseidon with sacrifices of many mares, and two nights later the traitors opened the postern gate by the eastern tower. Antenor and Aeneas were allowed to depart with their families and the Greeks entered. Blood and fire and pain."

"So your auguries were fulfilled again?" She ranked herself with Delphi or Dodona. "Did Aeneas sail to the west?"

"Arr! How can I know? I heard once that Antenor did, but

no bard ever sang of the doings of Aeneas. He never did anything worth remembering. Go, little boy, and let me sleep."
She was a shapeless heap in the shadows, huddled on her
blanket.

I should indeed be on my way, before evil stirred in the
ruins on the hill. I stretched my arms and yawned. "I need
the end of the tale. Agamemnon brought you here to Mycenae?"

"Aye," she said impatiently, "and in the same ship as Cassandra, as she foretold. Me and many others, to wash nobles
in their baths or hoe for them in their fields. Or be hoed by
them in their beds. Bear and raise their bastards—many a
Hector or Antenor now thinks of himself as a good Greek,
not knowing his grandmother or her mother hailed from the
Troad."

"And did you witness Agamemnon's murder?"

The old woman sighed. "Nay. Wish I had, but Cassandra
tended him in his bath that night. She died with him."

"Well, that is as I have heard," I conceded, rising to stoop
under the ruined ceiling. "But much of what you have babbled this night jams in my ears, Grandmother. Omens? Great
heroes copulating like cats? The bards do not describe the
wooden horse as you do."

"Then you must choose between truth and art. Truth is
usually safer. Begone!"

"I trust the bards who sing the words of the Muses—they
are certainly more melodious words than yours. But your
tale passed the night, and I thank you for your hospitality."

I thought she was not going to speak again, but then she
muttered, "Remember to take your guest gifts: a rich cloak,
a silver rhyton, a stool fine-inlaid with ivory."

"I shall send my host leader to collect them," I said. "May
the gods preserve you."

"They have preserved me too long already."

I paused in my crouch before the entrance hole. "Life can
never be too long, only too unpleasant. One last question,
Briseis, if that is indeed your name and not just another fig-
ment of your fancies. You most foully slandered many great
heroes in your maundering, and Achilles not the least. I fear

his shade howls most pitifully in Hades' halls at your un-
truths. Well, as you fear the gods at all, old crone, answer me
this: If Zeus in his wisdom had granted you one of those
great warriors to be your life's mate—if you could have
been wife to one of them all these long days, raised him a
whole tribe of sons and grandsons, grown old at his side
even until now—tell me which you would have chosen."

Her breathing rasped a few times before she muttered,
"Why even ask? The son of Peleus, of course."

"Truly? It seemed to my ears that you loved the hope of
sharing his throne more than the man himself." Receiving no
answer, I tried again. "Which one do you mourn the most,
woman?"

"Achilles!" she croaked. "Isn't that what I have been
telling you all night?"

"It was what you were saying, grandmother, but it may
not be what I heard!" Chuckling at her stubbornness, I
crawled out from her burrow into a fresh dawn and drew a
deep breath of sweet new air. Nothing stirred among the
shattered ruins of Mycenae. Musing on the strange lies she
had told me, I strode off on the long road to Athens.

But when Briseis, gorgeous
As sweet Aphrodite the golden, saw Patroclus
Gashed and torn with the mangling bronze, she flung
Herself on him and shrieked in her grief, and with her hands
She tore at her breasts and soft neck and beautiful face.
Wailing, the woman lovely as a goddess cried:
  "Patroclus, most precious to my wretched heart, I left you
Alive when I went from this lodge, but now, O leader
Of many, I come back to find you lying here dead.
Thus misery continues to follow misery for me.
The husband to whom my father and queenly mother
Gave me I saw lying dead before our city,
Gashed with the mangling bronze, and my three precious brothers,
All sons of the mother who bore me, were likewise all
Overtaken by their day of doom. But you, when Achilles
Killed my husband and leveled Mynes' city,
You wouldn't allow me to grieve, but comforted me
With the promise that you would have great Achilles make me
His lawful wife, and have him take me to Phthia
In one of his ships and joyfully celebrate there
With a wedding feast mid the Myrmidons. Hence I weep
For your death without ceasing, for you the forever gentle."

—Homer, *The Iliad*, XIX,
translated by Ennis Recs

POSTSCRIPT

The first cities of Europe were built in Greece during the Bronze Age, and the greatest of them was Mycenae, whose massive ruins still impress. The people spoke and wrote an early form of Greek. Theirs was a militaristic, slave-owning society rigidly controlled by palace bureaucracies—the inspiration for Sphelos, of course. They traded as far away as Sicily and Egypt, and they were certainly present in Anatolia, modern Turkey. We know nothing of their politics or why Mycenae was so important. The enduring legend that its king led a Panhellenic expedition to besiege and sack Troy is not supported by any physical or historical evidence. There is no evidence against it, either.

Troy today is not impressive if you expect a great city. All that remains are ruins of a fortress, a stronghold that was founded in the Stone Age and inhabited with hardly a break for three thousand years, into Christian times. Archaeologists distinguish forty-six layers of occupation. Its Bronze Age inhabitants traded with Greece, but they probably spoke Luwian, an Anatolian language.

Warfare was dominated by the chariot, the nuclear missile of its day, although we do not know how it was used. Achilles and Patroclus are archetypes of the warrior prince and his faithful driver, a deadly partnership that overran the known world from Europe to India in a chariot blitzkrieg about 1600 B.C.E. Their descendants and imitators founded elite military castes that were to rule for the next four centuries. The princes buried in the shaft graves of Mycenae were taller than males of the general population. Whether this was due to race or better nutrition is unknown, but the tradition that a hero had to be big persisted until Homer's day. We are not free of it yet. In modern elections the tallest candidate usually wins.

The cause of the sudden collapse of the Roman Empire sixteen hundred years ago has been a puzzle ever since, but

sixteen hundred years before that a similar calamity ended
Bronze Age civilization. It swept through Greece, Crete,
Turkey, and Syria, apparently in a very short time. The
palaces burned; many of their sites were never reoccupied.
Only Egypt survived. The pharaoh Ramses III turned back
an invasion by "People of the Sea," who may have been the
cause of the disaster or refugees fleeing it.

A dark age ensued, and virtually nothing is known of
events for the next five centuries. About 700 B.C.E. the first
glimmers of history appear with the introduction of writing,
a murky dawn that reveals Greek-speaking peoples settled
on the western coast and offshore islands of Turkey, having
brought with them from their Greek homeland the legends
of that long-ago Trojan war—which they may have used to
justify their own conquests. It was there and then, or a little
earlier, that Homer wove the best of the myths into the *Iliad*
and *Odyssey*. Of Homer himself we know absolutely nothing except that he was illiterate and at least the equal of
Shakespeare or Dante. All the great art, philosophy, and civilization we think of as Greek were still to come. Alexander
the Great was born in 356 B.C.E., so Achilles was as remote
to him as William the Conqueror is to us.

Homer undoubtedly blended many strands of tradition,
and five hundred years of oral transmission had contami-
nated his material with Dark Age customs. Thus he mentions iron tools and Phoenician traders, neither of which
belong. He has the god Hephaestus working bronze as if it
were iron. He is sadly wrong about the Mycenaeans'
weapons, religious beliefs, and funeral customs; he underes-
timates the wealth of the palaces, sends a princess out to the
stream to wash clothes, and has the Great King of Mycenae
stripping the armor off his fallen foes. I don't say Agamemnon would have spurned the loot, but to collect it himself in
the middle of a battle shows the mind-set of a village
brawler. Homer also used his own imagination, of course.
When he described robots in Hephaestus' workshop on
Olympus, he was inventing science fiction.

Epic poetry is capable of astonishing feats of folk memory, but historical accuracy is not its strength. The history in

Le Morte d'Arthur, *Beowulf*, the *Nibelungenlied*, or the *Chanson de Roland*, has been grossly distorted. Troy, like Camelot, rolled down the centuries gathering up all the best stories. The ancient Celtic hero Tristan was coopted to Arthur's court and given a seat at the Round Table. Homer's Ajax is a wonderful character but archaeologists insist that his tower shield is centuries out of date.

Diomedes, too, was drafted to Troy—a great hero, one of the Seven Against Thebes, king of Tiryns. But Tiryns is only an hour by fast chariot from Mycenae, where Agamemnon ruled, and although Homer tries to divide the Argolid between them, it is not big enough for both. I assume that Diomedes lived several generations earlier and was hijacked by Homer or one of his predecessors. Nestor likewise. The garrulous Gerenian horseman is Homer's favorite character after Odysseus; he explains a lot but never *does* much. I am personally convinced that Nestor belonged to an earlier era and Homer himself put him into the story, having the grace to make him a very old man.

The piracy is quite obvious in the case of Sarpedon, a hero from Lycia, in southern Turkey, who was probably brought to Troy mostly to be an impressive conquest for Patroclus. His earlier duel with Tlepolemos of Rhodes sounds like a rerun of a famous local quarrel, but his tomb must have been a revered landmark in Lycia, because as soon as the poor fellow is dead, Homer has Apollo carry his corpse home again. Achilles and Agamemnon may well have been real people. I'm not convinced they ever met.

Nevertheless there are many nuggets of authentic Mycenaean lore in the poems. The palace accounts in Pylos mention aristocrats called followers, with chariots and special cloaks, probably tasseled. Boar's tusk helmets are important in Mycenaean art, obviously a symbol of status. Here are the samurai, the warrior caste. When Odysseus quells the riot in Book II of the *Iliad*, Homer has him make a clear distinction between the gentry and the riffraff. When Priam is accosted by Hermes, the old man is terrified until he hears the young stranger speak and recognizes a gentleman's accent. In Book VIII Agamemnon rallies his troops by waving his red cloak.

I have no authority for assuming that the followers' mantles bore insignia like medieval coats of arms, but Mycenaeans did use regional symbols on their sealstones—lions for Mycenae, a bull for Crete among others. I have no evidence for a formal oath of knighthood, but there must have been an agreed code of conduct to explain Achilles' fury when Agamemnon broke it.

I did not invent the bathtub. When Odysseus's son Telemachus visits King Nestor back home in Pylos and is bathed by the beautiful Princess Polycaste, he emerges "looking like a god." In Homer's day a god was depicted as a young man wearing nothing except a cryptic smirk that made you wonder what he'd been up to. Excavations at Pylos found the bath itself and the bench Nestor sat on, and palace records which, although they do not mention the fair Polycaste, do list thirty-seven female bath attendants and their twenty-eight children. You really think those thirty-seven spent all their days gathering firewood? In other legends, King Aegeus of Athens, stopping in at Troezen on his way home from Delphi, fathered the hero Theseus on Princess Aethra with her father's connivance. Life was short in those days. Anything that increased the birthrate would have been acceptable, and a ruling elite that shunned intermarriage with lower castes would welcome periodic infusions of "noble" blood. Of course the custom would have been sanctified as a religious duty to silence any protests from the girls. Remember that the god of hospitality was Zeus, the worst lecher of them all.

Mycenaean women seem to have been relatively liberated. They certainly drove chariots, and priestesses owned land. Inheritance in the female line is implicit in many of the legends, although the idea would have astonished Homer and appalled the men of Periclean Athens. It explains why the suitors were so keen to marry Penelope and why neither Odysseus's son nor father was king in his absence. When Troy fell and Menelaus got his hands on Helen, he took her home to Sparta to be queen again instead of wringing her neck as one might expect.

Contrary to Homer, the Mycenaeans buried their dead and

believed in an afterlife, or they would not have provided grave goods. They worshiped all the gods of Classical times—except possibly Apollo, who may have been a Trojan import—plus others, mostly goddesses. What the people actually believed and how they worshiped are unknown. My efforts to fill in the gaps are based on a scattering of evidence and much guesswork.

Lyrnessos has not been found. I based Briseus's palace on excavations at Pylos, although there was probably nothing so grand in the Troad except Troy itself. What Homer calls a city may have been no more than a hamlet. His numbers for Agamemnon's fleet and army also seem far too large, although critics in Classical times considered them far too small.

Archaeologists have concluded that level VI.h at Troy best fits Homer's description and was destroyed at about the right date, but possibly by an earthquake. It was rebuilt as a meaner, dingier Troy VII.a, and soon sacked by someone— Mycenaeans? Peoples of the Sea? Or were they one and the same? Archaeology tells us that the terminal disaster came soon after the fall of Troy, and the legends say most of the heroes ran into trouble when they got home.

What overthrew their world so suddenly? Here is one theory, but remember you read it in a work of fiction. We know that their primitive agriculture degraded the soil and evidence at Pylos suggests new land was being cleared just before the fall. This would not be the last time in human history that governments took firm steps to make things worse. Poorer land required more slaves to work it and hence brought more war and more mouths to feed. The food stores were in the palaces, so when famine struck the nearest palace went up in a local Bastille Day. Breakdown in law and order brought less output and more famine, so the next raid was directed against the palace next door. Defense became an obsession, consuming more and more of the economy and creating the megalomaniacal walls of Tiryns and Mycenae. In our time we have seen the infinitely greater and more complex U.S.S.R. collapse in a few months.

Life in the Bronze Age was undoubtedly short and brutish

and to us would seem very nasty indeed, but it must have had its heroes and lovers, triumphs and tragedies, joys and sorrows. They were people like us, however strange we find their customs and beliefs. Homer, creating epic poetry, gives them grandeur. Laboring in a more realistic medium, I shall be content if I have made them seem human.

FURTHER READING

Homer, *The Iliad*, and *The Odyssey*.
New translations continue to appear. A good introduction and a glossary are valuable additions to the text.

Chadwick, John, *The Mycenaean World*, Cambridge University Press, 1976.

Drews, Robert, *The Coming of the Greeks: Indo-European Conquests in the Aegean and the Near East*, Princeton University Press, 1988.

———— *The End of the Bronze Age: Changes in Warfare and the Catastrophe ca. 1200 B.C.*, Princeton University Press, 1993.

Willcock, Malcom M., *A Companion to the Iliad*, The University of Chicago Press, 1976.

Wood, Michael, *In Search of the Trojan War*, British Broadcasting Corporation, 1985.

PEOPLE AND PLACES

There are several ways to transcribe Greek names into English. I put clarity and familiarity ahead of consistency. Names shown in *italics* can be found in Homer.

Achilles, leader of the Myrmidons, son of King Peleus of Thessaly

Abydos, town in the Troad, modern Canakkale

Actaeon, legendary hunter eaten by his own dogs for spying on Artemis

Adrestos, former king of Hire

Adramyttion, gulf south of the Troad, modern Edremit

Aegisthus, Clytemnestra's lover who slew Agamemnon

Aeneas son of Anchises, a Trojan hero and ally, leader of the Dardanians. Homer relates how he was saved from Achilles by Poseidon. Virgil's *Aeneid* tells how he survived the war and fled with his followers to Italy, where his descendants founded Rome.

Aesacus son of Priam, a seer. Although not mentioned by Homer, he is known from other sources.

Agamemnon son of Atreus, king of Mycenae, Great King of the Greeks

Ajax son of Telamon ("the Greater Ajax"), Greek hero, king of Salamis

Ajax son of Oileus ("the Lesser Ajax"), Greek hero, leader of the Lokrians

Akamas son of Antenor, Aeneas's charioteer. Homer tells how he was slain by Meriones.

Alcandre, wife of King Altes of Pedasos

Alcathous son of Aisyetes, king of the Dardanians. Homer relates how he was slain by Idomeneus.

Alcimus son of Polyctor, a young Myrmidon, Patroclus's charioteer

Alcmene, a woman in the palace of Lyrnessos, friend of Queen Nemertes

Alexandra, Automedon's concubine

Alkimedon son of Laërkes, Myrmidon, follower of Achilles

Altes son of Molion, king of Pedasos

Amphidora, bath girl at Lyrnessos

Amphimedes, master of bees at Lyrnessos

Amphitrite, slave girl at Lyrnessos

Anchialus, Greek casualty listed by Ajax

Anchises son of Capys, father of Aeneas. According to Virgil, he survived the sack of Troy and died in Sicily.

Andromache, wife of Hector

Antenor, a Trojan counselor, one of the anti-Helen party. Homer tells little of him, but other sources report that he and his family survived the sack of Troy, and he has long been suspected of betraying the city.

Anticleia, a woman in the palace of Lyrnessos, friend of Queen Nemertes

Antilokos son of Nestor, a knight from Pylos, friend of Achilles

Apaseusians, contingent of the Greek army

Aphrodite, goddess of love

Apollo son of Zeus and Leto, an Olympian, god of pestilence, prophesy, music, etc., but also patron god of Troy

Archer, the, Apollo as god of sickness

Archelochus, son of Antenor

Ares, god of war

Argives, inhabitants of the Argolid, the vicinity of Mycenae

Arkadians, contingent of the Greek army

Arkesilaos son of Promachos, a Boeotian captain

Artemis, goddess of beasts, the huntress

Ascanius son of Aeneas, a boy

Assaracus, legendary ancestor of Aeneas

Ate, goddess of folly

Athena, daughter of Zeus and chief Greek supporter among the gods

Atreus son of Pelops, father of Agamemnon and Menelaus

Aulis, a town in Greece where Agamemnon's host assembled.

Automedon son of Diores, a Myrmidon, Achilles' charioteer

Bakkhos, an Anatolian god identified with Dionysus

Bienor, Briseis's twin brother

Boeotians, a contingent of the Greek army

Boreas, the north wind

Briseis, wife of Mynes and queen of Lyrnessos, prize of Achilles

Briseus son of Mydon, Briseis's father, king of Lyrnessos

Caeneus, legendary hero mentioned by Nestor

Caïcus, river in Turkey, modern Bakir

Calchas son of Thestor, Greek seer

Carians, Trojan allies

Cassandra daughter of Priam, seeress and twin sister of Helenus

Chariseus, servant in the palace of Lyrnessos

Chloris, bath girl at Lyrnessos

Chryseis daughter of Chryses, wife of Pollis, Agamemnon's concubine

Chryses, Chryseis's father, a priest

Chthonia, goddess of the dead in Lyrnessos

Clytemnestra, wife of Agamemnon, who slew him after his return from Troy

Coön, son of Antenor

Cretans, contingent of the Greek army

Crethon son of Diokles, Greek casualty listed by Ajax

Cronos, father of Zeus

Ctesios, a Myrmidon

Ctimene, Briseis's slave

Daos, slave boy in Lyrnessos

Dardanos, legendary ancestor of both Hector and Aeneas; name giver to the Dardanelles

Delphi, site of oracle

Demeter, goddess of the Earth

Demodokos, bard in Lyrnessos

Demoleon, son of Antenor

Dictynna, an Aegean goddess sometimes identified as Artemis

Diomede, a slave woman, one of Achilles' captives

Diomedes son of Tydeus, king of Argos, Greek warrior

Dionysus, god of wine

Dodona, site of a famous oracle

Dryas, legendary hero mentioned by Nestor

Eëtion, king of Thebe

Elatos son of Altes, leader of the Lelegian host. Probably the Elatos of Pedasus Homer mentions as being slain by Agamemnon.

Elysium, abode of the blessed dead

Enispe, a town in Arcady, birthplace of Briseus

Enops, brother of Briseis

Enualios, god of war, either Ares himself or the son of Ares

Epistrophos son of Euneus, brother of Mynes

Erichthonius, legendary ancestor of Aeneas

Erinyes, the Furies who pursue the wicked

Eriphyle, slave woman given to Automedon

Eudoros grandson of Phylas, Myrmidon, follower of Achilles

Eumaeus, a cattle raider mentioned by Epistrophos

Euneus son of Selepus, father of Mynes and Epistrophos

Euneus son of Jason, brother of King Thoas of Lemnos

Eurybates, a Greek herald

Eurymedon son of Ptolemy, Agamemnon's charioteer

Eurypylos son of Euiamon, a Greek leader assisted by Patroclus

Exadius, legendary hero mentioned by Nestor

Gorgon, Briseis's dog

Griffin, Bienor's dog

Hades, the abode of the dead and also the king of it

Halizones, Trojan allies from the southern shore of the Black Sea

Hecamede, Nestor's concubine from Tenedos

Hector son of Priam, host leader of Troy

Hecuba, queen of Troy, wife of Priam

Helen, Menelaus's wife, whose abduction by Paris began the Trojan War

Helenus son of Priam, an augur

Helenus son of Oenops, Greek casualty listed by Ajax

Helios, the sun god

Hera, goddess, wife of Zeus

Heracles, legendary hero, god of strength

Hermes, god of travelers, commerce, and thieves. He conducted the souls of the dead to the realm of Hades.

Hermione, Helen's daughter

Hippodemia daughter of Anchises, queen of the Dardanians, a sister of Aeneas

Hippothoös son of Lethos, leader of the Pelasgian host. Homer tells how he was slain by Ajax.

Hippothoös son of Priam, a Trojan prince mentioned by Lykaon

Hire, a town in the Peloponnese, ruled by Euneus, although Homer does not say so

Ida, mountain above Lyrnessos, highest point in the Troad

Idiaos, Priam's herald

Idomeneus son of Deukalion, king of Crete

Ilium, alternative name for Troy

Imbros, an island, modern Gokçeada

Iphidamas, son of Antenor

Iphinoös son of Dexius, Greek casualty listed by Ajax

Iphis, Patroclus's concubine

Iris, messenger of the gods

Isos son of Priam. Homer tells how he was slain by Agamemnon.

Jocasta, mother and wife of Oedipus in older legends

Kikones, Trojan allies

Kilikes, tribe of the southeastern Troad, around Thebe

Klymene, one of Briseis's great-aunts

Knossos, city in Crete

Kopi, bath girl at Lyrnessos

Kreion, captain of the guard at Lyrnessos

Kyparisseeis, town in Pylos, possibly modern Kiparissía

Laodamas, son of Antenor

Laothoë daughter of Altes, wife of Priam, mother of Polydorus

Larisa, town in the Troad, possibly near the mouth of the Satniois River

Leda, former queen of Sparta, mother of Helen

Lede, mistress of textiles in Lyrnessos

Leleges, tribe of the southwestern Troad, around Pedasus

Lemnos, modern Limnos, an island west of the Troad, Greek ally

Lesbos, modern Lésvos, an island south of the Troad, Trojan ally, famous for the beauty of its women

Lethos son of Teutamos, king of Larisa

Leto, mother of Apollo and Artemis

Lokrians, Greek force led by the Lesser Ajax

Lycia, a country on the south coast of Asia Minor, opposite Rhodes (cf Lykia)

Lykaon son of Priam, grandson of Altes. Homer tells how he was captured by Achilles, sold into slavery on Lemnos, escaped home to Troy, and was killed by Achilles when they met again.

Lykia, a district in the eastern part of the Troad (cf Lycia)

Lyrnessos, a town near Troy sacked by Achilles, assumed to be close to the Hellenistic town of Antandros, modern Altinoluk.

Machaon son of Asclepius, king of Trikke, one of the Greek leaders

Maeonians, Trojan allies

Maera, old priestess in Lyrnessos

Megara, an aged handmaid to Queen Nemertes at Lyrnessos

Melantho, widow of the king of Larisa, now concubine of Menestheus

Melite, one of Briseis's great-aunts

Menelaus son of Atreus, Agamemnon's brother, king of Sparta

Menestheus, leader of the Athenians

Menesthius son of Areïthous, Greek casualty listed by Ajax

Menesthius son of Borus, Myrmidon, follower of Achilles, and Achilles' nephew

Mestor son of Priam, Trojan prince. Mentioned only in passing by Homer, but known from other sources to have died in the sack of Pedasos.

Methymna, town on Lesbos

Moirai, the Fates

Mycenae, Agamemnon's city in the Peloponnese, effectively the capital of Bronze Age Greece

Mynes son of Euneus, king of Lyrnessos, Briseis's husband

Myrmidons, the warriors of Thessaly, Achilles' men

Mysians, Trojan allies

Nemertes, mother of Briseis

Nestor son of Neleus, king of Pylos, an aged hero

Odysseus son of Laertes, king of Ithaca, Greek warrior

Oenomanus, Greek casualty listed by Ajax

Opous, birthplace of Patroclus

Oresbius, Greek casualty listed by Ajax

Orestes son of Agamemnon, revenged his father's death by killing his mother

Oros son of Ormenos, an Arcadian to whom Agamemnon gave Ctimene

Orsilochos son of Diokles, Greek casualty listed by Ajax

Paeones, Trojan allies

Palladium, a representation of Pallas Athena reputed to have been carved by the goddess herself

Pammon son of Priam

Panope, Briseis's name

Paphlagonians, Trojan allies

Paris son of Priam, his abduction of Helen began the Trojan War

Patroclus son of Menoitios, Achilles' companion

Pedasos, city ruled by Altes, sacked by Achilles, assumed to be modern Assos, where traces of Bronze Age ruins have been found.

Peisander son of Maemalus, Myrmidon, follower of Achilles

Pelasgians, a tribe of the southwestern Troad, around Larisa, Trojan allies. The name was used in other areas and may refer to pre-Greek aboriginals.

Peleus son of Aeacus, Achilles' father, king of Thessaly

Penelope, wife of Odysseus

Pergamon, the palace of Priam in Troy

Perimedes, Briseus' cupbearer

Perithous, legendary hero mentioned by Nestor

Pero, bath attendant at Lyrnessos

Persephone, goddess of the Underworld, wife of Hades

Perseus, legendary founder of Mycenae

Phaedre, a weaver in Lyrnessos

Philaios, Mynes' catamite in Lyrnessos

Philona, Queen Nemertes' personal slave at Lyrnessos

Phoebus, see Apollo

Phoenix son of Amyntor, Myrmidon leader, formerly Achilles' tutor

Phrygians, Trojan allies

Phthia, Achilles' home in Thessaly

Phylo, servant in the palace of Lyrnessos

Poias, smith at Lyrnessos

Pollis son of Eëtion, prince of Thebe, husband of Chryseis

Polydamma, bath girl at Lyrnessos

Polydorus son of Priam, grandson of Altes. Homer relates how he was slain by Achilles.

Polyphemous, legendary hero mentioned by Nestor

Ponteus, a slave in Lyrnessos

Potnia, ruling goddess of Lyrnessos. Potnia, "my lady," was later a term of respect addressed to women or goddesses, especially Athena, but in Mycenean times, Potnia was a generic term for the local goddess—"Our Lady of . . ."

Potnia Aphaea, aspect of Cretan goddess

Potnia Theron, aspect of Cretan goddess

Priam son of Laomedon, king of Troy

Pylaios son of Lethos, brother of Hippothoös

Pylos, Nestor's kingdom in Messina

Samothrace, an island northwest of the Troad; modern Samothráki

Sarpedon son of Zeus, leader of the Lycians, a major Trojan ally

Satniois, a river in the Troad

Scaian Gate, the main, south gate of Troy

Scamander, the river near Troy; modern Menderes

Selepus, grandfather of Mynes

Sime, formerly Briseis's nursemaid at Lyrnessos

Simois, river north of Troy, now the Dumrek Su, a tributary of the Scamander

Skyros, an island in mid-Aegean, sacked by Achilles, home of Iphis, modern Skíros

Smintheus, Homeric name for Apollo

Sokos, one of Aeneas's Dardanians

Spartans, contingent of the Greek army

Sphelos, brother of Briseis

Strophos, shortening of *Epistrophos,* brother of Mynes

Talthybius, a Greek herald

Telandros, alleged friend of Alcandre

Telephus, king of the Mysians; not in Homer, but known from other sources

Tenedos, a small island off the Troad; modern Bozcaada

Teuthras, Greek casualty listed by Ajax

Thallata, former bath slave at Lyrnessos, one of Agamemnon's captives

Theano daughter of Kisseus, wife of Antenor, priestess of Athena in Troy

Thebe, city ruled by Eëtion, sacked by Achilles, possibly near modern Edremit

Thermi, town on Lesbos

Thersites, a Greek soldier, a malcontent

Thessaly, modern name for Achilles' homeland, ruled by Peleus

Thetis, a sea goddess, mother of Achilles

Thibron, a Spartan, alleged friend of Alcandre

Thoas son of Jason, king of Lemnos, a Greek ally

Thracians, Trojan allies

Tiryns, a Greek citadel close to Mycenae

Tisamenus son of Orestes, later ruler of Mycenae

Titios, master of the king's vineyards at Lyrnessos

Tlepolemus son of Heracles, leader of the Rhodian Greeks, slain by Sarpedon

Trechus, Greek casualty listed by Ajax

Troad, peninsula south of the Dardanelles, site of Troy

Tros, legendary founder of Troy

Xanthus, a herald at Lyrnessos

Zephyrus, the west wind

Zeus, father and king of the gods